Praise for the Talon Duology

"An intricate and compelling new tale from one of the great original voices of fantasy. Full of fascinating ideas, engaging characters and magic."
Adrian Tchaikovsky, award-winning author of Shadows of the Apt

"*Talonsister* is wonderfully rich and inventive, it takes familiar things and places to make them new and interesting and the tone is perfectly balanced. I hugely enjoyed it."
Mike Brooks, author of The God-King Chronicles

"One of my favourite books of the year so far, *Talonsister* shows Jen Williams at the peak of her powers. An enthralling tale split across a cast of complex and fascinating characters, each flawed yet loveable in their own way... I was left bereft by its conclusion, and cannot wait for the second part."
David Wragg, author of The Articles of Faith

"*Talonsister* has all the hallmarks of a Jen Williams novel: a fast pace, humour, slick and sure worldbuilding, but most importantly it's driven by characters you immediately adore... I was utterly charmed by the world and people of *Talonsister* and I am certain you will be too."
Lucy Holland, bestselling author of Sistersong

"Dizzyingly inventive and packed with mythologies familiar and strange, *Talonsister* is Jen Williams at her storytelling best."
ANNA STEPHENS, AUTHOR OF THE GODBLIND TRILOGY

---

"*Talonsister* sweeps readers into a fantasy world both delightfully familiar and brilliantly unexpected, brimming with griffins and broken warriors and forests filled with uncanny beasts. Williams knows her craft, and her confidence and ingenuity shines through every twist and turn."
H. M. LONG, AUTHOR OF THE WINTER SEA TRILOGY

---

"This is an author going from strength to strength. An unforgettable magical fable from Britain's Queen of Fantasy."
FANTASY HIVE

---

"I thoroughly enjoyed *Talonsister*. It's perfectly balanced between whimsical and gritty, with characters so skillfully drawn you even have sympathy for the villains (well, most of them). A superb piece of fantasy storytelling by a writer at her peak."
JAMES OSWALD, AUTHOR OF THE BALLAD OF SIR BENFRO

---

"Like all the best fantasy *Talonsister* goes for the heart. Relatable characters in strange situations, a rich world painted with a wry sense of humour, and more cool creatures than you can shake a stick at."
PETER NEWMAN, AWARD-WINNING AUTHOR OF THE VAGRANT TRILOGY

# TITANCHILD

## JEN WILLIAMS

**TITAN** BOOKS

Titanchild
Paperback edition ISBN: 9781803367781
E-book edition ISBN: 9781803364391

Published by Titan Books
A division of Titan Publishing Group Ltd
144 Southwark Street, London SE1 0UP
www.titanbooks.com

This paperback edition: October 2025

10 9 8 7 6 5 4 3 2 1

This is a work of fiction. All of the characters, organizations, and events portrayed in this novel are either products of the author's imagination or are used fictitiously. Any resemblance to actual persons, living or dead (except for satirical purposes), is entirely coincidental.

© Jen Williams 2024.

Jen Williams asserts the moral right to be identified as the author of this work.

No part of this publication may be reproduced, stored in a retrieval system, or transmitted, in any form or by any means without the prior written permission of the publisher, nor be otherwise circulated in any form of binding or cover other than that in which it is published and without a similar condition being imposed on the subsequent purchaser.

A CIP catalogue record for this title is available from the British Library.

EU RP (for authorities only)
eucomply OÜ, Pärnu mnt. 139b-14, 11317 Tallinn, Estonia
hello@eucompliancepartner.com, +3375690241

Printed and bound by CPI (UK) Ltd, Croydon, CR0 4YY.

*To Mrs Mongon, Mr Mealing
and Mr Brannigan – with thanks
for opening that door.*

# PART ONE

## IN WHICH A GREAT POWER IS SUMMONED

# PROLOGUE

*2,000 years ago*

'The god-boar have breached the gate.'

Areel turned away from the window to see if Icaraine had heard him, but she was fussing over the baby, picking the child up and jostling him so he would giggle. It made Areel nervous, to see the priestess like that. They were in the middle of a war, one he was no longer certain they could win.

'Icaraine...'

'I heard you.'

She joined him at the window, the child – Malakim – now settled in the crook of one powerful arm. Areel glanced at it, then away.

'So they come,' Icaraine said, eventually. 'It makes them easier to slaughter. Our soldiers simply step out onto their own doorsteps to kill them.'

'Hmm.' They were in the tallest building in the Black City, the palace that had once belonged to the old queen. From here they had a fine view of the western-most gate – or at least they had, until the god-boar crushed it under their hooves. The room itself had once been the old queen's dining room, with views to every side of the Black City; now it was Icaraine's nursery, Icaraine's war room, Icaraine's most exclusive chamber. Scattered around the room were chains forged from Titan ore, each link as thick as Areel's wrist. The old queen's belongings were long gone, discarded when Icaraine had dragged the woman out by her hair some years ago. Queens were born perhaps once every five hundred years or so; they were larger than normal babies, with greater appetites. When two were born in the same period it tended to cause... problems.

'We should get you and the child out of the palace,' said Areel. The fighting was still distant, but he could hear the bellowing of the god-boar, and the roaring of the bears. Othanim soldiers flitted over the city, guarding against attacks from griffins and fire birds, both of which were deadly. 'Get you to the Undertomb, or out of the city altogether.'

Icaraine flexed her wings, smiling her wolfish smile.

'You are afraid for me, Areel?'

Areel frowned. He was aware that it sounded ridiculous, when Icaraine was fully two feet taller than him and entirely capable of picking him up one-handed.

'Or are you afraid for your lover, out there on the front line?'

'Felldir is strong, and fast,' Areel replied firmly, trying to make himself believe the words. 'None of these lesser Titans could possibly cause him difficulty. It's you I'm worried about, Priestess. Our people need their leader.'

Icaraine had been given the title 'priestess' by the old queen, a sop to keep her from challenging the throne. It hadn't satisfied Icaraine for long. Areel was beginning to think nothing could. In these days of war and domination she kept the title of priestess as a kind of grisly joke.

'You worry too much, Areel.' Icaraine turned her attention back to the child in her arms. The baby was wrapped in a white shawl embroidered with scarlet threads, only the pale blond hair on his head and one chubby arm visible. 'Malakim here will be the sword that cuts through all these lesser Titans. He will forge the chains that hold the human races where they belong – below us, always below us. We feed Malakim the bones of our enemies and he becomes stronger every day.' She grinned. 'The more of them that die, the more powerful we will be, Areel.'

As if encouraged by his mother's praise, Malakim reached out with one tiny, grasping fist. On the far side of the room, one of the Titan-ore chains slid across the floor towards them. It was only a couple of inches, but it was unmistakable. Areel felt his stomach roll with something he was beginning to suspect might be panic.

'There! Did you see that?' Icaraine kissed her baby on the very top of his head, taking care to avoid the multiple scarlet eyes. 'We will pull the very bones from their bodies!'

# 1

*It has been two years since the Othanim were first sighted off the coast of Wehha by Queen Ceni herself, and we have been on the back foot ever since. What are the Druin for, if they cannot protect our borders? Brittletain has become a battlefield.*

Extract from a letter signed with the
seal of King Eafen of Mersia

'My lord, we cannot keep this up! We must retreat!'

The Druidahnon glanced at the thicket around his feet. Elder Kirka's face was smeared with blood, the skin across her eyes green with the forest-fury. Around her, the Wild Wood teemed and seethed, both with the other Druin warriors and the magic of the wood itself as they commanded it; roots grew and slithered from the ground as vines shot, whip fast, into the sky. But it wasn't enough. The Othanim, the old enemy, only came within reach of their magics when they intended to kill.

'If we're not careful we shall retreat ourselves right into the sea,' he bellowed back. The Court of Bears was long lost to them, and they had been gradually pushed east, setting up their makeshift camps in the woods of Wehha. At any other time, they would have been a force to be reckoned with: the Druin rangers and warriors, the last of the armies of Londus and Galabroc, fighting alongside the last Titan bear, twenty feet tall with claws as long as a human forearm. But their enemy was too lethal.

The Druidahnon looked back up to the overcast sky, where clouds hid the Othanim until they were ready to strike. Even the weather had turned against them. *If my brothers and sisters were alive...* he thought. But they were not: the final generation of bear Titans had died in the first Titan war, and it seemed that their last scion would die here, in the second.

A darting shape left the clouds and struck. One of the Druin rangers was taken, kicking, into the sky. The Druidahnon reached for her, too late; blood laced the air, sharp and unmistakable, and then more Othanim fell on their ragged party like locusts.

'Get back!' This was Aeden, a Druin he vaguely recognised – not especially talented, but loyal. He had given up on his Druin arts and taken a spear from one of the fallen soldiers; he was using it to defend an injured comrade, poking desperately at the flying shapes around them. The Othanim were eerily expressionless, each of them wearing an elaborate silver helm that covered much of their faces.

The Druidahnon reached over with one vast paw and knocked two of the flying pests out of the sky at once. They crashed into the undergrowth, feathered wings broken, but three more took their place. He snapped his jaws at them, catching the leg of one and severing it in one neat bite. Hot Titan blood gushed down his throat, and he felt as though he could taste the hot jungle air of Houraki again, the dust of the Black City stinging his eyes. Elder Kirka's writhing vines shot up into the air, circling around the waist and legs of another Othanim, dragging him closer to the ground; Aeden buried the point of his spear in the man's gut. But still they came.

'It is hopeless,' cried Aeden. The small man's arms were shaking with the effort of holding the spear.

'No, my friends,' said the Druidahnon. 'There is still hope.'

He led them back, further east, while the Othanim continued to harry them, as persistent and seemingly mindless as midges over a swamp. Wehha was not a kingdom known for its hills – beyond the Wild Wood, it was a wet, marshy land – but there was one high place, and this was where he led them, opening Paths as easily as breathing. As they emerged onto each new Path, the Othanim would appear again, and they would fight them off as best they could. *That is the thing about war which the peace-born forget*, thought the Druidahnon. *How quickly it becomes drudgery. The sight of blood and reeking guts spilled on the floor becomes commonplace, and all that matters is the next breath you take. Survival.*

When they reached the hill itself, the Druidahnon was pleased to note that the mark of Hickathrift was still there – a great white horse with eight legs, carved into the chalk of the hill.

'My friend,' he murmured. He placed one great paw on the gritty chalk. Around him and above him, the battle continued. 'I promised not to wake you, but my children are dying.'

With one of his own wickedly sharp claws, he cut into the fur above his paw, digging deep into the flesh and splitting it open. He saw a brief flash of silvery blue, his own bone, and he shuddered with revulsion – but this was what was needed. You couldn't wake the bones of the earth without showing your own.

Blood gushed across the grass and over the chalk, staining it scarlet and black. Kirka, who had been trying to keep at his side, as if she could protect him somehow, looked with alarm at the wound.

'What are you doing? My lord, you have been hurt...'

'Be careful, Kirka, the ground here is liable to be unstable.'

'What do you—'

The grass under their feet rippled, then jumped. The chalk horse began to fall apart as the ground split and fell away. The Druin and the soldiers scattered, fleeing back down the hill. Above them, the Othanim darted back and forth from their cloud cover, but the Druidahnon noticed that a few of them had paused in the air, watching the breaking ground with interest.

*Where is she? Where is the one who called herself the bringer of light?*

Of their leader, there was no sign – from the messages they had received at Dosraiche before they were driven from their tree-city, Icaraine rarely left Londus-on-Sea – but the Druidahnon had believed she would come to him eventually. He was sure she could not resist watching the last of her old enemy die.

*I am afraid I will have to disappoint her, then*, he thought bitterly.

There was something crawling out of the hill, something even larger than the Druidahnon. The great old bear moved back, ignoring the searing pain in his wrist. Pieces of hillside crumbled into rubble.

'What's happening, lord?' Aeden had stumbled to his knees.

Kirka bent to help him up. 'It's the giants,' she said. Despite everything, there was a note of wonder in her voice. 'He's raising the giants.'

'Just one of them,' said the Druidahnon. 'I don't have enough blood for them all, and they sleep all over Brittletain. We shall have to hope one is enough.'

A vast figure rose from the hill, standing black and stormy against the clouds. It was roughly humanoid in shape, and covered in thick brown and greenish hair, which was clogged with mud and stones and grass. Overly long arms with grey skin hung at its sides, and from within the shaggy head of hair it was just possible to make out two great eyes, glowing red like embers in the fire, and the suggestion of a pig-like snout framed with yellowed tusks. It did not look pleased to be awake.

'Hickathrift!' cried the Druidahnon.

'𝔗𝔥𝔬𝔲 𝔥𝔞𝔰𝔱 𝔴𝔬𝔨𝔢𝔫 𝔪𝔢 𝔣𝔯𝔬𝔪 𝔪𝔦𝔫𝔢 𝔰𝔩𝔲𝔪𝔟𝔢𝔯.'

The giant's voice, unheard in Brittletain since its earliest days, was just how the Druidahnon remembered it: a rumble like a glacier collapsing.

'We need your help, my hairy old friend!' The great bear held his bleeding paw to his chest; he was losing enough blood to drown the people below him. 'Our island is being invaded.'

Hickathrift lifted his shaggy head. He was so tall that the Othanim hovering in the sky were much closer to him. Already they were pointing their spears and swords in his direction.

'𝕴𝖘 𝖙𝖍𝖆𝖙 𝖘𝖔?'

The giant bent back to the place where he had been buried, and drew from the ground a huge, notched blade that widened to a blunt end with a single, wicked-looking tooth. The weapon was streaked with rust and dirt, but it looked solid enough, and it was almost as long as Hickathrift himself.

'𝕬 𝖘𝖑𝖆𝖚𝖌𝖍𝖙𝖊𝖗 𝖙𝖍𝖊𝖓, 𝖎𝖙 𝖘𝖍𝖆𝖑𝖑 𝖇𝖊.'

Moving much faster than it seemed he should be able to, Hickathrift hefted his huge blade and swung it in a great arc through the air. The sky hummed with its passing, a hot, trembling sound, and Othanim fell from the sky in pieces. There was a ragged cheer from the surviving humans. Even the Druidahnon felt a flicker of hope as Hickathrift set about cleaving the winged Titans from the skies.

The elation was short-lived. Hickathrift struck many of them to the ground, so many that a mist of blood soon hung over the shattered hill, but the Othanim were quick and seemingly fearless. As the Druin and the Druidahnon did their best to continue fighting, their enemy drew back from them, instead creating a vast swarm that surrounded Hickathrift. The old giant began to bellow as they stung him like a cloud of wasps. Wounds from hundreds of swords opened up across his dusty grey flesh; his matted hair grew heavy and black with his own blood. Hickathrift howled with fury and struck repeatedly with his blade. The Druidahnon tried to reach him, to help his old friend, but very quickly the giant was on his knees. Blood coursed down the hill in waves. One of the Othanim, taking advantage of his weakened state, landed on the giant's snout and thrust her sword deep into Hickathrift's eye socket. The fiery red glow flickered and grew dark.

Slowly, like a great tree felled before its time, the giant crashed to the ground, his tusks bared to the sky in a useless, silent snarl. The Druidahnon felt his own heart thrum in his chest, as though it might splinter into pieces.

'Ah, my old friend, I am sorry. I woke you to your death.'

'We're done for.' Aeden was covered head to foot in Hickathrift's gore. 'This is the end.'

'No, not quite yet,' the Druidahnon answered. 'There is one last thing I can do. Children, go back to the Wild Wood, and hide. You must recover what strength there is left to us.'

'But, my lord,' Kirka did not look at him as she spoke; her eyes were on the enemy above, who were preparing for another attack, 'you can't mean to stay here alone? Now is the time to fight!'

'We have fought, and we have bled.' The Druidahnon looked at the bodies of the Druin scattered around him. It was too close to the pain he had felt in Houraki, as each of his siblings was cut down by Othanim blades. 'Now is the time to retreat, Kirka. It pains me to say it, but you must do as I ask. Go. Hide. Wait for the one who comes.'

Kirka looked at him sharply. 'Who? What are you talking about?'

He wouldn't elaborate. Kirka led the remnants of their fighting force back into the Wild Wood, with those Druin who still had some strength providing cover from the Othanim as they moved. The Druidahnon climbed the rubble of the hill, stepping around the body of Hickathrift, until he stood at the summit. It was harder going than he expected with his injured paw still leaking blood.

*Or perhaps I am just old*, he thought ruefully. *Perhaps it is time, after all.*

He stood up on his back legs, and bellowed a challenge to the Othanim that swarmed through the air like gnats. One of them peeled off from the rest and came to address him directly, taking off his helm as he did so. He was pale-skinned, with hair like burnished silver. He grinned widely at the bloody bear.

'You have decided to surrender, beast? Icaraine will be pleased when I take you to Londus in chains. She wanted to kill you herself.'

'Who are you?'

'I am Remielle, harbinger of the third battalion.'

'Do you ever wonder, little flying pest, why she makes you kill for her? You are no more than tools to her. That's the way it's always been.' The Druidahnon sighed. 'What happens when there are no more wars to spend you on?'

The Othanim only grinned all the wider. 'We will not stop until all of Enonah is within our grasp and every false Titan's bones are ground into powder. Now that the child is awake—'

Using the last of his strength to move as quickly as possible, the Druidahnon snatched the talkative Othanim out of the sky and snapped his head off with one bite. He chewed and swallowed, glad that the creature had done him the favour of removing his helm first, and threw the rest of the body onto the dirt below him. As he knew they would, the Othanim in the sky descended upon him in a storm, blades flashing as they screamed oaths at him.

'Yes!' he bellowed, raising his front legs even as he felt swords plunge into his flesh. *The bites of pests*, he told himself. 'You will not take me alive, you rogues! You blackguards!'

More came, flying into his side with enough force to make him stagger. He stayed upright with some difficulty; he could feel his blood flowing back into the earth as Hickathrift's had. He could feel the earth responding, quickening as it sensed what was about to happen. There would be a great deal of magic at hand, and he would only have one chance to use it.

*One life to give.*

One of the flying Titans got a good grip on his shoulder, and from there thrust a long blade into the Druidahnon's throat. There was a terrible tearing sensation, and the hot flood of life's blood as it began to rush out of him at speed. He heard them cheering, the Othanim, the shininess of their helms dulled with the blood of the last bear Titan. The Druidahnon lifted his head so that he could see the Wild Wood beyond the hill, so dark and so green and so still. When he spoke, he seemed to speak to the trees themselves.

'I call you here now, Walker of the Paths! I call you now, Forest Father! The Wild Wood needs its protector, Green Man!'

There was a tremble beneath his feet, and then the Druidahnon fell to his knees. He did not get back up again.

---

From her vantage point in the trees, Kirka watched him fall, a cold hand around her heart. Next to her, Aeden was weeping.

'He has left us,' he said. 'Left us when we needed him the most.'

'No, you fool.' Kirka spoke softly, too aware of the sorrow every Druin would be feeling in their hearts. 'He's giving us a reason to fight on.'

As they watched, the great form of the fallen bear began to crumble and fall apart, disintegrating into a vast cloud of wildflowers: buttercups, daisies, foxgloves, dog violets and clover, leaving only his bones behind. The wind picked up the blossoms and carried them to the waiting wood.

## 2

*I call you here now, Walker of the Paths.*

Cillian startled, almost losing his balance on the slippery roof. Next to him, Leven was a still shape in the darkness.

'Did you say something?' he whispered.

'What? No,' she whispered back. 'We're supposed to be quiet, remember?'

A steady rain was falling, chill and grey, soaking them to their skins. They were perched on one of the roofs of a complex of buildings that clung to the very edge of the sea cliffs of Blessed Gäul; just behind them was a sheer drop into the churning water. Cillian knew that if he turned and looked out across the sea, the maelstrom of the Titan's Eye whirlpool would be visible, with its rills and swirls of angry white water; he wouldn't even need to borrow Inkwort's eyes to see that monstrosity. But ahead of them the complex, with its tiled roofs and neat gravel-covered courtyards, was quiet. The guards were all hiding from the rain under the eaves. Somewhere down there was Gynid Tyleigh, the woman they had spent the last two years tracking across multiple countries, both Blessed and Unblessed. And more importantly, somewhere within this warren of buildings was T'rook, a young griffin neither he nor Leven had set eyes on before.

'I'm sure I heard... a voice.'

He looked around for Inkwort, in case the little jackdaw had made one of her rare attempts to communicate with him, but there was no sign of her. It was likely she was hiding from the rain, too.

'It can't have been Ynis,' said Leven. 'It's too soon.'

Thanks to a childhood spent in the mountainous region of Yelvynia, Leven's younger sister was an exceptional climber. It had been decided that she would go ahead of them, moving quietly through the buildings until she had some idea of where T'rook, her griffin-sister, was located. A soldier more used to being on the vanguard of every battle, Leven herself was to wait until Ynis gave the signal – which was to be one of her alarming, bird-like cries.

Cillian shook his head. 'It wasn't that. I half think I knew the voice. It was very faint.'

'Can't hear anything in this bloody rain.'

Cillian shook his head, droplets of rainwater flying from his horns. 'Perhaps it was just...'

*I call you now, Forest Father.*

This time Cillian gasped, almost rising to his feet. The voice in his head was louder, a kind of thunder that seemed to flatten every other thought. And there was a greenness to it that he almost recognised; he felt something inside him shift, responding automatically. Leven grasped his arm.

'Cillian, are you alright?' In the gloom he could just about make out her grey eyes. She looked worried. 'Is it... the thrawn?'

'No. I don't know what it is.' He took her hand and kissed it, tasting the mineral tang of rain and the scent of her skin, a scent he never seemed to tire of. 'Ignore me, love. We've more important things to do here.'

She didn't look convinced, but nodded. 'We'll want to be as quick as we can,' she said. 'We don't know what sort of state T'rook will be in when we reach her, but we'll have to move her out of here fast.' Leven went over the plan again. They'd discussed it many times over the last few days, but she was nervous. Two years of hunting out leads, chasing after rumours and hearsay, and it all came down to this single night. If they didn't get it right, that could be the end of it. Leven had confided in Cillian that if they showed their hand too early, it was likely Gynid would simply kill T'rook – out of spite, or a need to cover up her tracks. It was a miracle she hadn't killed the griffin already. 'Can you sense anything?'

Cillian held himself still, putting the mysterious voice from his mind for the moment. He did not have the connection with this land that he had shared with the Wild Wood of Brittletain, but since he had gone thrawn, his abilities were both powerful and unpredictable. Nearby he could sense human beings – their labyrinthine minds forever closed off to him – and a handful of dogs, kennelled close to the entrance to the complex. There were birds too, tiny warm points of life that clustered together in nests tucked away in a variety of dark, cosy places. Behind him, the vast unknowable sea, a world that swam with presences that made little sense to his dry, green mind. A sea eagle coasted over the waves, hunger drawing it further and further from land.

'Nothing important. How are you feeling?'

She grinned at him in the dark.

'Aside from the usual aches and pains? Spectacular. Very soon I could be hanging Gynid Tyleigh up by her ankles before asking her some pointed questions about what she did to my father. What she made me do to Ynis.'

'What she did to *you*,' Cillian said.

Leven nodded. 'A lot of pointed questions, at the end of my pointy blade. She's going to regret ever fucking—'

When the voice came a third time, it felt as though something enormous had crashed into him. There was a light the colour of the morning through dappled leaves, a rushing sound – desperation, magic, death.

*The Wild Wood needs its protector, Green Man!*

Someone was with him in the dark, someone huge, and another presence, somebody dangerous and strange. He realised that he had stood up; he was moving, shouting wordlessly. He heard Leven calling him, and then he dropped, falling into open space.

'Shit!'

The night lit up with the shining blue luminescence of Leven's Herald magic. She had sprung her wings and jumped after him, catching him by the back of his jacket before he could hit the ground. Now they were both hanging in mid-air, lit up like the caul of stars for all the guards to see. The warm human shapes he could sense in the night were all converging on their location, swords and spears and curved knives glinting with raindrops.

'Stars' arses,' hissed Leven. 'I told you I wasn't made for stealth!'

---

Ynis hung beneath a windowsill, her fingers gripping the clay lip, her feet braced against the slick stonework of the wall. There was grit under her hands and she disliked the smoothness of the surfaces, but compared to climbing the peaks of Yelvynia it was a sunny day in spring. This window looked in on a storeroom full of crates and boxes, so she swung herself along to the next one, moving silently in her soft leather boots. It had taken her some time to get used to these human nest-pits – or buildings, as her human sister insisted on calling them. The openings and exits were too small, and barred with doors or big stretches of glass, and inside they were so full of *things*. At home in the Bone Fall, the nest-pit she shared with T'rook was practically bare: there was Ynis's leather bag, her tools, the blankets she had made from furs and stolen feathers, her claw-knife. T'rook had scratched a few shapes into the rocks and ice that served as their walls; that was all they had in way of decoration. But humans...

Ynis heaved herself up so that she could peek over the sill into the next room.

There was no one in there, but the place was crammed with stuff. Fascinated, she pulled herself up further so she could look properly. There were tall shelves pushed against the walls, and odd pieces of furniture scattered about: a huge, overstuffed sofa that had evidently once been green, but was now covered in dubious stains; a leather armchair in the corner; a wide wooden table; a desk with a large oil lamp; a great ball with a map on it, spinning in its own frame. And as if this wasn't enough, every surface was scattered with more things: paper, parchment, ink stones, bottles of liquid of all colours, shallow clay bowls filled with grey ash, books, knives – these Ynis looked at very closely – and greasy-looking jars. On the odd bit of wall that wasn't taken up with a shelf there were more maps, and a few objects hung on nails that she didn't understand at all: an elaborate silver helmet that looked too big for a human and too small for a griffin, and the shining purple carapace of a huge beetle.

'What do they *do* with it all?' Ynis murmured to herself. The rain was growing heavier, although she barely felt it. 'They must spend all their lives looking at the things they've collected. Like magpies.'

The door on the far side of the room opened. Ynis ducked back down out of sight, where the shadows were darkest. An older woman shuffled into the room, moving slowly, as though every step pained her. As she came closer to the oil lamp, Ynis felt a dark thrill of recognition: she had no memory of this woman, but she had seen her in Leven's memories. It was Gynid Tyleigh, the alchemist they had spent two years looking for. *My human mother*, she reminded herself.

In Leven's childhood memories Tyleigh had still been a young woman, sharp-boned and fox-faced, with an untidy mess of red-brown hair. Now she was hunched and small and wiry, her hair shot through with grey and white. There were dark circles under her eyes, and she leaned heavily on a stick to walk. She had a long pipe of black wood stuck in the corner of her mouth, and as she shuffled across the room she puffed on it, chewing the stem. The smoke that came out of it looked strange – not like woodsmoke, but yellowish, greasy.

*It is her.*

Ynis tried to swallow down her excitement. If Gynid Tyleigh was here, that meant that T'rook must be close. They knew from the information Leven had gathered in Stratum that Tyleigh had an adolescent griffin, one that had been captured and kept alive on her specific instructions. They knew that Tyleigh had moved her workshop out of Stratum to some secret location. And they had finally found it. If they had still been uncertain, the gossip she had overheard by the kitchens had dispelled that: every day they butchered goats and sheep for Tyleigh's 'pet', and at night they could hear it screeching, loud enough to wake the ancestors they believed were the stars.

*I'm coming to get you, sister.*

As she watched, Tyleigh went to one of the shelves and pulled out a jar of something brown and fibrous. With a sharp, practised movement she struck the end of her pipe on the table, removing a small pile of blackened, smoking material, and replaced it with fresh stuff from the jar, tamping it down with her thumb. Ynis had learned about this foul substance in Stratum – it was some kind of weed that could be burned and inhaled. Tobacco. When she had it lit and smoking again, Tyleigh took a breath on the pipe, pulling the smoke deep into her lungs before letting it out. She picked up a book from the table and made to leave the room, her movements a little smoother than they had been.

Ynis scrambled to follow her, pulling herself along the ledge to the next room. Here she caught a glimpse of something like a corridor, dimly lit by a single oil lamp, and then her quarry vanished through another door. Beyond that the windowsill ended, and Ynis felt a drop in her guts – *what if I lose her here, after everything?* But there was a clay drainage pipe running down the brickwork, and she used this to climb up to where longer, narrower windows started. What she saw through them made her stop, heart pounding in her chest.

It was a much bigger room than the others she had seen so far, with a high ceiling and a lot of empty space. There were a few wooden buckets scattered about, dark with bloodstains, and a number of sturdy chains hung from the ceiling beams. In the middle of the room there was a large, free-standing cage made of a silvery-blue metal that looked familiar. And even more familiar than that, her sister stood inside it, her proud head held high, the feathers around her neck and chest puffed out with indignation. It was the same old T'rook – eyes like golden autumn leaves, feathers and fur brown and black and white, lethal blue talons – except that she was different, too. A little older, a little larger, the muscles across her shoulders and flank more developed, the small crest of dark feathers on her head a little longer. Ynis felt her throat close up with feelings she barely understood. *She has become an adult*, she thought, *and I missed it.*

One of the narrow windows was propped open by a book. Ynis scooted along so she that she could hear her sister's voice as well as see her.

'When I get out of here, human, I will eat your liver first.'

Gynid Tyleigh came into view, still puffing on her pipe.

'Is there any particular reason for that?' asked the human. 'Do you gain a certain strength from eating human livers?'

'No, I would simply enjoy rooting around in your guts while you are still alive.'

Tyleigh gave a laugh that was more of a cough, and winced.

'Do you ever get tired of thinking of new ways to kill me?'

'Is that some kind of weak human joke, you ground-stuck parasite?'

Hanging from the window ledge, Ynis smiled to herself. In some ways T'rook had clearly not changed at all.

Tyleigh sighed. 'Two years. I would have thought even a griffin would get bored. But it seems your reputation as the most stubborn breed of Titan is well deserved.' She shuffled over to a three-legged stool and sat on it. For a moment she leaned forward, clutching her stomach, then whatever ailed her seemed to pass, and she sat back up. 'Tell me what you know about the other Titans.'

T'rook snapped her beak derisively. 'I will tell you nothing. About anyone.'

'That's a shame,' said Tyleigh. 'I had some rabbits and goats brought over from Brittletain. A taste of home, I thought.' She grinned, a brief flash of teeth. 'For us both. And it's a bloody nightmare getting anything out of that poxy little island these days, what with the Othanim occupation. They are your old enemy, aren't they? I know about the war with them, the attack on the Black City. How you drove them underground. What are they? Who is their leader, this Icaraine?'

T'rook was quiet. Ynis imagined her sister knew as little as she did about the strange new Titans currently attacking Brittletain, but she would not want to appear ignorant in front of the human.

'Food scavenged by humans is not fit for a griffin to eat,' she said eventually. 'We hunt. We kill. We eat fresh meat, with the blood hot. As I will eat you when I get out of here.'

'Suit yourself,' said Tyleigh. 'All the more rabbit stew for me.'

Ynis leaned back, easing the tension on her arms for a moment – and all hell broke loose. From somewhere behind her she heard the sudden panicked shouting of men and women, followed by some very loud swearing that could only have been her human sister. Sapphire light, like water running over the heart of a glacier, splashed against the walls. Leven had summoned her Herald powers, and their cover was blown.

Ynis, who had learnt a number of interesting new words over the last couple of years, muttered 'fuck' to herself before scrambling back down the wall.

# 3

To the south-east of Stratum, there was a region of land known as the Breaks.

Hundreds of years ago, when the Imperium was a burgeoning state with some grandiose ideas, the emperor of the time had ordered this stretch of land to be mined for Titan ore. They were still unearthing plenty of Titan remains from the crater that would eventually become the city of Stratum, but the Imperium had always had eyes bigger than its belly, and they were keen to expand their efforts. Great machines were built that were capable of breaking open the earth, and the Breaks – then known as the White Steppe – became the landscape where all of these diabolical contraptions were tested. In the end, only minimal Titan remains were recovered, but the land itself was irretrievably broken. A desolate place.

Kaeto didn't know if many people had lived on the White Steppe before it was broken by the Imperium, but he thought it was extremely likely – people would, in his experience, attempt to live anywhere that wasn't actively underwater. The Breaks made him think of the town he had once lived in with his parents, which had been flattened to make way for the Indigo Sky Palace, one of the empress's favourite haunts.

Here, rather than a flat and featureless desert, he rode through a landscape of jagged broken pieces; vast edifices of blue and brown stone thrust up out of the ground, while to every side there were great chasms. He imagined that from above the place must look like an intricate piece of lace.

The horse he rode was one of his favourites, a feisty black mare with a wild look in her eye, but even she was quiet when they travelled through the Breaks. He wondered if she could sense the dizzying drops that waited for them if they took the wrong path.

'Nearly there, girl.' Kaeto put his hand on her wide neck, feeling the movement of her powerful muscles beneath the skin. 'And we don't have to hurry back.'

In time they came to a chasm that cut directly across their path. It was one of the largest in the region – the other side was, Kaeto knew, just over a mile away. And perched on the edge of it was a ruined castle.

There was a cry from somewhere in the sky above, and a shadow skittered across them, too big to be a bird. The horse whinnied and took a few hurried steps backwards.

'Come on, now.' Kaeto leaned forward so he could speak softly into her ear. 'You should be used to this by now. A big brave horse like you.'

'Chief!' Belise landed just ahead of them in a thunder of wings, bending her knees to brace for the impact. She didn't quite land as she wanted, stumbling forward on the stony ground, but a second later she was up and trotting towards him, a big grin on her face. 'I hope you've brought something interesting to eat. It's been bloody goat meat for weeks. Felldir says I have to learn to hunt because providing for yourself is a useful skill.'

'He's right,' said Kaeto. He looked up at the broken castle. Much of one half still stood on the edge of the cliff, while the other half had partly crumbled, catching on a series of ledges that jutted out into the crevasse below. Belise and Felldir had spent most of the last year making the place as habitable as possible, repairing what they could and adapting it for two people who were larger than the humans who originally made it. 'Where is he?'

'Up in the bell tower.'

Kaeto grimaced. The bell tower was the highest accessible point in the castle, but as a normal human without giant feathery wings to help should he lose his footing, it wasn't his favourite place to visit.

Belise grinned at him in an infuriating manner. 'I'm sure he'll come down for *you* though, chief.'

They took the horse to the space they had made into a stable – once a sprawling kitchen, the outer wall long since fallen into rubble – and Kaeto followed Belise into what was technically the interior of the castle, although there was rather too much sky on display through the partially collapsed walls, and certainly far too many glimpses of the chasm itself. As they made their way through the ruins, Kaeto noticed the small ways in which Belise and Felldir had been making themselves at home: a space cleared and dusted and filled with cooking implements; a bench for Belise to repair her weapons; a small collection of books on a shelf, all of which Kaeto had brought from Stratum for them; a neat stack of notes nearby that suggested Felldir had been learning about the two thousand years of history he had missed while confined to the Black City.

They made their way into the old hall where the pair of them spent much of their time now. Once, it had been someone's throne room, with high ceilings and fireplaces; now it contained the best of the furniture they had scavenged.

Felldir met them there. 'I heard your voice,' he said. 'We thought you might arrive today.'

Kaeto nodded, looked away. He had grown used to Belise's new body relatively quickly. She had accepted her change of circumstance with her usual pragmatic optimism, and hearing her voice, there was never any doubt that she was exactly who she'd always been. Felldir though... Felldir's presence still unnerved him, filled him with feelings he wasn't quite sure he understood.

Whenever he returned to the broken castle and saw him again, he remembered how he had first met the Titan: in a tower room, his hair loose, his eyes as yellow as a wolf's, his hands covered in dried blood.

Kaeto had provided him with new clothes, shirts, furs for the cold nights, proper leather boots and good, practical woollen overshirts. Standing in the hall with his long white hair pulled back into a neat braid, Felldir looked well-groomed, handsome, civilised; as though he were a relatively well-off warrior from some Unblessed land. But the wolf eyes remained.

Kaeto put the bag he was carrying down on the table, and Belise began unpacking it with the enthusiasm of the fourteen-year-old she actually was.

'I know I'm a little later than I promised.' Kaeto untied his riding cloak and threw it over one of the chairs. 'The Envoy office is extremely busy. Busier than I've ever seen it. Celestinia is eager for any information she can get about the Othanim, and everyone travelling through Stratum is either being watched or questioned. We've dispatched a special unit to San Rosen port to catch those refugees coming from Brittletain, and the stories coming out of that island are only making Celestinia more paranoid.'

'My people have gone to war,' Felldir commented dryly.

'Indeed.' Kaeto thought of how Gynid Tyleigh had warned him not to release Icaraine, the lethal high priestess of the Othanim. It seemed she had been talking sense after all. Not that Kaeto had had any real choice at the time. 'It's been my job to collate this information, cross reference, draw conclusions, present my findings.' He sighed and stretched his arms up to the ceiling until the small bones in his back clicked. It was good to be away from his desk, and away from the dungeons under Stratum.

'And what are your findings?' asked Felldir.

'We have many interesting fragments that don't yet add up to a full picture. Icaraine has taken Londus-on-Sea and her warriors attack the rest of the island apparently at random. Queen Broudicca is believed to be a prisoner in her own palace, and it's unclear what has happened to her numerous daughters, but it seems the island was in the midst of a civil war when the invasion—'

'There's soap,' Belise interrupted brightly. 'And sugar and butter. Fell, we can try making those pastries I was telling you about.'

Kaeto felt an odd constriction in his chest. *Fell?* She had a nickname for their Othanim friend. *As well she might*, he reminded himself. *He guided her spirit to this new body, which is as much a Titan as he is.*

'There's more in the packs we took off the horse,' he told her. 'Cheese, some jars of double cream. You'll want to get them into the cold store quickly.'

Belise gave him a quick nod. Rather than walking back the way they'd come, she climbed up a broken portion of wall to a sizeable hole, through which he could see a bright square of blue sky. She unfurled her grey feathered wings and was gone.

'How is she doing?'

Felldir smiled fondly, and again Kaeto felt that strange constriction in his chest. Was he jealous? Jealous of what, or who, exactly? He couldn't help noticing that there was a new softness to the Titan's face when he smiled. It made him look more human.

'She is a worthy student. Everything I tell her, she remembers, and when she does not immediately grasp something, she comes back to it from another angle.'

Kaeto nodded, pleased. Felldir had been teaching Belise about the Othanim, their history – which was now her history – as well as more technical things, like how to fly, how to land, how to hunt from the air, and how to sleep when your back had two extra limbs.

'She always was a fast learner.'

'She has missed you,' Felldir replied. 'You'll be staying the night?'

'Yes.' To avoid looking directly at the Titan, Kaeto went to one of the small tables and helped himself from a dusty decanter of wine. 'The Envoy office believes me away on some kind of top-clearance mission for the empress. I won't be missed for a little while at least. Would you care for a glass?'

Kaeto poured Felldir's wine into an oversized wooden goblet. Normal glasses looked much too small in his hands.

'That is good.' When Felldir took the goblet, his hand brushed against Kaeto's curled fingers. 'That you can stay for a while. Belise prefers it when you are here.'

'I would be here all the time, if I could.' Kaeto cleared his throat. Something about being in Felldir's presence made him admit things he wouldn't utter to another soul. 'But Stratum would have questions if I spent too long away. They might start looking into my recent movements more carefully. You've seen no one in the Breaks? Not even distant travellers?'

'No.' Felldir sipped his wine. 'You chose this place well. The only other living things we have seen are the red birds that roost in the bell tower, and the wiry little goats. And this castle is a good place to hide, should anyone come looking. It's not easy to traverse for people without wings.'

'Good. If the Imperium should find out I'm hiding two Othanim under their noses...' Kaeto tried to make it sound light-hearted, but the reality was grim. He would be executed for treason. If they took Felldir and Belise alive, no doubt they would be carted off to Tyleigh's new secret workshop, where she could cut them up into as many pieces as she liked. The empress's desire for knowledge of these new Titans allowed for no mercy.

The thought of Tyleigh turned the wine sour in his stomach. He had thought he'd left that snake to die in Houraki, but she was as tough and as unkillable as the cockroaches of Stratum. 'The empress and the Imperator have been reading all the reports I've given them. There have been a number of heated arguments. Imperator Justinia, predictably, believes we should act against the Othanim while they are distracted with Brittletain, crush them with our new Heralds and take their bones for ourselves. The empress, though... she has always been a careful woman. She wants to wait, to carry on gathering knowledge, learn what we can about the Othanim.'

'She will be disappointed,' said Felldir quietly. 'There is little depth to what Icaraine wants. An end to the other Titans, the enslavement of humans.'

'What would you advise?'

Felldir tipped the goblet back to drink the last of his wine. Kaeto had a moment to observe the fine line of his jaw, the smooth column of his neck. 'I would advise you to leave your Stratum and your empress behind. Come here, and the three of us will head west, to the lands beyond the Broken Sea.'

Kaeto smiled lopsidedly. 'I meant what would you advise the Imperium to do.'

'I do not care about the Imperium.' Felldir put the goblet down and fixed him with a look that made Kaeto's heart beat a little faster. *Does the wolf wish to eat me?* he thought. *Or does the wolf wish to...*

Belise came back in through the shattered doorway, her arms full of provisions.

'We'll be eating well tonight, Fell! There's a whole side of rolled pork in this bag, with a layer of fat that's going to make the best crackling. Chief, are you staying the night?'

'I am, and I was thinking about roasting that pig the whole way here. Help me set up the cookfire.'

---

Later, when Belise had eaten a frankly worrying amount of roast pork and blackened potatoes and passed out in her cosy nest-like room in the bell tower, Kaeto took himself to one of his own favourite haunts in the broken castle. It was a room still accessible on foot, but with one wall entirely missing, so it was possible to look out across the yawning chasm. The sun had set, leaving the sky rinsed almost green in the twilight, a shower of stars overhead.

All around him he could hear the occasional chirp of the birds that nested in the castle at night. He sat with his legs dangling off the side. After a little while, Felldir joined him, sitting next to him on the ledge in companionable silence.

'Do you ever regret leaving Houraki?' Kaeto asked eventually. 'You did not have to come with us, after all.'

'Sometimes, when I am instructing Belise, she asks me if something is a "trick question". Is this one of these?'

Kaeto laughed quietly. 'In the Black City I asked what you would do, if your obligation to Icaraine was finally ended, and you said you would die. You sounded glad of it. What's changed?'

'I was a fool,' said Felldir. 'I'd forgotten that the rest of the world existed, that there were things beyond the Black City that could still bring me joy. All that time I spent as a living curse, as a guardian that dealt only death. I had forgotten how to feel.' He gestured out at the ever-darkening night sky. 'This world is still so new, and I'd have missed it all. If I'd stayed there, I would not have discovered the joy of teaching a child.' Somewhere in the dark, a nightbird cried out. 'When Icaraine freed her Othanim army she freed me as well, yet it was you who truly gave me freedom, Kaeto. You showed me there was a new kind of life to live.'

A gust of wind barrelled up from the chasm below, blowing a scattering of feathers and old, fragile leaves onto their secluded platform. There was a rustle at their backs, and Kaeto realised that Felldir had extended one of his wings around him, sheltering him from the worst of the wind and debris. That feeling in his chest again: hard, brittle, exciting. A complication he could never have anticipated.

When the silence between them had grown too loaded to bear, Kaeto got to his feet, and Felldir withdrew his wing.

'I'm going to get some rest. I wish you a goodnight.'

The Titan watched him leave without speaking.

# 4

*You requested a full rundown of the abilities and restrictions of the Heralds. Here it is. I don't know why you couldn't have just retrieved the information from my extensive notes on the matter, going back years, but I suppose I can't expect people in your position to actually read. Do let me know if you'd prefer it written in crayon.*

- *Wings of blue light can be summoned at will. They last a few hours, so not suitable for travelling extreme distances or over the ocean.*
- *A sword of blue light can be summoned at will. Never needs to be replaced, never needs to be sharpened or carried. I think even you must see the benefits.*
- *Heightened strength and healing. What more could you want in a warrior?*
- *Memory loss. As far as I can tell, subjects lose all memory of anything that happened to them before the augments are grafted into their skin. As most of them are prisoners you've dragged out of a hole somewhere, this is no great loss.*
- *Inability to get pregnant or carry a child. I can only see this as a plus for soldiers. And certainly it means the Heralds can enjoy their leave without consequence.*
- *Eventual mental and physical degradation. After around eight years or so, it appears the ore-lines start trying to retake their original forms. This can lead to pain, confusion, and possibly*

*the resurgence of lost memories. Eventually, madness and death. Again, given many of your 'volunteers' are criminals, I think this is a reasonable payoff for a legion of untouchable warriors.*

Note from Gynid Tyleigh to Imperator Justinia

---

Leven dropped Cillian safely onto the courtyard flagstones, spreading her blue glass wings wide before folding them away again. Once they were gone, she summoned her magical blade to her hand; having both her wings and sword burning at the same time cost her too much these days. Ahead of them, three guards were racing into the yard, the light of her blade lighting up their armour with flashes of sapphire.

'Who are you?' one demanded, in a strong Stratum accent. 'You're trespassing.'

Another, slightly faster on the uptake, drew his sword slowly. 'That's a bloody Herald, that is. One of the old ones.'

'Bloody cheek,' said Leven.

'And she's got one of those horned devils from Brittletain with her,' the guard continued.

The first guard raised his voice. 'Are you here to see the bone crafter, then?'

'In a manner of speaking,' said Leven. Next to her, she could hear Cillian breathing rapidly. Something was wrong. Or at least, something was wrong beyond him falling off a roof.

'There's no one permitted to see the alchemist.' The second guard raised his sword as the third came around the side of his companions. 'No one's even supposed to know where she is.' He shot an irritated look at the first guard. 'We'll have to kill them now, so word don't spread.'

'I'd love to see you try.' Leven darted forward, knocking the man's sword into pieces with her own blade, before neatly crashing her forehead into his unprotected temple. He went down in a boneless slump. She threw herself sideways into the third guard. He grappled with her, trying to bring his sword around to stab her in the guts, but she swept downwards with the Titan blade, catching the backs of his legs and the outermost portion of his heels. The man opened his mouth to scream and she clasped a hand over it, pulling him down to the ground as she did so. Looking up, she saw the last guard trying to escape the attentions of a huge sea eagle that had flown down from the night sky and was currently trying to pull his scalp off with its talons. Leven tried to haul herself up, leaning on the guard's face as she did so, but already the Titan strength was draining out of her, taking her own human strength with it.

*It leaves me faster and faster*, she thought, despair mixed with a slow-moving panic.

'Cillian, we're supposed to be *quiet*. We don't want to give her a chance to crawl off somewhere else.'

'I think that ship has sailed, my love,' he replied. So far from his native earth of the Wild Wood, he wasn't able to move the ground beneath them as he had been, but the thrawn taint still allowed him access to the minds of creatures, and dominion over them. The sea eagle stopped its ear-piercing screeches at a look from Cillian, but the guard continued to bellow as the bird clawed his face ragged.

Taking a deep breath, Leven forced herself to her feet, hand on the knife at her belt, but as she watched the soft section of skin beneath the guard's beard suddenly split open, fountaining blood clear across the courtyard. He dropped to the ground and she saw Ynis standing in the shadows behind him, her claw-knife dripping red. The sea eagle, released from Cillian's control, flew back up into the night, no doubt confused by the fresh human blood spattering its feathers. Ynis watched it go with that quietly thoughtful expression Leven had grown familiar with.

'Come,' she said. 'I know where our mother is.'

'Wait a moment,' said Cillian. He went to Leven, pushing the hair back from her face. 'Are you alright?'

Leven gritted her teeth and nodded. Already the burning pain was coming; thousands of hot needles piercing her skin wherever the ore-lines were traced – face, body, arms, legs, even the delicate skin on the palms of her hands throbbed with it. And with it something else. An alien presence in the back of her mind.

'Fine. I'm fine. What about you? You looked as if you'd seen a ghost up there. What happened?'

'I don't know.' Cillian frowned. 'Something… I thought I heard something. A voice. It could be another symptom of being thrawn.'

'The concern you show for your mating partner is touching,' said Ynis, 'but have you forgotten why we are here, Leven? I have seen her.' Her usually calm voice grew ragged. 'I have seen my sister!'

'I hear you, Ynis.' Leven put the knife back into her belt and tried to push the pain out of her mind. 'Lead the way.'

---

Leven had expected more resistance, but they followed Ynis without further trouble, and even found the door to Gynid Tyleigh's rooms unguarded.

'The Imperium really thought they'd hidden her well,' she said to Cillian as they stood outside the chamber, her voice little more than a murmur. 'They barely bothered to guard the old witch.'

'It did take us two years to find her,' Cillian pointed out.

Leven grinned at him. 'I love it when you're reasonable.'

She kicked the door open, using the pain of her ore-lines as a kind of catalyst. Beyond it was a room crowded with furniture and objects that reminded her of the workshop under the central plaza in Stratum – chemicals, books, tiny delicate knives forged to cut and splice human flesh – and in the corner, Tyleigh herself, bent over a walking stick as she retrieved something from a shelf. She straightened up and turned, looking at the three people who had walked into her chamber with a distinct lack of surprise. She had a pipe in her mouth, which she took out with her free hand. There was a long moment of silence; it made Leven think of creeping out over a thin layer of ice, a lake with dark waters beneath. *There's no going back now.*

'I knew someone would come,' she said. 'What I'm making here is just too powerful. But Blessed Eleven? I wasn't expecting you.' She peered at Cillian's blue horns. 'Or a Druin. A *thrawn* Druin, no less. And a scrawny girl child. Interesting.'

'You remember me.' Leven found that her heart was pounding in her chest, all the pain of her ore-lines forgotten. She felt filled with lightning, with something that could not be contained much longer. The Wild Wood of her childhood suddenly seemed very close: snow on the ground, a terrible stone altar waiting for her somewhere in the trees. 'I thought maybe you'd forced yourself to forget. That would explain some of it.'

Tyleigh shuffled forward. Belatedly, Leven saw that the woman looked extremely ill, a husk of her former self. Her reddish hair was greying, and her skin was sallow, but more than that, she looked as though every movement hurt her. There was a terrible smell in the room. Tyleigh tapped the ash from her pipe out onto a nearby table. The bad smell increased significantly.

'You know who you are? Now that is unexpected,' Tyleigh said flatly. For a second, a tremble that was almost a spasm moved across her face, a brief glimpse of some emotion that was there and gone like summer rain. 'How can you know? Did that bastard Envoy tell you? I thought I had hidden your records, but I wouldn't put it past that snake to figure it out.'

'I remembered,' Leven said simply. 'I remembered what you did to me, over and over. What you did to my father. What you did to her.' She gestured sharply at Ynis, who was hanging back near the door, her claw-knife ready in her hand.

'Her?' Tyleigh's mouth turned down at the corners. 'I don't know that girl. She isn't related to that little brat that got eaten by the beetles in Houraki, is she?'

'Got eaten by the what?' asked Cillian, but Leven was already talking over him. She grabbed Ynis around the shoulders, bringing her towards their mother.

'Don't you recognise your youngest, Tyleigh?'

The old woman blinked rapidly, shook her head. She took a step backwards.

'That's... not possible.'

'You killed our father – worse, you made me kill him – you destroyed my memories, and you abandoned Ynis to die in the woods. When her name was Alaw.'

'And you have my sister,' Ynis put in. 'You will let her go, now.'

'Yes. Let the griffin go,' Leven took a long, deep breath, 'and then I'm going to kill you.'

'Wait. Wait!' Tyleigh scampered back awkwardly, leaning heavily on her stick. 'You must have questions, girls. You must have things you want to know. This is your chance to find out.' She moved back to the wall, where there was a small alcove with a lamp inside it. 'I'll tell you anything you want to know. And I know a great many things, believe me.'

She paused to cough, bent over so far that Leven thought she might just collapse onto the floor. When she straightened up again, there was blood on her hands and lips.

'What is wrong with you?' asked Cillian.

'Heh.' Tyleigh looked at the mess on her hand, then wiped it down her shirt. 'Put simply, my insides are slowly dissolving, the result of a particularly nasty and unique poison from the jungle just outside the Black City. An Envoy poisoned my tea, would you believe? I told them what he did clear enough, but Envoys are skilled with lies, and the truth is...' She paused to catch her breath. 'The truth is, we're both too valuable to the empress. Easier to keep us both alive.

Anyway. He did enough damage that I don't have much longer to live, Blessed Eleven. You needn't waste what little energy you have.'

'Even a slow death by poison is more than you deserve.' But Leven didn't move from her spot. Tyleigh was right; she had questions. Who else could ever answer them? When it came down to it, there was only one that really mattered.

'Why?'

Leven thought Tyleigh would protest, pretend not to know what she was talking about. Instead the alchemist pursed her lips, and looked to the windows. Rain was lashing against the glass, the wind picking up.

'Because I could,' she said eventually. 'I knew I could do it, and why shouldn't I? I could see so clearly how it could work, this infusion of Titan magic into a human body, and it would give me so much power – more power than I ever had as a Druin, even one that has gone thrawn.' She glanced at Cillian, openly curious. 'How are you finding it? There's nothing quite like it, is there? Forcing your will onto lesser beings.' She grinned, her teeth stained with her own blood. 'Those idiots have exiled you for it, haven't they? Because they haven't the strength to wield it themselves.'

'Hey.' Leven took a step forward. 'You don't get to talk to him.'

'If the bones of the griffins could give you power,' Ynis spoke from behind them, 'why didn't you do it to yourself? Give yourself wings?'

'Ha, you don't understand. And why would you?' Tyleigh leaned against the alcove, the yellow light from the lamp turning her face into a mask. 'It's not the Titan augments that are the power – it'll look like that to your average peasant idiot, of course, with the big impressive wings and the magical sword, the strength and the swift healing. No, the real power is being *the one person in all of Enonah who knows how to make a Herald.* Do you see? I didn't have to cut up my own skin to grasp the power, I just had to learn how to do it to other people.'

'And you thought experimenting on your own child was the best course of action, Echni?' There was a lot of coiled anger beneath Cillian's voice. 'Repeatedly wiping away her memories?'

Tyleigh looked at him with bright interest. 'What else was I to do? We lived in the middle of the Wild Wood, miles from anyone. I was already exiled from the Druin order, so I could hardly go to one of the queens and ask for test subjects. No. I had to work with what I had.' She gestured at Leven. 'And how are you, Blessed Eleven? How are you finding your, what is it now? Your tenth year with all your augments in place? I imagine things must be getting very difficult by now.'

'What is she talking about?' asked Ynis.

Leven shook her head. 'I'm fine.'

'Really? No pain in the ore-lines? Exhaustion? Any strange voices, noises, at night, when things are quiet?'

This time it was Cillian who looked at Leven.

'I'm right, aren't I?' Tyleigh sucked in air over her teeth, shook her head. 'I could never quite adjust for the inevitable damage when the ore-lines try to revert to their original forms. Always, after a few years, the same thing: pain, exhaustion, confusion. The resurgence of memories. A steady decline. Madness, death. I managed to stretch it out to eight good, solid years, and you were my testing ground, Eleven. By now you must have the remains of at least four or five different Titans in your ore-lines, all of them fighting to regain their own shapes.'

'That's all you have to say?' Leven asked evenly. 'Do you even remember the name you gave me, Mother? Or was it our father who did that?' Leven didn't want to cry in front of this woman, but speaking of the man from her memories hurt her much more than the burning ore-lines. 'Who was he? Where did he come from?'

Tyleigh snorted. 'Owain was a bloody fool. I should have looked for someone sharper, cleverer, more ambitious, but my choices were limited and I knew I needed my children to be strong. He was certainly sturdy, I give him that. Although you cut his head off easily enough, Deryn.'

'That's enough.' Leven had crossed the room in a couple of strides. The Titan magic had ebbed, but the dagger in her hand was real and sharp enough. She threw Tyleigh against the wall and put the blade to her throat. Under her hand her mother felt like a thing of bones and skin. 'I'm going to put you out of your misery.'

'Deryn!' Tyleigh seemed to shrink into herself. 'Do you really want to be the daughter who killed both her parents?'

'I'll live with it. You made me a killer, after all.'

Behind her, Leven could hear Cillian approaching. Ynis's footsteps were always silent, but she could sense the girl next to her anyway; curious, unmoved by the impending death of their mother.

'Wait! There's something else.' Tyleigh brought out an object from an inner pocket. It looked like a small flat lozenge of Titanore, silvery blue and inscribed with hundreds of tiny interlocking lines. 'This could save you, Deryn.'

Leven pressed the blade to her neck, but a hand closed over hers. It was Cillian's.

'What is it?' he asked.

'A new augment,' Tyleigh said quickly. She wheezed. Her breath stank like something rotten. 'Made from the bones of the Othanim. They are already our shape, you see, human in aspect – well, almost – and it won't rebel against you. The same powers – better, actually – wings and the sword, strength... It's what I've been making out here in the arse end of nowhere, and it *works*. No memory loss. It will heal you.'

'Stars' arses, you'll say anything to save your own neck, won't you?'

'It's true!' Tyleigh sounded almost indignant. 'A new army of Heralds for our, heh, glorious empress, but I'll give it to you, Deryn. Save your life. All it takes is this ore stone, grafted into your flesh, and it's done. No ore-lines.' She was gasping for breath now, a thin line of blood creeping from the corner of her mouth. 'I can't strip the ore-lines that already exist from your skin without killing you, but the Othanim ore should override them. *Will* override them.'

'Leven,' Cillian turned to face her, putting himself between her and Tyleigh. 'If there's a chance to... make things better—'

'No.' She gave a short bark of laughter. 'I'm never letting this butcher near me again. When we walk away from here tonight we leave her corpse behind.'

'Many griffins have died on her orders,' said Ynis quietly. 'That's enough for me to want to see her dead.'

'What about the other Heralds?' said Tyleigh quickly. 'They all faced the same fate as you, Eleven, but I've saved them. I'm in the process of saving them all – those that are left. Kill me now and you condemn them to the same fate as you!'

Leven stopped. For eight years of her life, her fellow Heralds had been the only family she had – the only family she'd ever known. They had faced death together. And been the deaths of so many others. Even if she never saw a single one of them again, she knew it was a bond that couldn't be severed. She thought of Foro the last time she'd seen him, his face gaunt, the terror and misery in his eyes. If she could have saved him from that, would she have? It wasn't even a question.

She stepped away from Tyleigh, her stomach rolling with disgust.

'Are you not going to do it?' asked Ynis.

'Look at her,' said Leven. 'She'll be dead soon anyway. It's not worth getting my dagger dirty.'

They left Tyleigh on her knees by the alcove, still grasping the ore-stone in her hand. Cillian opened the door to the next room, and Leven waited for Ynis, who was watching the old woman with an expression she couldn't decipher.

'Come on,' she said, 'let's go and get your other sister, the one with feathers.'

# 5

*Your Luminance, it is almost certain that a resumption of the ancient 'earth-shaker' plans would cause unrest in recently Blessed territories. It is the opinion of the Imperium's most celebrated geologists that the likelihood of finding more Titan bones remains slim. Or, as it was put to me, 'like trying to find a single star with no map'. They admit that there are likely new seams of Titan ore to discover, but it is very unlikely we will ever happen across such a density of remains as was discovered in the original Stratum site. Not to mention the fact that the earth-shaker machines have long since fallen into dust, and no one living knows how they were made.*

Envoy report on further Titan-ore mining,
presented to the Empress Celestinia

Kaeto awoke the next morning to the sound of an aggrieved goat's bleating and childish laughter. He lay for a moment in his scavenged bed, just listening. When he stayed at the broken castle, he slept in one of the rooms that could charitably be said to be on the ground floor. It had been a storeroom once, he thought, and it still carried the sweet elderly smell of ancient vegetables, but it was small and intact, and the bed he'd built for himself was comfortable enough. And so different from his quarters in Stratum, which were neat and functional, lined with drawers that held the secrets of the Imperium, the walls covered in maps – they were the first thing he saw when he woke, clinical reminders of the concerns of his employers. Their ambitions, their demands.

Here there was the simple brick of the wall, the quiet of a broken land... and the sound of Belise annoying a goat. He grinned to himself, and got out of bed.

Outside he found his assistant in an improvised pen near the chasm. Inside it there were several boulders carefully balanced on top of each other, and perched on the top of one was a black and white billy goat. Belise was standing with her wings tucked neatly along her back, her hands on her hips. She was a striking figure in the pale golden light of early morning, her black hair shining with a distinctly inhuman lustre, her pale skin almost silvery; she looked strong, otherworldly. So unlike the grubby urchin child he had found on the streets of Stratum with her wiry undernourished limbs, her mousy hair thick with tangles. He felt a pang at that. *She's gained so much, but there's no denying that some things have been lost forever.*

'Come on, you can do it,' she was saying to the goat. 'I've seen you climb more ridiculous things than that.'

The goat glared at her, its horizontal pupils narrowed in the early-morning sun. Then it hopped from one boulder to the top of another, an effortless springing step that even Kaeto found impressive. Belise laughed and clapped.

'Is Felldir teaching you to train goats?'

Belise turned at the sound of his voice, her usual easy grin in place, although he thought he spotted something else, too... bashfulness? He didn't think he had ever seen Belise even mildly embarrassed about anything.

'No, I just thought... They're really clever, chief. Cleverer than animals in Stratum, anyway. I thought it'd be fun to keep one around. He might not like that we spend a lot of time eating his friends but if I feed him regularly, he seems happy enough to be here. I was thinking he could be a kind of pet, maybe.'

A delicate pink blush coloured her cheeks, and despite her Titan face, with its alabaster skin and striking violet eyes, the expression that passed over her face was certainly that of a human fourteen-year-old. She was nervous; nervous that he wouldn't approve of the pet idea; that he might tell her it was frivolous, and unsuitable for an Envoy in training. A sharp sensation of guilt and sorrow passed through Kaeto's chest, softened slightly by the pleasure of seeing Belise enjoy such a simple, innocent thing. *I have taken her childhood from her.* Since they had returned from Houraki, it was a thought that had recurred often in quiet moments.

From its perch on top of the boulders, the goat bleated stridently.

'He wants to try another one,' said Belise. She went to one of the larger boulders, and, picking it up as easily as an apple, balanced it on top of another pile. Almost immediately, the goat hopped across, hooves scrambling against stone.

'I think a pet is a splendid idea,' said Kaeto. 'Does he have a name?'

Belise grinned lopsidedly. Her hesitancy vanished, much to Kaeto's relief. 'I'm calling him Fillipe. After that old geezer who sold herbs in the third ring market. You remember him, chief?'

'Indeed I do, and yes, I can see the resemblance.' Fillipe stuck his hairy chin out, as though insulted by the comparison. At that moment, a darker shadow fell over them. Kaeto looked up to see the familiar shape of Felldir descending from the sky, his wings spread wide. The Titan landed gently, his booted feet barely kicking up dust.

'Hey, Fell!'

'Good morning, Belise.' In his arms he was carrying a shallow bowl of red and black berries, which he passed to the Titan girl. 'I have found another bush of those berries that you like. There is a tiny patch of the bottom of the cavern that still gets sunlight, and much has grown there. I would like for you to see it, Belise. And perhaps we could have the berries with some of the cream that Kaeto has brought from your Stratum.'

Belise dug her hand into the bowl, bursting some of the berries on contact; she had not quite gotten used to the size or strength of her Othanim hands. She licked the juice off her fingers happily enough, and looking at the two of them together Kaeto felt something move inside him, a sudden release in his chest that felt both liberating and frightening. Here was everything he needed; it was madness that he hadn't seen it sooner. He thought of what Felldir had said the night before as the sun vanished beyond the horizon, about leaving the Imperium behind and heading west: away from Stratum, away from Brittletain even, and on to who knew what. It was madness, and yet it felt like sanity.

What if every morning could be like this one?

'Felldir,' he said, noting the pleasure he felt when the Titan turned his yellow wolf's eyes in his direction, 'if you have a moment later, I would like to discuss something with you.'

---

Later, when they had eaten the last of the cold pork with some sweet red apples, Belise flew off to play with her goat and Kaeto and Felldir were left alone in the broken throne room. Belise had insisted they light all their candles for dinner, and buttery light sank into the worn glass goblets, casting a dimpled glow against the stone walls.

'You had something you wished to discuss?'

Kaeto nodded, cleared his throat. He felt certain of his decision, but it was oddly difficult to concentrate when he and the Titan were alone together. Felldir wore his hair tied back in a neat tail these days, but it was very fine and had a tendency to escape the band; much of it had come loose over the course of the day, and strands the colour of moonlight framed his long, serious face.

'Last night you suggested that we go west,' he said carefully. 'And I think, more and more, that I might be of the same mind.'

Felldir raised his eyebrows.

'You are ready to leave your Imperium behind?'

'I... yes.' Kaeto swallowed hard. Why was this so difficult? 'I have a duty to Belise, especially given the... unique events that have befallen her, all of which are ultimately my responsibility.' Felldir was watching him closely, so he stood up, picking up his goblet of wine. For some reason it felt easier to be moving while he was talking. 'She needs guidance and care, which of course you have been giving her, for which I am extremely grateful, and while this war is going on with your people and Brittletain she will always be at risk. Anyone could see her at any point, assume she was an enemy, and act accordingly.' He took a sip of his wine, not looking at Felldir but aware of his golden eyes. 'While I am torn between this place and my duties in Stratum I cannot be sure of her safety. And it is time to... It is time to accept that to me, her wellbeing is of the utmost importance.'

'You love her,' said Felldir. 'She is your beloved child.'

Kaeto did not speak. He couldn't.

Felldir stood up from the table, pushing his chair back, and in a couple of strides he was next to Kaeto. Up close the Titan had an indefinable scent, something like the dust in the Black City and the sharp metallic tang of blood.

'You dance around it, Kaeto, and I do not know why. It is honourable to acknowledge your feelings. For anyone.'

'She's not mine,' Kaeto said quietly. The words felt like they were being drawn from him, like needles to a lodestone. 'I was never meant to have a child. I've brought her into danger, repeatedly, given her knowledge no child should have. My life has been darkness and secrets, doing terrible things in the shadows to serve a master

I never loved or even really admired. She should have had better choices than that. She should have had a loving, normal family, not whatever...' Kaeto looked away. 'Not whatever I am.'

'But you are the whole world to her, Kaeto.' Felldir looked at him curiously. 'Do you not see that?'

Again, Kaeto found he couldn't speak. Felldir laid one big hand on the place where his neck met his shoulder, the pad of one thumb brushing the skin of his throat. Kaeto felt a pull again, as though something else were being drawn from him – not words now, but another kind of truth. When he looked into Felldir's eyes, to his surprise he saw not his usual frank gaze or even hunger, but something more fragile. He almost thought it was fear.

He looked away, turning his body slightly so that contact between them was broken. He cleared his throat.

'So. I must leave the service of the Imperium. But it is not like leaving any other job, as I'm sure you can imagine. I carry the secrets of an empress in my head, and it is generally accepted that an Envoy either dies in service or is removed by the Imperator's own lackeys. A knife in the guts in a darkened corridor, a poisoned dart in a busy street. I have performed such *retirements* myself, many times.' He took a sip of his wine. 'I will have to disappear completely. If possible, I need to make them think I am dead. It will not be easy, and it will require a great deal of thought and planning.' He made himself look at Felldir again. He owed the Titan that much. 'It will take time, and I ask you to be patient with me. But it is something I am committed to. You, and I, and Belise, will go west. Together.'

In the light of the candles, it was just possible to see the hint of a smile touch the corner of Felldir's mouth.

'Very well. I can wait, light-bones.'

# 6

The water of the Old Father River was slate grey, matching a forbidding sky. From her hiding place, Epona could see Londus Bridge clearly enough, the winged figures at its highest point still uncanny despite two years of seeing them in the skies over her city. They had built a rough platform and there were human prisoners waiting at the edge, their hands bound behind their backs. Next to her, Jack crouched, a smear of river mud on one rosy cheek. She had the sword Caliburn slung across her back. For once, it was silent.

'Is there anyone you know there?' asked Jack. 'Can you see them well enough?'

Epona pursed her lips. She knew who Jack was asking about.

'My mother isn't there.'

'Are you sure?'

'I'd know her anywhere, even from this distance.'

Jack's posture relaxed slightly. They were hidden behind the structure of wooden frames at the base of the riverbank, their boots inches deep in gritty tidal mud. The struts were thick with it, studded here and there with pale freshwater barnacles. Someone had carved some words into the beam nearest Epona's head: *The Green Man Rises*. Beneath it someone, perhaps the same hand, had added an oak leaf. *Tell him to bloody hurry up*, she thought. *We need all the help we can get.*

'If we move quickly, we may be able to reach these prisoners in time,' said Jack. 'We will go quietly, and when we are discovered, I will cut my way through as many as I can while you free the captives.'

Epona stared at her companion. Jack had arrived at rebellion headquarters from the west just over six months ago, carrying news from Dwffd and Kornwullis, her magical sword slung over her shoulder. She had quickly become one of the key figures in their struggle against the Othanim, but still Epona could not quite figure her out. Insane heroics seemed to run in her blood.

'Are you out of your mind?' Epona hissed. 'There are two of us and... *hundreds* of them. We are just here to see what's going on. Not to go wading into a fight that will get us instantly decapitated.'

At that moment the sword gave a soft, slightly discordant humming noise – it made Epona think of some of the string instruments that the bards had played in her mother's summer court. It was not quite music, not quite a voice. It made her uneasy.

'Caliburn says that we could make it,' said Jack.

'Forgive me for not wanting to put my life in the hands of a piece of steel you found hanging about in a muddy lake.'

Jack looked slightly put out. 'Caliburn is an enchanted sword from the very beginning of our history; it has played a part in many of our greatest—'

'Yes alright,' Epona snapped. 'Look, we could go back to the hideout, get a small team together and come back. Perhaps with Caliburn we could take that group of Othanim on the bridge, but we'd need Druin. And people who can attack from a distance.' She straightened up a little, forgetting about the water seeping into her boots. 'Archers. Maybe two groups of them, hidden from the Othanim – that might keep them from being too comfortable in the sky—'

There was a scream and a splash. Epona looked up in time to see a prisoner being pushed from the bridge, their legs desperately pinwheeling in the air before they hit the water and sank like a stone.

'What are they—'

A second and a third were pushed off the ledge. Even from where they crouched on the bank, Epona could hear the merry laughter of the Othanim as they killed their prisoners. There was a joyfulness to them, as though they were children playing a game. A great wave of sickening helplessness moved through Epona – a feeling that had become extremely familiar in the last two years of Othanim occupation. Her hand went to the long dagger on her belt, gripping the hilt until her knuckles turned white.

'We would have been too late whatever we did,' said Jack. 'Please do not blame yourself, Princess.'

Helplessness was replaced with anger. 'I *don't* blame myself, Jack, I blame those flying fuckeries and the monster who rules them. And I told you not to call me that.' She sloshed away from the wooden scaffolding, turning her back on Londus Bridge. The last of the prisoners had already fallen. 'Let's head back to the Barrow. I've seen enough horrors for one day.'

---

The Barrow was a camp on the very edge of the Wild Wood. Once, it had been a sizable mound of chalky earth covered in deep green grass. According to the Druin in their group, it had been built by people thousands of years ago, possibly as a place to entomb their dead. Since then, the wood had seeped around it, growing hornbeam and poplar on its roof and concealing it from view – making it a very useful secret camp. There were two entrances, at the front and the rear, and inside there was a warren of tunnels and rooms. The main feature of the central chamber was a long stone plinth, which the rebels had adopted as the place to plan their attacks – attempts to rescue prisoners, sabotaging Othanim operations, passing information to other groups around Brittletain. All great, vital things, Epona believed – or at least, she had. Two years into the fight and it felt as though they had made very little progress.

'We're not getting anywhere.'

She stood at the end of the plinth, her hands pressed against the cold stone. Spread across its surface were maps, reports scribbled on old pieces of parchment, most of them held down with sticky clay cups that had contained mead or wine. Jack stood at the other end, the lamplight turning her face golden. She was an imposing figure, one it was curiously difficult to look away from; tall and well-proportioned, her arms lightly muscled and her posture always extremely correct. Her skin was creamy white and her cheeks slightly pink, so she always looked a little like she had just come in from a long journey across a cold country. She had golden hair which she usually wore pulled up in an untidy braid that ran from the centre of her hairline to the back of her neck. Her eyes were hazel, a warm tawny colour with a hint of green that refused to be pinned down. As a princess, Epona was used to being the person who drew the eye in a room, but Jack was something else. She was luminous. It was annoying.

Also gathered around the plinth were several of the rebels' key figures: Karayné-bog, the captain of Queen Broudicca's household guard (now disbanded), a man who gave the impression of being wider than he was tall, with a striking ginger beard that he had braided into points; Solasach and Yelm, two Druin who had survived the destruction of Dosraiche but had been separated from the larger Druin force; and Larth, a quietly spoken woman who wore the black eye-paint of Dwffd and a cloak made of bear hide.

Epona looked around at them all. She wished they didn't look as tired as she felt.

'Does anyone have anything new to report?'

Jack pulled a piece of parchment towards her across the plinth and held it up to the nearest lamp. 'Our people to the north have noted a lot of activity from the Othanim on the outer edge of the Wild Wood near the Greater Chalk Walkway. They have begun clearing trees away.'

Yelm scowled and crossed her arms over her chest. She had short curly horns, like a young ram, and darker freckles over nut-brown skin. 'The desecration of the Wild Wood continues.'

'What are they doing though?' asked Epona. 'Do they need the timber? If so, what for?'

'They just wish to burn that which we love,' put in Solasach.

'Could be they need a way through the wood,' said Karaynébog. He was pulling his fingers through his beard in short little jerks, making the ends of his braids stand on end. 'Although hard to imagine why, when they can fly wherever they like.'

'They *have* a way through the wood,' said Yelm darkly. For a moment the group grew quiet. It had been widely reported, and then confirmed by a spy within Londus-on-Sea itself, that several of the Atchorn group had joined forces with the Othanim. If the flying bastards needed a safe route through the Wild Wood, one of the Druin traitors could take them.

'I do not understand why,' Solasach said. He looked around at them, his eyes wide. He was a young man with a long, intelligent face. One of his horns had been snapped clean off in a skirmish with the Othanim. 'Why would those who were joined to the forest by the Druidahnon himself turn against Brittletain?'

'They like Brittletain well enough,' said Epona, 'it's the queens and kings they want to see dead.' She thought of her sister, Ceni, who had been queen in Galabroc and had taken Londus too, throwing their mother and younger sisters in the dungeon, all while the Othanim were beginning their assault on Dosraiche. Perhaps if Broudicca hadn't been distracted by trying to keep her eldest daughter from overthrowing her, they might have been able to save the Druin Mother Oak. They might have been able to save the entire island. Instead, their squabbles had left Brittletain vulnerable at exactly the wrong moment. Perhaps the Atchorn were right about the queens of Brittletain. 'And I suppose that the Othanim are the best chance of seeing that happen.'

Although, she reasoned, if she ever saw Ceni again, she'd happily reduce the number of Brittletain queens by one herself. At least her sister's occupation of Londus had been short-lived. The Othanim had unceremoniously tipped her out of her stolen throne.

'The number of people managing to escape the city has dwindled,' said Larth, her eyes downcast. 'We have people at all the known weak spots to take them away quickly if they get out, but we're definitely seeing fewer now. The tunnel under the old salt warehouse collapsed, so that's one less route for them to use, and they are watching the river much more closely than before.' The diminutive woman cleared her throat. 'We had a messenger return from Mersia. Their response is still the same.'

'They still think I murdered their queen.' Epona bit her lip. Since Ceni's schemes had landed her, Leven and Cillian in hot water, trust had been in short supply amongst the kingdoms of Brittletain – and it was ever a scarce resource. Even amongst her own followers, she knew there were those who still believed she had been the one behind Queen Ismere's gory death – and they admired her for it, despite her protests. 'Magog's balls,' she muttered. 'I don't suppose anyone has any good news? As a special treat?'

'Your sisters are well, and remain hidden,' continued Larth quietly. 'Awnie Taffler reports that they are, and I quote, a relentless pain in her rear end, but I take that to mean that the girls are in good spirits at least.'

'Thank you,' said Epona, meaning it. When the rebellion had snatched her from the dungeons of Londus, they had also managed to liberate her three younger sisters. Lanoshea, Ennua and Eefa, all under the age of ten when the Othanim had invaded, had since been packed off to be looked after by a distant relative. Epona was keen that they be kept some distance from the rebellion itself – as feisty as all three of them were, and as eager as they were to ride their own war chariots against the occupied city, they were still little kids. She missed them horribly.

Jack's sword hummed softly. Every face in the room turned to her. She cleared her throat.

'I don't quite understand what Caliburn means by this, but it is telling me that the Green Man has been summoned.'

Epona laughed. She thought of the words carved into the wooden strut she'd seen that morning. 'Well, thank you, Caliburn, but I was hoping for something a little more solid than rumours of a mythical figure sticking his oar in.'

'We don't use the Green Man's name lightly,' said Yelm, a slight tone of accusation to her voice. 'If possible, we don't talk of him at all.'

'Why not?' asked Karayné-bog. He was the sort of man who couldn't leave a question unasked.

'Because he is not some minor spirit or pixen you can call on for help or leave milk out for,' said Solasach. 'He's the very soul of the Wild Wood. He is chaotic, uncontrollable. He cares little for human lives. He is creation and death all in one.'

'Yes, but is he actually real?' Larth touched one of the papers on the stone and drew it towards her, before dismissing it again. 'I thought this discussion was for reports, supplies, the movements of real people. The war. Do we have time to listen to faery stories?'

'We *are* receiving information from an enchanted singing sword,' said Karayné-bog. 'I think it's possible we have already crossed that particular bridge.'

'Typical city dweller! Very happy to walk the Paths of the Wild Wood and seek our protection from the Dunohi, but asked to believe in something beyond the end of your stupid beard? Asked to take our magic seriously?' Yelm snorted. 'And suddenly it's all nonsense to you.'

'Caliburn's advice has always steered us in the right direction,' said Jack quietly. As ever, her voice cut through everyone else's despite its volume. Other voices rose in response, and very quickly the whole crowd was bickering. Epona watched them with a sinking feeling in her stomach. How could she lead these people? They were all so different. Brittletain had always been a place of factions, of tribes. Now they were all under threat and still they clung on to their differences, as though they couldn't fathom how meaningless they were in the face of the Othanim. She thought of the sound the bodies had made as they hit the murky waters of the Old Father.

'Enough!' She raised her voice. As short and slight as she was, every head turned to look at her. 'This is getting us nowhere and we've so much to do. They were killing people today.' She let the words sink in; watched the horror on their faces grow. 'Just throwing our people from the bridge into the river to drown – not for any particular reason. Just because it was fun. We have to...'

She paused at the sound of boots crunching against the pebble-strewn floor. A messenger appeared at the chamber door, her round face damp with sweat.

'What is it?'

The girl blinked. She looked caught between terror and excitement.

'We've got one of them,' she said. 'We've got one of the bastards.'

# 7

One of Karayné-bog's great projects over the last year had been a kind of spear catapult, with which pointed weapons could be launched into the sky via a contraption that was wound up with a crank. It turned out that the unfortunate Othanim had been caught by this machine's first real test – and the first where Karayné-bog's team had attached a light chain to the end of the spear. The Othanim now lay in the shallow pit where they had thrown it. One of its white wings had been torn through the middle by the airborne spear and was now half hanging off, a mess of blood and feathers with a sliver of silvery blue Titan bone poking through. Epona looked at the bone and thought of Leven, with her Titan-ore tattoos. *Where are you, my friend?*

'We'd tested it several times with nothing to really aim at,' one of Karayné-bog's assistants was explaining excitedly, ''cause there's only so much you can learn from shooting a tree with a spear, and there's no bird big enough to act as a substitute. But then we saw this thing flying over and we thought, yeah. Let's go for it! What harm could it do?'

'You could have pissed it off enough that it came down here and killed you,' said Epona, but without much heart. This was the first success they'd had in a long while, and they dearly needed one. *So why doesn't it make me feel any better?*

'It fought against us when we tried to drag it back in,'

the assistant continued, 'but eventually it seemed to lose its strength and it just fell. It landed on its leg badly. We think it's broken.'

The Othanim in the pit was female, smaller than most of the ones Epona had seen close up. She was short, with untidy dark hair and loose skin. She looked old, with deep creases at the corners of her wide mouth and her black eyes. *I assumed they didn't age*, Epona thought. *But of course, they must do.* Someone had tied her arms around her back; Epona made a note to find out who it was and give them a medal for bravery.

Her leg certainly looked broken, the whole thing lying awkwardly as though it had shattered into three pieces, but when the Othanim saw Epona, she grinned.

'The princess Epona,' she said. 'We have heard of you. The rebel princess.'

'How lovely,' said Epona dryly. 'It's nice to know I'm making an impact.'

'Like a rat, scratching at our back door,' said the Othanim.

'What's your name?'

'Bezryl.'

'Bezryl, I would love for you to tell us about your occupation of Londus. The number of people you have there, your patrols, when they happen. I would love to hear about your leader, what she wants from this place.'

The Othanim called Bezryl laughed. 'I will tell nothing to light-bones. Like speaking to an *animal*. An *insect*. You hear noises but you do not understand.'

'That is what we are to you? Insects beneath notice?' Epona tipped her head to one side. 'What about the other Titans? How do you feel about them?'

Bezryl sneered with her upper lip, exposing her long teeth. 'The griffins are little more than birds, hiding up in their mountains. And the Druidahnon is already dead.'

A cold hand seemed to grasp Epona's heart. Behind her she heard Yelm cry out, a low desperate noise of horror.

'Did you not know? We forget that your messengers are slow and cannot fly. The Druidahnon died on a hill, torn to pieces by our army. He is nothing but meat and bones now, lying on the grass for small scurrying animals to feed on. They feast on his guts.'

'That can't be true,' said Solasach. 'Can it? The creature is lying.' His voice shook. 'Our lord is the strongest of all Titans.'

'It pleases us to kill your leaders,' Bezryl continued. 'To leave you running around like headless beetles. Soon, we will kill your queen.'

Epona took a step towards the pit. Out of the corner of her eye she saw Jack look at her with concern.

'What did you say?'

'Oh yes,' Bezryl shifted in the dirt, her broken wing dragging in the mud. 'Icaraine the Lightbringer will feed your mother to her child soon – he will eat only the bones of the most important. A paltry feast, but we have very little to choose from on this stinking island.'

Epona curled her hands into fists, letting her fingernails dig into her skin. It was important not to lose your temper, important not to let them know you were afraid.

'When?' she asked, not trusting herself to say more.

'The child of the chains celebrates his fifth birthing day when the stars have turned to show us the Crystal Lute, the Branching Tree and the Broken Sword. The prince will enjoy crunching her bones between his teeth. She will scream, I expect.'

Epona turned her head away from the Othanim. She nodded to Jack.

'We won't waste time torturing this one. Kill her.'

Jack stood very still. From its scabbard on her back, Caliburn made a soft humming noise.

'I can't do that,' she said. 'I cannot kill an unarmed prisoner.'

'You can't, or the sword won't?' snarled Epona. 'Fine. Mother always encouraged me to be a hands-on kind of leader.'

She snatched up one of the long spears from where they lay in the dirt, and holding it with both arms, she extended it so that the steel tip lay against the hollow of Bezryl's neck.

The Othanim laughed. 'I am not afraid of you, little princess. You and your light-bones followers are little more than—'

'Rats, I know.' Epona pressed the spear home, the wickedly sharp point sinking into the soft flesh of the Othanim's throat. There was a strangled noise, and blood began to flow like a fast river, dark and somehow obscene. More blood surged up through Bezryl's mouth, and Epona saw fear on the creature's face after all. Her eyes grew wide and belatedly she tried to move – but it was much too late for that. 'How does it feel to be killed by a rat, great and worthy Titan?' Epona leaned on the spear with her full weight and it passed through the Othanim's neck into the dirt below. There was some more thrashing, and then it was over. Epona dropped the spear. Jack was staring at her, the flush on her cheeks especially pink.

Larth and Karayné-bog had been waiting off to one side. Epona gestured at them.

'Strip everything off that corpse. If she was carrying any more information, I want to know about it.'

# 8

'You're quite right, my friend, it was long thought that every portrait of the empress's unfortunate sister had been destroyed – there was even a large marble statue of her in the middle of Stratum once, and that was toppled and smashed to pieces when Celestinia took power. However, I had a source who insisted that one or two items of that period had survived. Extremely secret, of course, and actually owning any such thing would be a death sentence, but I can tell you that I have indeed seen a painting, one that was hidden in a cellar, behind a locked door, and covered with oil cloth. My friend swore me to secrecy, as you'd expect, but I see no real harm in describing to you what I saw (after all, the painting could be of anyone, couldn't it?). There was a young woman seated on the star throne, plain if I am being honest with you, but with a certain canny intelligence behind her eyes. Her hair was black and styled in oiled ringlets, and in her lap she held the sceptre of our ancestors. She looked... rueful, is how I would describe it. Faintly cynical. I think she knew her sister was plotting against her. Perhaps she'd begun to taste the poison.'

Transcript of a conversation between citizens of the Imperium under surveillance by the Envoy office

Kaeto's desk was covered in reports, as it often was when he'd been away – and the Othanim situation had increased them fourfold. He made himself a cup of hot sweet tea from the pot he kept warming on the stove – this was normally Belise's job, and he hadn't yet had the heart to replace her – and began to read through what had been left for him. It would be his job to sort out the useful and interesting from the pointless and repetitive, then bring that information in a palatable format to the Empress Celestinia. At least, until he had figured out how he could disappear.

From what he could see, the situation in Brittletain was dire. The island had apparently been at the start of a new civil war when the Othanim arrived on their shores, and this distribution of armies and resources had left them seriously on the back foot when the Titans attacked. The Othanim were first spotted on the eastern coast, over the Channel of Giants, yet Queen Ceni had continued her invasion and assault of Londus-on-Sea regardless. Only later, when the true Othanim force arrived at Brittletain's biggest city, had Ceni realised her mistake. She had already decimated more than half her mother's army, and with her own heavy losses she was woefully unprepared when Icaraine came knocking. Witness reports from the refugees managing to get out of Brittletain mentioned a battle that turned the waters of the Old Father River red. It wasn't clear where Queen Ceni was now. Everyone seemed quite certain that Queen Broudicca was still alive somewhere in the dungeons below Londus.

The great Druin tree-city, Dosraiche, had been destroyed. That gave Kaeto a pang of regret. The alien magic that was native to Brittletain had always felt pleasingly mysterious. It was disappointing to learn that it was as easily snuffed out as anything else. From what they'd gleaned from the Britons now in Blessed territory, pockets of Druin remained, likely hiding out in the deepest parts of the Wild Wood.

Other reports were more prosaic. They had several Envoys along the coast of Gaül on the lookout for signs that the Othanim forces were moving on from Brittletain, but so far that didn't appear to be the case. It seemed that Icaraine's only interest was the obliteration of the remaining living Titans. And yet...

Nothing he'd received so far suggested the griffins were involved.

There had been a Herald-led project in the very north of Brittletain, involving the slaughter of griffins and the retrieval of their remains. It occurred to him that Boss, the leader of the original Herald regiment, had been there. Perhaps she would have some unique insights into the griffin situation, having seen them up close. She might not know anything of use, but it was worth seeking her out to be sure.

He left his office and made his way down the secret corridor out into the larger Imperator complex through a concealed exit, but was startled to find two Heralds waiting for him there.

*Careless*, he told himself. *You're getting careless.*

'Envoy.' One of them gave a short half-bow, which put Kaeto on alert immediately. 'The empress wishes to speak to you.'

Kaeto smiled easily. He glanced up and down the corridor, calculating his exits. A meeting with the empress was one thing, but an unscheduled one?

'We have our regular meeting the day after tomorrow...'

'All the same, she'd like to speak to you this morning.'

These Heralds were the new kind, freshly minted by Gynid Tyleigh in her workshop, wherever that was; not even Kaeto was privy to that information, possibly because the last time he had seen Tyleigh she had been dying in agony from poison he'd given her. Rather than the familiar silver-blue ore lines of the original Heralds, these new volunteers bore only a single lozenge of the ore, buried beneath the skin; usually on the forearm, or the base of the neck, leaving a dark blue discolouration. They were stronger, more powerful than the retired Heralds, and as the process was significantly less painful and intrusive, they survived it with their memories more or less intact. And yet, Kaeto disliked them. They were soldiers, genuine volunteers: Imperial loyalists through and through.

The younger Herald, a man with a shaved head and skin the colour of milk, put his hand on Kaeto's arm. Just lightly, barely exerting any pressure, but the threat was there anyway. He smiled.

'If I am going to see her this morning, I should bring the reports I have already processed,' said Kaeto. 'I will just go back to the Envoy office and retrieve them.'

The grip grew a little tighter.

'There is no need for that, Envoy Kaeto.'

In the end there was little he could do. He walked down the corridor flanked by the pair of them. Kaeto had killed Heralds before, but always at a distance, in secret. He had a knife concealed in his boot, laced with a poison that would knock out an opponent for a day or more, but he had only the one, and he could not be sure the poison would affect them, or even that the blade would break their skin. These new Heralds were tough.

The taller Herald glanced at him as though she could read his thoughts.

'The empress is waiting for you in the Blue Room, Envoy. She will be concerned if we are late.'

---

The Blue Room wasn't truly blue; the name referred to the stained-glass window that dominated the chamber. Constructed from shards of blue, black and purple glass, it was made to resemble the night sky, with a crescent of golden moon and clouds painted in pale cream moonlight, while the ancestor stars were represented by golden studs. In the daytime, sunlight passed through the window to cast a soft azure light over the rest of the room. It was the chamber where the empress was traditionally housed while visiting the Imperator complex, and it was accordingly lush. Kaeto stood with his hands clasped behind his back, keeping his face relaxed, although on the inside every alarm was sounding.

The empress sat, tiny figure that she was, on a golden chair with pink upholstery. The doll she habitually carried with her sat on an identical chair to one side; today it was dressed in silver lace, its painted face hidden behind a glittering veil. Imperator Justinia was also present. She stood behind a long table, her arms crossed over her chest. As ever when she was in the presence of the empress she looked irritable, but Kaeto sensed that there was a special bit of irritation, just for him. Ire, even. The Heralds had taken the knife from his boot; he felt its absence keenly.

'There you are, Envoy,' said Justinia. 'I hope you feel suitably honoured. Our empress has left the Indigo Sky Palace especially to see you.'

'I am always honoured to be in the presence of either of you,' he replied evenly. Justinia, he noticed, had a sword at her hip.

'We have a special mission,' said the empress. She turned her wrinkled-moon face up to his, her head cocked slightly to one side. She was wearing a tiny pair of smoked spectacles – she spent so long staring up at the heavens that she often found daylight quite uncomfortable. 'Something... unique. As befits the only person in the Imperium to have had such direct dealings with the Othanim.'

'Truly, my experience with them was brief,' he replied. A prickle of sweat had broken out across the back of his neck. 'I spoke only once to Icaraine the Lightbringer.' His mind's eye served up the memory of Belise's bones, presented to him like a gift. 'And only a little with the other living Othanim in the Black City.' This was an outright lie, and it felt as comfortable as velvet gloves. His reports to the Imperium on their return from Houraki had been missing several key details, while his version of the poisoning of Gynid Tyleigh was a finely stitched web that would fall apart at the slightest touch: she had accidentally poisoned herself by brewing tea with the wrong plant, it had caused her to hallucinate and imagine all manner of terrible things. What an unfortunate slip-up by one of the Imperium's greatest minds. He had also failed to tell them that it had been his own action that had freed Icaraine, claiming instead that she had freed herself. But as always with the Imperium, if a thing was useful, they tended not to look too closely at its flaws.

'Tyleigh insisted that you were quite close to the creature. You and your assistant both.' The empress dipped her head towards her doll, as though it had whispered something to her. 'Once again, our condolences on the loss of your assistant. We understand that you valued her highly.'

'Thank you, your Luminance.' Kaeto gave her a half-bow. 'It is a great shame that Bone Crafter Tyleigh's recall of events was so fractured and confused by the poisons of Houraki. I'm glad that she has recovered enough to continue her services to the Imperium.'

The empress chuckled dryly. 'As limited as your contact with the Othanim may have been, Envoy Kaeto, that still makes you the most experienced by some margin.' She shuffled forward slightly on her chair. Her feet did not reach the floor. 'We want you to go to Brittletain itself and broker an agreement with this Icaraine.'

Kaeto cleared his throat. 'I beg your pardon, my empress?'

'Everything we've gathered about the Othanim so far suggests they have gone to Brittletain because they have a longstanding grudge against the griffins and the bear Titan,' put in Imperator Justinia. 'Your own reports detailed this war between the Titans that apparently took place two thousand years ago. It seems the Othanim wish to finish what they started. But nothing suggests that they won't start looking for other targets once they are done with that dreary little island.'

'It is hard to imagine that such creatures will be satisfied with Brittletain,' the empress said, smiling faintly. 'To us, they feel like locusts.' She reached across to pat her doll's hand. 'They won't stop feeding just because their favourite food is gone. So we must come to an agreement with them now, before that happens.'

'Forgive me, Empress, but I am not sure that the Othanim can be reasoned with.'

'Oh, but I'm afraid you are incorrect there, Envoy.'

The sense that something was wrong tripled. Kaeto suddenly had the impression that there were hidden depths beneath this conversation, depths that contained sharks and other things very keen on eating him.

'You have made contact with them,' he said.

'Yes. Little notes sent back and forth. A gentle query here and there, all very careful. They are willing to speak to a representative of ours.' The empress sounded pleased with herself. 'They are willing to talk about the future. Isn't that marvellous? There are certain criteria that must be met, but that is to be expected from such a powerful entity.'

*Here it is*, thought Kaeto. *Here comes the shark.*

'And what criteria are those?'

'We *know*, Kaeto,' Imperator Justinia said, her tone weary. She never did have the patience for the empress's little games. 'We know about your two friends, out in the Breaks.'

'And isn't that useful?' said the empress cheerily. 'You happen to have exactly what she wants.'

'I...' Kaeto swallowed hard. Panic swirled inside him, a lethal riptide. 'I'm not sure I know what you're referring to.'

'Icaraine the Lightbringer wants her subject back,' said Justinia. 'It seems she has unfinished business with him, too. And the other Othanim, whoever that is, will be a bonus. A goodwill gesture. A gift. In return she will listen to our proposals.'

'Did you really think, Kaeto,' the empress said, 'did you really think that you could return from Houraki with such a story and not be put under surveillance? We have known about your broken castle since the very beginning. We have simply watched and waited for it to be useful.'

'Listen...' His instinct, so ingrained it was like breathing, was to lie, to spin some fabrication out of thin air – anything at all to turn them away from what he needed to hide. But they knew. They already knew. He decided to try something new. The truth. 'Listen, they are doing no harm where they are. They have no loyalty to Icaraine, and no intention of ever harming the Imperium. She wants to kill them because they have defied her. What use is that to anyone?'

'It's useful to *me*, Envoy.' The empress chuckled. 'Perhaps you have forgotten who the ancestor stars blessed with their light?'

There was a long moment of silence. The azure glow from the window grew dimmer, then brighter again as a cloud passed in front of the sun.

He bowed deeply.

'Forgive me. I will of course go at once to the Breaks and prepare for the journey to Brittletain.' There had to be time to warn them. 'We can be ready to leave for the coast in a few days, assuming that the diplomatic messages are ready.'

'Kaeto, I'm surprised at you,' said Justinia. 'Being this slow on the uptake isn't an appealing characteristic in an Envoy. We already *have* them. Your Othanim friends have been captured and are already on their way to the ship that will take you across the Titan's Eye Sea.'

*Captured.* The word sunk a hook into his heart. Had they fought back? Felldir might not fight to save himself, but to protect Belise? And of course Belise would have fought. Her alley-cat instincts had never truly left her. Had they been hurt?

'Our new Heralds did a fine job,' Justinia continued. 'Very different, I imagine, from fighting an entire Othanim army, but even so, it was a useful test of their abilities.'

'Envoy Kaeto.' The empress sat forward in her chair. 'You look as though you have been hit on the head with something heavy, so let me explain this to you in a simple way. Either you accompany our Othanim captives to Brittletain and engage Icaraine the Lightbringer on our behalf... or you will be taken from here now and executed in the middle of Stratum plaza for treason. Do you understand?'

# 9

*Sometimes, when dealing with her is especially onerous, I entertain myself by thinking of the poor soul in Houraki who found her, crawling along that jungle path with her clothes soaked in blood and a fury in her heart. Tyleigh is hardly the most charming soul at the best of times, and I remain faintly amazed that whoever came across her during her agonised escape from the Black City didn't just put her out of her misery, or themselves out of theirs, at least. But credit to them, they got her to a healer, and reluctantly I must give credit to her, too: only a will of iron could have moved someone so grievously hurt.*

*Whether she accidentally poisoned herself or the Envoy was involved, the damage to her digestive system is extensive. My estimate is that it won't be long until I am put out of my misery.*

Extract of notes from the senior healer assigned<br>to Gynid Tyleigh during the new Herald project

The chamber where T'rook was being kept was gloomy and squalid. As they stepped beyond the door, Ynis noted many things she had not spotted from her perch at the window: a long worktable at the back of the room covered in what appeared to be jars of blood and feathers; a rack of strange metal tools she did not like to guess the use of; and several large drawings tacked to the walls of griffins that had been cut open, their guts and bones spread open and pinned in place – these made her think of Brocken, whose body had been taken from them before they could bring it to the sacred Bone Fall.

Her eyes only rested on these things for a moment; her full attention was for her sister, who had risen up on her back legs, her scaly blue talons ringing against the bars of her cage.

'*Ynis?* Is that you?'

'Sister!'

Ynis ran to the cage even as T'rook began beating her wings, making the drawings on the walls flutter, but when she yanked at the bars they would not budge.

'Get me out of here!' T'rook was calling, her voice ragged and furious. 'I must see the sky, and then I will slaughter every ground-stuck stinking human I set my eyes on.' Her golden eyes focussed on Leven and Cillian, who had come into the room behind Ynis. 'There! They are so brazen, but they won't be when you let me out. I will taste your blood, ground-stuck meat bags!'

'I don't know what I expected,' said Leven.

'Listen,' Ynis stuck her arm through the bars and grabbed a fistful of T'rook's chest feathers, forcing the griffin to look at her. 'This woman is my human sister. And this is the man she is rutting.' There was a strangled cough from behind her, which she ignored. 'We cannot eat them. Or maim them.'

'What? What are you talking about?' T'rook gave a harsh squawk. 'The Edge Walkers have made your brain-shell soft.'

'It's true.' Out of nowhere, Ynis felt like she might be close to tears. The smell of her sister, the cold softness of her feathers, and reality of her human family... it was too much. Her frail human emotions were betraying her again. She focussed instead on the task at hand. After two years of fruitless searching, they were nearly done. 'I will explain, but when we're far away from this place. You must promise.'

T'rook took a step backwards, breaking the contact between them. There was a wary look in her eye.

'I will swear,' she snapped. 'For now.'

'Here.' Cillian had been searching through the detritus on the tables and came forward with a brass ring. On it was single key as long as his hand. 'This looks to be the one.'

In seconds the door swung open, and T'rook leapt out, colliding with Ynis. For a moment she was uncertain on her feet, talons scratching and skittering against the smooth stone floor. Then, she spread her wings with obvious pleasure. Several items from the tables were dislodged, briefly filling the chamber with the tinkling music of broken glass.

'Stars' arses, I half thought we'd never get here.' Leven was grinning. 'But we can't hang around. Tyleigh will have alerted more guards and I'm not sure what I've got left to fight them.'

'Tyleigh!' The feathers on T'rook's neck stood on end and she reared up on her back legs. 'The witch! Show me to her and I will eat her bones! I will *feast* on that murderer, that torturer, that lowest of crawling snakes, I will—'

'Sister.' Again Ynis went to T'rook, sinking both hands into the ruff of feathers and fur. 'There is no time. We have to go, now.'

'We are to run from a fight?' T'rook tossed her head. 'Never!'

'Not so much running from a fight as running into several other fights,' said Leven in a mildly exasperated tone. 'Ynis, can you direct T'rook to the camp? Cillian and me will meet you there.'

---

It was extraordinary to be in the sky again.

Two years of both feet on the ground at all times, two years of watching her human sister flying instead of her on her blue glass wings. And here, finally, she was back where she belonged, the scent of T'rook in her nose, the solid familiar weight beneath her, and nothing but the stars above them. Ynis grinned into the dark, even as the tears tracked down her cheeks.

'You are heavier than you were,' commented T'rook. 'And longer. Your limbs are all over the place.'

'I'm older,' said Ynis. 'And you're older, too.' She freed one hand to wipe at her face. This high up, her tears were turning icy. 'I haven't grown all that much, not really, but you have.'

'You have grown *soft*. Why are we fleeing from the enemy? She is the one who caused Brocken to be murdered. To be butchered. She has kept me in a cage, Ynis. Like a *bird*.'

Ynis opened her mouth, then closed it again. She could think of no way to explain to T'rook that Leven needed Tyleigh alive to save the other Heralds – it was simply not something that T'rook would comprehend or sympathise with. To her, humans were prey animals to be scattered or eaten at the edge of griffin territory. What did she care about some humans she had never even seen?

And there were other reasons to keep Tyleigh alive. Ones that Ynis was not yet ready to admit to herself.

'She is already dying,' she said eventually, aware that this was not enough. 'She is a sickly prey creature, not worth dirtying your talons for. Right now, we have to fly rather than fight. But soon,' she leaned forward so that her head was close to her sister's, 'soon we'll be back in Yelvynia. We can see our fathers.'

Below them, the landscape rolled away in tones of blue and black and grey. Ynis could see patches of water in the fields, where the rain of the last few days had collected, and they reflected the stars back up at her. It was a gift, almost. Like flying in an endless sky.

'Yes,' rumbled T'rook finally. 'I will be glad to be there. With you, my sister.'

---

They had made their camp on a hill that overlooked Tyleigh's compound, a thickly wooded place that would be easy to hide in if the alchemist's guards came looking for them. Cillian had said nothing, but Leven could see easily enough the relief in his face; to be under the canopy of trees again, even if they weren't his trees, soothed him on some level he couldn't quite articulate. Unsurprisingly, Ynis and T'rook had reached the place before them, and her little sister already had the fire going.

'There is stew,' said Cillian, fetching the pot from where he'd hidden it from scavenging animals. 'Rabbit and carrot, mainly.'

'I prefer my rabbits with fur on,' T'rook said, her beak held high. 'Not in pieces with all the flavour boiled out.'

'Well, there's stew for us, anyway,' said Leven. She took the pot from Cillian and wedged it near the fire where it would warm. The only griffin she had been close to before was Festus, who had accompanied Ynis on her initial search for T'rook before returning to Yelvynia. He had been large and robust, with striking blue feathers and eyes the colour of summer oak leaves. He had tolerated the presence of humans with a kind of baffled grumpiness. T'rook looked actively irate. *I can hardly blame her,* Leven thought to herself. *She has been imprisoned and tortured by humans for two years. We're lucky we haven't been disembowelled. And it's all my mother's fault.*

'We will hunt.' Ynis stood up from her place by the fire. Her posture was stiff, as it often was, her shoulders up by her ears. 'There will be larger prey away from the hill. I have seen deer down on the slopes.'

'Now? At night?' Leven frowned. 'Surely the animals will be hidden away at this time.'

'T'rook can see well in the dark,' said Ynis shortly. The griffin stood up too, and Leven saw with a little trickle of dismay that they were both eager to be away again.

'Won't it be safer in the morning?' Leven began to dig through her pack. 'There's dried meat in here; it's salty but it's still good...'

A warm hand touched her elbow. Cillian spoke quietly enough that only she could hear.

'Let them go. They have a lot of catching up to do. They'll be back soon enough.'

She stopped. Ynis was already on T'rook's back and in a flurry of wind and feathers, they were back in the sky again, lost to sight in moments.

'I know you're right.' Leven turned to Cillian. 'I just worry. This whole area must be crawling with Tyleigh's people and they'll be looking for the griffin, for all of us...' She stopped. 'What is it? What's wrong?'

The Druin half smiled, shook his head. 'I'm not sure I can tell you,' he said. 'I don't understand it myself.'

'Here, sit down. Did you hit your head when you fell off that roof or something?'

They sat by the fire together, Cillian looping his arm comfortably around her waist. Before he spoke, he leaned against her so that they were cheek to cheek, and she took a moment to enjoy the scent of him, as she always did: green and wild and earthy.

'I heard a voice in my head,' he said eventually. 'When we were waiting in the dark. It was so loud, and so clear, for a moment. It felt familiar, yet it also sounded... wrong. Like it was warped by distance, I don't know.'

'What did it say?'

'It said, "I call you now, Walker of Paths. I call you here, Forest Father. The Wild Wood needs its protector, Green Man."' He paused, biting his lip. 'That's all it said. I think it was the Druidahnon. I always thought I'd know his voice anywhere, but I couldn't tell you for sure it was him. It was like two voices speaking at once.'

Leven pressed herself closer to him. She felt colder than she had moments before.

'Who is the Green Man?'

At that moment, Cillian's little jackdaw friend Inkwort flew down out of the branches above them. They hadn't seen her all day. She strutted about in front of the fire making her *tchk* noises until Cillian threw her some seeds from his pocket.

'I hardly know how to explain it. Him.' Cillian sighed. 'He's the spirit of the Wild Wood, I suppose, like the Dunohi, but... more secretive. More hidden. You might run across the Forest Souls when you're travelling the Paths – and you would know, you had a fight with one – but the Green Man? I know of no Druin who has seen him, but we all know he exists. He is a... a spirit of chaos, of death and rebirth, of growth and decay. He cares nothing for us, but he *is* us.'

'This is making even less sense than usual.'

Cillian gave a small snort. 'I'm doing my best, believe me. It's said that the Green Man is the Wild Wood itself, that he can command it. There are ancient beings under the ground, and they will come if he calls them...' He trailed off, shaking his head. 'If the Druidahnon is calling the Green Man, then things must be very bad indeed in Brittletain. Leven, I have to go back. I have to go back as soon as I can. Even though I...'

The thrawn. His horns remained a faint dusty blue and he was still able to command animals to his will – both things that meant he was exiled from the Wild Wood. When they had been there two years ago, it was as though the forest itself had turned against him, and it had caused him a great deal of pain.

'T'rook is free,' Leven said quietly. 'We've done what we meant to do, Cillian, finally. I'm only sorry it took this long. We'll go back as soon as we can.'

'What about Tyleigh?'

'Fuck Tyleigh to the stars and back,' said Leven firmly. 'I never want to see or hear about that creature again. If she can help my fellow Heralds, that is all to the good, but I am done with it. She won't be seeing me or my sister again.'

That night when Leven lay down to sleep, the warm shape of Cillian next to her, she felt the now familiar sense of another presence, seeping in at the edges as her own mind relaxed. Along with the pain and the weakness, this was another symptom that had been gradually growing worse over the last year.

*Quiet dreams tonight please*, she thought. *Or at least, memories that are my own.*

It wasn't to be. As she drifted off into an exhausted sleep, a rush of colour filled her head, along with a flurry of alien sensations: she was a beast with four legs; she was tall and strong and beautiful; a single pearly horn burst from her forehead and narrowed to a lethal point. Ahead of her was a landscape of black rock, roiling smoke and lethal red fire that oozed through cracks like streams, and she was lord of all of it. Heat battered at her, filling her black mane with soot, and she revelled in it. This was her land. This was her heart. Let them hunt her if they could: they would never survive it. Her very bones were magic, and they would all fall before her.

And then she was something else, something enormous that lived in the very depths of the sea. All was salt and blackness, a great pressure all around that was both deafening and silent. Soon, it would be time for her to leave the safety of the inner-dark and breach the surface. There, on a beach of blue sand, she would lay her eggs and watch over them for a hundred turns of the sun.

Next she was a creature of speed and ferocity, crashing through the forest like a storm. There were others like her, following close behind, and their tusks were already streaked with gore from an earlier fight. *They mean to kill me*, she thought, and the being that inhabited her laughed. *They mean to try*, it answered.

---

Leven woke, as she often did, in the early hours of the morning, her head pounding and a sour taste in her mouth. Her ore-lines were burning and prickling, and when she moved to get up, for a long handful of seconds she felt rooted in place, as though all the strength had seeped from her limbs overnight.

When eventually she could move, it was all she could manage to struggle into a sitting position. Cillian was by the fire already, preparing a meal for them all. She was glad he hadn't seen her struggle.

*We'll get back to Brittletain*, she told herself. *That's all we need to think about for now.*

# 10

*It is said that the Arch-Druin Merriden raised many of the standing stone circles that are peppered all over Brittletain; he was from a family of stone masons and had a particular affinity for the material. It was his job to find them, the stones that would be receptive, wherever they happened to be. One such stone was in the sea off the coast of Kornwullis; it is said Merriden sang to the kraken until they lifted it out of the sandbank for him and pushed it to shore.*

Extract from *Tales of the Arch-Druin*,
a children's book circulated by the Druin conclave

'It's hopeless.'

Epona threw her sword down onto the dirt of the Barrow entrance, feeling a sudden spiteful resentment for its weight. All that day and into the dusk she, Jack and a small group of scouts had carefully explored the perimeter of Londus-on-Sea, looking for new weaknesses, ways in, places where the Othanim forces might be overwhelmed, but they had found nothing of use. It might have been something, she mused, if they'd managed to find a fight while they were out there, some reason for her to have carried her sword all that way. But the Othanim were clever, mobile, and heavily armoured. And the rebels were just too few.

Jack stood up straight, her hands on her hips. Caliburn was a much larger sword than the one Epona carried, large enough that it had to be worn slung across her back, but it never seemed to weigh her down.

'There were some places where, with the right numbers, we could punch through their defences,' she said. 'It'd be risky, and bloody, but possible.'

'The right numbers,' Epona said. She lifted her arms over her head, stretching until she groaned. 'What a wonderful thought. Unfortunately, we're still severely lacking in allies. The queens of Brittletain are scattered.'

Queen Gwenith, who had allied with Ceni when Epona's sister overthrew their mother, had melted away into the hills when Ceni was driven from Londus. She had by all reports lost a large portion of her army when the Othanim decided to pursue. Epona had no idea if the queen of Dwffd was even still alive. Queen Verla of Kornwullis had shut her borders and not replied to any of Epona's messages – a fact that hurt Epona more than she was willing to admit. She'd thought they had forged some sort of understanding when she, Leven and Cillian had visited Verla's court. The kingdom of Mersia was even less forthcoming – Prince Eafen had been crowned king, and the city had closed itself off from the rest of Brittletain. To even approach the city was to be targeted by Wodencaester's elite archers. Not all of their messengers had returned. And abandoned by Ceni, Galabroc had reportedly fallen into chaos.

'The Druin, too, are all over the place now that Dosraiche is lost to them,' Epona continued. 'Who else is there? No one with a particular urge to help us take back Londus, I can tell you that.'

There was a faintly discordant hum from Caliburn.

'Caliburn says you should not leave your sword in the dust,' said Jack.

'Ah, Caliburn the ever-wise,' said Epona archly, but she picked up the sword. 'Jack, we have to find a way. We have to figure it out or...' Her throat felt solid with grief. 'I can't let that monster kill my mother. I can't. Bronvica is still imprisoned, I've no idea where Togi is, and Ceni, well... What happened to my family? I thought we were so strong.'

Around them, the Barrow was quiet. The sky had the purple cast of early evening to it, and the sweet scents of spring were in the air: there was blossom on the boughs, white and ghostly in the gloom. Epona looked up at the sky just in time to spot the shape of an owl passing overhead, close and clear enough that she could see, for an instant, the light brown spots on the underside of its flight feathers.

'Griffins,' said Epona. 'Where are the griffins?'

Caliburn made another sound. Jack looked faintly embarrassed.

'Caliburn says they're in the north.'

'Yes, thank you, I know that, we all bloody well know that. What I mean is, they can't be happy about all this, right? The last messages we got from the Druin in the north suggested that the Othanim were heading towards griffin territory. If we had them on our side, if we could get them to fight for Londus, we might have a chance.' Absently, she wiped the scabbard with her hand, brushing away the dust. She knew a little about griffins. When she had stayed with Ceni in Galabroc as a child, the griffins were a constant shadow over that northern territory, a predator that waited just out of sight. The only interaction a human was likely to have with a griffin was one that ended with their insides being abruptly on their outsides. And how would she ever get in contact with them? A messenger was unlikely to survive setting foot in Yelvynia.

'Even the Druin have nothing to do with them,' she said. 'If we had the Druidahnon, he might be able to talk to them, one Titan to another.' She sighed. 'But I don't think that flying turd was lying. I think he is dead. All that power, just out of reach.'

Caliburn's discordant hum was louder this time, but Epona spoke before Jack could translate.

'And you can tell your bloody sword to shut its hole.'

'No, wait, I think this could be useful.' Jack's eyes took on a faraway look as Caliburn sang louder, the notes becoming more complex. 'He says that in the days when he was forged, when his first and true master followed the Paths, when Merriden first raised the stones...'

'Can he please get to the point?'

'He says that there once used to be an accord between the kings and queens of Brittletain and the griffins. Not a particularly friendly one by the sounds of it, but there was at least an agreement that in certain circumstances they could... speak. There was a way to let them know, to summon them. But according to Caliburn it hasn't been done in a thousand years or more.'

Epona looked at Jack for a long moment, long enough that the other woman flushed again, her cheeks turning a deeper shade of pink.

'Come inside,' she said. 'I want to hear everything Caliburn has to say. For once.'

---

The nearest stone circle to the Barrow was a day and a half's ride away. The small group of rebels arrived dishevelled and wild-haired, too aware that travelling so openly was to invite attacks from roaming Othanim. It was late afternoon and unseasonably warm, making the grass of the meadow hum with bees and other insects. Epona slipped down from her horse, her heart thumping in her chest, and looked over at the circle.

'They're an odd collection, that's for sure.'

The stones of the Yernagate circle were of all sizes; the smallest was no bigger than a sheep, and the largest stood taller than a man. There were seven of them; Solasach wandered over to the nearest, resting the fingers of one hand against the grey, pitted surface. He looked worried.

'Talking to the trees, the animals. Even the fungi. On a good day? That I can do. But stones? You need a stronger Druin than me.' It was a version of what he'd been saying all throughout their journey. 'The minds of stones go *deep*. Deeper than most of us can go.'

'I know you can do it, Solasach,' said Epona. 'Besides, we don't have anyone else. And you have Yelm here to help you.'

The short Druin woman looked uncertain, but she nodded briskly. 'It was always your special talent, Solasach. Talking to those without voices.'

Jack, who had dismounted her own horse and was striding through the long grass, paused at the edge of the circle and drew Caliburn from the scabbard on her back. The others turned to look at her. In the bright sunlight, the magical sword burned and flashed like wildfire. 'You work,' she said to the Druin. 'Princess Epona and I will keep watch.'

Solasach nodded, still looking uncertain, before kneeling in front of the stone he had chosen. Yelm faced him on the far side of the stone, and together they both laid their hands, palms flat, against the rock. As Epona watched, Solasach closed his eyes and began to murmur, his mouth moving rapidly through words she couldn't hear. She joined Jack and leaned in so that she could speak without disturbing the Druin.

'Does Caliburn have any idea how long this might take?'

'He says that he once saw a team of Druin working to wake the circle for three days and three nights. There were ten of them, and they relieved each other so that there was always at least one Druin per stone the entire time.'

'Shit. We don't have that kind of time.' Epona glanced at the sky. There were clouds moving in through the blue, and the wind was picking up. 'All it takes is for one of those flying bastards to spot us down here and we'll have our hands full.'

'There are other dangers.' At Epona's look, Jack shrugged. 'You must know the same stories as me, Princess. The standing stones are waypoints for the dead. They travel through here. And they listen. The stones might not be the only thing the Druin awaken.'

Epona shivered, remembering the stone circle she and Leven and Cillian had travelled through on their way to Kornwullis. There they had encountered a spirit who travelled with a company of wolves. He had seemed to know Cillian, somehow. She remembered how cold it had been as the ghost passed them on by, the great sense of sadness and loss she had felt when he disappeared from view. He hadn't felt dangerous, not truly, but the dead of Brittletain were varied. And lively.

'We'd better keep our eyes open, in that case.'

---

For the rest of that day and well into the evening the Druin knelt by the stone, their heads bowed, their hands pressed to the rock. At one point, as the moon sunk back behind the hills, Yelm slumped sideways and would have fallen onto the grass had Jack not been there instantly, grabbing onto her shoulders and hauling her up. She took the Druin over to the small cookfire they had set up and gave her a clay cup of hot, sweet tea. Solasach remained where he was, crouched in the dark with his single unbroken horn pointing at the sky.

'How's it going?' asked Epona. It was very difficult to keep from grabbing Yelm in an attempt to shake some answers from her, but the woman appeared to be only partially conscious; her eyes were open a crack, and she didn't speak for several minutes. When she finally did, her voice was slow and hoarse, as though she'd spent the last few hours shouting at the top of her lungs.

'He's gone deep, right into the marrow of the stone,' she said. 'So many cold things in there. But he's doing it. Asking the stones to remember their promise.' She smiled a little. 'I couldn't follow all the way. It was just... too cold. But I think he's close to getting them to listen.'

Epona rubbed a hand over her face. Once, she had worn blue paint in stripes across her cheeks and forehead, a sign of her status as Broudicca's daughter. Since the war with the Othanim she had kept her face bare – to wear the paint of royalty was to single herself out as a target. Sometimes she missed those stripes, but more often she was amazed she'd ever done something so frivolous.

'Right. Good.' She glanced at Jack, who looked tense. 'Then we keep doing what we're doing and hope that Solasach can hold on a bit longer.' She stood up and took off her fur-lined cloak, passing it to Yelm. 'Put that over his shoulders. Help keep him warm.'

'He won't feel it,' Yelm said slowly. 'He's too deep.'

'Do me a favour and do it anyway. It'll make me feel better, at least.'

---

It was in the very earliest hours of the morning that Solasach stood up from where he knelt, startling all three of them, and stumbled out of the stone circle, falling over into the grass. A bare second later, the stones themselves and the patch of ground inside the circle began to glow with a soft green light. Epona jumped up from the fire, knocking her fourth cup of tea over.

'What is it? What's happening?'

The glow grew brighter and brighter, until the circle was difficult to look at directly, and then a beam of light as wide as the circle itself shot up into the air. It pierced the sky and splashed against the clouds, a vast tower of greenish brilliance. The meadow was abruptly lit up like it was daytime; Epona could see every blade of grass picked out in unnerving detail.

'Solasach!'

She ran over to his side and dragged him away from the beam. When she glanced at his face, she saw that his nose was bleeding. He smiled at her weakly.

'They remembered what they promised, an age ago,' he said. 'They've opened the ghost-way.'

'That doesn't sound all that reassuring...'

Jack appeared at her side, and together they took Solasach back to the fire. When he was seated and Yelm had taken his hands in hers, trying to rub some warmth back into them, Epona walked back towards the beam. It had a faint, musical hum, almost like the sound Caliburn made.

'What happens now? Do we just wait until the griffins come to us?'

All around them, the little meadow danced with light. Birds called to each other, confused about the time of day, and the clouds caught in the beam overhead looked solid somehow, like something sculpted from grey-green marble. *It must*, Epona thought, *be possible to see the beam for miles around*. She thought of the moths that battered themselves against the lamps in her mother's old rookery.

Next to her, Jack drew her sword.

'What is it?'

Jack lifted her chin in one jerky movement. 'Look.'

Lit by the eldritch glow of the ghost-light, two winged figures hung in the sky above them. One of them held a spear in his hand. As they watched, he lifted it into a throwing posture.

'Ah, *shit*,' said Epona.

# 11

'I thought you said we could not have our vengeance?'

Ynis leaned close over her sister's shoulder, watching the complex below. The roof where they were perched was the furthest from the lamps, but it still seemed incredible to her that the guards below hadn't spotted them. Their human eyes were weak, especially at night.

'This isn't vengeance. This is... something else.'

There were more guards than there had been when they'd broken T'rook out of her cage, and they appeared to be more on edge. She thought of the one whose throat she had cut. Perhaps that played on the minds of the men and women below.

'You did not tell the human woman where we were going,' continued T'rook, a note of suspicion in her voice. 'You told her we were hunting. We are not hunting. Are we?'

'She's my human sister,' Ynis said absently. 'She doesn't know anything about hunting.' A man had appeared in the courtyard carrying a large, covered bowl. Wisps of steam escaped from it and she caught the scent of something hot and savoury. During her time travelling with Leven and Cillian, she had learnt that humans spent a great deal of time *cooking*, and they had apparently taken the art a lot further than her rudimentary experiments with fire and boiling water. She could smell salt, garlic, fat and cream – rich things. Meat, possibly lamb. The food below was meant for someone important. There was only one important person in this complex.

'Ynis. Why are we here? I did not want to come back here.'

The man with the bowl had left the courtyard and was moving down a narrow alley between two buildings. In moments he would be lost from view. She slipped down from T'rook's back, treading softly on the roof slates.

'I know you didn't. And I'm sorry.'

'I would only come back here to eat that human woman's guts, but that is not why we are here, is it?' In the dark, T'rook's golden eyes were full of a quiet, banked fury. Ynis felt a pulse of shame. She had brought her sister back to the place of her torture, her imprisonment; had put her in danger of being caught again. All things that would have been unthinkable days before. 'Why have we returned, sister?'

'Wait here for me,' said Ynis, already moving away towards the edge of the tiles. 'If they spot you, fly back to that bridge we saw and I'll meet you there.'

Familiarity with the complex and her own quiet desperation made her bold. She jumped down to a lower roof, taking as much of the impact in her knees as she could, and then she climbed down via a series of windowsills, moving quickly and near silently. Once on the ground, she kept to the darkest shadows, her breathing as shallow as possible and her claw-knife held steady in one hand. If anyone stumbled across her in the dark, she would open their throat.

From there, she crept around the edge of the courtyard, waiting for a pair of guards to pass – they were close enough to touch – and then she moved down the narrow passage in a half-crouching run. The man with the bowl had vanished from view, but quickly she realised that it didn't matter. The passage led to another, smaller, neater courtyard, and at the top of a set of shallow steps there was a building that looked different to the others. Ynis recognised that this was what humans thought of as a home. There were plants in pots outside the windows, and the lamps inside radiated a soft, inviting light. More to the point, sitting on the steps was Gynid Tyleigh herself, her evil-smelling pipe in one hand. She was bent over, making her look hunched and small. Her untidy hair hung in her face, and she was staring into the distance. The bowl of food sat next to her on the step, still steaming away and apparently untouched. For the first time she looked truly unguarded. Ynis found herself studying the human's face. Was this what she would look like when she was an old woman?

Ynis stepped forward into the soft circle of light from the windows. Tyleigh looked up, her face already rearranging itself into an expression of annoyance.

'I said I wasn't to be disturbed, you useless piece of—' She stopped. There was a long moment of silence, during which Ynis could feel her heart thudding sickly in her chest. 'Well. I didn't expect to see you again, Alaw.' She blew a stream of blueish smoke out through her nostrils and grinned. 'Have you come to kill me? Or do you have questions your impatient sister didn't ask?'

'I was raised in the nest-pit of Flayn and T'vor. They fed me and protected me even though I did not hatch from an egg as any true yenlin does. Despite you, I know what it is to be loved by a parent.'

'Yes, fascinating,' said Tyleigh, leaning forward a little. 'No one living has the experience you do with the Titans. Do you realise that? Come back with me to the Imperium, to Stratum, and you'll live like a queen for the rest of your days. The empress will pave your path with gold to get at your secrets.'

'Did you ever love us, Echni?' She half expected to find the question painful to speak aloud, and she suspected that Leven would have, but she felt very little. Only a genuine, cold curiosity. *And this is how you are like her*, whispered a voice in her head.

'Love you? I was going to give you both the greatest power in all of Enonah. How's that for love?'

Ynis shook her head slightly. 'That's not the same thing at all.'

And here it was. The reason she had returned, despite everything. Something must have changed on her face, because Tyleigh sat up, her eyes wide, the pipe in her hand forgotten.

'So *that* is why you are here,' she said, her voice suddenly warm with a mixture of satisfaction and wonder. 'How delicious.'

'You know what I want,' said Ynis, only the slightest tremor in her voice. 'Will you give it to me or not?'

# PART TWO

## IN WHICH CHOICES ARE MADE
## THAT CANNOT BE UNMADE

# 12

*We didn't achieve everything we hoped, but if I'm honest with you, it went a bloody sight better than I was expecting. Funnily enough, that section of the wall has been on my docket to fix up for years, but Broudicca never used the dungeons enough to make it urgent. Bloody lucky for us all I didn't get round to it, as the fire-egg took all the black powder we had, and it was only just enough to make that hole. I can only thank the Green Man that no one inside was blown to tiny bits. But like I was saying – we got Epona out, we got the little girls out. Broudicca's cell we couldn't breach, and the flying bastards were on us in minutes. It's something, at least. Causing the Othanim even a little bit of trouble warms my heart on cold nights, I don't mind telling you that.*

Letter from Karayné-bog to a member<br>of the rebellion in the west

An inky black sea churned against the ironwood flank of the ship, spraying sea foam and salt into the cool air. Kaeto leaned against the rail, looking down at the sleek wet wood and thinking viciously about blowing it up. Just a little bit of his old grey powder in the right place, somewhere not too damp, and the ugly behemoth of an Imperial ship would shortly be at the bottom of the ocean. The Heralds, gods curse them, might escape into the air for a while, but even with Tyleigh's improved augments the journey back to the continent was longer than a day. He doubted they would make it. Meanwhile, Felldir and Belise would fly on, their wings a natural part of their bodies, and together they would make it... somewhere. Anywhere.

The reality was that before boarding the ship, Kaeto had been forced to change his clothes, and his luggage had been thoroughly searched. Even the poisons he had sewn into the inside of his vest had been found and destroyed, and the travel chest itself swapped out for one that didn't have several hidden compartments. He had raved and raged at the time, pointing out, quite reasonably he thought, that to send him into this particular diplomatic mission with no way to defend himself or extract answers was at best incompetent; at worst, suicidal. But the Heralds who had been assigned to watch him were unmoved.

Even if he could destroy the ship and survive, he would need to free Felldir and Belise beforehand, and his access to them had been extremely limited. To his great surprise and creeping dread, the Othanim of Londus had themselves sent a set of Titan-ore chains to Stratum, and these were what secured the Titan prisoners in the hold below. The chains were remarkably fine, each link no larger than the tip of his smallest finger, yet they were strikingly heavy and quite unbreakable. He had seen Felldir and Belise twice since he had come aboard. Once at the start of the voyage when he'd insisted on a tour of the ship – something he had done as a matter of course in the past as part of his Envoy duties – and once when he had briefly slipped away from his Herald chaperones. It had been the dead of night, and although a Herald had been assigned to watch his door, he had a great deal of experience when it came to moving through places without being seen. Down in the depths of the ship he made his way to the iron cage in the hold, and talked his way past the guard, who clearly hadn't been given the full details about Kaeto's role in this particular mission. Belise had been asleep, slumped on a rough cot, her beautiful wings restrained with criss-crossing lines of blue-green metal. Felldir had been similarly restrained, but he met Kaeto's gaze with his own wolf stare.

'I'm sorry,' Kaeto said. 'They were one step ahead of me all along. I'm a fool.'

Felldir shook his head, looked away. 'It is *her*. I am the fool, for thinking that I could ever be free while she is alive.'

'If I can't get you out before we arrive at Londus, what will happen?'

'Nothing good, as Belise might say.' Felldir shrugged. 'Icaraine may just have me killed, but I think it much more likely she will simply keep me in these chains, as a kind of pet. She enjoys her pets, and I was hers for a very long time.'

'I won't allow it,' Kaeto said fiercely, feeling faintly ridiculous. 'I will find a way out of this for all of us.'

At that moment the guard had returned, an expression on his face that suggested the Heralds had given him rather more information on Kaeto's exact status on this voyage, and so he'd made himself scarce, although not before catching a glimpse of the fond, sad smile Felldir had given him. It was like a dagger to the heart.

Now, the coast of Brittletain was visible on the horizon, and despite everything Kaeto found himself unable to look away. He could see a line of white – the famous chalk cliffs of the southern coast – and scattered above them, the occasional wink of green light, shifting and uncertain. He wondered if these were the wych lights he had read about, and he felt a shiver of awe at the thought: in all of his years working for the Imperium, he had never come so close to the haunted isle of Brittletain.

'Here I am,' he murmured to himself. 'I'm here by knifepoint, but I'm here.'

It was early evening before they came to the mouth of the Old Father River, the setting sun pouring blood into the water, splashing the ramshackle buildings of the port in pink, queasy light. Kaeto was in the bow of the ship, watching closely as the vast Imperial vessel bullied its way up the wide waterway. As far as he could tell, these outer edges of the great city of Londus-on-Sea looked to be deserted; he could see no one moving, and the place was eerily quiet. From his vantage point on the deck he spotted an old market stall beyond the crumbling harbour wall. The produce it had once contained had long since rotted away – he could see the whole skeleton of a sizeable pig laid out on the counter like it was taking a nap.

One of the Heralds, the one with the milky skin and closely shaven head, was standing with Kaeto, his arms crossed over his chest. His name was Thirteen. The original battalion of Heralds who had carried those numbers were all dead or missing, so in typical pragmatic fashion, Imperator Justinia had decided to reuse them. This particular Thirteen looked disgruntled.

'Where are they then?' he said aloud. 'I thought we'd get an escort of some sort. Don't they realise who they're dealing with here? The empress will be insulted if we're not given due respect.'

Kaeto smiled faintly. If the empress could hear this young idiot talking about her in such a familiar tone, she'd have the skin flayed from the soles of his feet. He briefly entertained himself with the thought of carrying out that order.

'*You're* the expert in these things,' carried on Thirteen. 'What do you make of it? Have they forgotten we're coming or what?'

'All I know is that we know very little about them,' Kaeto said. 'And everything we do know suggests we ought to be extremely wary.'

'Fat lot of use you are.'

'Believe me, Herald Thirteen, I'd be very glad to be useful elsewhere at this moment.'

The ship made its sedate way up the river. Around them the crew moved restlessly. Kaeto had the impression they had been unnerved by the silence, too. He was reminded of their journey to the Black City, how the people of Houraki had refused to speak of it, and how their guide Riz had died there, his blood and entrails strewn over the black stones. Why was he doomed to visit cursed places?

There was a shout from the front of the ship, breaking the silence and startling Kaeto more than he cared to admit. Several members of the crew moved to the port side, looking at something in the water with troubled expressions on their faces. One of them had a long staff with a hook on the end which he lowered into the water.

'What is it?'

Kaeto crossed over to the rail and looked down. There, roiling against the side of the ship, were two bloated human bodies. The skin that was left to them was green and the flesh white – fish, Kaeto supposed, had been nibbling at the softer parts. The man with the hook had managed to snag the larger one through a ragged leg bone.

'What are you doing?' asked Kaeto sharply. He had worked all his adult life with dead bodies, but the thought of bringing these corpses onboard filled him with disgust. 'Do you mean to bury them when we're back on dry land?'

The crewman closest to him gave him a dubious look.

'No, sir. There are far too many of them for that.'

With a growing sense of dread, Kaeto peered closer at the river. Now that he was looking for them, he realised he could see the shades of the dead all around. Paler shapes in the green-brown murk were half-rotten arms and legs, shifting pieces of rag and hair. With the passage of the Imperium ship the water was churning them up, pulling them from the mud.

'We don't like them to touch the ship if we can help it, sir,' said the one with the hook. He pulled the body out, away from the side of the ship, then, disengaging the hook, gave it a push. The corpse rolled slowly in the water and was lost. 'It's bad luck, you see.'

'That's a lot of dead people,' said Thirteen. He had joined Kaeto at the rail. 'Are these Queen Broudicca's army?'

'No,' said Kaeto, feeling a mixture of disgust and impatience. Belise would never have asked such a stupid question. 'The invasion of Londus was two years ago, those bodies will have long since skeletonised. These people here, they are the citizens of Londus.' Another body passed by, this one obviously that of a child. 'Just ordinary people. Murdered by a tyrant.' He thought of Belise in the hold of the ship, restrained with chains made of Titan bone. He was taking her into harm's way. Again.

'There are always casualties in a war,' said Thirteen, in what he likely imagined was a worldly-wise tone.

'Spoken like a true soldier,' spat Kaeto.

---

Night had fallen before they entered the court of Icaraine the Lightbringer. They had very little warning; the sails billowed as though caught in a sudden, unpredictable gale, and there was a deafening flurry of wingbeats. Kaeto, who had just been below eating his supper and was on his way back out onto the deck, ran up the steps to find the ship in a state of chaos. The Othanim were swarming, and in the midst of them, tall enough that she threatened to sink the whole ship, was Icaraine. The last time he'd seen her she had been wearing armour and a helm made of Titan ore, but now she wore armour of gold inlaid with bright blue enamel – he wondered if it had been made from the riches they'd stolen from Queen Broudicca's castle. Her black hair was bound back from her face with gold rings, and for the first time he saw her face clearly: her eyes were large, with thick dark lashes that almost distracted from her yellow pupils, and she had a large, fleshy mouth that split into a wide grin the moment she saw him.

She was beautiful in a terrifying way; she gave the impression that she might bite off one of your limbs for a snack.

'Light-bones! I remember you.' Her voice was still painfully loud. 'The one who came scampering to me in the night when I was trapped in the Undertomb. Yes. Desperate you were, and that was music to my ears.'

Belatedly, Kaeto looked for the Heralds. He spotted Thirteen and two of his fellow soldiers; they had summoned their wings but not their swords, which was a piece of common sense he hadn't expected from them. They did, however, look greatly unnerved – apparently sneaking up on Felldir and Belise had not prepared them for the reality of the Othanim horde.

'High Priestess Icaraine.' Kaeto bowed low. 'You honour us with your presence.'

'I'm sure I do.' Icaraine cocked her head to one side like a curious dog. 'I was surprised to hear from your empress. Humans think so highly of themselves, they think they can talk to their gods. That they can *ask* things of us. I thought I would enjoy crossing the sea again to pull this little human empress out of her palace. I have heard she is so small I could eat her in one bite.'

'That is quite possible, your majesty,' said Kaeto. He noted the look that Thirteen gave him – the Herald would no doubt snitch on him the first chance he got – but Icaraine laughed hugely, smashing one great fist against the mast in merriment. There was a twang and a snap as a rope somewhere above them came loose.

'But then,' continued Icaraine when she had recovered herself, 'your little empress told me that you had one of my people. That little worm Felldir who wriggled away when you, light-bones, let me out of the Undertomb. She had the audacity to *offer* him to me. As though he wasn't already my own. But...' Icaraine came a few steps closer, each footfall shaking the entire ship. When she was looming over Kaeto, she stopped. 'We are busy here, on this rain-soaked little island. I do not have time to go chasing after worms. Not when I have griffins to kill, and Malakim grows ever hungrier. So do you have him, light-bones? Do you have my beloved little worm?'

Kaeto felt his heart sink. Would she demand he be brought up to the deck immediately, and execute him then and there? Everything was moving too fast.

'We have him, your majesty, and orders to bring him to your court. I assume...' He cleared his throat again. 'I assume you have taken up residence in the queen's castle?'

'Yes, bring him there.' Casually, Icaraine walked over to a member of the crew, who was cowering by the forecastle. She picked him up by the head, muffling his screams, and then tossed him over the rail into the water. There was a shout and a splash. Icaraine shook her head. 'You see? The old entertainments, they are starting to bore me. But once I have Felldir back...' She turned to Kaeto and grinned. 'I can really start to enjoy myself.'

# 13

Leven stood on the edge of a rock pool and watched the ship that had carried them across the Channel of Giants leave, ruefully considering the amount of coin it had cost her to buy the skipper's silence. They had kept T'rook below decks, largely covered in blankets – much to the griffin's vocal disgust – but she had no doubt the crew knew exactly what they had been transporting. She had to hope that the payment was enough to stop word getting back to the Imperium, although she supposed that mattered less than it once had. She had no intention of ever returning to Stratum. If Tyleigh was right that she had very little time left, then she would spend it here, in her native home of Brittletain, with Cillian and her little sister. Her family.

'We're leaving,' said Ynis.

'What?'

It was very early in the morning, the violet light of dawn turning the water of the rock pools into silvery mirrors. Cillian had been heading up the rocky beach, his eyes on the dark line of trees at the edge, but he stopped to look back at them. Ynis was already on her griffin-sister's back, her face set in a belligerent expression Leven had grown very familiar with over the last two years.

'We will hunt,' Ynis said shortly. T'rook fluffed up the feathers on her ruff and looked away, as though the conversation was making her uncomfortable. 'Now we are home.'

'Can't it wait?' Leven scrambled up out of the rock pools, scattering droplets of water like diamonds. 'We've just got here.

There's plenty of food in our packs and it's been a grim sea journey for T'rook, she'd probably like a rest.'

'Humans are always resting,' T'rook commented dryly. 'It must be the proximity of the ground. It pulls you down. Makes you eager for sleep.'

'And it's dangerous here,' continued Leven. 'All those rumours we heard on the continent? We know at least some of them are true. A new Titan, a murderous one.' She glanced at Cillian, but it wasn't yet bright enough to read his expression. 'Supposedly they are killing griffins. Wait, and we'll hunt together.'

'No,' said Ynis. 'This is the best time to do it, so we shall go now.'

Leven scowled. 'Will you not even pretend to listen to me? How will you find us later? Cillian and I can't just hang around waiting for you...'

'I can find you anytime I like,' said Ynis. 'By the fate-ties.' She leaned down and spoke something into T'rook's feathered ear, and then the griffin was moving, up in the air before Leven could say another word. She watched the pair of them disappear over the treeline, her hands on her hips.

'Stars' arses. Are all children this annoying?'

'Yes,' said Cillian. She could hear the laughter in his voice. 'Or I certainly was, anyway.'

'Ever since we left Tyleigh's compound she's barely sat still,' she continued. 'Flying off on T'rook at every hour of the day and night.'

'Can you blame her?' Cillian continued trudging towards the treeline, and after a moment Leven joined him. 'We spent two years trying to find T'rook. She's eager to spend time with her.'

'It's not safe here,' said Leven, but without much force. The sun had come up more fully, and the small rocky beach was gathering light. She could see Cillian's face clearly, and he looked worried. Belatedly it occurred to her what a momentous thing this was for him, returning to Brittletain when the Wild Wood had banished him for going thrawn. She put her hand on his arm, gently. 'How are you holding up?'

They paused at the edge of the treeline. Ahead of them were densely packed trees in their bright spring foliage; Leven thought she'd never seen a green so *green* – it almost left an afterimage on her eyes when she blinked.

'I suppose we're about to find out,' Cillian said, eyeing the trees warily. 'The last time we were here, the Wild Wood was thrumming with... distress. With hate. Some of that was towards me, but much of it originated with the murders of the griffins in the north.'

'The Imperium covering itself in glory again,' said Leven.

'When I forced the Dunohi to bend to my will, I committed an unforgivable crime,' he continued, his voice soft. 'It changed my relationship with the Wild Wood forever. It's possible – very possible, in fact – that it won't let us in. Which could, uh, complicate our journey. I need to find the Druidahnon. I need to find out why I heard his voice.'

'There's always the coastal path,' said Leven, trying to sound unconcerned. 'If there's one thing Brittletain has, it's a lot of coast.'

They needn't have worried. When they stepped into the forest it did not turn dark or cold; the smaller animals did not attack them; birds didn't swoop down on their heads. Instead, it remained quiet. Normal, as far as Leven could tell.

'Are you sensing anything?' she asked.

'No,' said Cillian in a tone of wonder. 'The wood is there, but it's quiet. All I'm getting is a sense of... distraction? And movement. It's very strange.'

He stopped on the narrow path and crouched down. He placed his fingers on the dirt and leaf litter. To Leven's surprise, she saw a little shiver of movement pass through the leaves and twigs, as though Cillian had blown gently on them.

'What was that?'

He shook his head. 'I'm not sure. I don't think...'

The shiver came again. This time the scattering of twigs and leaves moved with purpose; as one, they all turned so they were pointing the same way. Leven jumped a little, startled.

'Is this a Druin thing I don't know about yet?'

'They're all pointing south-west,' he said, before moving his hand across the path. Everything within ten inches of his fingertips quivered and span. 'It's like the wood wants us to move this way?'

'Why would it want that?'

Above them, there was a flurry of movement as a small flock of sparrows left the oak they were perched in and flew off, also heading south-west. Leven met Cillian's eyes as he stood up.

'Do you think that was a coincidence?'

Once, when Leven was at the peak of her powers, when she had been roaming the Unblessed lands with the rest of the Heralds, she would have been very difficult to surprise and almost impossible to ambush. But in the last few years the pain and the exhaustion from her ore-lines meant that it was often difficult to concentrate on what was directly in front of her, let alone what might be sneaking up behind her. So when a trio of armed women stepped out of the woods to their right, it was a complete surprise. She attempted to summon her sword, but nothing came – instead she felt an uncomfortable sweep of pins and needles move down her sword arm.

'Who are you? What are you doing here?' The woman in the lead was carrying a bow, the arrow already strung, and as she spoke she lifted it to aim at Cillian's chest. She had tightly curled hair, with powerful arms and shoulders. 'Explain yourselves.'

Leven raised her hands, imagining what the pair of them looked like to these Britons: an obviously thrawn Druin with his discoloured horns, and a woman whose skin was covered in silvery-blue ore-lines.

'We're friends,' said Cillian quickly. 'Just looking for a Path to travel on to the Dosraiche.'

Behind the woman with the bow, a girl who appeared to be no more than sixteen or seventeen turned to the solid-looking woman next to her.

'They don't know,' she said, her voice low. 'How's that possible? How can they be here and not know?'

'Wehha is not welcoming to strangers these days,' said the woman with the bow. 'Who are you? Othanim spies?'

'Spies?' Leven began to laugh, then thought better of it. 'We're just travellers. Let us pass.'

'Or what?' snapped the woman. 'You'll not go far with my arrow in your throat.'

'Wait.' The eldest woman stepped forward and placed a hand on the archer's shoulder. 'Look at them, Molly. That one's a Druin. Perhaps they can help.'

'Help with what?' asked Cillian. Around them, a strong breeze moved down the path and through the trees. Leven couldn't help noticing it was blowing towards the south-west.

Molly lowered the bow, although she looked unhappy about it. 'We have a Druin in our camp,' she said shortly, 'and he won't stop screaming. Can you shut him up?'

# 14

*We don't know why Merriden erected the Ghost-Ways exactly, but we do know it was an enormous task, selecting the stones and the locations of the circles, transporting everything and weaving the magics... Of course, he had the giants to help him lift the stones, which would have saved some time, but certainly it was more work than one mortal man should have been able to do in a single lifetime. Whether Merriden was mortal or not is another question. What we do know is that they worked: pass through a stone circle at the right time, or even in the right mood, and you might come face to face with a long-dead spirit, wandering after something she has lost.*

*There was an intriguing note on a scroll from the First Age – one long-dead Druin believed that Merriden and Arthwr cooked up the idea between them. If that legendary king was involved, it's possible there is a purpose to them we have yet to discover.*

Note from a Druin archivist,
working on the Dosraiche records

The spear hit the ground with so much force that the front half of it was fully buried in the hard earth. Epona froze, for a heartbeat unable to take her eyes from it. The spear had struck only a handspan away from her foot.

'Run!' Jack was shouting. She had drawn Caliburn and was standing with her feet planted on the ground, both hands wrapped around the hilt. The song of the sword's voice was no longer soft or discordant. Instead, Caliburn rang with an eerie music – Epona almost thought she could discern its meaning. *Stand and fight, defeat the enemy, advance into glory...* She shook her head and drew her sword.

'Get down here and fight, you flying cowards!'

One of the Othanim did just that. Bathed in the shifting greenish light of the ghost-beam, the Titan landed in the grass hard enough that the ground shook. He was the one who had thrown the spear, although he made no effort to collect it. He advanced on Epona with his hands up, ready to wrestle her to the ground. Epona raised her sword, her heart thundering in her chest – she had rarely been so close to an Othanim – when Jack crashed into the side of the creature, Caliburn biting into its shoulder where the armour didn't quite cover it. The Othanim bellowed with rage, and a splash of purple-black blood scattered over the grass. Roots erupted from the ground beneath his feet, curling and twisting around his ankles and lower legs like the earth itself wanted him, and Epona remembered the Druin. When she turned to look for them, she had time to see Yelm, her face creased with concentration as she manipulated the roots. Then Solasach, just behind her, was snatched up into the air by the other Othanim. There was a ragged, desperate scream.

Epona ran forward and drove her sword at the Othanim's neck, but her aim was off and her blade slid across his armour with an unpleasant screech. Jack had pulled Caliburn free for another attack, her eyes glowing faintly with the magic of the sword, but the Othanim crashed one gauntleted fist into her chest, sending her reeling, before leaping back up into the sky. Epona cursed wildly, wishing they had Karayné-bog's spear-throwing contraption with them.

'Help him!' Yelm was shouting. 'They're going to pull him apart up there!'

The two Othanim had Solasach gripped between them – one had hold of his remaining horn, apparently trying to break it off – and they were both laughing. Epona felt the rage inside her rise like bile, like something that had to be expelled. Was this what she was leading her people to? Fights they had no chance of winning?

'Caliburn says we should retreat,' gasped Jack. She grabbed Epona by the arm and began dragging her away. 'We're outnumbered.'

'There are four of us!' shouted Epona, shaking her hand off. 'And two of them!'

'But they can *fly*,' continued Jack. 'We can't reach them, not here. We need archers, we need—'

'I'm not leaving Solasach to be torn apart by those things,' said Epona. She turned to Yelm. 'Can you reach them? With your roots?'

Yelm opened her mouth to reply, although Epona could already guess the answer, when they were all frozen by a deafening screech. Behind them, the ghost-beam flickered as something large and furious moved through it – and then it expelled a griffin moving at tremendous speed. Epona glanced up in time to see the Titan's furry belly, dotted with black, white and grey markings, its taloned feet tucked up close to its body, before it collided with the two Othanim. There was another piercing shriek and another, much larger splatter of blood. Abruptly, an Othanim head was spinning through the air. Solasach fell.

'Look out!'

There was a thump and a crunch as the Druin landed in the grass, rolling awkwardly. For a second Epona felt her heart leap up into her throat. Then she heard him bellowing with pain – if he could shout about it, he likely wasn't seriously hurt. Meanwhile the griffin above them had the second Othanim in its talons. Epona was treated to the sight of the creature's torso being torn open as easily as she might break apart a loaf of bread.

'Fuck me,' she murmured. 'We really do need the griffins on our side.'

Yelm had run to Solasach and was kneeling by him, murmuring calming words. Jack was wiping Caliburn on the grass, cleaning him of Othanim blood, but her eyes were on the griffin. Its wings were beating furiously as it methodically tore the rival Titan to pieces; a hand, the lower half of a leg, a sloppy rain of entrails – all splashed onto the ground ahead of them, steaming in the early-morning light.

'The summoning worked,' Jack said unnecessarily.

'It did. The question is, will the griffin treat that flying shitrag as an appetizer before it starts on us?'

Caliburn rang out, an echo of its former music. Epona got the impression it had been enjoying itself.

'Caliburn says the griffins are bound by the old pact not to attack the humans who call them via the ghost-ways, assuming they are not attacked themselves, or insulted. Or mildly inconvenienced.'

'Then I'll just be my most charming self,' said Epona. She stepped forward, waving her arms over her head. 'Greetings! You do us a great honour by responding to our summons, esteemed friend! And by saving our skins, as it turns out.'

The griffin dropped the last of the unfortunate Othanim and hung for a moment in the sky, vast wings beating with casual power. Epona had the sense of being a tiny prey creature, a mouse perhaps, caught in the gaze of an owl who hadn't quite decided whether she was worth the energy or not. It was not a comfortable feeling. Bloody feathers from the dead Othanim were scattered all across the grass in a sinister snowfall.

'What do you want?' called the griffin.

Epona cleared her throat. 'Perhaps you could come down here? Our voices do not carry as well as yours!'

There was a long pause, during which Epona found herself pondering how embarrassing it would be to be killed here, after everything, by a disgruntled griffin. Leven had always wanted to see the griffins in the north. She swallowed down a nervous bubble of laughter.

'Very well,' the griffin said eventually. 'If it will make this indignity pass more swiftly.'

The Titan alighted around ten feet away. Up close, Epona was struck by several things: that occasionally spotting a griffin in the sky didn't prepare you for the sheer size of them on the ground, and that this particular griffin was wearing an odd assortment of what appeared to be armour made from Titan bone, including a griffin skull that sat atop his own head. She bowed low, in the way her mother had taught her when she was old enough to officially attend the queen's court. All that formality might finally be useful.

'Thank you, Master Griffin. I am Princess Epona of the kingdom of Londus. May I ask who we have the honour of speaking to?'

'You have the quite unheard of honour of speaking to Witch-seer Scree,' said the griffin. He paused to run his beak over a loose feather on his chest. 'I can't imagine what a ground-stuck torrosa such as yourself has to say to a griffin, but I hope for your sake it is something that can be said quickly. I am the leader of the Edge Walkers and I am extremely busy.'

'The Edge Walkers?'

Jack murmured in her ear. 'Caliburn says they are an old death cult of the griffins.'

'Death cult?' snapped Scree. 'I had heard that humans had a better grasp of words and ideas than your average mountain goat, but clearly that was a ludicrous rumour. Death cult indeed. The Edge Walkers are griffins of exceptional talent who have been tasked with the vastly important work of shepherding our dead from this life to the next – of walking the very line between life and death.'

'They also, apparently, have exceptional hearing,' said Epona before very quickly bowing again. 'Witch-seer Scree, given how neatly you dispatched our flying guests I suspect you can guess why I have asked to speak to you today.'

'On the contrary, I cannot think of a single reason why a prey animal such as yourself – even one with such a pretty title – would need to talk to a griffin.'

'No, I imagine your previous conversations with humans were very brief indeed. The Othanim, my lord witch-seer. You cannot have failed to notice the invasion happening on our island?'

The Titan snorted. 'I know more about the Othanim than you could even guess, child.'

Epona nodded, keeping a smile plastered on her face. This was turning out to be even harder than she had anticipated.

'They have taken Londus-on-Sea, my lord, and Wehha and Mersia are under constant attack. They head gradually north, and have destroyed Dosraiche, the great stronghold of the Druin.'

'These places mean nothing to me.'

'But their plans mean something, surely? My lord, they are here for your people – to wipe the griffins out and enslave the humans of Brittletain.'

'They have made forays into Yelvynia,' Scree said dismissively. 'We have forced them back, as we did thousands of years ago.'

'It must be taking its toll on you... on your people?'

Scree tossed his head, making the bones of his cloak rattle. 'The problem with the Othanim is the same as it was all that time ago – there are many of them. And over the last two thousand years, the numbers of griffins have waned. But it is no matter. We have the situation in hand, little human. If that is all you wanted to say...'

'But we could work together!' Epona took a step towards the griffin. All at once she did not feel so afraid. Instead she wanted to grab Scree by the chest feathers and shake him. 'Don't you see? Together, we could kick these bastards out. My mother could take back her throne...'

As soon as she said it, she realised it was the wrong thing to say. Scree gave an abrupt screech of amusement.

'The concerns of your queens are about as important to us as the concerns of bats, of beetles. To be dragged away from the Bone Fall for such nonsense... The ghost-way summoning is not to be used frivolously. Do it again and it shall be your entrails I drop from a great height.'

'It is not frivolous!' Epona was dimly aware that she was shouting. Next to her, Jack was saying something quietly, some word of warning. 'Our people are dying. They are throwing them in the river just to watch them drown! They kill whoever they find, not because it gains them anything but because it amuses them. My mother is going to be eaten. We *need* your help.' She laughed a little, feeling despair lap at the back of her throat. 'We looked up to you, the great and terrible griffins. But what use is a hero who will not help those weaker than himself?'

Witch-seer Scree bristled and took a few steps forward until he was looming directly over Epona.

'You forget yourself, human. We owe prey animals nothing.' Then his voice softened slightly, and he looked away. 'If you would take my advice, you will seek out your Green Man. He has been summoned. He could be your most powerful weapon.'

'What?' Epona blinked. 'What are you talking about?' She glanced at Jack. The woman appeared to have turned a shade paler.

'We all felt it,' continued Scree. 'Even those dull-witted griffins who are not Edge Walkers sensed that the Druidahnon had died, and in doing so had summoned the Green Man. The Wild Wood knows it too. It is waiting.' Scree fixed her with one piercing blue eye. It was the colour of glaciers, cold and unyielding. 'Soon, one will appear who must be consumed by the green wood and wield its power. That is your best hope of casting the Othanim out.' He sighed. 'It might well be our best hope, too.'

With that, Witch-seer Scree leapt up into the air, banking sharply before heading back to the ghost-beam. Epona saw him enter the green light, saw the eerie shadow briefly cast by his wings, and then he was gone, winking out of the day like a pebble dropped into a cloudy pond. A second or so later, the beam itself vanished.

# 15

Belise held herself still, waited, and watched, just as Kaeto had taught her. She did not want eyes on her – they rarely did, in their profession – but she was aware that was more difficult than it had been in the past. In the past, she had been a scrawny street kid, one of thousands on the streets of Stratum. Now she was a seven-foot-tall Titan with violet eyes and feathered wings she had only just learnt to use.

Even so, it was good to be quiet. They had been brought back to the castle, she and Felldir in chains still, with Kaeto nearby, thrumming with anxiety she suspected only she could spot. And now they were in what must have once been a very beautiful throne room; the light from the windows fell over broken tables, soiled rushes on the floor, paintings and tapestries that had been slashed and ruined. The throne that Queen Broudicca had once sat in was gone. Icaraine lurked on the dais itself, a vast figure who watched everything too keenly.

There was another human in the room, a tall woman with warm brown skin and long dark hair in braids. She was kneeling on the ground by the throne, her head down so that her braids fell forward to cover her face. The Othanim who were Icaraine's closest advisors clustered to either side, talking amongst themselves, while Felldir knelt in the centre of the room, his head bowed. Someone else, she noted, might have been humiliated by that, but not Felldir. He carried his dignity with him always, as much a part of him as his skin and bones. She had not been made to kneel yet. She would not have a problem with it. Survival was more important than dignity. But she took note of Icaraine's thick neck, and where a well-placed dagger might do the swiftest damage.

'Felldir, my little pet, my scurrying beetle,' Icaraine cooed. 'How I've missed you.'

There was a rumble of laughter from the gathered Othanim. Standing off to one side, Kaeto was watching everything with his hands behind his back. He looked very small and powerless amongst the crowd of Titans, and that made Belise angry. She swallowed it down, promising herself she would dwell on it later.

Icaraine had hold of Felldir's Titan-ore chain in one giant fist, and she gave it a quick jerk. Felldir lurched forward, one of his wings reflexively spreading to balance himself.

'Come closer. I want to see what the years have done to your face.'

Hand over hand, Icaraine began pulling Felldir closer to her. He scrambled to his feet to avoid simply being dragged over the filthy floor. When he was close to the dais, she lifted the chain, forcing him to stand on his toes, his head tilted back. Icaraine peered at him, her nose wrinkling as she gave several great snorts. His white hair, now loose from its braid, shifted in the fetid breeze.

'You smell of them, Felldir. Like light-bones. The smell of cattle, of creatures that hang around waiting to be slaughtered. Do you enjoy that, my pet? Rutting around in the dirt with the animals?' Icaraine looked in the direction of Kaeto, a wolfish grin splitting her face. 'Human. If you live to see your Stratum again, you must tell your little empress thank you. I had thought it a ridiculous gift, to be given back that which is already mine, but I find that I enjoy this. It is delicious to have my Felldir back, and to see how you cringe and wince when I play with him.'

An expression passed over Kaeto's face that Belise was fairly certain she hadn't seen before. It hurt her to see it, so she focused her attention on Icaraine. Understanding the creature at the heart of the Othanim was vital.

The first and most obvious thing was the sheer size of the Othanim priestess. She was many times larger than even the biggest of her winged warriors, her arms and legs like tree trunks. Felldir had told her once that Othanim the size of Icaraine were not born very often, and when they were it caused a great deal of upheaval in their society – the ruling queen was often ousted, there was usually a war. Othanim like Icaraine were capable of creating soldiers that were utterly devoted to them.

At that point in the conversation Kaeto had spoken up. It had been winter, and they were all three of them crowded around an open fire in the broken castle. Belise had felt safe, then.

Kaeto had said that the Othanim sounded like bees in a hive, with Icaraine as their queen. He said that she was an anomaly, a mutation: a creature that by rights shouldn't exist, but did.

*You shouldn't even exist*, Belise thought, her eyes trained on the giant Titan.

'Your majesty.' Kaeto stepped forward, and Belise switched her attention back to him. She recognised what he was doing now, attempting to distract Icaraine from Felldir. 'Your majesty, her Luminance the Empress of the Imperium wishes to extend the hand of friendship to the peoples of the Othanim. It is her hope that our two mighty nations can benefit from a close relationship.'

Icaraine made a sceptical rumbling noise in the back of her throat, but her grip on the chain holding Felldir loosened. The human woman kneeling at the foot of the dais looked up, and Belise caught a glimpse of pale blue eyes.

'What could your human empire offer a Titan? What could ants offer you, Envoy Kaeto?'

Belise noted that the murmuring from the other Othanim in the throne room had stopped. They were watching closely. They did want to know what the humans could offer, despite what their priestess claimed.

Kaeto bowed again, acknowledging that he was in the lowlier position here. Clever.

'Your majesty, the Imperium will of course appear to be a mere upstart empire in the eyes of the ancient and storied Othanim, but in truth there is much we could offer you. In the two thousand years that you have been... absent, Enonah has changed. There are new alchemies, new nations, centuries upon centuries of history that you will not be aware of. Who can say what piece of information could aid the Othanim in their goals?'

Icaraine snorted again.

'Given how many Blessed nations we carry under our banner, the Imperium is also exceptionally well supplied. If you need armour, weapons, food, medicines, gems, livestock – these are all things we can give to you, and quickly. If you require aid on the battlefield, our Heralds are uniquely suited to assist in your fight against the griffins.'

'Little ghosts of what we are,' said Icaraine, clearly amused. 'As birds are to griffins.'

Belise glanced at Thirteen and the other Heralds, who were stood in formation just behind Kaeto. They appeared to be staring straight ahead, no readable expression on their faces – these were real soldiers – but Belise thought she caught the slightest twitch of Thirteen's eyebrow. He did not like Icaraine's tone.

'There is also, if I may offer it, the information network of the Envoys,' Kaeto continued smoothly. 'We work in the shadows, watching and waiting, and occasionally, when my empress demands it, we move in subtle ways to bend events to her desires. This is a service we could offer the Othanim, too.'

'I have never seen much use for stealth myself,' said Icaraine, and there was a flutter of laughter in the chamber. Belise herself smiled a little. It was difficult to imagine a creature the size of the priestess trying to sneak her way down a shadowy corridor. 'And what does your little empress want in return for these trifles?'

'The greatest token one could wish to receive – your friendship, your majesty.'

Icaraine laughed. 'You mean the promise that we will not fly to Stratum next and begin eating your children. I promise nothing, Envoy, but your presence here is currently a source of great amusement to me. You'll be given a room in this castle, a place of great honour, and you will be called upon regularly, most likely when I am bored. Ceni, you will see to this.' The kneeling woman bowed even lower, her forehead almost brushing the floor.

'Yes, my queen.'

Icaraine's eyes flickered to Felldir again, who had been standing quietly to one side. 'You care for my little pet, don't you, Envoy Kaeto? And your discomfort is quite delicious to me.' Abruptly the giant Titan stood up, her head almost brushing the ceiling. 'Where is Malakim? I wish to see him.'

Belise felt a prickle of something move down her back and along her arms. In the old days, when she had been training as Kaeto's assistant in Stratum, he had told her about this feeling: a kind of intuition, a sense that something important was revealing itself, usually in a way that would be missed by other people in the room. He told her to be on the lookout for that feeling at all times, because it could often be the key. When Icaraine spoke of Malakim, her voice changed, taking on a tone that felt quite at odds with everything they knew about her so far. She had stood up to make this pronouncement, and there was an energy about her that was almost... anxious? Whoever this Malakim was, he was extremely important to Icaraine. Perhaps important to all Othanim.

There was movement at the back of the throne room, and a concealed door behind the dais opened to reveal an Othanim with a young child. They led the child over to the dais, their posture oddly stiff. Once the boy was stood next to one of Icaraine's thick legs, the Othanim scampered back into the crowd, as though glad to be away.

'There you are, my sweet,' beamed Icaraine. One huge hand came down to scoop the boy up, and she set him on her knee. 'I have some new friends to introduce you to.'

Belise had been expecting a great war general, or even a lover, but a child? And Malakim did not even look like an Othanim child. Although larger than a human boy, he looked to be on the small side, and to her eyes no more than seven or eight years old. He had no wings, feathered or otherwise, and he was very pale and slight. His hair was a wispy, silky blond, just about covering a slightly bulbous head, and the head had to be large because... Belise blinked, making herself look at him properly and observe, as Kaeto would want her to. The head had to be large because Malakim had six crimson eyes, like a spider. They ran in pairs: the first where you would expect to find a pair of eyes, with the other four above, sunken into his forehead. They were red from edge to edge, and he didn't appear to have any eyelids – at least not in the way that humans or the Othanim did. All at once, Belise wished more than ever that she could speak to Felldir. He might know what this was, and what it meant.

'You see this little worm, Malakim?' Icaraine leaned down so that she could coo into the child's ear. At the same time, she gave Felldir's chain a yank. 'Do you see? Felldir was given an important task, because he was trusted once, a long time ago. He and his lover Areel were the closest of Mother's allies, my right and left hand. Then Areel died in the war, and Felldir lost his way. I gave him purpose, when we were imprisoned in the Undertomb by upstart Titans, but in the end, he failed in his duty. And when I was freed, he *hid* from us.' She gestured abruptly to a pair of Othanim by the throne. 'Unchain him.'

They did as she asked, and Felldir stood a little straighter. Belise felt her own heartbeat quicken. If Icaraine killed Felldir now, there was little Belise could do to stop her.

*I'll kill her though*, she thought, holding the idea close to her like a flame on a cold night. *Before the end, she'll regret fucking with us.*

The child Malakim looked at Felldir – or at least, Belise assumed he did. It was very difficult to tell what he was doing with those insectile eyes.

'Don't you want to play with him?' cooed Icaraine. 'He's my pet, but he can be yours too, Malakim. Why don't you show Felldir the worm your little trick?'

The boy took a step back, pressing himself against his mother's leg. Belise felt a brief moment of a street child's contempt for him – being shy wasn't a quality that got you very far in the alleyways of Stratum. But then the boy slowly raised one arm, reaching out towards Felldir, and his fingers twitched. Felldir grunted and bent, as though he'd been struck an invisible blow. Icaraine laughed, delighted.

'Good boy, my sweet.' She bent her head to Malakim and kissed his downy hair. 'You get stronger every day. Malakim is a special child, Envoy Kaeto. He can feel the bones of Titans. He can touch them with his mind. Eventually, he will be able to break them.'

'That is... quite remarkable.' Kaeto's face was carefully neutral, but Belise could guess what he was thinking. The child was a weapon, one that could destroy the griffins, or bring them to heel. No wonder Malakim was so important to Icaraine. Not only was he her beloved child, he was her means to winning the war, too.

Malakim seemed to have overcome his initial shyness and had taken a few steps away from his mother. His outstretched hand flexed, and Felldir bent double, his eyes squeezed shut against some inner pain.

'Very good, very good, Malakim,' said Icaraine, clearly pleased. 'But we don't want to wear you out. It's time you went back to bed...'

Malakim apparently had other ideas. The boy looked to the crowd of Othanim and swung his arm at them. They skittered back, but one was not quite fast enough, and they were jerked roughly forward, wings unfolding as they resisted Malakim's power. There was a ripple of nervous laughter from the Othanim that were comfortably out of reach. It occurred to Belise that they were frightened of the kid. As well they should be; their bones were the same as Felldir's, after all.

'That's enough, my sweet,' said Icaraine, her tone faintly dangerous. 'Mikeal, please take Malakim back to my rooms.'

But Mikeal, presumably the Othanim that had brought the child into the throne room, was nowhere to be seen. Belise considered what it must be like to be Malakim's babysitter: you would be under constant scrutiny from Icaraine, who was herself incredibly dangerous, and if Malakim had a tantrum of any kind – as little kids often did – your very bones would be in danger. It had to be an enormously unpopular job.

'Mikeal? Where are you? Attend to my child. Now.'

Belise stepped forward, as best she could in her Titan-ore chains. 'It would be my honour to serve your child, my lady.'

Kaeto was too clever to turn and look at Belise directly, but she felt his attention on her all the same. She could almost hear what he was thinking.

*What are you playing at?*

'You?' For the first time Icaraine's gaze settled on her. It was like a physical weight. 'The one who hid with the worm? I don't know you.'

'There is no reason you should, my lady,' said Belise brightly. 'I was left behind when you and your army left the Black City – a problem with the pod I slept in. The same problem meant I knew very little of who or what I was when I did escape the thing, and so I followed Felldir. I didn't have much choice.' She made herself look at Felldir; made herself scowl at him. 'If I had known that he had betrayed the Lightbringer, I would have killed him myself.'

This was a risk. It was possible that Icaraine would command her to kill Felldir to prove her loyalty, and then... And then a great many bad things could happen. But Belise had come to believe that Icaraine would see such a quick death as a waste. She wanted him to suffer.

'If you'll allow me, my lady, I would gladly serve the child Malakim. In order to make up for my foolish mistakes, and to prove my loyalty to you.'

Icaraine grunted. Malakim himself was watching with bright interest, his eyes like bubbles of blood.

'Very well.' Icaraine seated herself on the dais once more and gestured to the Othanim to release Belise's chains. 'You will be his companion. Your life belongs to him now. What is your name?'

'Belise, my lady.'

'Beleeze. It will be your duty to see to his wants and needs, and to keep him entertained. If he becomes unhappy with you, you can share Felldir's fate.' Icaraine grinned. 'Or Malakim will show you his displeasure himself.'

Belise nodded, then realising that wasn't enough, bowed low.

'It will be my greatest honour, my lady.'

'I'm sure it will. Take him away to my rooms.'

There was a murmur from the gathered Othanim as Belise walked the length of the throne room. Kaeto watched her pass with only the faintest twitch of an eyebrow to betray what he was thinking. When she drew level with Felldir, she paused, and making sure Icaraine could see it clearly, she spat on him.

'Traitor,' she said.

Malakim himself seemed unsure what to make of her. He looked up at her with an expression she couldn't read. *The creepy little shit. You can tell so much about how someone is feeling through their eyes*, she thought. *I'll have to learn new ways with this one.*

She gave him her sunniest smile and held out her hand.

'I think we're going to be good friends, Malakim.'

After a moment he took it.

# 16

*There are said to be giants buried all over Brittletain. A lesser-known Titan, these creatures vanished long before the god-boar, the unicorns and the kraken, apparently choosing to retire from mortal life to an eons-long hibernation beneath the ground. It's not known how many there were, in the days when they roamed across the hills and forests of Brittletain, but even if they were very few in number, the Titan-ore deposits in the dirt and stone of that island must be great indeed. Another reason we must bring the blessings of the Imperium to its shores, sooner rather than later.*

Excerpt from *The Lore of the Deep Forest:
An Examination of the Myths
and Facts of Brittletain*

Molly and the two other women – who introduced themselves as Niala and Kessen – led Leven and Cillian deeper into the wood. They did not follow any Paths, and they did not ask Cillian to open any for them. In truth, he felt half reluctant to even try. It had been so long since he'd manipulated the Wild Wood in that way, and the last time he'd been here, it had been angry with him. Instead, they walked until the sun was beginning to taste the edge of sky, and they came to a great hill rising out of the trees. At the base of it they met a number of ragged people armed with spears, who glanced at Molly and the others before waving them through. From there they came to a cave entrance, a tall and narrow fissure in the hill; over the top of it hung a vast skull with a pair of tusks curling upward from its jaw. In the last of the light, the Titan bone looked almost purple. With a shiver of recognition, Cillian realised he knew where they were.

'The Keeper of the Names,' he said. 'She lives still?'

Kessen, the older woman, looked at him keenly. 'You know her, Druin?'

'No. But all Druin know of her. I've never been to the crystal cave.'

'Ah.' Kessen's mouth quirked into a smile. 'It's quite a sight. Not as magnificent with all of us cluttering it up, but the Keeper has been kind enough to take us in.'

From inside the cave, there came a sudden, wailing shriek. Cillian felt Leven tense next to him, her fingers twitching with the urge to summon her blade.

'That's our Druin problem,' said Kessen. Molly and the younger girl, Niala, had melted away to speak to the people standing guard, but Kessen waved them through the entrance impatiently. 'We picked him up around a week ago on a hunt. He was crouched in the branches of an oak, would you believe? Perhaps that is normal behaviour for a Druin, I'm sure I wouldn't know, but he was screaming and shouting fit to wake the Green Man himself, and with those flying bastards all over the place it's not safe to be so noisy.' She sighed. 'There was something of a *discussion* over whether we should bring him back with us, but this is still the Wild Wood, and the Druin have kept us safe here for years. It was eventually decided we should do the same for him.'

'What is his name?'

'Tonnroc. We got that much out of him, at least.'

They emerged through the short passageway into the wider cave. Both Cillian and Leven stopped short in amazement. Aside from the floor, the place was formed entirely of purple and blue crystals, vast edifices of glittering rock that thrust from the stone in jagged clusters. Here and there, winding steps had been carved into the crystals, leading up to smooth circular tunnels which from the ground appeared to be entirely dark. It was an extraordinary, beautiful place, filled with eerie lights that burned deep inside the crystals. The effect was somewhat at odds with the teeming activity on the floor of the cave; here there were several campfires burning, and around each were gathered groups of tired-looking people, cooking and talking, their belongings and bedrolls in piles next to them.

'What is this place?' asked Leven.

'An absolute pigsty, is what it is,' boomed a voice from behind them. Startled, Cillian turned to see a diminutive woman squinting up at them. She had dark, wrinkled skin, and her head was entirely bald. White paint had been daubed across it in white spots, and her eyes sparkled with ire or mischief; Cillian couldn't tell which. He cleared his throat.

'Keeper of the Names, Speaker of the World,' he said carefully. 'We're honoured to be in this sacred place.'

'I'm glad someone is.' The tiny woman bustled past them towards one of the fires. Without a word to the people gathered around it she grabbed the spoon out of a cooking pot and ate a mouthful of stew. When she was done, she passed the spoon back to a woman kneeling on a bedroll. 'Needs more salt. If you're going to cook in my cave, at least do it properly.' She turned back to them and pointed abruptly at Cillian. 'A Druin then. Looks like you've been naughty, from the state of your horns, but I have to tell you, lad, I don't think anyone gives a single shit about such things these days, so you can wipe that sheepish look off your face. If there's one thing a Druin shouldn't have, it's a sheepish look – it goes too well with the horns, and then what have you got? People will start saying *baa* at you.'

Next to him Cillian heard the faint strangled noise of Leven trying not to laugh.

'Still, useful. We've got one Druin here already – you can probably hear him, the poor wee duck,' continued the Keeper. 'Hollering fit to wake the giants. I don't suppose you could have a word? He won't listen to any of us lesser mortals.'

'I'd be glad to.'

'Good lad. He's along there, up the third set of steps.' She nodded towards the back of the cavern. 'It's not ideal, keeping him in one of the crystal tunnels, but Galehort is practically deaf these days. I imagine he thinks a pigeon has got in somewhere.' When neither of them moved, the Keeper waved a hand at them brusquely. 'Go on then. The sooner the better. He's putting people off their tea.'

They made their way through the groups of refugees, who looked tired and wary, holding their children close. The smells of smoke, roasting meat and unwashed people seemed at odds with the vault of crystals over their heads. *We really are at war*, thought Cillian. *And not with each other, for once.*

'Who is Galehort, exactly?' In the flickering light from the cookfires Leven looked tired. There were dark circles under her eyes, and she moved carefully, as though her muscles ached. Cillian knew she wasn't sleeping well.

'A giant,' he replied. 'One of seven said to be sleeping beneath this hill. It's the Keeper's job to remember their names and their deeds, and to keep them aware of what's going on in the waking world.'

'Giants sleeping under the hill. Of course there are,' said Leven. 'I don't know why I asked. And how does she keep them updated exactly?'

'The tunnels carved into the crystal lead down to each sleeping giant. The Keeper calls her news whenever something significant happens, and the tunnels carry the sound down to them.'

'Do the giants ever answer back?'

'I don't believe so. They were never very talkative, according to the legends. At least, not with humans. The Druidahnon said there were one or two who you couldn't shut up after a few barrels of mead.' Thinking of the old bear brought back the urgency of their mission. They had to find him; they had to find out why Cillian had heard the Druidahnon's voice. 'Come on. We can rest here for the night, and tomorrow I will have to try opening the Paths again.'

'If Ynis doesn't return by moonrise, I'm going to look for her myself,' said Leven firmly. She shook her head at the look he gave her. 'I'm worried about her, Cillian. Something is up. I know I've only been a big sister for a couple of years, but I like to think I've developed a few instincts.'

They climbed the crystal steps carefully, their boots finding little purchase on the slippery surface. As they did so, the Druin in the tunnel began wailing again, and Cillian felt all the hairs on the back of his neck stand on end. The sound was pure grief, pure despair. When they got to the mouth of the tunnel, they could see a humanoid shape slumped in a sitting position, his branching stag horns caught in the light of a small yellow candle.

'Tonnroc?' Cillian called softly.

The Druin stopped wailing and turned his face to the tunnel entrance.

'We're lost.' His voice was barely more than a whisper. 'We're all lost.'

'My name is Cillianos, Tonnroc. I was given my horns at Dosraiche too. This is my wife, Leven, a traveller from... from very far away. What is wrong?'

'You... you're a Druin, too?'

'Yes.'

There was a beat of silence. Underneath it, from the far side of the tunnel beyond Tonnroc, Cillian thought he could hear another sound, so large and so quiet it almost felt like the movement of blood around his own body. It sounded a little like snoring.

'I haven't seen any others,' whispered Tonnroc. 'Not since...'

He fell silent.

'What happened to you?'

'I was part of a small group of Druin. We were bringing supplies through the Wild Wood, and we were using the Quiet Paths. The darkest ways.' He paused, swallowing down a sob. 'Do you know what I mean?'

'Yes,' said Cillian. 'The Paths that skirt the Wildest Wood. That would have been very dangerous.'

Tonnroc nodded. After a moment, he picked up the candle and crept towards them. With his face lit by its glow, Cillian could see that he was young, with a patchy beard on his chin and a deep wound on his temple that had been stitched shut with thick black thread. The hand holding the candle was trembling, and he peered at the two of them with watery red eyes.

'I'm not a ranger,' he said. 'I hear the wood too clearly. My place was in Dosraiche, doing quiet work. Keeping the histories. But we needed every Druin out there. And because I can hear the wood so clearly...' He shuddered, making the candle flame quake. 'I could help keep the others safe. That's what they said.'

Cillian turned to Leven slightly. 'Tonnroc would be able to tell if they were about to run into the Dunohi, and in the Wildest Wood that is a very real danger.' He turned back to Tonnroc. 'You were doing an important job.'

The young Druin rubbed the heel of his hand against his eye, wiping away more tears.

'We were on the marsh that runs between the Chalk Hare and the reed downs. There was very little cover there, and the Othanim, those creatures, we knew they were in the area so we had to be so careful. So quiet.' He gave another hiccupping sob. 'My mind was deep, deep in the wood, watching and listening for the Dunohi, watching and listening, watching and listening. I hardly saw the ground under my feet, or the sky. You know what it's like when you're in the green.'

'I do,' said Cillian. 'What happened?'

'*I didn't see the sky,*' said Tonnroc again. 'And I was deep in the green. So when it happened, it was like being drowned. Drowned in grief. Like falling, like the ground dropping away from me. I felt his pain, I felt the blood running out of him. He gave up his life for a spell. *I felt him leave us.*'

'Who?' asked Cillian. He felt cold all over, a creeping dread seizing his throat.

'The Druidahnon,' said Tonnroc. He shook his head, sobs bubbling up again even as he tried to speak, but Cillian was already standing, already backing out of the tunnel. 'And I screamed; I felt him leave us and I couldn't stop screaming. They were nearby, the Othanim, and they came like I'd bloody called them—'

'No.' Cillian felt Leven touch his arm but he moved past her. All at once he couldn't bear to be in that dark tunnel a moment longer. 'That can't be. The Druidahnon wouldn't... he can't be dead.'

'They killed everyone. It was a slaughter.' Tonnroc was still talking, babbling now as though they'd somehow uncorked him. 'The Othanim tore them apart. I saw the pieces, falling. And all the time, all I could feel was the loss, the absence. The Wild Wood itself in mourning.' He took a watery breath. 'The Keeper said they likely spared me because I frightened them, with the noise I was making. Maybe she's right.'

Cillian stood at the top of the crystal steps, his heart racing. Behind him he could still hear Tonnroc talking, tripping over his words as he tried to convey the horror he'd experienced.

'It can't be,' he said again, but he knew already in his heart that it was true. When he'd heard the Druidahnon's voice in his head, he had sensed the desperation there, and the ending of something. He just hadn't dreamt it had been the old bear lord himself who was ending. *And I was gone from the Wild Wood when it happened. I wasn't here for him*, he thought. *Why would he speak those words as he was dying? What do they mean?*

'Cillian, I am sorry.' Leven had left the tunnel and stood beside him. 'And even sorrier you had to find out that way. Are you alright?'

'No,' said Cillian. 'I'm not. But if he was dying when I heard him speak to me, Leven, I think he was using his death to fuel a spell. Using it to summon the Green Man.'

'The nature spirit you told me about? Spirit of chaos and death, and all that?'

'And life and rebirth, yes.'

'And is that... good?'

He shook his head. 'I hardly know. I suppose he thought that it couldn't make things worse. Leven, what are we supposed to do without the Druidahnon? What are any of us supposed to do?'

# 17

'Roots fuck me sideways, I'm tired of fighting these bastards.' It was three days after they had spoken to Scree. The rebels had combed through every report they had in search of news about a newly summoned Green Man, but there was very little to go on. Solasach had knocked his head in the fall and was being tended by their tiny group of healers. Although Yelm told them everything the Druin knew about the Green Man, in Epona's opinion it mostly amounted to superstition and rumour. No living Druin had ever seen him, and no one seemed to have a clear idea of where he might be if he suddenly reappeared – in the Wild Wood somewhere, Epona assumed, but they may as well go looking for a particular acorn in a vast oak forest. Slowly, they had accepted that as impressive as it had been to awaken the ghost-beam, what Scree had told them wasn't much use. Instead, they had gone back to what they had been doing for the last two years: watching the city and harrying the Othanim where they could. All the while, Epona was aware of Bezryl's threat: that Icaraine would be feeding her mother to her child in less than a month.

'We're all tired of it,' said Jack.

Mist was rising off the Old Father as the first rays of sun began to heat the water. Epona and Jack were on the upper floor of a deserted tavern, watching the river from the window. The place still smelled of spilt ale and tobacco smoke, and it was making Epona twitchy. She felt like she could turn around too quickly and catch the ghost of an old patron downing a pint. On the river itself was a vast ship with a broad hull and navy-blue sails. The name of it, according to the sloping golden words painted on its side, was *The Wandering Eye*.

The ship had docked some days ago, the first significant traffic the port had seen in years – the last had been the desperate exodus of practically every boat in the harbour when the Othanim had arrived – and Epona had decided she had to see it for herself. Who would come to Londus now, when it was crawling with winged monstrosities? Now that she could see it, the answer was obvious. There were stars painted in gold across the sails, and the figurehead at the prow was a comet.

'The bloody Imperium,' she said for the third time that hour. 'As if we haven't enough on our plate. One invader clearly isn't enough.'

'It vexes you,' said Jack, a mild question in her tone.

'All these years of keeping them out, and they sail right up the river on their biggest ship.' Epona sighed. 'Mum's going to be furious.'

There were humans on the ship, a normal crew from the look of them, and they kept their heads down as they moved across the deck. They were being watched by a crowd of Othanim from a nearby roof. Clearly shore leave wasn't on the cards. Epona got up, went to the back of the room and peered down the stairs. As well as observing the new ship, they were there to meet a contact, and they were late. Sometimes, contacts from within the city would stop turning up to their meetings, and Epona never knew if they had decided it was too risky, or if they'd been caught by the Othanim. Every time one was late, she began to get an awful, gnawing feeling in her stomach. She returned to the window, glanced at the ship once more and felt her heart leap in her chest.

There was a figure on the deck with shining blue wings of light. For a second, she thought it was Leven – but no. As she watched, they lifted into the air, taking with them a length of rope they clearly intended to tie to the mast. The Herald was male, with a bald head that looked almost painfully white in the dawn glow.

'There are Heralds here,' said Epona. She felt rather than saw Jack look at her. All of the rebels knew that Epona had travelled with the Herald who had come to Brittletain; once or twice she had overheard them swapping tales about it. 'Leven could be here. If she... if she went back to the Imperium.'

'Would you want her to be here?'

'What? No, of course not. If she's here on that ship, then she's an invader too, probably in league with the Othanim.' Epona rubbed her thumb along her lower lip, her eyes still on the ship. What would she do if Leven suddenly appeared down there, climbing up out of the hold with her eyes squinted against the sunshine? Would Leven be a potential ally, someone they could get information from, or even convince to sabotage the Othanim? Or would she be fully loyal to the Starlight Imperium, the adventures they had shared in the Wild Wood put aside in the face of these new Titans? The reality, Epona suspected, was that she and possibly also Cillian had perished in the north of the Wild Wood, caught by her sister Ceni's warriors or torn to pieces by griffins. She frowned. 'I feel like it doesn't bode well for us though, that the Imperium have sent Heralds to Icaraine. They're certainly not here to fight the Othanim.'

'You were close to her? The Herald.'

Epona looked at Jack finally. She was surprised to see that the woman had a faint pink blush across her cheeks. The sun streaming in through the windows was beginning to heat up the room, she reasoned.

'We were friends,' she said. 'And I wish I hadn't lost touch with her. I know we'd be doing a bloody sight better with this rebellion if she had been with us for the last two years.'

Jack stood up. Caliburn gave a soft whine, but unusually, she didn't translate what the sword was saying.

'I'll go and look for our contact,' she said. 'He can't be far.'

She left, the sound of her boots on the stairs fading into the distance. Epona turned her attention back to the ship. They were offloading crates, the men and women of the crew carrying one between two, and she felt a curl of suspicion settle in her stomach. What did you do when you were trying to get someone onside? You sent them gifts. It was exactly what her mother had sent Leven to do – except, of course, that Ceni had used that particular mission to her own ends.

Sooner than she expected, she heard Jack's boots on the stairs again, along with another, lighter step.

'He was just in the alley,' she said. 'Getting up the courage to cross the street.'

Their contact was a boy called Jerran. He was ten years old, slight for his age, with big dark eyes under a mop of unruly hair. When the Othanim had murdered most of her mother's staff in the castle, they had spared a handful of servants – those who were young, old or especially weak. No one who could cause much trouble, in other words.

'I was gonna do it,' said Jerran. The boy looked on the verge of tears, which made Epona feel guilty, which in turn made her feel weary. 'I was just being careful.'

'As you should be, Jerran.' Epona crossed to the boy and placed her hands on his shoulders. 'Never come if it's unsafe. Right? That's the first rule.'

'Yes y'majesty,' he mumbled, looking at his boots.

'Good. Come and sit and tell us about this ship. We've brought some food for you.'

The gods only knew what the servants were eating inside the palace, because Jerran fell on the bread and fruit they'd brought him like he hadn't eaten for a week. In between mouthfuls they got the pieces of the story out of him.

'And who came off of the ship?'

'There was a human man, and two more of those flying shits.' He paused, his eyes growing wide. 'Sorry, y'majesty.'

'It's alright, Jerran. If I couldn't cope with some fruity language, I would hardly be Broudicca's daughter.'

Reassured, he continued. 'The funny thing was, the flying wossnames, they were in chains. Weird ones. I saw when they were brought into the throne room, and they were both all tied up.'

'They were?' This made little sense to Epona. 'They were prisoners?'

'I guess,' said Jerran. 'One of them is still in chains in Icaraine's rooms. A big miserable-looking fella with white hair. The other one is a girl with black hair. She's been let out of the chains now and she stays with the other thing. The monster.'

'Icaraine's child?'

Jerran nodded, although he didn't look sure at all. 'If you say so. It looks awful to me. Like its head is half bug.' He shuddered. 'The girl, she looks after it.'

'Why would the Imperium be transporting Othanim prisoners?' asked Jack.

'I don't know. As a favour to Icaraine? I've no doubt the empress is looking for ways to be indispensable. What about the human that came with them, Jerran?'

'Old. Well, older than you two.' Now that he had food inside him, he was much cheerier and more talkative. 'Black hair and beard, wore dark clothes. He was very calm. He didn't speak much. It's more like he was watching them all, you know. He didn't look very happy to be there.'

'Did you see him close up, Jerran?'

He nodded.

'Was there anything else about him you can remember? Any other little detail?'

Jerran shrugged, then seemed to think about it. After a moment he shrugged again. 'Well, he wore really plain clothes, black and dark red, with a hood. But he had a big piece of jewellery on his chest too, which I thought was a bit odd. You used to see merchants down by the docks who wore jewellery like that, big gold rings and necklaces and so on, but he didn't look like one of those to me.'

'What did it look like, this jewellery? Was it a necklace? A brooch?'

'A brooch, yeah,' said Jerran. He paused to take another bite out of the loaf they'd brought him, chewing noisily. 'It was gold, and star-shaped, with rays coming off of it, and in the middle there was a big green stone.'

Epona sat back in her chair. Caliburn was singing, but she didn't need Jack for this one.

'A green comet,' she said. 'The emblem of the Envoys. That makes sense, I suppose. They're said to be skilled at a number of different things. But it's interesting that the empress didn't send a diplomat. That suggests to me that they're hedging their bets a little. The primary function of an Envoy is assassination, but the Othanim won't know that. Perhaps this Envoy will be open to a bit of communication.'

'What are you thinking?' said Jack.

'Jerran,' said Epona, patting the boy on the shoulder again. 'How would you like to earn some mead?'

# 18

*The sword has been lost for an age, and I tend to think that was a conscious decision on its part. After the death of its master, it found every warrior lacking, and yearned only to return to the depths of the lake where it was made – that was the account given by Orlash, his master's lover, and she spoke to the sword and understood its words. So it would not surprise me greatly if somehow the sword contrived to be returned to the lake, and rests there still, only to leave when a warrior the equal of its old master calls upon it. And the Green Man only knows when that might be.*

Extract from the writings of Elder Druin Jathinos,<br>Dosraiche's Master of Histories

Leven watched the moon rise with impatience. Cillian was still inside the cave, talking with the Keeper and Molly about the war and its impact on the Wild Wood, but she had taken herself outside to wait for Ynis. She knew that her sister was right about the fate-ties, that she could follow them back to her at any time, but would she want to? Now that she was home with the sister she had grown up with, did she have any real reason to stay with Leven and Cillian? *To stay with the woman who murdered her father and left her to die in the woods,* her mind added viciously.

Beyond the cave there were a handful of refugees; they were drinking from a bottle they were passing around, and talking in low voices. They looked exhausted. Leven, who had experienced the aftermath of battle more times than she could count, recognised the look. These people had seen terrible things, and terrible things could happen again at any moment. One of them, a young man with a dark beard, caught her eye and beckoned her over. He passed her the bottle, which turned out to be full of the sweet honey wine the Britons were so fond of. *I'm a Briton too*, she reminded herself. *Even if I don't remember much of it.*

'What's your story, friend?'

Leven smiled and passed the bottle back. 'My husband and I have been travelling awhile, looking for a member of our family. We were away when most of this was happening.'

'Away from Brittletain?' asked one of the group. He was an old man with a leather patch over one eye; his one good eye was glaring at the Titan-ore markings on her skin. Leven hoped he would just take them to be elaborate tattoos.

'Our sister was *very* lost,' said Leven.

'You were lucky,' said the man with the beard. 'I've thought about trying to make it to one of the big ports. Get on a ship going anywhere. But very few ships come to Brittletain now.'

'Nowhere will be safe from them flying bastards soon, you mark my words,' said the one-eyed man in a dark tone. 'What's to stop them from flying over the sea to the Blessed nations? Or even heading west across the Broken Sea? They are a plague. They won't stop at Brittletain.'

'Where have you all come from?' asked Leven.

'Mersia,' said the bearded man. 'When they came, King Eafen drew back all his warriors to the city and left the rest of us to be massacred.' He paused and tugged at his beard. His eyes looked too bright, and Leven knew he was remembering things he would rather have forgotten. 'And they didn't stay, that's what I don't understand. They came, they killed... hundreds of people, and then they left again. It's like they don't want the land.'

'They just want the blood,' the old man added.

'Skirmish fighting,' said Leven. 'It's a way to grind you down. Half the battle is with the idea that you could be attacked at any moment.'

'How do you know so much about it?' snapped the older of the two.

Leven clenched her jaw, thinking of her time with the Heralds. Once, it had seemed glorious, to be part of that unit, taking the Imperium's blessings from one nation to the next. Yes, the people resisted, but change was always resisted at first; that's what Boss used to say. These days, when she thought of those years, odd images came back to her with alarming clarity: the upturned face of a terrified child as they flew in low over her village; bodies in the river, streamers of blood turning the cold water red; enemy soldiers screaming as the Heralds snatched them up only to let them fall to their deaths. *I know too much about it*, she thought.

'I was a warrior, once.' She cleared her throat and looked back up at the night sky. The moon was a silver curl, icily brilliant, and there was still no sign of Ynis. With thoughts of the Othanim and her own reckless slaughter in her mind, she suddenly knew she could not wait any longer. She nodded to the two men. 'Thanks for the drink.'

As she walked away, the younger man called out to her, 'Stay close to the cave, friend. It's not safe out there.'

Leven moved into the trees without looking back, keen to get a good amount of distance between them so they didn't see the light from her wings – the last thing she wanted to do was spook the guards, who were twitchy and had a number of powerful longbows between them. When she was satisfied she was far enough away, she summoned her wings, wincing at the wave of pain they brought with them, and let them bear her up into the sky.

It was a cold and clear night. In the distance, she could see lights on the ground in a few places; settlements, she guessed, or the camps of survivors, but not as many as she expected to see. Most, she suspected, would be under cover by now if they were lucky, or had decided to endure a night without a fire in the hope they wouldn't bring the Othanim down on them. The problem she had was that although Ynis could track her with her Edge Walker skills, she had no such way of following her sister – a fact that Ynis was using to her advantage more and more these days.

'No matter,' she muttered to herself. 'I will look for her anyway. It's all I can do.'

The reality was she might not have that long to do it. The Herald powers did not last like they used to, and sooner than she'd like she'd have to return to the crystal cave.

But she suspected she could raise her chances of finding her wayward sister. She knew the sorts of things that she liked to hunt, and the sorts of places she liked to be at night. Ynis liked to have the open sky over her if possible, because it reminded her of her home in the north. She liked high, cold places where you could see a long way. Places where you could hunt small, scurrying things.

Leven turned in a slow circle, letting her eyes travel over the varied landscape of Brittletain, until she spotted exactly what she was after. Another hill – Cillian had told her these were called fells – cresting above the thick blanket of the Wild Wood. It appeared to be largely free of trees. Instead, she could see craggy rocks, their jagged edges lined with silver moonlight. She was fairly sure she could make it there and back before the Herald magic ran out, and if she didn't find Ynis there, well. She would just have to accept that.

It was still and largely quiet as she flew above the canopy of the trees, the blue light from her wings flickering across the leaves below her like a shoal of luminous fish. Ynis wasn't the only one on her mind. Cillian had been deeply shaken by the news of the Druidahnon's death, although being him, he tried to hide it. He had spent some time with the traumatised Druin, talking softly about the permanence of trees and things like that, and had quietly listened to what Tonnroc had to say, but there had been a stiffness to him that suggested he was holding onto a lot of pain – pain he would attempt to deal with in private. Leven didn't quite understand the relationship between the Druin and the Druidahnon, but she knew they were connected through the Wild Wood, which was also in the middle of some sort of mysterious magical crisis. To Cillian, it must seem like all the roots he relied on were being brutally ripped up and exposed to the sky.

She forced herself to fly a little faster – if Ynis was not somewhere on this fell, then she would be glad to get back to Cillian. He needed her too. Probably more than Ynis did, if she were being honest with herself.

And then she saw it. A flicker of movement in the air over the fell, which was much closer now. Almost immediately she lost sight of it again, but she had no doubt it was T'rook; griffins did not venture this far south. It was too dark to see if Ynis was on T'rook's back just yet.

'Hey!' Leven spread her wings and swept closer to the griffin. The blue light from Leven's wings revealed that Ynis wasn't on her back after all. 'Where's Ynis?' She bit down on the urge to mention that it was past her bedtime. T'rook looked startled. 'Is she down on the hill?'

'No,' said T'rook. They flew around each other, almost dancing in mid-air. It felt exhilarating to be sharing the air with a creature the size of T'rook. 'She is not here. You should go back.'

Leven smiled, shook her head. Already the ore-lines were starting to burn, and she didn't have time for T'rook's obstinance.

'Come on, she needs to rest. We all do. We've found somewhere that's safe. I can lead you both there.'

She looked down at the rocky hillside below, only for a bright light to appear over the crest of the hill, shooting towards them.

Her first thought was the Othanim, and her sword almost flickered into existence, summoned instinctively. But it wasn't the Othanim.

It was Ynis. And she had wings.

Leven almost dropped out of the sky in surprise. Ynis's wings were very like hers, formed of something that looked like bright, shining crystal – as though someone had crafted a vast eagle's wing out of glass – but they shone with a cleaner, paler light, blue like glacier ice. As Ynis spotted Leven, the expression of pure joy that had been there abruptly vanished, to be replaced with one of anger and guilt.

'What are you doing here?' she snapped.

'*What did you do?*'

Ynis backed away, a little awkwardly. She was clearly still getting used to the wings. She had no ore-lines on her, but Leven knew that Tyleigh's new augments didn't need them. There was a rising tightness in her chest, a fury and a horror unlike anything she had ever felt.

'I have always wanted to fly,' Ynis said, her voice trembling slightly. T'rook had moved away, reluctant to be between the two of them. 'So I went back to her. I had to.'

'You went back to that *butcher*?'

Before she really knew what she was doing, Leven was tackling her little sister, her hands on her shoulders, wings beating furiously. She wanted to drag her from the sky, to force her onto the ground – to make her take it back, somehow. Dimly she was aware there were tears running down her cheeks. Ynis, taken unawares, fell back towards the ground, and in an eyeblink they were rolling in grass and gorse. Leven pushed her sister into the dirt, attempting to hold her still as Ynis tried to wriggle out of her grasp.

'You don't know what it's like,' hissed Ynis. 'To be wingless is to be *nothing*. My whole life, I've been less than them because

I couldn't fly. I've had to ride around on my sister's back like a parasite. And then...' She gasped, caught somewhere between tears and laughter. 'And then when I found my human sister, she could fly too! How is that fair?'

'That woman is a monster.' Leven's wings flickered, winked out, then reappeared. 'You saw what she did to me, Ynis! Over and over again. And you saw what she did to our father. How could you? How could you go back to her and let her...' She swallowed. The idea was too horrible to speak. 'She destroyed my life. And left you for dead.'

'She's changed it. The process.' Ynis scrambled away from Leven, her bright wings flexing behind her. When she was clear of her sister, she rolled up her sleeve. Visible in the light from the Herald magic was a blue patch of discoloured skin, roughly square. Behind her, T'rook alighted on the ground, her proud head bowed. 'It was easy. It only hurt a little, and I haven't lost my memory. Flying is the heart of griffinhood. I have yost now. I can return to my fathers on the wing. *I can fly with them.*'

Leven dragged herself upright. She felt cold, and sick.

'You've given Tyleigh exactly what she wanted. Now she has tainted us both.'

'No,' said Ynis. She stood up straight and spread her wings out to either side. 'She has made me who I was always meant to be.'

'Stars' arses, you idiot.' Leven took a shaky breath. 'She doesn't know this won't drive you mad in the end, or slowly kill you over time. How could she? She's using you as a test subject, just like she did me.'

'I don't care,' said Ynis hotly. The quiet pragmatic teen Leven had come to know over the last two years seemed to have disappeared. In the light from her wings Ynis looked older, and furious. 'I am going back to Yelvynia. I will fight alongside my griffin brothers and sisters.'

'Wait!'

Ynis leapt up into the sky and shot away like a star, taking her light with her. T'rook, who was still on the ground, eyed Leven warily. For a long moment, neither of them spoke.

'It has been hard for my human sister,' she said eventually. 'For so long. I do not understand yet what she has done to herself, but I cannot blame her for it.'

'How long has she had the... the augments?'

'Since the night you broke me from my cage.'

Leven shook her head. The strength was draining away from her, and it felt as though she were being filled back up with despair.

'Why didn't she tell me?' she asked. 'Why did she lie?'

T'rook sniffed. 'There are some things humans cannot understand. Even flying ones.'

# 19

*The rest of Brittletain may have forgotten, but I have not. My mother and my dear brother perished at the hand of Princess Epona, no doubt directed by Broudicca herself. Let the Othanim feast on Londus – that is what I say. This request for help is worse than a joke. It is an insult.*

King Eafen of Mersia's response to a<br>messenger from Princess Epona's rebellion

There was screaming from the courtyard again.

Half reluctant, Kaeto went over to the thickly leaded window and peered through the warped glass. There were two Othanim down there on the cobblestones. One of them had a young man held by the arm – a servant by the look of him, wearing ragged clothes and an apron. The Othanim laughed and pulled him up by the wrist, letting him dangle a little, and the young man shrieked, babbling some plea for them to leave him alone. The second Othanim took a knife from his belt – he was speaking, his mouth moving, but Kaeto couldn't hear the words – and seized the man's other arm. He ran the blade across his flesh, almost gently, but the blade was very sharp; immediately the young man's arm was covered in a sheet of blood. The screaming grew louder, more desperate. From the northern side of the courtyard, three more Othanim were approaching, cheerful expressions on their faces. They had been bored, but now they had found some entertainment.

'They'll have no servants left if they keep this up,' he said to the empty room. He imagined what Belise might say if she were here. Perhaps she'd ask why they did it when they had no interest in cooking or cleaning themselves; or perhaps she'd point out that Kaeto had done worse to people in the service of the Imperium. But she wasn't here. Since they had met Icaraine in the throne room, he'd only seen brief glimpses of Belise, always in the company of the child, Malakim. He worried for her, even as he knew she was doing the right thing. Outside, the unfortunate servant was enduring the attentions of five Othanim. One of them unfurled her wings, lifting him partially up into the air. Blood spattered onto the cobblestones.

He was still watching, horribly transfixed, when the door to his chamber swung open to admit a young, powerfully built woman with dark hair and green eyes. She looked strikingly similar to the woman who had knelt beside Icaraine in the throne room, only younger. She had blue paint across her eyes and mouth, and her clothes were the worn, hardy garments of someone who spent a lot of time outdoors. She eyed him warily, and closed the door behind her.

'You are one of Ceni's sisters,' he said, feeling some pleasure at the expression of surprise that passed over her face.

'Ceni said you'd be a clever bastard,' she said. 'I am Bronvica. You're alone?'

'Very much so, I'm afraid. Icaraine lets you roam the palace?'

She came into the room, looking into every corner as though to check for Othanim spies anyway. 'We're *servants*,' she said, her mouth twisting as though the words were sour. 'It amuses her, to have us running around. Ceni especially, because Ceni was a queen. The big brute keeps her especially close. Me though? I am less interesting to her.'

'That must be a relief.'

Bronvica snorted. 'I suppose it is. Here, I have a message for you.' She took a rolled-up scroll from within her sleeve, and passed it to him. He didn't move to read it.

'If the reports I received were correct, Queen Ceni attempted to overthrow your mother and take Londus for herself.'

'So you know all about our family drama. It's almost flattering that the Imperium would take such an interest.' Bronvica snorted again. With her muscled arms and broad shoulders, there was something about her that put Kaeto in mind of a horse. 'She didn't just attempt it, she succeeded. Stormed Londus-on-Sea with her army and several others, dragged Mother off the throne by her hair and declared herself queen of Londus and Galabroc both. She must have held the throne for all of a week before the Othanim showed up. Are you going to read that?'

'And what side were you on in this family drama?' asked Kaeto.

Bronvica narrowed her eyes. 'My place was with the household guard. My warriors and I fought Ceni as we were ordered to. Many of my men and women died under Ceni's chariot wheels. Does that please you, Imperium?'

'I am just wondering why you are still talking to her, in that case.'

Bronvica laughed. 'Sisters are complicated. Royal sisters, even more so. And if you haven't noticed, we have larger problems these days. Large, winged problems.'

'Hmm.' Kaeto looked at the scroll in his hands. It was sealed with a blob of blue wax, although there was no insignia embedded in it. He broke the seal and unrolled it. There were two lines written in a sloping script, in the bottom right-hand corner of page.

*The spring can be chilly in Londus, especially in the castle. Be sure to have the servants build up the fire.*

Outside, he realised, the screaming had stopped. He went back to the window and looked out. The unfortunate man and the Othanim were gone, but there was a large pool of blood on the cobblestones. It had started to rain, diluting the blood.

'Well?' snapped Bronvica.

'You don't know what it says?'

She scowled at him, and he realised he was pushing her a little too far. Being a servant was one thing, but being ignored was something else entirely. He went to the empty fireplace, and quickly used the dry logs stacked to one side to build a small fire, feeding it scraps of straw until it was burning merrily. All the while, Bronvica glared at his back. He could feel it, like a hot hand on the back of his neck.

'Felldir, the Othanim I brought with me in chains. Have you any news of him?'

For a long moment, Bronvica said nothing.

'I've not seen much of him,' she said eventually. 'Icaraine barely lets him out of her chambers. Ceni would know more. But there have been... rumours. She does not treat him well.'

Kaeto felt a tightening in his chest. His Envoy training told him to ask about the rumours, to push to get every detail. But he couldn't bring himself to do it. Instead, he held up the parchment in front of the fire, letting the light filter through the thin material. As he had suspected, there was more writing on the parchment, invisible until a strong light shone through it. He had used such inks himself in the past, although the trick was too well known in the Imperium to be truly useful. The new script was in the same hand, and it read:

*Greetings, Envoy. Is it satisfying to be in my country finally? Or frustrating that the only way you could achieve it was for someone bigger and badder to beat us first? I shouldn't waste parchment on these sorts of questions, but I've always been too curious for my own good. And I find myself very curious about the nature of your visit. Reaching out to a new power to make an alliance is the obvious guess, but I suspect it is more delicate than that. Are you gathering information? Certainly. And if you've any sense, you'll be thinking about how you might beat them should the Othanim turn up at your door. There was a phrase I read in one of my mother's old books: the enemy of my enemy is my friend. I find I have been thinking about that a lot, recently. I wonder if it's a phrase that has meaning to you, too. There is a garden in the palace, the southern-most edge of which runs along the river. We have access to it. I don't know how much freedom Icaraine allows you, but if you could contrive to be in that garden at midday, two days from now, we could talk in person. You're a resourceful man, I'm sure you could manage it.*

    *Yours,*
    *E*

'E,' Kaeto said thoughtfully. He looked up at Princess Bronvica. She looked back at him sullenly. Apparently her appetite for chat had been exhausted. 'Broudicca has seven daughters,' he said. 'I assume not all of you were captured when the city fell? Epona then.'

'She and I were both in cells in the dungeon when the Othanim attacked,' said Bronvica. 'Someone got her out – I don't know how, but there was an explosion. She's on the outside now, leading a rebellion.' She puffed out her chest a little, looking suddenly defensive. 'You might think to tell Icaraine about that, a way to gain her favour maybe, but it'll do you no good. Icaraine knows, and she doesn't care. The rebellion is just a mild nuisance to her.'

'You're in contact with Epona? On the outside?'

'Messages are passed along. That's all we can do. The Othanim seem unconcerned about us, really. If they kill us, it's because they're bored – not because they've caught us doing something we shouldn't.'

Outside, the rain grew heavier, bringing with it a rushing sound that felt oppressive. It did not rain often in Stratum.

'I will meet with her, if I can,' he said. 'But she shouldn't expect help from the Imperium.'

'She doesn't expect help from them, she expects help from *you*. The poor sap who was sent into the lion's den to pull its teeth.' She walked to the door stiffly.

'The paint you wear on your face,' he said, uncertain why he wanted to keep her in the room a little longer. 'It is something only the royal family wear, am I right? Why do they let you wear it?'

Bronvica gave one of her laughing snorts. 'They don't know what it is, Envoy. And they don't care to, either.'

Kaeto watched her close the door behind her. After a moment, he went and threw the parchment into the merrily burning fire.

# 20

Belise sat patiently, her legs crossed on the grass. The rain of the previous day had cleared away to reveal a pale blue sky, bright and cavernous, yet it hadn't grown much warmer. She missed the flat heat of Stratum, the sense that the sun was waiting to punch you in the face every time you left the cool marble buildings of the Imperator complex. Here there was sunshine, but a washed-out version of it, and sooner or later it would rain again. In front of her, the child Malakim was also sitting with his legs crossed, a piece of slate in his lap covered with a sheet of fine white parchment. He had a colouring stick in one bony fist, and he was patiently filling in every bit of the white. The colouring stick was red.

'What is that you're drawing, my prince?'

The boy looked up at her, his six red eyes glistening in the daylight. So far, he hadn't spoken a word to her. She wasn't even sure he could speak, which could make things difficult.

'It's a good colour, isn't it, red? Is it your favourite?' It occurred to her that perhaps his strange insectile eyes only let him see in red – perhaps for Malakim, everything was drowned in ruby tones. It would explain the 'drawing'. 'Here, let me show you something.'

Gently, she slid the sheet of parchment from his slate and picked up the black drawing stick. With it, she drew six shapes in the red – they weren't quite circular, they were pinched on either side, and she lined them up in two columns. And then she added a nose, a sly little mouth, a chin, a pair of ears. Master Kaeto had taught her the discipline of drawing when he'd first taken her in and had set her to copying anatomy from a variety of old books. When he needed a body sketched as part of a report, she could do it quickly and confidently, and over the years she'd become adept at it. She turned the paper around so that Malakim could see it.

'It's you,' she said, tapping the page and then pointing to Malakim. 'That red is almost the colour of your eyes, isn't it?'

He picked up the sheet in his pudgy fists, his mouth pursed. After a moment he turned it one way, and then the other, trying to make sense of it. Belise thought about how he had been entombed with his mother for two thousand years, caught in a kind of cocoon, neither ageing nor dying. She wondered how much of that he had been aware of, and what it might have done to his mind. Back in Stratum, she had known of several prisoners in the bowels of the Imperator complex that had gone into their cells as intelligent, reasoned men and women, and come out a handful of years later as broken, shivering wrecks.

'Do you like it?' she prompted. It was good work, she thought, and she was a little annoyed he hadn't been instantly delighted by it. He looked up at her sharply, each of his six red eyes narrowed. In one jerky movement, he tore the parchment in half, then tore it again, throwing the pieces onto the grass.

Belise watched the pieces fall, not reacting. One of the great disciplines in an Envoy's life, Kaeto was always telling her, was knowing when to react. And when to wait. Sometimes a quick reaction would save your life. And sometimes it would end it. Being a good Envoy was about knowing which was which.

Malakim stood up. From the expression on his face, he was wrestling with some strong emotion. He threw out an arm towards her, his fingers clutching at the air, and Belise felt her body go rigid. Her heavy magical bones were thrumming as an alien power wrapped itself around them. She made a small involuntary grunt – it was a deeply unpleasant sensation. She opened her mouth to try to say his name, to talk to him in a reasonable tone that would soothe this particular tantrum, but nothing came out. Her lungs wanted to draw in air, but her ribs would not obey. Meanwhile, Malakim's face had returned to its more familiar configuration: slack, disinterested, blank. His fingers curled inwards, and Belise turned on the grass, like a toy boat pushed by the currents.

This was even worse. It was one thing to be hurt, but to have no control? Belise gritted her teeth and pushed back, attempting to wrestle control of her body back. It was painful, like her bones were trying to push their way through her muscle and skin, but she found it was possible to move of her own accord, just a little. Slowly, she lifted her head to look at him, trying to keep her anger and defiance from showing on her face, although she suspected it was there anyway. His red eyes met hers, and abruptly the pressure on her bones vanished. She slumped into the grass, only gasping a little.

The boy looked at her for a moment longer, his narrow chest rising and falling rapidly as though from some great exertion. Then, he turned and ran back across the grass. Belise watched him go, catching her own breath.

'I suppose you didn't like it then,' she said in an even tone.

## 21

Ynis flew, and it was glorious.

She had spent much of her childhood in the air, clinging to her sister's back as they hunted, travelled and played, but this sensation was entirely new. The freedom of the air on all sides of her, the sheer joyful space of it all, with no tension in her arms and legs and shoulders, telling her that the slightest slip might see her plummet to her death. No, finally she had wings of her own and the sky was hers. She remembered telling T'rook once that if she had wings she would never come down, and that now felt very possible. Why would she give up these clouds, this frigid air, the sense of the world below her as a tiny, insignificant thing? She was a griffin. She was *yost*.

It had been three days since they had left Leven and Cillian behind. They had flown through squalls of rain, sleet and brilliant winks of sunshine that left them both dazzled. They were heading north-west, then north, and already Ynis was excited to see the ragged tips of her beloved mountains, to see the faces of their fathers when they saw what she could do. Even Queen Fellvyn would have to welcome her back – there could be no more exile for her and T'rook, surely.

'What is that?' called T'rook. 'Down there. Some human nonsense.'

Below them was the Wild Wood, livid with spring foliage, but in the middle of the section they were flying over was a brutal stripe of bare earth, wide enough, Ynis guessed, for ten griffins to walk side by side. Crawling over it were giant, winged humanoids – the Othanim Titans that had apparently invaded Brittletain while they were looking for T'rook – and several small groups of humans. From what she could see, the Titans were tearing up the trees while the humans scurried around after them, digging up the remaining roots and filling in the ground; making it flat, making it walkable. There was more activity around the trees that had been ripped from the earth, but Ynis couldn't make it out. She was more concerned about the Othanim, and whether they would spot them flying over.

'What are they doing?' demanded T'rook.

Ynis shook her head. She didn't know, not quite, but it made her feel sick and worried. The Wild Wood was part of Brittletain just as the Bone Fall was, and to see it being torn down and churned into the earth was like watching some long, protracted act of violence. She thought of the things they'd seen beyond Brittletain, in a world without a Wild Wood or griffins, and a word floated to the front of her mind.

'They are building a road,' she said. 'Although I don't know why. Flying creatures do not need roads.'

'Human nonsense,' T'rook said again, dismissively.

'I don't think it is, not really,' said Ynis. They flew on, following for a little way the line of the road until they came to the place where it ended. The activity here was at its fiercest. 'Those humans are there against their will. I saw chains on their legs, and the Othanim had things to hit them with.'

Next to her in the air, T'rook grumbled, 'The sooner we get back to Yelvynia, the better.'

---

That night, they sheltered under a gathering of pine trees on top of a low hill, the pine needles on the ground making a spongy, soft bed. With great reluctance, Ynis put away her shimmering wings and let her feet feel the ground again. She made a small fire, which T'rook curled up in front of, her beak tucked under her wing. Ynis assumed her sister had decided to go straight to sleep, something she often did after a long day of flying, so when the griffin spoke, she startled a little.

'Your human sister was very angry.'

Wind gusted across the hill, scattering pine needles into the fire. Their rich green scent increased: a smell of home.

'She was,' Ynis agreed. There was curiosity in T'rook's tone, as well as a little judgement. Ynis couldn't tell if the judgement was for her or Leven. 'My human sister has been able to fly for years and years. Since she was my age, almost. She doesn't know what it's like to be ground-stuck.'

'Will you return to them, one day?' asked T'rook.

'Why?' Ynis turned to look at her sister. The beak had retreated even further inside her wing. 'I... was never meant to find her in the first place. I was looking for you when I found her.'

'You explained the fate-ties to me. So Leven must be important, yes? Is that not how they work?'

Ynis sighed. 'Maybe she was important to help me find you.' After a pause she added: 'She'll never understand me. Not the way you do.'

The griffin puffed out her feathers in a combination of pride and exasperation.

'That might be so,' she said. 'But you were hatched from the same clutch of eggs. That is important, too.' T'rook drew her head out from the wing. Her eyes reflected the firelight, golden and full of movement. 'You are angry that she doesn't understand. And you are full of that fury now. It keeps you warm. But I think to myself, what if we had left Yelvynia angry with our fathers? And our fathers angry with us? How much harder would that have been to bear?'

'It's not the same.'

'Fionovar the Red said that it was foolish to let a wound fester out of spite.'

Ynis laughed, the sound too loud under the trees. 'Now you're quoting Fionovar at me?' She wanted to summon the wings again. They brought her a peace she didn't experience on the ground. 'Why can't all of you just let me be happy?'

T'rook snapped her beak a few times, a gesture Ynis knew well. It meant she was tired of the argument and getting impatient.

'Do not twist my words. It brings me great joy to fly with you, sister, as you must know in your heart. Let's go to sleep. There is no talking to you in this mood.'

Ynis snorted, ready to point out that it was T'rook who was the moody one, but the griffin tucked her head back under her wing, more fully this time, and Ynis knew she wouldn't get much more out of her.

She ate some dried meat from her pack, washed down with a sweet barley wine they had bought on the road to Tyleigh's compound. Thinking of her mother, she rolled back her sleeve. On her forearm there was the squarish discoloured patch of skin that indicated the location of the Titan-ore nugget. She had lied to Leven when she said the process had been painless: Tyleigh had numbed the area with a cloth soaked in something that smelt incredibly pungent before using a scalpel to slit open a section of her skin. A tiny wound really, less than an inch long, but she had certainly felt it; like a bee sting, or a scratch from a particularly vicious bramble. But the real pain had been when Tyleigh had pushed the lozenge of Titan ore into the wound. Ynis had hissed and bared her teeth. Tyleigh had chuckled.

'Deryn made much more of a fuss than you,' she had said. 'But back then my methods were... untidy.'

Under the pine trees, Ynis pressed the pad of her thumb to the small patch of blue skin. There was no scab, or even a scar. Once the lozenge was under the skin, the flesh had just sealed up by itself, knitting together like nothing had ever happened. When Ynis had stared at it, astonished, Tyleigh nodded seriously. 'Something about Titan bone works to keep the flesh together. It explains why they are so difficult to kill, doesn't it? And why the Heralds are so strong. You will still want to be careful though, Alaw. It doesn't make you invulnerable.'

Such a small thing. And it had given her wings. There was a sword too, although she had yet to summon it. Perhaps when she was hunting goats in Yelvynia she would summon the weapon, but for the moment...

She looked up. The quality of the darkness had changed in a way she couldn't quite pinpoint. On the far side of the fire, her sister was already snoring, her feathers orange and yellow in the firelight.

'Hello?'

Ynis stood up. The place where the trees were thickest was growing darker as she looked at it, shadows bleeding out of nothing, moving like tendrils of ivy up trunks and along branches. The temperature dropped, and Ynis shivered. She recognised this feeling – it was very similar to walking the Edge, the place between the living and the dead. When she had been looking for T'rook with Festus she had experienced this same cold over and over again, but she hadn't summoned it this time. There was also a scent: a high, mineral stench, like water that had been left to stand for too long. It was a green, rotten smell. The Edge no longer frightened her – if anything, it felt like home – but this? Her hand drifted to the claw knife on her belt automatically. If anything threatened T'rook, it would find itself full of holes soon enough.

She stepped beyond the fire towards the dark. There was a trickling noise, somewhere in the shadows, like water running over stones – and then, to her surprise, the quick *ribbit* of a frog, followed by an answering call. She wondered if they had missed a spring or a stream somewhere.

'If someone is there, speak.'

The watery sounds increased, followed by a wheezy laugh.

'The child summons us, then has the cheek to be put out.'

Ynis didn't recognise the voice, but it sounded unspeakably old. The scent of stagnant water increased sharply, and a soft green light began to glow, hanging suspended in the air like a tiny star. Around it, Ynis could see the pine trees she expected as well as a thick, marshy bog. Wet tussocks glimmered under the light, surrounded by black water. Reeds sprouted where previously Ynis was sure there had been grass, and at the edge of this pool of muck was a figure – or three figures, joined together. They looked like corpses, but their skins were brown and hard, almost like bark. One of them bared long teeth the colour of mushroom gills at Ynis.

'So much power it has, to summon the Lich-Way to it. Why are you so close to the dead, girly?'

'I didn't summon you,' said Ynis. 'What is this? What are you?'

'We are bog bodies, darling,' said the figure on the left. A tiny green frog was perched inside its empty eye socket. 'And the Lich-Way is a place of the dead, and of the past. All things that were flow through here. Very slowly, mind.'

'The Druin come here sometimes,' continued the figure in the middle, 'when they're desperate or don't know what's good for them. But you're no Druin, child. You look to be many things at once.' The bog body twisted her head to one side, as though trying to get another angle on her. 'Child of many worlds. The human and the griffin, the living and the dead. You smell of the Bone Fall. How is that possible?'

'I have grown up among the griffins,' said Ynis. Even now, even with the wings waiting to be summoned, it cut her deeply that she couldn't say *I am a griffin*. 'They raised me and trained me as an Edge Walker.'

'Oh that's what it is!' The one on the right leaned back, sending slow ripples across the viscous surface of the bog. 'Why didn't you say so? Edge Walkers know this place. It's practically next door to the Bone Fall, in a manner of speaking. You must be wanting some advice, yes? Advice from your dear old dead aunties. Much more useful than advice from those bird brains. No disrespect.'

Ynis shook her head. She didn't know what to make of any of this. 'I don't need advice. Especially not from you.'

'But there *is* something.' The bog body in the middle leaned forward, pulling her sisters with it. Runnels of water ran from various holes. 'You carry the dead with you constantly now. There, just there. In your warm flesh.' She raised an arm that looked like a branch and pointed at Ynis. 'Your arm, child. What's under your skin?'

Instinctively Ynis curled a hand around her forearm, covering the place where the Titan-ore lozenge rested.

'That's none of your concern, dead thing.'

'Oh but it *is*.'

It felt colder again, colder than it had moments before. Ynis's breath clouded white in the stagnant air. Somewhere, in the darkness beyond the bog bodies, there came a rumbling, roaring noise that set all the hairs on the back of her neck standing on end.

*There is danger here*, she thought. *It might be similar to the Bone Fall, but it's not the same. The dead here are not at peace.*

'That's a stolen power you wear inside your flesh,' continued the bog body. 'And it has already caused you trouble, hasn't it, little egg?'

'My sister,' she replied, then stopped. She didn't know why, but the urge to tell these creatures what had happened was strong. 'My sister is very angry with me about it. But that's her problem, not mine.'

The bog body on the left chuckled wetly. 'So eager to cut all your ties, when you've only just rediscovered them, are you? You'll need them, girl, before the end. You'll need them again.'

'What does that mean?'

The rumbling sound in the distance grew sharper suddenly, angrier. As one the bog bodies drew back, their arms circling each other so that they were pressed very close, their heads touching.

'Time to go, girly, if you know what's good for you.' Ynis was no longer sure which bog body was speaking. 'We don't normally give warnings, see, spoils the fun, but you're practically one of us. Send us back while you still can, before something comes out of the swamp that you can't command.'

'And tell that green boy he needs to pull his finger out,' said another one, a note of exasperation in her voice. 'We've been waiting a long time. Tell him that.'

'What? What are you talking about?' There was a growing shadow beyond the swamp, something huge and shaggy. Points of light that might have been glowing eyes travelled before it. The waters of the marsh were shivering, sending slow ripples in every direction. More frogs plopped out of the bog bodies and vanished into the murk. 'I didn't summon you here, so I don't know how to dismiss you. Are you listening? I don't—'

The soft green light that had been hanging over the swamp winked out, sending everything back into the dark. For an alarming second, Ynis thought they were still there: the talking dead, and the thing behind them that was journeying out of the shadows. But then she blinked, feeling the warmer night air on her bare arms, and realised that the stink of the place was gone, along with the subtle sounds of water. The Lich-Way, whatever it was, had vanished back to wherever it normally lurked.

Ynis stood for a long time, looking into the shadows, before turning back to where she'd left T'rook. At some point during her time with the bog bodies, the fire had gone out.

# 22

*The krakens and the giants are long lost to us. Creatures of the sea and the deep earth. Who knows what secrets they carried, what hidden knowledge they kept? The age of the mightiest Titans has passed.*

> Extract from the writings of Elder Druin Jathinos,
> Dosraiche's Master of Histories

Miles beneath the dimpled surface of the sea, Leven slept. Very little of the sun's light reached this place, yet it could not be said to be dark. Creatures that carried their own luminescence made their sedate way across the grey sand, a procession of yellow, green and blue lights casting an eerie glow on the constellation of rocks and corals. Leven, curled up in her favourite alcove, watched their comings and goings with one vast, lidless eye. The taste of the sea, so much more than just salt, washed through her gills, bringing with it the stories of a thousand years: shipwrecks, whale falls, storms and earthquakes – all of it reverberated through the salt.

It was peaceful to lie there, to contemplate the teeming ocean floor and taste the sea's history, but she was being called back to the shore again; she could feel it as keenly as she could feel the tug of the currents and riptides. It was a force that held the very heart of her being in an iron grip; she could no more resist it than she could resist the water that pressed all around her. With a great flex of her finned tail, she pushed herself out of the alcove, briefly scattering all the creatures who had forgotten her presence – easy enough to do, since she had not moved from her hiding place in ten turns of the world – before stretching languidly across the sand. It was pleasurable to feel the small rocks and pointy boulders scraping across her leathery skin; some of the barnacles and sea urchins that had taken advantage of her long sleep to find a home were rudely ejected into the larger ocean. Once that was done, she found an area of softer sand and corkscrewed her way through it, luxuriating in the cool shifting softness of it.

When she emerged, she had a brief moment of confusion. Her body seemed much, much too large. Had she always had a tail? Wasn't she supposed to be a tiny fragile thing, something that needed air to live; something that would be crushed into paste simply by touching the ocean floor?

No. No, that life was a dream, some lurid fantasy brought on by eating a whale carcass that had been left to rot a touch too long. Leven was herself: the largest being in the sea, the most powerful, and of her Titan cousins, the most at peace. As she swam away from her sleeping place, powering towards the shore like a dart, she thought of those others and the conflicts they nursed between them. The vain unicorns and the aggressive god-boar, the haughty griffins and the self-important bears. The Othanim that thought themselves above the rest. It was all so tiresome. But, she reminded herself, they didn't have the sea to soothe them. This was what came of spending all that time breathing air. Leven tried to avoid it, where she could.

There was no avoiding it today, however. The sea grew shallower the further she swam, becoming warmer as the ocean floor crept closer to the sun. Once or twice, she was aware of other beings of great size in the waters around her; a pod of whales, their hides a patchwork of white and blue and black, sent her greetings in their sonorous voices; she tasted the scent of one of her own kind, who had passed this way three turns ago. That was another reason the other Titans were so prone to conflict. They did not give each other space. Leven barely kept company with her own kind outside of breeding season, and even then, she preferred to keep the liaison as brief as possible.

Eventually she felt the soft golden sand kiss her belly, and when she raised her head it broke the surface. The sun was all around, an obnoxiously bright dazzle, and she flushed water through her nostrils in playful admonishment. The sea birds that had been brave enough to stay on the sand when she broke the surface upped and left in a cacophony of outraged squawking.

Here, then, was the exhausting bit. Dragging herself up onto the beach, Leven rolled onto her side and unfolded the first of her land-limbs, usually kept tucked up tight under the barrel of her chest. The second, a powerfully muscled leg, stretched creakily from her pelvis. Once they were free and some feeling had returned to them, she rolled onto her other side and repeated the process. It occurred to her that in the strange dream she had had, she had not needed to unfold her limbs for use on land. They had simply been there, ready at any moment to climb over sand or rock or grass. What a curious idea.

All four limbs free, she raised her vast body on them, feeling her feet sinking into the soft sand as they took her considerable weight. Leven never felt heavy in the sea, so this sensation was always something of a novelty, and she let herself enjoy it, sinking great clawed toes into the ground. Here, very near here, her eggs were buried. It was time to dig them up. Soon, her children would be ready to break the shells and take their first little nips of the air before descending into their true home. There, Leven would nurse them for a while, showing them the skills of the sea-Titans until it was time for them to seek out their own part of the ocean floor. She had performed this cycle more than twenty times.

The beach was not entirely silent as she made her way along the sands. To her right there was the great wood where the bears lived, and it was full of birdsong, a bright happy noise that she had to concede she missed when she returned to the sea. There was another sound, one that made her furrow her brow, just a little. It was akin to the noises humans made, those tiny scurrying creatures who Leven most often saw hanging over the edges of their boats, their eyes and mouths wide as they stared down at her, but louder, brasher. It did not matter. Beyond this dune was her nesting place, and if there were humans there, they wouldn't be for long; either they would run at the sight of her, or she'd give them a little encouragement.

But when she crested the dune, everything was wrong. The beach where her eggs were buried had been upended. Instead of smooth golden sands, there was a great hole, and around it, a gathering of laughing Othanim. They had exposed her eggs and shattered them. One of her children had been dragged part of the way out of the broken shell, its dear little head curled against the sand as though it were asleep. One of the Othanim looked up and saw her, its face splitting into a wide grin.

'Excuse us, Mother,' it called. 'Icaraine the Lightbringer requires food for her child, and even these tiny half-formed bones will make a good meal.'

A rushing feeling entered Leven's chest, a sense of fury bigger than anything she had ever felt. There would be time for sadness later. Now there could only be a slaughter to answer for a slaughter, and she would drink the blood of each of them, except that something had hold of her, a soft pressure on her shoulders... She tried to wrench herself away from it, but it held her in place, gripping even tighter as she thrashed.

'Leven. Leven, we're here.'

Wasn't it enough that they had killed her children after she had waited ten turns for them? Was she to be denied her rightful revenge too? Leven dug her clawed feet into the sand and pulled, ready to drag herself down the dune if necessary. The laughter of the Othanim was a searing pressure in her ears.

'Leven. Wake up, my love.'

*No!* She struggled against it, but the beach with its broken eggs was fading, and her sense of her own body with it. Suddenly she was small and helpless and weak, and her head rested against hard wooden boards. There was a human crouched over her, thick ram's horns curling out of his temples. She knew him, she realised. Knew him better than anyone.

Leven sat up, groaning.

'What happened?'

'You were having another dream,' said Cillian, his green eyes pensive. They both knew that dream was an inadequate word for what she was experiencing. 'But we've arrived at the stones now, and these people need their cart back.'

They were on a narrow dirt track in the Wild Wood. Off to one side, Leven could see a fast-running stream with four large boulders on each bank. The trader who had lent them the use of her cart was looking over her shoulder at them from the driver's perch.

'Is she alright?' she asked, her eyebrows raised. 'She don't look so well.'

'I'm fine, thank you.' Blushing faintly, Leven scrambled to the end of the cart and jumped down. She knew that it was only sensible to travel this way, but falling asleep in the back like some old duffer was a humiliation she could do without. As she stood on the dirt trying to get her bearings, she could still taste the salt in her mouth, and her body felt subtly wrong. *I miss my tail*, she thought, half smiling at herself. The remnants of rage and sorrow clung to her uneasily, slowly fading like an afterimage of the sun caught in her eyes. In its place came her own flavour of those feelings – an anger at her sister, and a sadness that they had parted on bad terms. Ynis had flown away and she had no idea if she'd ever see her little sister again. *Perhaps those two years together are all I'll get.*

Cillian joined her as the trader's cart rumbled off down the track.

'This is the place?' she spoke quickly so that he wouldn't continue the trader's line of questioning.

Cillian nodded. 'It's one of the oldest stone circles in the Wild Wood. It was here long before the stream. If he's... If I can make contact with the Druidahnon at all, which I'm not convinced I can, then I think this is the best place to do it.'

'Because stone circles are linked to the dead?'

'They are between places,' said Cillian. As they made their way down to the stream, Inkwort flew ahead, alighting on one of the weathered stones. They were all covered in luxurious thick green moss that shone like emeralds in the dappled sunshine. 'Sometimes, the dead will wander through.' Inkwort squawked at them impatiently. 'I need to know why he spoke to me, Leven. That was powerful magic he was using. There had to be a reason.' He took a deep breath, his face troubled. 'What if he needs me to find the Green Man? Or finish the summons? I can't let him down. Not after everything.'

Leven glanced at the blue tint on Cillian's horns. Although the Wild Wood seemed ambivalent to his presence, she knew that being thrawn haunted him. That the things he'd done when they were last in this forest played on his mind. They had been for the sake of survival, but she knew that made little difference to him.

They approached the edge of the stones and stopped.

'So what will you do?'

'I'll meditate inside the circle,' said Cillian. 'And when I've made a connection with the stones, I'll reach out to him. It may take hours, or days.' He glanced at her, and she was struck by how serious he looked. He was worried about what the Druidahnon might ask of him. 'It's never safe here, as you know by now, but it's especially not at the moment. Will you be able to watch over me?'

Leven snorted. 'Please, I'm not completely useless yet. You take as long as you need. I'll just get myself comfortable and keep an eye out.'

# 23

Cillian paused at the edge of the circle. Inkwort, who had been watching him closely with her milky blue eye, pecked at the moss in a pointed way.

'Do you think he'll be in there somewhere?' he said in a low voice. On rare occasions the little jackdaw would speak to him. 'Or are we wasting our time?'

Inkwort strutted away, tsk-tsking.

Behind them, Leven had settled into the grass. She looked weary, but when he turned to give her a wave she waved back, her face brightening. Cillian stepped into the circle, already quietening his mind for the long meditation ahead. He would start by standing in the water, where the heart of the circle had once been, and—

'There you are!'

The familiar booming voice was almost like a blow to the head. Cillian stumbled backwards, not quite out of the circle, as the vast shape of the Druidahnon came forward. In life he had been an impressively solid presence, and even in death he was powerful, seeming to bend the world around him.

'Where have you been, lad? Did you not hear me call you?' The Druidahnon leaned over him. His eyes shimmered with a blue-green light. 'I've been waiting, Cillianos.'

'My lord.' Cillian tried to gather his wits. Inkwort had flown into the circle and settled on the giant bear's right shoulder. Birds, and particularly jackdaws, had a slippery relationship with the dead. 'My lord, what happened?'

'The Othanim happened, didn't they? Those diabolical feathery miscreants.' The giant bear shifted his shoulders and Inkwort gave an indignant chirp. 'No offense, no offense, my dear friend. Wait a moment, where is the other one? What's she doing standing out there like a tit in a trance?'

Leven had stood up and come over to the edge of the circle, her eyes wide. Cillian remembered that of course she had never seen the Druidahnon before. He could be an overwhelming sight, even in this ghostly form.

'We thought this would be... well, we thought it would be Druin business, my lord. I also thought it would take a while to find you.'

The Druidahnon harrumphed. 'All of this concerns her too.' He raised his already loud voice. 'You there, girl! Get into the circle, we have things to discuss, and I can't be having with shouting it all at you. Think of my poor old dead lungs.'

Leven glanced at Cillian. 'If you say so.' She stepped into the circle gingerly, as though she expected it to set her on fire, and came over to stand next to Cillian. He reached for her hand, and as her fingers slipped through his he felt stronger, more himself.

'Now then,' said the Druidahnon. 'What was I saying? Oh yes, the Othanim, dreadful creatures that they are. I had thought we had solved the problem all those years ago, but perhaps we just delayed the inevitable. Some of my brothers and sisters insisted that the only way to have a lasting peace was to kill them all, and I will admit to you that it crossed my mind. When we'd chased them back to the Black City and had them pinned down in that awful place... When I saw what she had made... But to me it seemed like a thing we could never take back, a piece of violence that would stain us forever. What if peace cost us our souls, eh, what about that? That's what I said to them, and my brothers and sisters, they were not bloodthirsty bears. We were all tired of the war. I suppose we thought we could put the problem far away from ourselves and forget about it. Foolish.'

Cillian rubbed a hand over his face. He did not know what the Black City was, and he was finding it even harder than usual to follow the Druidahnon's train of thought.

'And here they are. I like to think they were disappointed to find only myself left of the great bear clan – my bloodkin cheated them out of that slaughter, at least, by dying so long ago – but in truth it was always the griffins they hated the most. Isn't that strange? You would think they had the most common ground between them – or common sky, ho ho. Yes, the Othanim will head north, and on their way they will gladly tear apart everything that Brittletain is. We cannot let it happen, Cillian, my boy.'

'I heard about what you did,' said Cillian. For some reason it seemed important to say this to him. 'I spoke to another Druin. He wasn't there with you, but he felt it happen, through the trees. My lord, why?' Cillian pressed his lips together. A deep well of sadness had opened up inside him. 'Why did you leave us?'

'Oh, I was old, Cillian, I was old.' The giant bear let himself fall forward onto all four legs. Even as a ghost, he shook the ground beneath him. 'My fighting days are long lost to me, truth be told, and I've clung on to this life longer than I should. The world is changing around us, and the Titans have largely faded into dust and memories.' As it sometimes did, his mood changed with the suddenness of a riptide. 'I was old, and desperate enough to do something drastic. The Green Man is the only one who can save the Wild Wood now, Cillian.'

He stopped speaking. A silence grew between them. The old bear's eyes gleamed and a cold wind blew through the circle, even though the trees on either side stood unmoving. Next to him, Leven shifted from one foot to the other, restless. After a while, Cillian realised the Druidahnon was waiting for him to say something.

'And where do we find him, my lord?'

The Druidahnon snorted. 'Find him? Find him, Cillianos? You do not have far to look.' He bellowed with laughter, his mood changing again. 'He is *you*.'

Cillian blinked. 'What?'

'You are the Green Man, my boy. Or at least, you will be. You just have to let him come through.'

'Hold on,' said Leven. 'The Green Man, as in the wild spirit of chaos and death? That Green Man?'

'I don't know what you mean.' Cillian backed away a little, Leven's hand slipping out of his grasp. He had never felt afraid in the Druidahnon's presence before, yet he was terrified of what the great bear might say next. 'You must be mistaken.'

'Pish, I've never been mistaken about anything in my life,' said the Druidahnon. 'Save for the Othanim, perhaps, and that, I think you'll agree, was a complicated problem. No, Cillianos, it is you who must wear the mantle of the Green Man. You heard me when I called, didn't you?'

'I did, my lord, but...'

'This is your purpose, my boy. Not an easy one, by any means, but special talents require a special destiny.'

'What does this actually mean?' Leven took a step forward, moving in front of him slightly. This was her pragmatic side, the part of her that had fought for the Imperium for eight years, throwing herself into the heart of the fight to do what needed to be done. She wasn't about to let Cillian be rushed into something strange that she didn't understand, and he loved her a little more for it. 'Are you just giving him some sort of, I don't know, title, that means he's responsible for taking back the Wild Wood? Because if so, you can shove that up your big hairy—'

'I don't think that's what he means,' said Cillian quickly. 'Is it, my lord?'

The Druidahnon sighed, a sound like a gale blowing on some

high, forgotten hill. 'No, it's not, my lad. I only wish it were as simple, or as painless. All of my Druin carry a little of the Green Man within them, it is simply part of your connection to the Wild Wood. And you've long known that your connection is deeper and stronger than most. Now more than ever. Is that not right, blue-horn?'

Cillian's face burned. Here it was then, the judgement he had been waiting for since they'd returned to the shores of Brittletain. In a way, it was a relief. He deserved to be punished.

'I am thrawn,' he said quietly. 'I have failed you.'

'He did what he had to do,' said Leven. There was a dangerous tone to her voice. 'He did it to save me, and to save Princess Epona. So if you must blame anyone, you can blame me.'

To Cillian's surprise, the old bear chuckled. 'Deryn, always so ready for a fight. Put away your talons, girl, I know more than you can imagine about your journey through Brittletain. After all, my friend was with you.' On his shoulder, Inkwort gave a self-important *tchk*.

Cillian said, 'Inkwort?' at the same time Leven said, 'How do you know my real name?'

'I knew all the children of this isle, for what good it did me. Especially those with Druin blood in their veins.'

At this, Leven grew quiet.

'Now then, Master Cillianos, you might not want this destiny, but it is yours, nonetheless. I saw it the day they brought you to Dosraiche, a sliver of green in you that went down to your core. But it is still, ultimately, a choice you have to make. The Green Man cannot inhabit you if you will not have him. I know you have already seen his signs, Cillianos. The whispering of the wood. The living things that pointed towards me to show you the way. He's growing impatient, lad.'

'I don't like the sound of this at all,' said Leven. 'Inhabit him? Is this Green Man trying to take over his body?'

'In a sense, Cillian will not be himself anymore.' The Druidahnon sounded solemn again. 'He will be *more*. And with that he will have all the power of the Wild Wood in his blood – the Dunohi and the giants and the root-dragons, the green-fury and the pixen and the Lich-Way. All will answer to him, and with that power he will be capable of ending the Othanim. But Cillian, my lad, this path is the leaving behind of the mortal world.' The old bear glanced at Leven, a considering look in his black eyes. 'You will not be human. You will not even be Druin.'

'Are you telling me he turns into a giant stag or something?' demanded Leven.

'No, Deryn, but you might find that easier to stomach, I'm afraid.'

There was a long moment of silence.

'What the fuck does that mean?' Leven said eventually.

'It cannot be me,' said Cillian. 'I am thrawn. I'm exiled from the Druin. There will be hundreds of Druin more worthy, more capable. And besides which... I have my own life now, lord. You told me once that I had too much green in my blood, that I needed to know my own people better and spend less time with the trees. Now you're telling me the opposite?'

'These things you have learned, your love for this woman, they are all vital parts of your becoming, lad. But as I said, it is still a choice. One that only you can make. If you should decide to take up the mantle of the Green Man – to save the Wild Wood, to save Brittletain – then Inkwort will show you the way.'

'You can't ask him to do this,' Leven said. She took hold of Cillian's hand again and squeezed it. 'Get someone else to do it. I don't care who.'

'I need to think.' Cillian looked up at the old bear. Light filtered through him like a dusty window. 'I need *time*, lord.'

'Take it,' said the Druidahnon. 'Only remember that it is very short indeed.'

# 24

'We don't talk about the unicorns much, possibly because they weren't especially likeable. They were dangerous, for one thing; even more so than the griffins, or the god-boar, both of which were famously territorial (still are, in the case of the griffins, of course). They were vain, spiteful creatures, drawn to extreme places – the fiery, stinking flanks of volcanoes, or the blizzard-choked lands to the far north. According to several legends it was possible to woo a unicorn, to bring it over to your side, usually via lavish gifts and endless praise. They were especially fond of mirrors. But if you wronged them in some way, or they perceived some tiny insult from your behaviour, you'd likely find a three-foot-long Titan-bone horn suddenly protruding from your chest.'

Transcript of a lecture given by Elder Druin Jathinos,<br>Dosraiche's Master of Histories

Getting into the gardens unobserved turned out not to be a problem at all. It seemed that Bronvica was right; the Othanim barely seemed to notice the humans in the castle unless they were bringing them food or being killed for sport. Kaeto had asked the Othanim guard on his corridor if he could go; the Othanim had looked at him like he was a fox that had suddenly got up on its hind legs and ordered a drink. It seemed that as long as Icaraine could summon him whenever she liked, he was free to go where he wanted. And really, what reason did they have to keep an eye on him? Save for the Heralds, he was alone, and the lands beyond Londus would hardly welcome him with open arms. If he returned to Stratum with empty hands, he'd soon be short a head. His options were limited, and they knew it.

No, the real problem was what they were doing to Felldir.

His head down as he followed the overgrown path, Kaeto thought about the last time he had seen the Titan. He had been taken to Icaraine's quarters, ostensibly to discuss the empress's offer of friendship, but when he arrived in the rooms – which were filthy, filled with rotting food in unwashed bowls and discarded feathers – the high priestess of the Othanim seemed to barely notice he was there. She had been occupied with Felldir.

The big Titan was dressed only in a ragged cloth wrapped around his hips and groin. His white hair hung in his face, dirty and unwashed. He still had the Titan-ore chains around one ankle, which were attached at the other end to a ring in the wall. This was hard enough for Kaeto to look at, but when he came fully into the room to stand where Icaraine could see him, he noted that the pale skin of Felldir's back was scored with hundreds of livid red lines.

*She scratches him*, Belise had said when he'd had a brief moment to talk to her afterwards. *She'll just hold him down with those huge paws of hers and slowly run her fingernails down his back.* Belise had frowned; even on a new face, he recognised the stubborn lines that appeared on her forehead whenever she was frustrated or angry about something. *And he doesn't do anything about it. Just lets her do whatever she wants.*

The phrase haunted Kaeto. *Whatever she wants*. How could he get Felldir out? How could he get all three of them out and away from both the Imperium and the Othanim? So far, no obvious solutions had presented themselves.

He took a deep breath, taking in the sweet scent of the roses that grew in the garden, drawing himself back to the present. Clearly no one had tended to the place in some time and the flowers had run wild, thorny bushes crawling over the path and up the walls. He followed the path to the far corner, then paused. He could smell the silty, mineral scent of the river strongly here. The stone wall that encompassed the garden was partly broken, old masonry crumbling away like sand. It wasn't a huge gap, but it was large enough to let a small person through, and as he neared the corner he saw a slim shape move out of the shadows of the bushes. Kaeto paused, missing once again the familiar weight of the dagger in his sleeve.

'Princess Epona, I assume?'

The family resemblance between her and her sisters was striking, yet there was something about Epona that set her apart. She was small and compact, her dark hair cut in a brutally straight line from one ear to the other, and her eyes were the blue of cornflowers. She had a presence and a weight of personality that Kaeto could feel the moment she smiled thinly at him. Here, he thought, was a woman who could go toe to toe with the empress herself. She was wearing a hooded leather mantle, scratched and scuffed from long use, and a short sword at her belt. Her hand hovered over the grip.

'And you are Envoy Kaeto, the empress's loyal lapdog.' She grinned suddenly, sharply. 'That's what I'm supposed to say, right? I need something from you, but my pride dictates that I spend some time mildly insulting you before I come out with it. And you will sneeringly comment on Brittletain being a damp little backwater shithole, not worthy of licking the Imperium's boots. Or we could skip all of that and discuss the important business of getting these fuckers out of my castle.'

Kaeto bit down a smile. He liked this woman, and in his position that wasn't necessarily a good thing.

'Is Brittletain extending the hand of friendship to the Imperium? Because your nation has refused the blessings of the empress many times in the past.'

Epona laughed. 'Don't be soft. Is that what you're here for? Forming an alliance with those flying rat-bastards?' Her tone was light but Kaeto sensed a steely interest underneath. 'They'll come for you next, you know. It doesn't matter what you offer them. They're not interested in treating with humans, not really. To them, we're little more than ants.'

'Or beetles,' said Kaeto, thinking of the Undertomb. 'It is true that I am here on behalf of the Empress Celestinia. She believes that the Imperium and the Othanim can be friends. That in fact the Imperium has a great deal to offer these new Titans.'

'Perhaps Brittletain has a great deal to offer the Imperium. If we were friends rather than subjects, I mean.'

Kaeto tipped his head to one side, narrowing his eyes. 'I'm not sure I believe that, your highness. The Othanim have been here for some time. They made short work of your biggest armies. I suspect that Brittletain is on its last legs, fighting a fight where it is desperately outclassed. I suspect the peoples of your warring kingdoms are in hiding or dead, and you and your friends are the last scraps of a hopeless rebellion.' He glanced at the hole in the wall, where he could see the shadow of someone waiting. 'I might personally have sympathy for your situation, your highness, but if you want the Imperium to transfer allegiance to the underdog here, I'm afraid you've very much misread the empress's intentions.'

Epona looked back the way he had come, past the rose bushes and towards the main keep of the castle. A certain weary seriousness was on her face now. It made her look older. 'I said that the Othanim think of us as little more than insects, but that's not entirely true,' she said. 'An insect, like an ant, would be able to crawl into this castle unobserved, coming and going freely. But the truth is, they watch us more closely than you think. Those who serve in the castle are given certain freedoms, as are visitors such as yourself. It might be easy to think that you are more or less forgotten about.'

Kaeto had indeed been thinking that, but he did not react.

'But they know who is supposed to be here, and who is not. Believe me. If they see a face within the castle walls they do not recognise, well... it doesn't end well. Over the last two years I have sent over twenty people to their deaths, Envoy Kaeto. The second they spot someone who shouldn't be here, they tear them apart. And the men and women and children who remain in the castle to cook and clean and, I don't know, wipe their arses, they are not warriors. They're young or weak or old. The Othanim are not silly. You, though... you and your Heralds. You're a different kettle of fish entirely.'

'Kettle of fish. What an interesting phrase.'

She took a step towards him. The rueful good humour vanished from her face to be replaced with something much closer to desperation. 'My mother, the rightful queen of Londus, is imprisoned in the dungeons here, Envoy Kaeto. I know that Icaraine plans to feed her to that creature she calls a child. I need to get her out. I know you have no reason to help me, and I am having difficulty conjuring one up from nothing. But I once knew someone from the Imperium, and she was good. She would have helped me. If she were here now, she'd fly over this wall and take them all on, because it would be the right thing to do. So the least I can do is ask, right? If one person from the Imperium can be good, then maybe others can, too.'

*Fly over this wall.*

'Who was your friend?' asked Kaeto, genuinely curious.

'A Herald you named Eleven. I thought they were valuable to you, but apparently you don't keep a very close eye on them.'

A memory resurfaced: standing in the Imperator's office, listening as Blessed Eleven demanded that they help her friend, Foro. Blessed Forty had begun to suffer from the degeneration of ore-lines, a condition they had decided to keep from the Heralds and the people of the Imperium in general. He remembered the stubborn set of her jaw and her honesty; there had been no subterfuge in the woman at all. At the time, he had dispatched Blessed Forty, and very shortly after that he had been sent to Houraki with Tyleigh. By the time he'd returned, Blessed Eleven had vanished from the city, and he had not given her a thought since. It appeared she had come to Brittletain, of all places.

'What happened to her?' he asked.

'She was captured by my idiot sister Ceni, then escaped. I don't know what happened to her after that.' Epona glanced at her feet. *She suspects her friend is dead*, Kaeto thought.

'If she survived that, it is likely the ore-lines would have killed her by now,' he said gently. 'The magic sewn into the skin of Heralds is volatile, and doesn't last. At least, it didn't used to. I would not rely on Blessed Eleven to come to your aid, Princess Epona.'

She looked up at him sharply, any vulnerability that might have briefly been there fled. 'And what about you? I have spies in the palace, Envoy, as I'm sure you would in my situation, and I have had them watching you especially closely. I don't think things are as clear cut as you are making out. Who are the two Othanim who came with you on the ship? Why were they in chains, and why does Icaraine torture the male?'

Kaeto returned her gaze without speaking.

'Then there's the female one, the one watching over that creature with all the eyes. We've seen you talking to her. You *know* her, don't you?'

The princess's eyes scanned his face rapidly, watching, he knew, for any change.

'Yes,' she said eventually. 'More than that. She's important to you. Who are they? What is going on here?'

'So many questions, your highness. None of which I need to answer. I am meeting you here as a courtesy, after all. Not even that, really. A curiosity, shall we say.' He realised that she had made him angry, simply by being able to spot what he'd been trying to hide.

'Listen.' Epona took a step forward and grabbed his wrist. Her hand against his skin was hot, her grip fierce. '*Listen*. You say that the Imperium will not aid Brittletain, and let's be honest, I didn't expect it to – I'm no idiot, Envoy. I know exactly what a giant pile of shit we're currently lodged in. But maybe I'm not talking about our nations. Maybe I'm talking about you, and me.' She squeezed his wrist hard enough that it hurt. Behind her, the shadow by the wall drew closer, as if concerned by the tone of her voice. 'I want to get my mother out. I want to save her from being killed by a monster. You can understand that, right? And I think you need help, too. I'm not sure why yet, or how, but I think you're very alone here, Envoy. And I also think you know what it's like to face down a monster that wants to eat you. Am I close?'

Another memory, this one much worse. Icaraine, out of her tomb, leaning forward with her hand open to show him the tiny, picked-clean skeleton of Belise.

He pulled his hand away.

'You have my sympathies, your highness, but there is nothing I can do for you. I will take my leave of you now.'

Epona's shoulders rose and fell with a deep sigh; of anger or despair, Kaeto couldn't tell.

'If you change your mind, Envoy, Bronvica can get a message to me. She'll be in the stables if you need to find her. There are two or three horses that the Othanim haven't butchered yet and she's determined to keep them alive.'

Kaeto nodded once and turned back to the overgrown path, leaving the princess among the roses.

# 25

The promised rain had come, and stayed, and was now outstaying its welcome as far as Belise was concerned.

Malakim had his own chamber adjoined to Icaraine's rooms, and this was where she sat, looking out of the window at the fat grey river beyond. The rain was so heavy it was creating a mist at street level, and the castle of Queen Broudicca seemed to sit in its own lively fog, while a freezing damp oozed through the stone walls. Belise was chilled and bored, a miserable combination. She was beginning to wonder if she had made the right choice in volunteering to look after the boy. Since she had drawn the picture of him, he had barely acknowledged her existence. Perhaps if she'd stayed with Felldir, she could be helping him. Even a cell in the dungeons seemed to offer more possibility than these chambers with the rain falling endlessly outside.

Belise was not used to being bored. In Stratum there was always something interesting to do: track a traitor, dissect a body, poison someone.

From the room next door there came a muffled grunt, and then the pealing sound of Icaraine's laughter. Belise stood up, suddenly eager to move.

'What are you up to, my prince?'

Malakim was sitting in the corner with his head down, not looking at her. The boy didn't eat, as far as she could tell, but she'd had her lunch in these rooms. She was tempted to take her plates back down to the kitchens and see what she could overhear. The servants took care not to talk in front of her – she was no longer as inconspicuous as she'd once been – but you never knew when someone might slip up. It was something to do.

Yet when she bent to pick up the plates, she saw that Malakim was bent over something he was holding in his hands.

'What have you got there?'

Six red eyes glistened and pulsed, a movement Belise had come to recognise as Malakim's version of blinking. He lifted his hands a little, and she saw that he had a creature held there – an insect. It was a greenish brown, with big back legs and a long face with busy mandibles. On the top of its head were two big, shiny brown eyes, almost red in the gloomy light of the chamber. Belise had seen similar creatures in Stratum called crickets. Malakim had hold of the thing by one spindly leg; it clearly couldn't move without pulling its own limb off. Queasily, she thought of the beetles in Houraki. Once, she'd had no fear of any insect, but these days they brought her out in a cold sweat. She forced herself to smile brightly at the boy.

'That must have hopped in through the window to get out of the rain.'

Malakim held the cricket closer to his face, peering intently at it. There was a sharp scent in the chamber, unpleasant and somehow grassy. Belise remembered that if you caught the crickets in Stratum they released a stinky fluid to try and get you to drop them again.

'Do you want me to find something to put it in so you can keep it?' she asked. 'A box, or a jar? The kitchens will have something.'

Malakim didn't appear to be listening. He reached out with one pale finger to touch the cricket's head. The insect strained to get away from him.

'Mine,' said Malakim. 'Like mine.'

*He speaks.* His voice was tiny and scratchy, and oddly older than Belise had been expecting.

'Like yours?' Belise looked at where he was pointing. 'Oh, its eyes? You mean its eyes are like yours?'

He looked up at her, his eyes glistening again. She had the sense that he was daring her to say the wrong thing, which was something she very much wanted to avoid. She hadn't forgotten the crawling horror of her own bones not obeying her.

'Nothing else... is like me,' he said. 'All of you. Mother. Eyes the same. Not me. But this.' He cupped his other hand around the cricket as though it were something precious. 'I see. Me.'

Belise nodded slowly. 'We can find more like that if you like. There will be lots of bugs in the gardens. We can build something to keep them in.' She paused, wondering too late if the word 'bug' would upset him, but he just continued looking at the cricket. 'Do you want to show it to your mother?'

Icaraine's quarters smelt strongly of ale and wine. Ceni was there, pushing the remains of several broken bottles to one side with a broom, leaving a long streak of maroon on the flagstones. The former queen of Galabroc looked dishevelled and tired, the cuffs of her shirt dark with dirt. Icaraine herself was crouched by the great hole in the outer wall – they had removed it to allow her to move freely in and out of the castle. Icaraine had trouble fitting through doors meant for humans.

As always when Belise entered the high priestess's rooms, she looked for Felldir, a tight feeling in her chest. One day, she was sure, she would find his body in here.

'Malakim, my sweet,' boomed Icaraine. 'Come and see how my pet entertains me today. I think you'll enjoy it.'

Uneasy, Belise followed the child over to the missing wall. Once they were closer, she saw that Felldir was out there, flying in the rain, although he still wore the Titan-ore chain around his ankle, and it was still attached to the wall. He had flown until the chain was taut, and was hanging in the sky, grey wings beating as the rain soaked them. Even in the short time Belise observed him, she could see that he was tiring. His wings moved slower and slower by the moment. His skin looked white and slippery, like marble, and every injury Icaraine had inflicted on him stood out like a brand.

'There, you see? He'll be back down here again in a moment,' said Icaraine, chortling. 'The pathetic little worm hasn't got the stamina! Have you, worm?'

She was right, Belise saw. Felldir faltered, dropping out of the sky. He fought against it, big wings lifting him back up again, but it didn't last. He dropped again, and Icaraine leaned out and grabbed the ore-chain, yanking him closer.

'Where'd you think you're going, worm?'

She had a lance in her other hand. It looked ridiculous in her fist, but when she hit Felldir with it, Belise heard the hard, meaty thud it made, and she saw the way Felldir jerked as it made contact.

Icaraine laughed. 'Get back up there, you little shit.' She struck him again, and from somewhere Felldir found the strength to flap his wings again. He rose uncertainly into the rain, his white hair plastered to his face. *How long has this been going on for?* Belise wondered. *And how long before she gets bored of it?*

'Lightbringer.' Belise stepped forward. 'Prince Malakim wishes to show you something.'

Icaraine's head whipped around, her flat yellow eyes narrowed. This was dangerous. Getting Icaraine's attention at any time was unwise, but especially when she was 'playing' with her favourite pet.

'What? What is it, Malakim?'

The boy came forward, the cricket still cupped between his hands. As he made his way over to the window, walking into his mother's shadow, Belise felt a tightening in her stomach. Dread flowed through her like cheap wine. He looked so tiny in front of his mother, so insignificant. Was this really the thing she was using to shield herself? The thing she was using to save Felldir and Kaeto?

Malakim held out his hands as Icaraine leaned down to look. Her huge brow furrowed.

'What is it? What are you showing me?'

'Like me,' came Malakim's tiny, scratchy voice. 'It. Like me.'

He opened his hands, letting go of the cricket's leg. The creature jumped immediately, awkward in its movements thanks to its crushed limb, and it landed on Icaraine's knee. For a few seconds everyone in the room stared at it, unmoving.

'Like me,' Malakim said again.

There was another beat of silence. Then Icaraine's vast hand came down on it, obliterating the cricket in a second. She hooted with laughter, apparently not seeing how the child flinched.

'That will be you and the griffins soon, my sweet,' she said. 'You'll crush them as easily as I just crushed that bug. You'll eat their bones.'

Malakim did not move or say anything. When Icaraine turned back to the window, her thick fingers closing once more around Felldir's chain, Belise put her hands on Malakim's shoulders and led him back towards his chamber. Ceni, her own hands still clutching the broom, watched them go.

---

Three days later, when Belise had had time to scour the gardens and retrieve unwanted jars from the kitchens, she brought Malakim back to his rooms to show him the fruits of her labours. There were two crickets – which one of the human children in the palace had told her were more rightly called grasshoppers – a fat spider speckled all over like a bird's egg, a moth, and a shiny black stag beetle. This last had been an especially difficult catch for Belise – every time she got close to it, she remembered the Undertomb and the sound of thousands of beetles moving together, whispering like the sea – but she'd persevered. Now each had its own jar filled with grass or twigs. As Malakim inspected them, she watched him closely. Since his mother had smashed the cricket, he had returned to his truculent silence.

'What do you think?' she asked. 'We can keep looking, if you like. There's bound to be more things out there for us to find.'

Malakim's pale hand rested on top of the jar that contained the spider. He looked like he was struggling with something.

'Thank you,' he said eventually. 'Thank you.'

## 26

*T'vyn the Trickster had the finest crest the world had ever seen. It shone gold to match his wings, and when he fought his enemies, he danced through the air so that the sun would leap from it, blinding them*

An extract from *The Tales of T'vyn*,<br>as written on the Silver Death Peak

They reached the border of Yelvynia as the sun reached the highest point in the sky. To Ynis, the jagged line of the mountains felt like some ragged piece of her heart that had been missing for the last two years, and from the piercing cry her sister gave, she knew T'rook felt the same. The pair of them flew wingtip to wingtip, Ynis's shimmering blue wings throwing an uncertain light on the fog that clung to the foothills even in the middle of the day.

'How does it feel, sister, to be home?' T'rook called.

Ynis grinned. There were no words for it. Not for returning to the mountains with a pair of wings on her back.

'It feels *right*,' she said, and left it at that.

Yet there were other things to consider, things Ynis had not thought about in years, and as they coasted over the bracken and rocks she began to feel a little uneasy. After all, she and T'rook had been banished from Yelvynia after a fight with a pair of adolescent griffins; a fight where Ynis had used her claw-knife to tear the crest feathers from a griffin's head. They had been told they could never return. What would happen if they flew into the heart of Yelvynia now? Could they assume that all would be forgiven just because they had been away for so long? After all, the griffins of the mountains knew nothing of what they had been through, or even that she and T'rook had lived within sight of the Bone Fall for a time.

'Queen Fellvyn will not have forgotten our beaks,' said T'rook, as though she could hear the thoughts in Ynis's head. 'But we are yostra now, fully grown. If those ground-stuck parasites we fought with have not crawled away into a cave to die, we can challenge them and win back our honour.' She gave three short caws, a traditional griffin battle cry. 'I will savour the taste of their guts!'

Ynis thought of the sword that hovered invisible by her right hand, ready to be summoned at any moment. It was true that they would think twice about calling her a stinking prey animal now. Even so, T'rook's words did not reassure her. Would their fathers still be living with the shame of exiled hatchlings? Would they even want to see their daughters after all this time?

'I will not turn away from a fight with them,' she called over the wind.

The further they travelled into Yelvynia, the thicker the fog below them grew, until it was almost as though they were flying above the clouds. The sun striking off the vapour was dazzling.

'I wonder if we will see Festus,' said Ynis eventually. The handsome green and blue griffin who had helped her locate Leven had returned to Yelvynia when they'd spoken about travelling across the sea. He was fierce and brave, but he was still a young griffin, and the idea of leaving Brittletain in the service of humans was clearly a peck too far even for him. Even so, Ynis remained grateful for the help he had given – and she had not forgotten her sister's crush, either. She glanced over at T'rook to see her staring straight ahead. 'Do you think we will?'

'I am sure I do not know,' she snapped. 'And I do not care. Ynis, there is a shadow below us. Do you see it?'

Ynis looked. Below them was the bank of fog, an almost blinding white in the midday sun. Occasionally the foothills rose out of it like the backs of vast sea creatures. She could see their shapes, cast crisply by the sun.

'I can see *our* shadows,' she replied.

'No, not that.'

There was a shape, a patch of the fog that wasn't as bright as the rest. It was moving very fast, even faster than they were, and Ynis narrowed her eyes trying to make sense of it, when something enormous struck her from her left, bodily shoving her from the sky. Her wings flickered with the shock of it, and for a few heart-pounding seconds she fell, a yawning stretch of nothing beneath her. She heard T'rook squawking with outrage and fear – then her wings caught her and she was sailing up, up. In the sky there were two more griffins, fully grown adults wearing silvery-blue armoured plate and chainmail. They were shouting to each other.

'It's a small one, some sort of runt! They must be getting desperate if they're sending their yenlin to hunt for them.'

'Are you sure? Its wings look wrong to me...'

'It still counts. If we kill it and take it back, we'll be ahead of the other patrols.'

Below them, the grey shape beneath the fog revealed itself to be another armoured griffin, broad white wings lifting her out of the mist with barely any effort. Ynis swallowed hard; the air suddenly felt very thin in her lungs.

'I'm not your enemy!' she cried. Even shouting at the top of her voice she sounded tiny, a squeak of a mouse in the face of these griffins. 'I'm not a Titan!'

'Leave my sister alone!' T'rook was there, wings spread in front of her, shielding her from the others. Ynis felt a surge of annoyance in the midst of her gratitude. Would she always need T'rook to protect her? Her right hand tingled, itching to summon the blade. 'Back off, you stinking torrosa!'

'Get away,' one of the other griffins snapped. 'You shouldn't be flying out here alone, young one. The Othanim have been known to swarm lone griffins and bring them down.' He snapped his beak in a commanding fashion. 'We will take care of this one.'

'I am not Othanim, I am a...' Ynis faltered. What was she, that these griffins would understand? They wouldn't know what a Herald was. 'I am an Edge Walker!'

The griffins exchanged a puzzled look. One of them laughed.

'Who told you that word, Othanim? Are you such a coward that you'd spin ridiculous lies?'

'It's true,' said Ynis. 'You can ask Witch-seer Frost, of the Bone Fall. She will know me.'

'Nonsense.' The first griffin leapt forward, his claws suddenly looming very close. 'Enough of this. Let's kill it and take it back. If it's a new kind of Othanim the queen will want to have a closer look at it.'

'Wait!' The white griffin that had risen from the fog had reached them. She was wearing a silvery chest plate and cuffs of silver around her shaggy legs but no helmet. There was a line of grey scar tissue along the top of her white head, and a few tufts of silvery-grey feathers where a crest might have been. When she opened her beak Ynis saw that her tongue was purple, and a cold sensation moved through her body. She recognised this griffin.

'I know these two,' the white griffin was saying. 'You idiots, this isn't a Titan. Look at it. It's a tiny, scrawny stinking human. Still playing at flying, I see.'

'You!' thundered T'rook. 'We should have torn your throat out that day.'

The other two griffins hung back in the air, looking uncertain, while the white one came forward, talons outstretched.

'I will admit that your pretence at yost has improved,' continued the white griffin. 'I don't know where you got those wings from, yenlin, but they smell almost as bad as you.'

'T'oro, what are you talking about?' demanded one of the other griffins.

'These are the hatchlings of T'vor and Flayn,' she said, disdain dripping from every word. 'If they can even be called that. They were cast out of Yelvynia when they attacked me and my clutch-brother.' She narrowed her eyes. 'That stinking prey animal tore my crest from me.'

'It's not Othanim?'

'That thing's bones are soft and yellow, just like its heart. But it is exiled from Yelvynia, and returning is an extremely foolish thing to do.'

'This is our home,' said T'rook hotly. 'We should never have let you force us out of it.'

'You'll come with us now. And the queen will decide what to do with you. Hopefully she will allow me the honour of pulling your guts out.'

T'oro swept closer and the other two followed. She had grown a lot since Ynis and T'rook had been thrown out of Yelvynia. Ynis was still scrawny, even for a human sixteen-year-old. The sword hummed on the edge of her awareness, but she had never wielded a blade like it, and T'rook was still an adolescent. If they resisted, things could go badly. She met T'rook's panicked golden eyes, and shook her head, just a little.

'That's right,' T'oro snapped her beak triumphantly. 'Fall into line like good little birds.'

# 27

'I just can't see any reason why you would. Why you should, even. Let your old bear find someone else. It's as simple as that.'

They had wandered some distance from the stone circle and made camp at the base of a cliff. Behind them, there were caves and tunnels to disappear into if the Othanim should suddenly appear in the sky, but otherwise the Wild Wood was quiet. Inkwort perched on a nearby boulder. Cillian found that his eyes kept returning to the little jackdaw. Since they had found out that she was, for want of a better word, a spy for the Druidahnon, he had not been able to relax around her. *My lord saw everything we went through*, he thought. He wasn't sure how he felt about it.

'What if this is the only way to expel the Othanim from Brittletain?' He felt weary saying the words, as though each were a rock weighing him down. 'The Druin are almost lost, Leven. He wouldn't ask me if he wasn't desperate.'

Leven made a disgusted noise. She was sat on the far side of their little fire, her shoulders slumped. There were dark smudges under her eyes, and her skin was shockingly pale under her ore-lines. He knew that they hurt her all the time now, not just when she summoned her wings.

'People in charge always have other options. They just don't want to share that information with you. Believe me, after eight years fighting for the Imperium, I know. My point is, Cillian, it doesn't have to be you. He has plenty of other Druin to choose from.' She leaned back, absently rubbing her fist against her chest. 'The answer is no. Seems pretty straightforward to me. I don't know why we're still talking about it.'

It was late, and the stars were out. All around him, Cillian could sense the Wild Wood, and something just beyond it. A presence waiting, and watching. It wanted to come through, he realised. It was hungry to walk the world again.

'Do you *want* to become the Green Man?' Leven's tone was slightly exasperated. She was tired, he realised. When Ynis left, she had taken a great deal of Leven's resolve with her. Each day was a struggle: against her failing body, against the resurging memories of the Titans that were etched into her skin. When he looked at her, he felt a rising panic somewhere behind his breastbone. What if he lost her? The idea was unthinkable. 'Do you want to become some weird inhuman forest spirit with tree trunks for legs? Is that what we're talking about?' She blinked slowly. 'Will you become something like the Dunohi? A skull-faced ghost with an unpredictable temper?'

'I don't want to become the Green Man,' he said. He leaned over and took her hand in his. It was cold. 'I want to stay here and be human with you. That's all I want. To live in the Wild Wood, to wander the Paths, with you. But what if there are no Paths because the Othanim tore them all up? What if they burn the Wild Wood down? What if I have a chance to stop that?'

'Let someone else do it,' she said, too quickly. She squeezed his hand. 'It doesn't have to be you. So just stay with me. Please.'

He looked at her for a long moment: the smoky grey of her eyes, the flecks of white in her dark hair. Then, he smiled. 'I will. I'll stay with you, Leven.'

---

Later, when he was sure Leven was deeply asleep, Cillian sought out Inkwort. The little jackdaw had hopped inside one of the cliffside caves and was perched on a sizeable stalagmite. Around her there was a soft yellow light that glittered faintly. Cillian couldn't see where it was coming from.

'I should have known you were no ordinary jackdaw,' he said. 'Is the Druidahnon still watching through you?'

'He has left my mind for the time being.' Inkwort's voice was soft. 'He believes this should be your choice alone.'

'Does he?' Cillian seated himself in front of the stalagmite, his legs crossed under him. 'Because he isn't an easy person to say no to.'

'Is this not what you always wanted, child?'

'What? No, of course not.'

Inkwort dipped her beak into the feathers at her breast, sifting some dust from them. 'I seem to remember a very green boy who wanted nothing more than to be alone with the Wild Wood. To walk the Paths and know its innermost secrets.'

'I was a fool.' The wind picked up outside, and somewhere in the cave above them came a high, keening noise; the sound of air moving through some natural chimney, he supposed, yet it felt like a voice speaking an ancient language. Even here, he could feel the Green Man waiting. 'The Druidahnon was right to send me to Londus. Since that day I've learned what it means to care for other people. To care about things other than the trees. How can he want me to walk away from all that?' He sighed and looked down at the stony floor. The lines and cracks almost seemed to form a face. 'I have Leven now, and she...' He paused, a hard knot of sorrow briefly closing his throat. 'The ore-lines are killing her. I don't know how much longer we have together. I won't leave her, and I won't spend what time we have left as some sort of inhuman demigod. She deserves to have all of me, now more than ever.'

'Cillianos.' Inkwort hopped down from the stump so that she was perched before him, her head turned to the side to look at him with one blue eye. The golden light followed her, as though it came from her feathers. 'What is the Green Man?'

'He is the Wild Wood. He is the god of this place. A spirit of chaos and the green, of rebirth, life and death.' Cillian shrugged. 'He is not me.'

'Listen to yourself.' Inkwort pecked at his boot sharply, punctuating her words. 'Life. And death. A spirit of life and death.'

'What are you getting at?'

'Roots and stars, and the Druidahnon thinks you clever! If anyone can change what is happening to your wife, Cillianos...'

Cillian leaned back, a cold prickling sensation moving down his back. The wind whistling in the cave almost sounded like laughter.

'You think I can save her?'

'I think it is your best chance, Cillianos,' said Inkwort. 'She is worth taking a chance on, yes?'

He thought about the first time he'd seen Leven, standing next to Epona in Queen Broudicca's hall. An interloper, her skin marked with magic that was an insult to the Druidahnon himself, her body lean and capable and somehow so sure of herself, even as she stood in a court that feared and hated her. Back then he'd been horrified by the task ahead of him: to guide this butcher from another land through Brittletain's most sacred places. But things had changed over those weeks in the Wild Wood. Dislike had somehow become respect, and attraction, and the tight feeling in his chest when he looked at her became an overwhelming need to know what those ore-lines would feel like beneath his fingertips. When they ventured beyond the northern border of Brittletain he had felt more lost than he ever had in his life, yet when they kissed for the first time, under the Caul of Stars, it felt like coming home. He lifted his eyes to regard the little bird seated in front of him.

He couldn't lose Leven.

'Tell me more,' he said.

Leven fought her way out of a fitful sleep. In the dream she was beneath the ocean again, this time a creature of ceaseless rage and appetite. She sighted a lone whale, caught in the golden light filtering through the surface of the water. In seconds she was upon it, her huge jaws dislocating to allow her vast array of serrated teeth better access to the animal's tough leathery skin and the savoury blubber beneath. It thrashed, and she coiled herself around it, ready to drag it down to the depths with her own body weight, when she realised she was caught within her own bedroll, and the chill of the ocean was the chill of the early morning. Their fire had gone out.

She sat up, wincing at the newly awakened pain in her orelines, and saw that the bedroll next to hers was empty. The camp was empty too, but when she explored the nearest cave, she found a stalagmite covered in green shoots, tiny plants forcing their way up through the cracks in the rock. Frowning, Leven came back out into the daylight, a horrible suspicion crawling through her gut.

'Cillian?'

# 28

*I don't know what led me to it, except that we had tried everything else, and we could not let Icaraine's child waste away to nothing. If we did that, then what had all the bloodshed been for? The old queen and her people slaughtered, for a new queen that produced only sickly children? It was unthinkable. So we tried it. I suspect now that it was a mistake.*

Extract from the private writings of Areel,
on a scrap of parchment found in the Undertomb

'Do you see, light-bones? Do you see how mighty we are? The Imperium has nothing to offer us.'

Kaeto had to admit it was impressive. Icaraine and her guard had taken him out of the castle to a stretch of land to the north of the city. The great Wild Wood began there, a dark chaos of greenery with trees even older and larger than those in the jungle of Houraki. In the middle of it was a wide stretch of... nothing. Or more accurately, a surface of broken stone and dirt. This great rupture in the Wild Wood stretched on out of sight, heading directly north. Humans and Othanim crawled all over it, carting away felled trees, breaking up boulders and digging, digging everywhere. As they watched, a trio of Othanim rose up into the air, the trunk of a great oak suspended on ropes between them.

'A road,' said Kaeto. 'I will admit, your majesty, this surprises me. What use do a winged people such as yourself have for a road?'

'Humans have such small minds. You are almost like griffins, in that way.' Icaraine had bound her long hair with Titan-ore chains, which glistened under the weak sunlight. They made Kaeto think of Felldir. 'Malakim cannot fly, Envoy, and Malakim must come north to eat the bones of the griffins. So we build a great road for him.'

Kaeto bit down a number of responses to that. 'You couldn't just carry him? Forgive me, your majesty, but surely you alone could carry him one-handed.' There was a fresh scent in the air; sap, tempered by dust.

'You know something of us, I think, Envoy? The Othanim are quite unique among the Titans. One of the reasons we are superior.'

'I know a little.' Kaeto thought of Tyleigh's speculative reports, of Felldir sitting in the broken castle, explaining his people to Belise. A pang of sorrow moved through his chest. The castle in the shattered lands felt very far away. 'I'd be grateful for any enlightenment you care to shed, of course.'

Icaraine grunted. 'Malakim is my child, so he is unusual. The children of queens are always unusual, in one way or another. I will admit that at first, when he emerged without wings, I was concerned. I thought him malformed in some way. And he was so small. So tiny. A pale little grub. Almost like a human child. Can you imagine? We gave him medicines, and every food conceivable to make him larger, stronger, more Othanim. Nothing worked. He remained tiny and weak. Until one day my advisor Areel brought me a tincture for the child, a strange shifting substance that glittered. It smelt like death, and it frightened me.'

Kaeto glanced up at the Othanim, startled. He found it hard to imagine Icaraine knew what it was to be afraid. She chuckled.

'Oh yes. Using Titan bones for magical purposes has always been a taboo, Envoy. Rather like cannibalism, all Titans know in our hearts that it is wrong. I knew what that smell was, and I didn't like it. But Malakim ate it. He grew that day, right before our eyes. It made him strong. He opened his eyes, all six of them, for the first time. And then he stopped, and would not eat. For thirty years, he took no interest in food, until one day he was ravenous again. Areel brought the tincture, more of it this time, and Malakim drank it down, demanded more. When he'd finished all we had, Areel brought the raw bones themselves, and my little sweetie, he crunched them between his teeth.' Icaraine smiled fondly.

'Whose bones were they?' said Kaeto. The words were out of his mouth before he'd known he was going to speak. *Not a good sign.*

'Devoted followers,' said Icaraine, apparently unconcerned by the question. '*Very* devoted. That time, when he'd eaten his fill, he was twice as big as he'd been, and he spoke his first word. And when Areel went to leave, my little Malakim reached out his hand and...' Icaraine lifted her own hand into the air and slowly formed a fist. 'Stopped him. Just grabbed his bones with the force of his will. So. I'd always known that Malakim was special, and now I knew exactly how special. He was born to rule over all of them, Envoy. He eats them, and he commands them. It is who he is. What he is.'

'The other Titans took exception to this, I imagine.'

Icaraine ignored this. 'He eats rarely, my son, but when he does, he changes. We don't know how he will change, exactly, but he might one day be larger even than me, and carrying him won't be an option. He will eat again soon – now that he can speak, he can tell us when he begins to hunger. When he does, I want him to taste the bones of griffins. They must all die, to feed my son. And so we will wipe them out, finally. Malakim will rule all of Enonah.' She turned her head towards him. It was like being regarded by an avalanche. 'Tell me, Envoy. How does your Imperium fit into this world? What can your tiny empire offer my son?'

Kaeto fixed his eyes on the distant road. He noted that Icaraine's voice had softened while she had spoken about Malakim. Now, it was full of a more familiar slyness.

'It is true we cannot offer much in the face of power over Titans,' he said slowly. In this conversation, there was danger from two sources. There was the threat of Icaraine's dissatisfaction, and the empress's fury if he overpromised. Yet he could sense that Icaraine was looking for something from him, which suggested there might be a way forward, if he could just find it. He thought of the Princess Epona, standing ragged and furious in the rose garden that had once belonged to her mother. 'But your numbers are limited.' He gestured to the road. 'Your majesty has wisely identified Londus as the busiest port in Brittletain, and the best place to build a new kingdom of the Othanim. Imagine how much faster you could build, your majesty, if your workforce was made up of thousands of willing workers from the Imperium, instead of prisoners taken from Brittletain. Your own people would be free to do as they wished. Supervise, instruct, invade.' He thought of the musical tower he had sat in with Felldir in the Black City. Felldir had told him that once, his people had given concerts in those filigreed towers, letting the music of the wind add to their songs. What had become of those gentle Othanim? Lost, he assumed, more than two thousand years ago, when Icaraine and her mutant child took power. Eaten. 'You ask what the Imperium could give you?' He gestured to the road again, dismissively this time. 'A skilled workforce, your majesty. One that could build a better road than that.'

She narrowed her yellow eyes at him. Despite the chill of the day Kaeto felt a prickle of sweat break out across the back of his neck. Then she looked away, a rumble of something like a chuckle in the back of her throat.

'Perhaps you are right.'

Despite everything, Kaeto let his shoulders relax a little. This was undoubtedly a dangerous thing to promise Icaraine, something the empress might well refuse entirely, but it had bought him a little more time.

'My pet is ill, by the way,' Icaraine continued. 'An infection, we think. He lies feverish in my chambers, like a sick dog.' She curled her lip. 'A disappointment. I thought he would last much longer. Titans are difficult to kill, after all, but all those years of waiting and guarding weakened him.'

'I am... sorry to hear that, your majesty.' All feelings of relief fled. He didn't have more time; he had even less than he'd thought. Felldir couldn't survive much longer.

'What interests me is that in his delirium, he sometimes calls your name.' She peered down at him again, a hungry expression on her face that he didn't like at all. 'Kay-toe, isn't it? You came to know each other well in the Black City?' She leaned down until her head hung inches from his. The heat radiating from her was intense, like a boulder left under the Stratum sun. 'Humans have loved our kind before, Envoy. It never ends well.'

Kaeto opened his mouth, then closed it again.

'Anyway.' She straightened back up. 'You do not need to be sorry. When Malakim eats again, which will be very soon, perhaps my little pet Felldir will be his appetizer. A more honourable fate than that worm deserves.'

When he was returned to his rooms, Kaeto left again immediately, heading down through the warren of corridors until he came to a courtyard bracketed by stables. Princess Bronvica was just where Epona had said she would be. There was a tall chestnut horse in one of the stalls, and she was brushing it down with slow, rhythmic strokes. Her face, in the seconds before she realised Kaeto was there, looked content.

'What do you want?' she asked brusquely. She rested the flat of one hand against the horse's shining flank.

'I want you to get a message to your sister,' he said. 'I think we can help each other.'

# 29

Epona flattened the parchment with her fingers, reading what was written there for a second, and then a third time. It wasn't much, not really, in the face of everything they were up against, but it felt like the first crumb of real hope in a long while. She had been inspecting Karayné-bog's new flying spear contraptions when the message arrived, and he was standing impatiently at her side, clearly desperate to know what it said, yet too in awe of her to ask. Jack was there too, and Solasach, his head still bandaged.

'Well?' demanded Karayné-bog. 'What does it say?'

Epona pressed her lips together to keep from smiling. Clearly awe only lasted so long. She cleared her throat, and read the message from the Envoy aloud.

*To the lady of the roses,*

*Having had some time to ponder your words, I think it is possible after all that we have something to offer each other. Unfortunately for the both of us, I am currently here without the tools I need to perform my duties adequately, and the castle itself offers little opportunity to replace them. I wondered if you might be good enough to acquire the following for me:*

*A length of flax*
*Henbane*
*Monk's Hood*

*Hellebore*

*Yew bark*

*There is a mushroom, we call it the Burning Star in Stratum, but I do not know the name for it here. It is pale, with a moss-green tinted cap and white gills.*

*Sweet oil*

*A small blade, as sharp as you can manage (I could steal this from the kitchens, but I fear they will not be sharp enough for my purposes)*

*A set of pins*

*In return for delivering these items to me, I will meet you once again in the rose garden, where we will talk further about liberating those closest to us. In a further act of goodwill, I will tell you that the high priestess's child is the key: it is for him that she invades Brittletain, seeking to feed him the griffin bones he needs to grow. Do with this information what you will.*

*We will arrange our next meeting when I have the materials I require.*

*Yours, in haste,*

*K*

'I'm fairly sure the mushroom he calls the Burning Star is the Death Cap,' said Solasach. 'A horrible way to die. What could he need it for?'

'He's an Imperial envoy, he probably spends his days poisoning people for entertainment,' said Epona. 'What about the other things? Are they easy enough to get?'

'Mostly, yes,' said Solasach. 'We may have to look deeper into the Wild Wood to find some of it.'

'Getting a blade into the palace will be harder,' said Jack. 'If a messenger is found with it, they could be in serious trouble.'

'Let's get it done,' said Epona firmly. She passed the note to Solasach. 'I'd like to get these items to him by the next sunrise, if possible.'

Karayné-bog folded his arms across his chest. 'Oh aye, taking orders from the Starlight Imperium now, are we? Just scurrying around after them like good little blessed subjects? Who's to say he's not just using us to fetch and carry? What is he going to do for us, exactly? We already knew the child was important. I don't see what good this information does us.'

'Boggy, if you weren't so clever with your hands, I'd give you a good kick up the arse.' Epona absently ran her hand over the spear contraption. They were on a sheltered hill near the Barrow, with each pointed steel tip aimed at a gap in the tree cover overhead. 'This is just the beginning of the dance, don't you see? Envoy Kaeto needs something from us beyond these tools, and we need something from him. He has Heralds at his disposal.' Epona clenched her jaw, thinking of Leven's glittering sword: a blade that could be conjured from nothing and just as easily hidden again. She imagined it cutting through the neck of an Othanim warrior; imagined its head spinning off to strike the ground. '*Heralds*. It could be the edge we need.'

Solasach frowned. 'What about what the griffin said? About the Green Man. There has been murmuring amongst the trees. They say he is close.'

'I don't think that's a power we should court,' said Jack. She was standing in the dappled sunlight filtering through the trees, and for the first time Epona noticed that she had a spray of freckles across her nose. They made her look younger, despite her serious expression. 'The Green Man is unpredictable. We have no idea what could happen if he entered the fray.' She glanced away from them all, into the trees, and Caliburn hummed. She looked uneasy.

'Oh fuck the Green Man,' said Epona breathlessly. Why couldn't they see what this meant? Why did they have to be so resistant? 'There's no bloody sign of him, for a start. We can't hang around for mythical figures to do this for us. We have to take the chances we get. I'll draft a message to the Envoy to go with the supplies. When you've found what we need, Solasach, come to me and—'

There was a discordant hum as Jack drew her sword. A second later, Epona heard the sound too: the crash and crunch of someone running through the undergrowth. She turned towards it, her hand on the pommel of her own short sword, but it was Larth who emerged from the trees next to them. She was panting, her face dotted with sweat.

'What is it?'

'They're bringing something big down that abomination of a road of theirs,' she said. She paused to wipe her forehead, smudging the black paint she wore across her eyes.

'How big? Is it more timber?' They had all watched the butchering of the Wild Wood over the last two years with increasing fury, and had on occasion sabotaged the building works, although the human slaves had borne the brunt of the Othanim's fury for that, and so they did it sparingly.

Larth shook her head. 'I don't think so. It's a covered cart so I don't know what it is exactly, but it has to be something important.' Her eyes darted once to Solasach before returning to Epona. 'The Atchorn are with it. Whatever it is, they are the ones who are bringing it to Londus-on-Sea. And your sister is there, too.'

'Togi,' said Epona, not bothering to disguise the bitterness in her voice. 'Right then, let's go and have a look, shall we? It's got to be important if it's got that weasel showing her face.'

---

They entered the city through the secret ways they had mapped since the Othanim arrived, moving silently down empty alleyways and through abandoned buildings. Sometimes they went below, into the scattering of tunnels that punctuated the underworld of the city – places built, as Epona understood it, by the handful of criminal gangs that made Londus their home, places they used to hide things they shouldn't have. Each time they came, Londus felt emptier somehow, and older, less vital – as though, without the lifeblood of its citizens, the city was dying.

*Who are you kidding?* Epona thought as they crept out onto a sheltered balcony. *Londus is already dead. You're walking through its ghost.*

The balcony overlooked one of the main thoroughfares to the castle, the road that saw the most traffic from those working for the Othanim. Epona sat down with her back to the wall, hidden in the deepest part of the shade. It was still possible to see the road through the balustraded wall. Jack and Larth crouched either side of her. There was a distant rumble, as of cartwheels on cobblestones, growing closer.

'The Atchorn must see how it goes with the Othanim,' said Larth quietly. Her Dwffd accent was melodious and sweet, even in a near whisper. Sometimes in the evenings she would sing in the Barrow, her voice echoing around the stones like harpsong. Even gruff old Karayné-bog would weep, sometimes. Sometimes, Epona would join him. 'They are mice playing at friendship with the cat. When Icaraine has no more use for them, she'll use their horns as toothpicks.'

'They've always been deluded,' Epona replied. She remembered being caught by them just outside of Kornwullis; they had smelt like fanatics, even then. 'I'm surprised at Togi, though. I'm not about to say that she was blessed with more sense than Ceni, but she was always quite concerned with preserving her own skin.'

As she spoke, the cart appeared from around the street corner. It was one of the biggest Epona had seen coming into the city. Usually they carried timber from the Wild Wood or stone, but this one was covered over with a large piece of rough spun cloth, spotted with large maroon stains.

'Dried blood,' Jack said quietly. 'Are they bringing bodies back for the Othanim to eat?'

Epona focused on the Druin at first. There were ten of them, four with the blue-tinted horns of those who had turned thrawn; exiled from the Druin order itself, it seemed they no longer troubled themselves to follow the Druin code. All of them looked as though they had recently been in a pitched battle, with torn clothes and freshly bandaged wounds. One of them was limping along with a stick under his arm, which struck her as odd. Why wouldn't he ride in the back of the cart if his leg was injured? Unless Jack was right, and it was full of the dead. Epona scowled. The thought that the Atchorn would be squeamish about the dead when they themselves were working with the murderers made her even angrier. She wished suddenly that she had a bow with her; she would cure that Druin of his limp in an instant.

'And there's your sister, Princess,' said Larth.

Togi came around the corner after the cart, walking a little way behind the Atchorn.

'That's Togi all over,' said Epona. There was an odd tightness in her chest, a constricted feeling that made it difficult to swallow. To look on the face of someone you knew so well, who had once chased you with a wooden sword through the rose garden, told on you when you spilled ink on the rug, or carried you up the stairs when you had a splinter in your foot... And had stood in a line of warriors calling for your mother's blood. 'She doesn't like to get too close to others.' She pressed her lips together, aware that she was on the verge of saying too much. Jack glanced at her, a line of concern creasing her forehead.

Togi had grown out her red hair, which was the same acidic orange as a carrot, and it hung down to her shoulders. She had braided parts of it, just as their mother did, and there was a long sword strapped to her back, its pommel winking in the sun. Epona studied her sister's face, looking for signs of regret, or fear – anything to tell her that Togi knew she had made a mistake. But she could read nothing there.

'Watch out,' said Jack, nodding at the slim strip of sky above them. 'Othanim are coming.'

The three of them drew further back into the shadows as a number of winged shapes briefly blotted out the sun. The Othanim brought with them their eerie laughter, like the chimes of discordant bells. Epona wished once again that she had access to her bow. Or better yet, that Jack did – she was far and away the better shot.

'If we're lucky,' she hissed, 'they might pick off a couple of Atchorn for sport.'

The Othanim, though, did not seem particularly interested in the Druin or Togi. Instead, they descended on the cart itself, two of them alighting on its sides and plucking at the sheet that covered the contents. They were saying something, speaking in merry voices to the Druin. Epona saw one or two faces turn downwards or away. One woman with horns like an ox rubbed a hand over her mouth, as though she were trying not to be sick.

The two Othanim with the sheet seemed to be squabbling over it, and then one rose suddenly into the air, the corner of it clutched between his fists. In the bed of the cart there were enormous blue and silver bones; they glittered like jewels in the sunlight. Epona realised she was on her feet suddenly, her heart in her throat. They knew, of course they already knew, but it was something else to see the evidence so plainly. From its place on Jack's back, Caliburn the sword hummed mournfully.

'He really is gone, then,' said Larth, her tone despondent. And then, more fiercely, 'Fuck them. I pray to the Green Man that all of them die with my knife in their guts.'

They were the Druidahnon's bones. As they watched, one of the Othanim reached down into the bed of the cart and pulled at a vast skull lined with fangs. It was too big for the creature to move on its own, so one of its companions came to help it, almost lifting it into the air. They were still laughing merrily.

'It's an honour guard,' said Jack. 'The Atchorn must have insisted on accompanying his remains. Perhaps they have some tiny speck of respect left after all. Princess Epona, will you not sit back down? I would feel more comfortable if you sat.'

'The *bastards*.' Epona did not sit. 'The note from the Envoy said the child needs to eat Titan bones to grow. I bet that's why they've brought his... his remains here. The kid is getting hungry.'

The Othanim dropped the skull, finding it too heavy and slippery to keep hold of. It rolled in the back of the cart, scattering femurs and leg bones and the ribcage. *Once, he was the mightiest hero on this island*, thought Epona, *and now he's a plaything for the Othanim*.

'I was right though, and this proves it. We can't rely on mythical figures to come and save us.' She made herself look at the Druidahnon's skull one last time before turning away. 'We have to save ourselves. Whatever it costs.'

# 30

*We've no evidence for the existence of root-dragons, save for the odd wood carving in an orchard, but the legend states that they will come when the land itself calls them. Even the Druin doubt they were ever real, but some of the wilder stories about Arch-Druin Merriden have him riding one across the Broken Sea to the cursed lands to the west, although supposedly this one was made of seaweed rather than the roots and branches of the Wild Wood.*

Note from a Druin archivist,<br>working on the Dosraiche records

On the way back to the Barrow, it rained, the kind of rain Brittletain specialised in: a great vertical flood, driving into the packed dirt of the paths and pounding them to churned mud in a matter of moments, rinsing through the trees and turning the air cold enough to raise goosebumps. Larth ran on ahead, her head bowed against the downpour, her bouncing curls rapidly turning to a dark wet cap.

'Of course it's pissing down,' laughed Epona, not sure Jack would hear her over the thunder of the rain. 'Sometimes it's satisfying when the weather matches my mood.'

Jack grabbed the edge of her cloak and pulled it up over Epona's head, creating a kind of shelter. Fat, hard drops of rain drummed against the thick wool.

'What are you doing?'

'I can't just let you get soaked,' said Jack, sounding faintly embarrassed.

'Jack.' Epona bit down a sigh. 'I know you're very committed to this *knight serving her lady* bit, but it's really unnecessary.' It was warm under the cloak, and the solid weight of the tall woman's side pressed against hers was reassuring.

'It could be that I'd do this for anyone,' said Jack. 'I have a cloak, and you don't.'

Epona felt her cheeks grow warm. She'd assumed this was a chivalry thing because she was a princess and Jack was a warrior in her service... *Oh gods*, she thought, *do I think I'm a maiden out of a story or something?* Squirming with embarrassment, she decided to try and change the subject.

'Where are you from, Jack? You've been with us for months now, yet I feel like I barely know anything about you.'

It wasn't easy, keeping up a casual tone whilst also raising her voice to be heard over the cacophony of the rain. For a long moment, Jack didn't say anything. Epona wondered if her words had been lost in the weather.

'I'm from a tiny village in Wehha,' she said eventually. They were walking slowly, the world outside the cloak reduced to a wet grey hum. 'It's called... Butterwart.'

'Butterwart?' Epona tried to hold down a laugh, and failed.

'You won't have heard of it.' She could hear the smile in Jack's voice. 'It truly is tiny.' She took a deep breath. 'On the day I was born, a strange man came into the village and seated himself on the ground outside my mother's cottage. When people questioned him, he told them he was there to witness the coming of a child with a great destiny. He said his name was Merriden.'

'Merriden?' Epona tried to peer up at Jack's face, but the angle didn't quite work. 'He was claiming to be the Arch-Druin?'

'That's what he said.'

'But Merriden was alive during the times of King Arthwr. When the Druidahnon...' She paused, thinking of the bones they had just seen. 'When the Druidahnon was little more than a cub himself. Probably.'

'I know,' said Jack. 'The villagers scoffed at him, told him to stop being so daft and get up out of the mud, but he wouldn't. My father came out and told him to move on before he was forced to box his ears. He was a mild man, my da, but I was my mother's first child and he was worried sick. Still, this Merriden wouldn't move.'

'What did he look like?'

Jack's low melodious voice was making Epona think of story time at the castle when she was very small. It would be pleasant to think that, for a little while, it was just the two of them and this outlandish story; no war, no invasion, no rebellion to lead.

'As you'd imagine,' said Jack. 'He was wiry, with a wild beard and hair. Blue eyes like robin's eggs. Horns carved with strange shapes.' Her tone lightened. 'I was told the story, you see, many times. Practically every villager had their own version they liked to spin.'

'What happened?'

'When I was finally born, and he heard my cries, he got up from where he was sitting and went to the brook that ran behind my parents' cottage. He waded in and began digging around in the silt until he brought up a large rock, which he brought back to the house. By that time he had a little crowd around him. There wasn't a lot to do in Butterwart. A wandering madman *and* a new baby? It was an exciting day.'

'Ha.'

'By then, the sun was setting. He tapped the stone on the ground, and it split open. Inside it were two small lizards, a white one and a green one. They scampered out onto the dirt outside my parents' house and fought each other until the green one was dead. When that was done, he asked to see the baby.'

Jack grew quiet for a moment.

'Well? What happened?' asked Epona. She had been impatient when listening to stories as a child, too. 'Did your parents show you to the old weirdo or what?'

'Everyone was very impressed with the lizard thing. Called it proper Druin magic. So yes, my father brought me out, swaddled in a blanket and quiet, very quiet. The old man—'

'Merriden,' said Epona.

'Yes, Merriden. He touched my forehead with his finger, and he told everyone standing there that I was the hero promised to the land, destined one day to save its most desperate people. I would find a sword, he said, and with it, one day I would... kill the Green Man.'

'Well that...' For once, Epona wasn't quite sure what to say. 'Huh. I think I understand why you didn't mention this before.'

'I know it's ridiculous.'

'The best stories are.'

'I just don't understand it. Why would anyone need to kill the Green Man?' Epona had the impression that Jack would have thrown her arms up in exasperation if she could. 'It's haunted my life ever since, that prophecy, and...' She cleared her throat. All around them, the rain rumbled on. They were closer to the Barrow now, the dark shapes of the trees on both sides becoming more familiar. 'I'd rather you didn't tell anyone about this,' she said. 'I don't talk about it often.'

'Everyone knows about Caliburn though,' said Epona. 'He's not exactly subtle.'

'Yes, the part about the sword was true at least. When I was old enough, I left Butterwart.' She chuckled. 'Why wouldn't I? And I wandered for a time, until I found a lake... I suppose a number of things have happened since then, many of which would make good stories, I suspect, but... this one answers the question of where I'm from, Princess.'

'Hmm, well.' From somewhere ahead of them, light was beginning to break through the clouds, and the drumming of the rain on Jack's cloak lessened. 'When I asked, I expected you to say something like, I don't know, *I was born in Kornwullis, ate a lot of fish*, not *an ancient legendary Druin came back from the dead to tell people I will one day kill the ultimate spirit of life and death.*'

'As I said, I don't tend to talk about it.' Around them, the rain sputtered and stopped in the sudden way it sometimes does. Jack pulled the cloak back, and Epona blinked in the weak sunshine. 'And it's not important right now. Please don't mention it to the others.'

Ahead of them, the Barrow squatted beneath the trees, the moss and grass that covered it especially green after the rain. The guards at the entrance looked bedraggled.

'Fine,' said Epona. 'Although it might become relevant if the Green Man does show up.'

She meant it to be a joke, but the words felt like pieces of lead on her tongue. When she met Jack's eyes, the other woman looked serious.

'Let's hope not,' she said.

# 31

Leven stayed by the cliffs until the sun set. When it grew dark, she built up their campfire again, pausing regularly to go and stand by the edge of the trees, listening. She had long since given up calling for Cillian – if he could hear her, he would have come – but she thought there was a chance he would return. She ate some of the bread and sausage from their pack, washing it down with some of the watered wine they had left, and watched the darkness grow deep and thick amongst the trees. It occurred to her that she had never been in the Wild Wood alone. When she had arrived in Brittletain, over two years ago, she had been expressly warned that such a thing was enormously dangerous – especially for a stranger, for a woman who knew nothing about forests or even the natural world. And this was a time of war, when the skies themselves were full of a monstrous enemy who might decide they wanted a little sport. Leven lifted her right hand and looked at it, turning it so the ore-lines glittered in the firelight. At least if they tried, they wouldn't find her unarmed.

She tried not to think about Cillian, what he was doing or what he might have decided. The night before, he had looked her in the eye and seemed certain about his choice, but who was to say what long thoughts had come to him in the night? Or if the Druidahnon himself had returned in some ghostly form, to make him feel guilty all over again? She stood up, fists clenched, and stomped around the fire for a bit, anger getting her feet moving even as her ore-lines prickled and stung with each step. The darker it got, the closer sleep came, and with sleep came the dreams that felt less and less like dreams. She didn't want to give in, but she was often exhausted, and sooner or later, her body would begin winding down regardless of what she wanted.

Eventually she dragged her bedroll – and Cillian's – into the cave mouth, reasoning that being under a ceiling of rock was at least mildly safer than sleeping out in the open. If Cillian didn't return in the night, she would fly somewhere, anywhere, and when she'd found civilisation and her bearings, she'd look for him. That's what she would do. She hadn't lost him, like she'd lost her sister.

Sleep took her quickly despite her anxieties. She spent the night running through a different forest, one populated by trees with wide, hair-covered leaves and purples vines that hung from the branches overhead in great loops. There were small animals everywhere, furry things with big eyes and clever fingers, and she was lord of all these creatures. If they disagreed, she would run them through with her horn.

Leven woke up shivering and unrested. A thin lilac light was creeping in the mouth of the cave. The sun hadn't quite risen yet, and the Wild Wood was alive with the sounds of early birdsong. She stood in the mouth of the cave, looking over the remains of their campfire, a cold dread seeping through her limbs. Despite the unsettled dreams, she felt more awake than she had done in days, and the precarity of her situation was stark. Cillian would never have left her like this if he had a choice. He would never have abandoned her in the forest if he wasn't in trouble himself.

'Stars' arses,' she murmured. 'What a fucking mess.'

At the sound of her voice, there was sudden violent movement in the undergrowth to her right. A small shape, no bigger than the palm of her hand, tumbled out of the holly. It looked up at her with tiny, bright eyes, like glossy blackberries.

'Oh, it's you,' said Leven, except that it wasn't. Even in the dim light of the predawn, she could see that this wasn't a pixen she had met before. It was covered all over in spines, had a short, pointy nose, and long-fingered hands that clutched each other in front of a pale blue vest. It looked up at her with its head tipped to one side, as though trying to figure out what she was. 'What do you want?'

Seemingly out of nowhere, the pixen produced a tiny acorn cup, the interior of which was painted gold. He held it up to her expectantly.

'Still after that, are you?' Leven sighed, and looked around. The sky hadn't grown any brighter, as though the day itself were holding its breath. 'Fine.' She crouched, and with her finger and thumb she carefully plucked the acorn cup from the pixen's hands, before holding it between her own lips. With the short dagger at her belt she pierced the skin on her arm, taking care not to get too close to anything important, or too deep, and then she pressed the acorn cup to the flowing blood. It filled, quickly overflowing, and she passed this down to the pixen, only spilling a little.

The tiny creature grabbed it eagerly and all at once there were hundreds of the things, streaming out of the undergrowth, all apparently intent on getting their hands on the acorn of blood. Leven startled, lifting her feet one at a time to avoid accidentally squashing them into paste.

'Hey! Alright, calm down.' There was a tug on her leg, and then another. The pixen were at her heels, pushing her forward, and as she watched, the others began to flow forward into the forest. She saw many pairs of beady eyes blinking up at her, checking to see if she was following or not. Leven took another look at their meagre camp. It looked very sorry in the lilac light, which seemed to leach all colour from the ground. She picked up her pack, frowning slightly at the thin line of warm blood that ran down her forearm to soak into her shirt.

'I guess I'm coming with you then. The stars know I've no better options.'

---

The morning light didn't get brighter, but it did get stranger. As Leven followed the pixen deeper into the wood, the lilac tone of the dawn turned mauve, gilding the leaves and trees and branches in silver fire. When she glanced up at the sky beyond the canopy of the forest, she saw that it was a deep, luscious purple, the colour of an orchid she had seen once in the Imperator's office. There were stars out, but they were too bright and too yellow, and she didn't recognise them. As an Imperial soldier, the shapes of the ancestor stars were as familiar to her as the ore-lines on her hands. A new kind of fear blossomed in her chest, one that was bound up with wonder.

'Where are you taking me?' she asked, but she knew that was the wrong question. She was already somewhere *else*.

The pixen didn't answer; Leven hadn't truly expected them to. Instead, they ran on ahead or kept pace with her, a rushing tide of oddness that brushed against her feet or tangled in her hair until she carefully pulled them free and put them back on the ground. A few of them, she noted, could fly. They bobbed about on sparrow or bat wings – one had the gossamer glass wings of a dragonfly.

The trees they passed looked taller and stranger than any Leven had seen in the Wild Wood. They had bark like stone, and were hosts to vast numbers of fungi of all shapes, sizes and colours; pixen were perched on them, watching her with bright interest as she passed. The leaf litter and gorse under her feet softened to become soft pads of green, grey and orange moss, until with every step her boot seemed to sink two or three inches. The pixen had grown livelier, and she could hear the tiny piping squeaks of their voices as they called to each other. Here, the air was heavy with the perfume of flowers, a thick and heady scent that was almost oppressive. Leven sneezed, and many of the pixen laughed.

Just when she had convinced herself that the pixen had led her into the woods on a lark and she would likely be lost forever in this strange, eerie land, she spied a human figure in the gloom ahead. It looked to be a woman, tall and thin. She wore a strange dress made of a very fine grey lace, which glimmered and shifted in the half-light.

'Hello? Who is that?'

The woman lifted her head, and Leven felt a brief stab of recognition. Could it be...?

The pixen in the lead had reached the woman and were cavorting around her skirts. She did look familiar, but she clearly couldn't be someone Leven had met before; her eyes were filled with inky blackness from lid to lid. Now that she was close enough to touch, Leven saw that her dress wasn't made from lace at all, but spider's webs. There were still spiders all over her, spinning away as they worked on their creation.

'I think I might still be dreaming,' said Leven. 'My dreams have certainly been unusual lately, but this feels like a new level.'

The woman smiled.

'We remember you.' Her voice sounded like several voices at once. From within the neck of her dress she removed a long silver chain. On the end of it was another acorn cup, the inside also gilded with gold, and it was then that Leven realised who she looked like. The spiderwebbed woman was strikingly like Verbena, the consort of Queen Verla, the ruler of Kornwullis. Verbena had been dreamy, distracted, and dressed in a weird hotchpotch of rags, whereas this woman's expression was sharp and watchful. Other than those differences, though, they could have been sisters.

'I... thought I remembered you too, but perhaps I don't. Who are you?'

The woman dropped the cup on the chain, then held out one hand – her nails, Leven noted, were very long and sharp – and one of the pixen deposited the bloody acorn cup in her palm, tipping it so that Leven's blood flowed across it. In one quick movement, the woman licked the blood off her palm with a tongue the same colour as the sky. She nodded, satisfied.

'It is you, Deryn of Echni, Eleven of the Imperium, and... you have a third name, but not yet. I am Mab.'

The pixen coursed around them like a small violent whirlpool. Leven could feel them trampling over her boots.

'How do you know me?'

'Like the Druidahnon, I know all the children of this isle, Deryn. And if I forget, I can find your name written through your blood.'

'What am I doing here?'

'Don't you know?'

Leven shrugged.

'My children have led you here because they are grateful for the taste of your blood, and they believe you need help. What has happened to you?'

'I...' How to even begin telling that tale? 'I have cursed magic in my skin. Despite my warnings, my little sister went and had the same thing done to her. The cursed magic is killing me slowly, with visions of the lives of long-vanished Titans...' Leven paused and laughed. None of it was funny, but she felt oddly giddy all of a sudden. The perfume in the air grew more potent. 'My husband has wandered off and left me in the middle of this lethal forest to become the Green Man, whatever that is, although my impression is that it's not great, at least not the sort of thing you want your husband to suddenly turn into...' Mab tipped her head to one side, an unreadable expression passing over her face. 'And I think he would have come back for me by now if he wasn't in trouble. Oh, and this whole nation is now at war with a new Titan who's turned up out of the blue. And my sister ran away. I don't know if I'll ever see her again.' Leven took a deep breath. 'I think that's it. I feel drunk. Do you feel drunk? I think there's something in the air here.'

'We know the Green Man,' said Mab, ignoring the question. 'He has spent time here, with us, in the past. We have not always seen eye to eye. Since the Druidahnon called him, he has been restless. We have heard his hooves thundering in the wood, the horns blowing.'

Leven tried not to frown. The idea of Cillian with hooves concerned her.

'He rouses himself to war,' continued Mab. 'He's impatient for the mortal who will carry him to come forward.'

'Yes,' said Leven, no longer resisting the frown. 'That's my impression. But I don't see why it has to be *my* mortal.'

'He will try to consume your husband,' said Mab matter-of-factly. 'It's his nature, to take and to change. It is not his fault, not truly. You may as well ask a patch of earth not to grow weeds.'

'I'm sorry, I...' Leven looked down at her boots where they had sunk into the colourful moss. It was difficult to think clearly, yet the strange lilac light had given everything a startling clarity. One of the pixen at her feet wore a hat made of a mushroom cap, and she could have counted every single spot on it. 'I'm really not clear on who you are. Are you another sort of Titan I don't know about? Because I know you're not human. Or are you just a really big pixen?'

There were some titters at that from the creatures on the ground.

Mab just smiled. 'I am the queen who walks in the lilac wood,' she said, as though that explained everything. 'Come with me, Deryn. There is something I should like to gift to you, in your time of trouble.'

# 32

*One of Arch-Druin Merriden's most popular prophecies concerned a 'lady of the green'. It has largely been ignored in modern times as fanciful, even romantic nonsense, but I believe it holds the seed of something interesting. Supposedly there would someday come a woman who had lived many lives, a warrior and a wife and a mother, a friend and an enemy of queens, who would be wedded to the Wild Wood itself.*

Extract from the writings of Elder Druin Jathinos,<br>Dosraiche's Master of Histories

'First of all, Cillianos, there are some things you should know before you make this choice.'

They had walked through the night and into the dawn, Inkwort flying ahead or resting on his shoulder as she saw fit. Often, as she was flying, she would open Paths, and they followed a route that he had never seen or even guessed at. He saw places that were entirely new to him. Often, the woods they travelled through felt older, more dangerous. Once or twice, Cillian had waded through snow as high as his waist. *We are skirting the Wildest Wood,* he thought.

'By all means,' he said, trying and failing to keep some of the sarcasm from his voice. 'It sounds like there's plenty I don't know, after all.'

The latest Path had led them to a ruin Cillian didn't recognise. There were two old stone walls, forming a corner, and a lower wall heading off to the east that crumbled into pebbles after around ten feet. The wood crowded in on all sides, and much of the stone was covered in thick ivy, while a tall oak tree loomed over the remains, its roots making the ground uneven. Inkwort alighted on the low wall, strutting and peering about.

'Here will do,' she said.

'For what?'

'For the telling,' she replied, in what Cillian considered to be an unnecessarily ominous tone. He sighed, and found a space to sit by the wall so that the ruin loomed off to his right. All around them, the wood was ringing with morning sounds, birds calling warnings and greetings to each other. Cillian's thrawn senses seethed, longing to reach out to them. He ignored it.

'Are you comfortable?'

'Yes,' he said, although he shifted impatiently in his spot. 'Whatever it is you have to tell me, can you just spit it out? I want to get back to Leven as soon as I can. It's not safe in the Wild Wood for a lone traveller, as I'm sure you're aware.'

The little bird hopped onto his knee. This close he was able to admire the sooty blackness of her wings, the soft dusting of her grey hood.

'Why can't I sense you?' It was something he had wondered since he had first met the jackdaw at the Dosraiche. 'Normally I have a... sense of living things. Like a patch of warmth in my mind where you are. But with you it's like you're muted, or hidden.'

'Cillianos,' she said, 'you cannot sense me for the same reason the acorn doesn't sense the oaken wood.'

He opened his mouth, about to ask what she could possibly mean by that, when she darted forward and pecked him firmly in his left eye. Cillian yelped and scrambled up, both hands going to his face. He was dimly aware of the whirring of wings as Inkwort took off again.

'Fuck! Ow. Why did you do that? Fuck, *my eye*.'

Cillian bent over, feeling tears streaming down his cheek – at least, he hoped they were tears.

'Open your eyes, Cillianos,' said Inkwort from somewhere near his left shoulder. 'Open your eyes and see, child.'

'I *would*,' said Cillian, his voice raised. 'But someone just tried to peck one of them out.'

Even so, he gradually took his hands away from his eyes, blinking rapidly. The sting was fading, leaving behind a faint tingle. When he opened his eyes, squinting against a further attack, everything felt a little too bright. And then he saw that the landscape around him had changed.

'What's happening?'

'To accept the Green Man – to make this choice with an open heart – you must know some things about yourself. We are in your earliest memories now, seeing things that have been lost to you for the longest time.'

They stood at the edge of a busy little village. The handful of houses that he could see had roofs thatched with straw, one-storey structures slumping towards the ground as if it were too much effort to stay upright. It was a bright, hot summer's day, and a few people stood by the well in the middle of the settlement. They were talking quietly, laughing and exchanging gossip.

'This place is...' He didn't know, he realised. He didn't know where it was, but it was known to him, nonetheless.

'How much do you remember, Cillianos, of the time before you arrived at the Dosraiche?'

'Very little,' he said. 'I remember my mother, faintly. She was kind to me, but mainly I remember how she got sick, and couldn't pick me up to carry me around anymore. This place was where I grew up?'

Inkwort settled on his shoulder. 'Behind you, on the very edge of the village, is your mother's cottage. We shall go there.'

Cillian turned, a queasy feeling of unreality rushing through his gut. This place was known to him, and with that recognition came a flurry of sensations he had almost completely forgotten: being small and close to the ground, adults towering over him; drinking well water from a smooth clay cup, so cold it still had pieces of ice in it; chasing a neighbour's kittens, the warm sleepiness of one curled in his lap. His throat felt thick, as though he were close to tears. He cleared it, trying to bring himself back to the present.

'How are you doing this?' Ahead of them was a winding, overgrown path, bracketed with gorse and holly. He remembered that he used to enjoy seeing the red berries of the holly in winter, and the yellow of the gorse in summer. 'I've seen something like it before, I think.'

Inkwort made a *tchk* noise. 'I doubt that, Cillianos.'

'No, I have. Leven's sister Ynis used Edge Walker magic to lead her back through her own memories. She prepared a paste from griffin bones, and Leven slept, and as far as I can tell, dreamed her memories back.'

'Hmm,' said Inkwort. 'I suppose that is one way to achieve the effect. A crude way. As the Druidahnon's psychopomp, I have access to much superior magics. I have given your eyes the ability to see. To truly see, as birds do.'

Cillian didn't know what to say to that. They followed the path around until they came to another cottage, this one even more slumped than the others. There was grass growing through the straw on the roof, and ivy almost covered the tiny windows. Beyond it was the familiar dark green presence of the Wild Wood. Seeing it made him feel calmer.

'Alright. So this is my mother's cottage. What is it I need to know about all this, exactly? I don't see how this relates to the Green Man.'

'We've come to you and told you that you must take on the mantle,' said Inkwort. 'In another time, in another world, the Othanim were never released from their prison. They never came to Brittletain, and you were spared all of this. It is a world I should have liked to live in.' Inkwort fluffed up her feathers, making her look bigger, fiercer, as though the words she spoke were dangerous to her. 'Over the years we spoke, the Druidahnon and I, about telling you all this sooner. Preparing you in some way. But neither of us could decide on how we would do it. In the end, we decided that it was better, kinder, to let you live your own life without this knowledge hanging over you.'

Cillian felt the first coil of real fear move through his gut. Inkwort sounded afraid. She sounded sad. It was the most he'd ever heard her speak, he realised.

'But you were so *green*, child. There was never any question you would be Druin, and even for one of them you were isolated, too deeply connected to the roots and the branches. The Druidahnon decided that he would send you out into the world with the Herald, to get some humanity into you. This I did argue against.' Inkwort snapped her beak together derisively. 'He did not listen. And now you have these other *complications*.'

'You mean my wife.' His tone was slightly dangerous. 'The woman I love.'

'Yes. Perhaps we should have let you embrace the greenness as you so clearly wanted to. If you had lived free in the Wild Wood, the Green Man's embrace would have been a more comfortable thing. Look.'

They had arrived at the far side of the cottage where there was a sprawling garden full of growing things: Cillian saw apple and pear trees, beans and peas, mint and carrot and potato plants. There was a woman in the garden, standing with a baby in her arms. She had freckles, and long brown hair loose over her shoulders. Of the child he could only see the top of a head covered in wispy hair.

'Your mother,' said Inkwort, unnecessarily. 'Braela, as she was known.'

Cillian waited for the gut punch of recognition, but none came. He had known the village, the shape of the cottages and the position of the well, but for this woman he only felt a vague familiarity, as though he had seen someone like her before somewhere. As he watched, she kissed the top of the baby's head in an absentminded way. *My head*, thought Cillian.

'I don't know her,' he said.

'She was a flighty, silly girl, was Braela,' said Inkwort. 'Easily distracted. But she did love you.'

A thin, whistling noise came from the inside of the cottage. The woman glanced at the open back door, and then, carefully, knelt and placed the baby on a patch of brown dirt that had been cleared for further planting. It was in the sun, and the baby wriggled his limbs in pleasure at the warmth. The woman disappeared back inside, where she was lost in the shadows.

'Watch,' said Inkwort.

For a few moments, nothing happened at all. The baby gurgled and stretched, throwing off some of the wrappings and freeing one pudgy arm. Overhead, a crow cawed rustily, over and over.

'I don't...'

Cillian stopped speaking. All around the baby, little green shoots were pushing out of the dark earth, tiny plants reaching up towards the sun. In moments he was surrounded by them; a sweet-smelling green halo. His mother returned, her arms full with a basket of potato peelings – which she dropped at the sight of the baby. Cillian saw her hands fly up to her mouth, covering the perfect 'o' of shock there. Her eyes were very wide.

'You see?' said Inkwort. 'Always so green.'

When Braela had recovered herself, she reached down and snatched the baby up. Underneath him there were more plants, all slightly squashed. Cillian thought they were sweet peas.

'I knew a little of this,' said Cillian, not quite able to pull his eyes away from the new patch of green in the dirt. 'The Druin elders said I was precocious. Naturally gifted, they said.'

Inkwort snapped her beak, her version of a tut. 'None were so gifted as you, child. Look.'

The light grew so bright then that Cillian winced. When he was able to see again, they had moved. Now they were on the edge of the Wild Wood, the cottage some distance behind them. A small child stood at the treeline, no older than three or four. He had brown hair and serious green eyes. Cillian looked down at himself without horns – he realised he couldn't recall what it was like not to have them. The little boy wore a rough-spun tunic and held a broad sycamore leaf in one hand. It was autumn, and the leaf was somewhere between orange and yellow and gold. His mother was nowhere to be seen.

'I've wandered off,' said Cillian. He thought of Leven, who would by now know that he had gone. *I'm always wandering off*, he thought.

The little boy tottered forward, his free hand raised in front of him, and a Path opened up. The wood directly in front of them was no longer a collection of broad oak and sycamore, but pine and poplar, the ground soft with needles. Little Cillian took the Path without concern, and they followed him. When Cillian turned back, the way to the cottage was gone. They were in an entirely new bit of the Wild Wood.

'I don't know this place,' he said. The smaller, hornless version of himself had climbed a mild incline to reach the place where the pine needles were thickest on the ground. He seemed entirely at home.

'You did once,' said Inkwort. She flew up to rest in the bottom branches of the pine tree closest to the boy, who had sat down. He was patting the needles and smoothing them. 'You used to come here to sleep under the trees. The first time you did it, the whole village went out looking for you. Your mother nearly lost her mind – she thought you'd wandered off to be eaten by a wolf or a bear, or snatched away by the Dunohi. In the end, they had to send for a Druin to come and search for you.'

'I don't remember any of that,' said Cillian. The little boy had curled up on the needles, his eyes closed. It seemed he really was going to have a nap in the middle of the Wild Wood.

'The Druin searched for you for some time. You had found one of the lesser-known Paths, apparently. Your mother was much too soft to punish you once you were home. All she did was cry and hold you. The Druin were a little upset, but they were intrigued, too. A child opening the Paths with no instruction? With no horns? They kept their eye on you after that.'

'They had me earmarked for the order this young?'

Inkwort flew back down from the branch, a whirring of black wings. The boy slept on, undisturbed.

'They did. Braela was against it at first, but things started to get harder for her.'

Cillian blinked, and the forest vanished. They were in a cramped room that served as both kitchen and living room; there was a stove and a big glazed sink, as well as a long scarred table covered in bunches of dried herbs, various tools, and dirty cups. It was night-time, and Braela was sitting by the light of a candle; she was not doing anything that he could see. Instead, she stared into the distance, an unreadable expression on her face. One arm hung down the side of her chair.

'What's wrong with her?'

For the first time, Inkwort seemed uncomfortable. 'Your mother... this wasn't the life she had expected for herself. Oh she loved you, more than anything, believe me. But it was hard.'

There was a noise from outside, a kind of snort. It roused Braela from her dreamy state, and she stood up and went to the window. There was a light dusting of snow outside, turning everything crisp and unfamiliar. Cillian went and peered out with her; it wasn't easy, as the ivy framed every side. Next to him, his mother gasped.

On the dirt outside the window were a collection of wild animals: deer, rabbits, foxes, squirrels, mice, badgers – Cillian's eyes skipped from one to the next in amazement. There was even a wolf off to one side, and at the back, a vast dark shape that could only have been a bear. And they were all standing together, looking at the cottage. It was an incredible sight, not least because half of these creatures were the natural predators of the other half, but there was something eerie about it too. When his mother backed away, tears in her eyes and her face the colour of chalk, he found he understood. She was alone here, with a small child, and a crowd of animals were watching the house.

Alone.

As though he'd summoned the child, a small shadow appeared at the door to the living room. Cillian looked to be around five or six, and his hair had grown long, almost reaching his shoulders. He looked like the sort of child that actively avoided soap.

'I never knew my father,' said Cillian. 'I don't remember her ever mentioning him, and not long after I joined the order, she died, so I never found out. But it seems wrong that she was here by herself. Didn't she have a mother, someone who could come and help? Aunts, uncles? Where are the rest of her family?' All at once it seemed strange that he had never really thought about it. *Too concerned with the wood*, he thought, guilt like a heavy stone on his chest. *That's what my mind was always caught up in.*

'Wilful, your mother,' said Inkwort. She was perched on the back of the chair. In the shadows of the room, she was a simple dark shape, the light from the candle reflected in her eye like a tiny golden dot. 'So wilful. They wanted a particular type of life for her, one she felt she couldn't fit into, so she ran away from them. She chose this life, a life of freedom and independence, but it wasn't always easy, Cillianos. She regretted some things, but never you.'

Cillian turned to look at the bird more closely. Something about her tone was strange.

'What is it?'

'I have one more thing to show you,' she said quietly. 'But it is from before you were born, so you will have to borrow one of my own memories. Come on.'

The young woman had gone to her child, and Cillian's last glimpse of her before the scene changed again was of her kneeling, her arms around him, and the child's hand nestled in her dark hair. And then they were once again in the Wild Wood. It was spring, the air full of the scent of blossom, and the trees were all wearing their sharpest, greenest clothes. Cillian took a deep breath. It was a relief after the tiny, oppressive kitchen.

'There she is.' Inkwort's tone was, Cillian thought, judgemental. 'Not a thought in her pretty head.'

*And she was pretty*, thought Cillian. There on the path in spring, with her hair loose over her shoulders and her eyes – they were hazel, he realised, a warm tawny colour quite unlike his own – sparkled with some inner mischief. She wore a travelling pack and a long, battered coat. Her boots were caked with mud. He wondered when this was exactly – how much time she had before she fell pregnant with him. *Did I take this from her? Did she ever wear that carefree expression again after I came along?*

'What's she doing out here?'

'Just walking. Enjoying the wood. It was always her favourite thing to do. Look here now. Watch.'

Braela had wandered off the dirt path and was crunching down a slope covered in holly bushes and leaf litter. She had spotted a glinting light through the trees, and as they followed, Cillian realised it was a pond, deep and clear and dark. Green rocks lined the bottom, and here and there, a yellow frog swam in jerky movements through the water. There was a stillness to the place that almost felt unnatural; Cillian could hear no birdsong, no insects humming. And on the other side of the pond, there was a man. Cillian stopped at the sight of him, his heart in his throat. This was no mortal man. This wasn't even a Druin.

His mother had stopped too, her hazel eyes filled with an expression that was difficult to look at.

'Yes,' said Inkwort. She sounded regretful. 'There is one final thing you should know, Cillianos.'

# 33

*The story they tell about Queen Consort Verbena is that her ship was lost in a storm, and she washed up on the shores of Zenore only to be picked from the rocks by Queen Verla herself. It's very romantic, and the people of Kornwullis especially like to share the story with grockles (travellers from outside the kingdom). A quick glance at any reasonably accurate historical record, though, reveals that the real story is slightly more prosaic, if, in my opinion, just as romantic. Verbena was the daughter of a minor warlord operating out of one of the islands beyond the Broken Sea. Queen Verla met Verbena while trading with the islands, and spent a year sending the young woman gifts – the finest pearls, silks, spices, all the treasures that pass through the famous ports of Kornwullis. But Verbena was ever dreamy and away with the pixen, and although she expressed her thanks for the gifts in a sweet and polite manner, she never seemed to quite understand that the queen of Kornwullis was wooing her. Eventually, desperate, Verla sat and wrote all her feelings into a poem (reportedly asking members of the royal crew for help with the spelling of certain words) and a month later, Verbena arrived at Zenore port, all her worldly belongings with her.*

Extract from the writings of Elder Druin Jathinos,<br>Dosraiche's Master of Histories

'I was married too, once,' said Mab.

She was walking a pace or two ahead of Leven. The spider-webs of her dress floated and trailed behind her in a breeze Leven could not feel, and her hair, which was black, glittered like the stars overhead.

'We've only been married for a year or so,' said Leven. Even now, when she spoke about it, she found herself smiling, her face flushing with pleasure. 'We were outside of Blessed Gäul, searching for someone, and we came across an old temple on top of a hill. It looked out across the forests there, and there was a tree growing right in the middle of the place – a great old oak, bursting up through the flagstones so that its branches became the roof. We both felt something there. I can't describe it, really. We thought it had been abandoned centuries ago, but while we were exploring, this tiny old woman appeared from nowhere. She told us that she was the priestess, and did we want her blessing? And I said...' She paused, grinning. '"Will you marry us? I think this is the place we're supposed to be married." In the Imperium, you see, you're supposed to ask your partner first, that's the tradition, and then you spend a year promised to each other, but none of that seemed very important. Not in that place. So, this ancient priestess married us under that oak tree, and that was it. My sister was there, and she asked me if this was normal for humans.'

Leven stopped. She didn't know why she had said all that aloud.

'Your sister is not human?'

Mab turned her head slightly to look at her from the corner of her eye and Leven noticed for the first time that the queen of the lilac wood had horns too – not Druin horns, exactly, but two small raised points of bone at her temples.

'Not exactly. She was raised by griffins. It's complicated.'

The wood was growing darker as they walked, and again Leven wondered what had happened to the dawn. Overhead, the tall trees were reaching towards each other, forming a kind of twilight tunnel.

'My husband, Beron, was a complicated man,' said Mab in her voice that was many voices. 'Wilful, quick to anger. The finest hunter the world has ever seen, and the most enthusiastic drinker. He was competitive too, in everything he did. Always looking to find a way to best his rivals. An edge. And because of this, he made a mistake.'

Leven watched the back of the woman's head, the stars in her hair the only thing lighting the way. She felt as though she were walking into a dream.

'What did he do?' she asked. Her voice sounded very distant to her own ears, while the pixen chirped and chittered from all around. She was beginning to feel like she understood what they were saying. Almost.

'He made a deal with someone he should not have,' said Mab. 'We are not mortal as you and your husband are, but the risks are very similar.'

A cold hand walked down Leven's back. 'The Green Man? Your husband made a deal with the Green Man? What for?'

The tops of the trees were too dark to see, and the sky had vanished entirely. Leven had the sudden realisation that they weren't in a wood anymore; they were in a cave. The fungi that the pixen were perched on clung to rugged stone walls, curving softly inwards, and there was a strong mineral scent of underground water.

'The usual reasons men do,' said Mab, as though this explained things. 'Beron thought that if he had the power of the Green Man at his disposal, he would truly be the greatest hunter that has ever lived, or ever will live.' Mab stopped walking, and Leven arrived alongside her. The expression on the woman's face was rueful. 'He was already a legend, Deryn of the Wild Wood, but it wasn't enough. He had to be *more*, and in doing so, he lost everything. Everything that mattered, anyway.'

'What happened?'

Mab turned her black eyes towards her, and Leven saw that they were speckled with light, like the night sky.

'The Green Man consumed him. He went into the green, never to return. What Beron was, the essence of him, became another part of the Green Man. He broke Beron down and grew something new from him.'

'I'm sorry.'

'Do not be. Beron was ever stubborn, and we rarely agreed. Our marriage was a wild and thorny thing long before the Green Man raised his shaggy head. A sliver of him will always exist as part of the Green Man, but I do miss him, all the same. Which is why I want to help you, Deryn.'

'You do?'

'I want to give you something.'

The tunnel had narrowed, the ceiling drawing down towards them. The scent of flowers had faded, to be replaced by something ripe and earthy. There was a faint hint of sweet decay, as though somewhere nearby a pile of fruit was turning to mush. The pixen, Leven realised with a start, had vanished. It was just her and Queen Mab.

'I believe that all of us who are not men share something, Deryn. I will not say that I want revenge on the Green Man, for I am no fool. You cannot revenge yourself against a spirit of chaos. But perhaps I want to make things a little harder for him.' She smiled in the gloom, a small sharp thing as lethal as a dagger. Leven found herself wondering if Mab was speaking the whole truth.

'There is little that you can do, Eleven of the Imperium, to stop your husband from joining with the Green Man. Even now, he is close to taking that step.'

Leven swallowed hard. She should never have slept last night. She should have stayed awake to watch over him. She stopped walking, her hands balling into fists. 'Then why am I even here? I need to get back. I need to find him.' Leven took a step backwards. 'Why am I letting you waste my time like this?'

'Deryn, come.' Mab beckoned with a single finger, and Leven shivered. She could no more have resisted that summons than she could have pulled her own arms off. 'It is not much further.'

They began walking again. The ground under their feet was soft black dirt, almost as fine as sand.

'The pixen will not come here,' Mab said almost conversationally. 'It frightens them.'

'Where are we?'

'The Holloway. This is my place between places.'

Leven snorted. 'Brittletain has so many layers and secret places I can't keep track. It's like a bloody honeycomb.'

'It is a jewel with many facets,' agreed Mab. 'We are here.'

The queen of the lilac wood came to a stop. Just ahead of them was a small alcove, and in it what looked suspiciously like a shrine. There were fat red candles balanced on flat rocks, melted wax oozing down the stone like spilled blood, and in front of these sat the largest longbow Leven had ever seen. It was made of warm, earth-coloured wood and there were shapes carved into the surface that gave off a faint pearlescent glow. It was so large Leven could not imagine anyone human being able to lift it.

'Beron's bow,' said Mab.

Leven wondered, her heart tripping in her chest, if Queen Mab was going to give her the bow. What would she do with it? Even with her Titan augments it would be too heavy and large for her to draw, and she had no experience of using such a weapon. A horrible crawling embarrassment turned her cheeks pink.

'I am honoured,' she said. 'But I can't possibly take that.'

Mab laughed, a rich throaty sound that was surprising out of her thin, pale face. 'I do not mean to give you his bow. That is not an instrument for mortal hands. Here.' She crouched slowly and pushed her hand into the black dirt just in front of the bow.

For a few moments she rummaged around, pushing up dirt and blackening her nails, until finally she stood up triumphantly. She held out her hand to Leven. On her upturned palm there was a small white rock, no bigger than a snail. It had a small hole in it which passed all the way through the middle so that she could see the white skin of Mab's hand.

'What is it?'

'It is a hag stone. Take it.'

Leven plucked it off of the woman's hand. It was cool and hard and completely unremarkable. Once again Leven felt mildly dizzy with the strangeness of the situation.

'I... thank you?'

'Keep it safe, and keep it with you.' Mab looked entirely serious; even a little concerned, as though she were already doubting the sense of her decision. 'When the time comes, use it. You will know when.'

'And how do I use it?' Leven held the stone up, turning it this way and that in her fingers, looking at it from all sides. It didn't have any strange markings on it like the bow did. 'Maybe in Brittletain you all know how to use rocks with holes in, but I don't. The Imperium mostly use rocks to throw at enemies, and that hasn't been their style for a long time now. And this? Even if you threw it really hard, I doubt you'd stop anyone. Might piss someone off, I suppose.'

She held the stone up to her eye, meaning to peer through the hole, but Mab's hand was suddenly clasped around hers, the fingers icy cold. Her grip was extraordinarily strong, completely immovable.

'Don't,' breathed Mab. 'Just... don't. Do not look through the hag stone here. Do you understand me?'

Leven swallowed. 'I do. I do.'

'Good.' Mab released her grip. 'You will go back now, Deryn of Echni, Eleven of the Imperium. I have done what I can for you. We will both have to hope it is enough.'

'Wait.' Abruptly, Leven felt panicked. Whoever or whatever Mab was, she was clearly a being of great power. Here was a chance for her to make an alliance, something that would truly help Cillian. She wished intensely that Epona was there with her. She knew how to deal with queens. 'Can you tell me where Cillian is? Can you come with me, back to the Wild Wood? The Othanim are destroying Brittletain. Surely you can help?'

But Mab simply smiled, and the world around Leven melted away. All at once she was back in the Wild Wood, and it was full of mid-morning sunshine.

'Ah, fuck,' she said.

## 34

In their previous lives growing up in the mountains of Yelvynia, Ynis and T'rook had rarely seen large groups of griffins. It was a place of scattered nest-pits and communal spaces; even Queen Fellvyn's home rarely saw many visitors, as she did much of her official queening on the wing. But as they flew over the mountains with their escort, the sun setting off to the west, Ynis saw that a great many things had changed while they had been away. The irregular copses of pine and cedar had been cleared away; instead, they saw regular towers made of wood and griffin spit, glowing with eerie green marsh lights. Griffins were perched on top of them, their eyes staring out into the dwindling night. They wore armour that reflected the orange blaze of sunset in fiery flashes. As they passed, Ynis saw them look at her with particular attention; her wings were so bright she was hard to miss. She saw feathered manes puff out with indignation, or fear. *None of them recognise me,* she thought, *and why would they? Humans all look the same to them, and I have been gone for more than two years. And I am a winged thing now.* The thought that she'd finally gained her wings at the exact moment that winged humans had begun attacking the griffins did not fill her with joy.

T'oro, for her part, ignored the attention they were getting from the watchtowers and led them higher into the mountains. Here, the skies were busy – griffins flew back and forth on urgent business, some clutching prey animals in their talons, others wearing heavy armour. Ynis saw one with a dead Othanim, the creature hanging from the griffin's claws like a butchered carcass.

'What has been happening here?' asked T'rook.

'I suppose you have been too busy grubbing around on the ground looking for worms to notice,' said T'oro. 'But we are at war with the ancient enemy, and Queen Fellvyn has ordered us to readiness. We watch the borders at all times. All sightings of the Othanim are reported to the Council. And the war-nest was built. Do you see it?'

They coasted around a craggy outcrop of rock, revealing the far side of the Silver Death Peak. Clinging to it like a barnacle was a vast structure, built of wood mulched down with griffin spit. It was bulbous at the centre and lined with hundreds of windows and entrances, through which endless numbers of griffins were coming and going. Along the top were more towers, stretching out across the rocky face of the mountain like human hands with the fingers spread wide. There were more marsh lights too, green and yellow points of luminance in the dark that shivered in the wind.

'Who could possibly need a nest-pit that big?' said T'rook. 'Every griffin in Yelvynia must be here.'

'It's not for hatchlings, you fool,' said T'oro. Ynis saw her sister glance meaningfully at the other griffin's neck, as though she might merrily tear it out. 'It is so that Queen Fellvyn can speak to us all at once and instruct her bravest and most valuable warriors – like us.' She tossed her head towards the other two griffins, who had remained silent on the flight back. 'We are part of the patrols that keep Yelvynia safe for little yenlin like you.'

T'rook snapped her beak dangerously. Ynis spoke before her sister could do something unwise.

'Have many of these Othanim come so far north? We saw some in Brittletain. The humans there are at war with them too.'

'Humans at war with Titans?' T'oro squawked dismissively. 'You might as well say that grass is at war with the goats. The Othanim come in small groups. There seem to be endless numbers of them, but all that means is more fresh meat for us. Here, we will head straight to the Crown. I'm sure Queen Fellvyn will want to deal with you both as quickly as possible.'

They flew up, heading towards the upper section of the war-nest. There was a wider opening there, the bottom half of which was lined with what Ynis initially thought were human skulls, but as they got closer, she saw that they were too big, and the bone was a silvery-blue colour: Othanim skulls. As they landed, Ynis let her wings disappear and paused to take in their surroundings. Beyond the entrance there was a vast chamber, the walls lined with balconies on which stood more griffins. They were talking or feeding, or in some cases, tending to wounds. The floor was covered with feathers that looked strange to Ynis's eye. When she bent down to pick one up, she realised immediately from the feel of them that they weren't griffin feathers; they were slippery, oily almost. They had been plucked from the wings of Othanim – Othanim that the griffins had killed, she assumed.

As they walked deeper, the other two griffins peeled off, heading to an alcove at the base of the walls where a small group was tearing into the carcass of what looked like an elk. When they got there, they murmured to the other griffins and all of them looked back at their group, their eyes seeking her out. The back of her neck prickled. This was a very poor time to be human-shaped in Yelvynia.

Towards the back of the place T'oro had referred to as the Crown, a large clay tablet had been set into the floor. Several griffins moved around its edges, peering down at it with troubled expressions. It took Ynis a moment to recognise one of them, because she was wearing an elaborate golden headdress and cuffs of Titan ore around her thick forelegs, but then she looked up and spoke, her golden eyes narrowing.

'What is this?' asked Queen Fellvyn, her voice cutting through the general hubbub of the hall like a talon through rabbit meat.

'My queen, I bring you trespassers,' T'oro said eagerly. The white griffin puffed out her chest and folded her wings neatly along her back. 'There is no reason for one as important as yourself to remember this pair of stone-lickers, but I could never forget them. This human once cut the feathers from my head when I was taken unawares, and you in your wisdom banished them from Yelvynia. And yet they have had the temerity to return!'

The queen sighed noisily and murmured something to a small tan-coloured griffin next to her, who nodded and flew up to one of the balconies. Now that they were closer, Ynis could see that the clay tablet on the floor had been carved with a map of Yelvynia, and was inscribed in places with griffin cloud-writing. It looked as though they were keeping track of Othanim incursions. There were a lot of them.

'And there is more!' T'oro raised her voice, just in case she hadn't yet secured the attention of every griffin in the hall. Ynis placed her hand on T'rook's shoulder, taking strength from her sister's solid presence. 'The human has made magical wings somehow, which leads me to believe that it is working with the Othanim. Perhaps it is a pet to them now, a small version of themselves they keep for their amusement. If it pleases you, my queen, I would be very happy to rip their throats out, saving you the trouble. If anything—'

'The children of Flayn and T'vor,' said Queen Fellvyn. 'I thought I was clear when I told you never to return to this place?' T'rook opened her beak, but the queen spoke over her. 'Putting that briefly aside – does T'oro tell the truth, human? Or has she eaten too much dagger root?'

Ynis cleared her throat. 'I have wings, your majesty, but they are not griffin wings or the wings of Othanim. They are a human magic.'

'Humans do not have magic,' Fellvyn said witheringly. 'None worth speaking of, at least.'

'This magic is... from a foreign land.' Ynis thought of the Herald that had attacked Brocken, her shining golden armour winking under a winter sun. 'It is made from the bones of Titans.'

There was a chorus of outraged squawks from the hall. Ynis heard a few griffins calling 'Outrage!' and 'Death to it'.

'You see how it dares to insult us,' said T'oro, her eyes glinting with excitement. 'To walk into the war-nest and speak such abominations.'

'I've heard enough from you,' said Queen Fellvyn in a dangerous tone. T'oro lowered her head, baring her long grey scar. 'Explain yourself, human cub. I see no wings on your back. I do not have the time for such nonsense. If this is some kind of jest, I will have all three of you torn to bits and fed to my fledglings.'

Ynis took a step away from her sister and summoned the wings once more. The chamber filled with their shifting sapphire light, and the griffins grew quiet.

'This is a magic created by my human mother,' said Ynis, raising her voice so that all in the chamber could hear. 'She took griffin bones from the Bone Fall and made an ore from it, which she stitched into the skin of my human sister.' Ynis paused. Even now, speaking of her human family felt like a betrayal of herself. 'She is a bad person, a stone-licker and a parasite, but respected by humans for her powerful magic. The humans who carry this magic are called Heralds.' She spread her wings as wide as they would go, feeling a strange moment of mingled guilt and triumph. 'The ore that I carry under my skin, though, was made from the bones of the Othanim. Not griffins.'

Queen Fellvyn came forward, stepping around the map in the floor until she towered over Ynis. Blue light played over her golden headdress and pooled in her eyes. 'Where have you been, yenlin?' she said in a much quieter voice. 'Have you been in the south? Have you seen what they are building?'

Uneasy about the attention they were attracting, Ynis let her wings vanish. 'Yes. We flew...'

There was a clamour over their heads, a whirring of wings and the sound of a voice raised in excitement.

'My yenlin!'

Flayn landed at the queen's side with a distinct lack of grace, sending up a cloud of Othanim feathers, before throwing himself amongst them. Ynis found herself enveloped in her father's scent, her face pressed into his fur. Somewhere close by she could hear T'rook making low trills of delight; she hadn't heard T'rook make such a noise since they were both yenlin and cosy inside their fathers' nest-pit. Her eyes filled with tears.

'Father.' She put her arms around his neck and breathed deeply. Feathers, dust, gorse blossom and grass: a scent out of yenlinhood. It was hard to speak. 'I... we've missed you.'

'I never thought I'd see you again! Look at you both, you're so big!' Flayn pulled back from them a little to get a better look, then ran his beak through T'rook's ruff of feathers, chasing some errant bit of dirt. 'You are a mess too, Ynis.' He rested his forehead against hers briefly. 'What a day this is. I never thought... T'vor will not believe it.'

'Where is he?' asked T'rook. 'Is he here with you?'

'T'vor flies the patrols, while I offer Queen Fellvyn my humble advice on the war. I barely see him, but you know what he is like. If there is a fight, he will find it.' There was a darker tone under Flayn's joy, but he moved quickly on. 'You must tell me where you've been. And why is everyone talking about wings, Ynis? What has happened to the pair of you? I will want to hear all of it, you realise.'

Behind them, Queen Fellvyn noisily cleared her throat. Flayn fell silent.

'Yes, we would all wish to hear this,' she said. 'For there must be some great reason for their return, given it flies in the beak of my banishment and exile.'

'My queen,' Flayn bowed his head. 'Surely, I could be allowed some time with my hatchlings? It has been years since we have flown together.'

'How dare you!' piped up T'oro. 'To ask this of our queen when your torrosa yenlin have disobeyed her decree, returning as they do with filthy human magic that mocks all griffinkind!'

'Do close your beak,' said Queen Fellvyn abruptly. 'You do not speak for me, T'oro. If I require your tongue, I will rip it out myself.' When she turned back to them, she looked tired. 'Go. Speak with your yenlin. I will have questions shortly.'

# 35

*We owe our empire to the star that fell and blessed the land. This is the story we tell ourselves, the reason we pay tribute to our ancestor stars and encourage our finest minds to trace their paths across the night sky. This is a picturesque way of framing the reality: once, a star fell, a piece of debris from the sky we cannot guess the origin of, and it landed with such force that it simultaneously gouged an enormous crater in the land and killed many thousands of Titans in an instant. In that crater, we built our greatest city, Stratum. And from that crater, we retrieved a fortune's worth of Titan bone, founding the Imperium.*

Extract from *Imperium: The History and the Alchemy* by Edzio Hawk

'Where is he?'
Thirteen looked at Kaeto with flat dislike, his arms crossed over his brawny chest. The Herald was paler than ever, his bald head traced with blue veins. The cool climate of Brittletain clearly didn't agree with him.

'I don't see why you are so concerned,' Thirteen said, his lip curling. 'We've handed the prisoners over. What the big bitch does with them is up to her.' The sneer stretched into a smirk.

'Or were they true, the rumours? I should like to know how that works – even a little Othanim like him could pick you up like a ragdoll. Or maybe that's what you like, I don't know.'

Kaeto thought of the blade in his sleeve – newly supplied that morning by Princess Epona – and pictured the satisfying spurt of blood that would result from burying it in this dreadful little man's throat. He would gurgle and retch and choke, and it would all be immensely gratifying, but then he'd have to clean the mess up. And he knew the Heralds were sending messages back to the empress. Slitting the throat of one of the Imperium's most expensive warriors would doubtless cause endless paperwork.

'The Heralds are valued for their strength, prowess in battle, and access to Titan magic,' he replied. 'Not for their diplomatic acumen, it seems. What happens, Thirteen, when Icaraine the Lightbringer has finished with the presents our empress has sent her? How long do you think she'll tolerate our presence once Felldir is dead and she has to look for something else to entertain her? Do you want to be the next toy in her bedchamber? More to the point, once she's bored of us, our ability to negotiate any kind of alliance goes out the window. Is that enough explanation for you, or would like me to break it down into smaller words? Perhaps I could draw some pictures?'

This was, he knew, pushing it too far, but he could see from Thirteen's face that the Herald hadn't got further than picturing himself in Icaraine's clutches – his pale skin had turned even whiter.

'They've taken him to the old state room where they used to put visiting royalty,' said Thirteen. 'The servants, I mean. The other flying arseholes won't touch him.'

Kaeto left him there in the corridor and hurried away. When he arrived at the room, he saw a young woman, little more than a girl really, leaning against the door frame. Her apron was covered in blood and her hands were trembling. When she looked up at him, she flinched, as though expecting more violence.

'How bad is it?'

'She is a *monster*.'

He brushed past her into the chamber. There was a canopied bed in the room, which was itself large and well lit. He could tell that this had been the place that Broudicca housed visitors she wanted to impress. The view took in the river and the formerly bustling city to great effect. On the bed was Felldir. Kaeto felt his heart twist in his chest.

There were two servants with him. One of them was elderly, with knotted, shaking hands. The other was a young girl, no more than fourteen or fifteen. They were both trying to bandage what remained of his right wing; it appeared to have been sawn away at the largest joint. Kaeto saw jagged bone, torn skin, and everywhere, bloodstained feathers. Several nebulous ideas about how they might all escape vanished into nothing.

*He needs you*, he told himself. *This is no time to panic or lose hope.*

Taking a deep breath, he strode over to the bedside.

'When did this happen? How much blood has he lost?'

The old woman looked up at him with watery eyes. Her mouth was trembling. 'A couple of hours ago, lord. She sent for tools from the stables, and then we heard him screaming...'

'Where is the other part of his wing?'

'She kept it.' The old woman looked like she might be sick. 'Just picked it up and started plucking the feathers from it like a chicken.'

Of course. If there were bones to be had, Icaraine would be keeping them.

'He won't stop bleeding,' said the girl. Her blonde hair was pulled back into a tight bun at the back of her head and little wisps of it had come free, floating in front of her face. She sounded both exasperated and shaky. 'I can't see what to do with him. I've had to patch up wounds before, but a broken wing? Do I look like a Druin?'

Kaeto put a hand lightly on her shoulder. 'What is your name?'

'Flo,' she said. The expression on her face said that she hoped he was someone who could make sense of all this. His heart went out to her; he feared no one could do that.

'Flo, please go to the kitchens and have them make up boiling water in the cleanest pans they have. Get them to bring them up here. I'll also want a pestle and mortar. Then I want you to go to the stables and find whoever is left there – we'll want leather belts off of harnesses, and twine if they've got it.' He turned to the old woman. 'You. Go to that wardrobe and bring out any clothes that are left. And start tearing them up.' He glanced at the woman's wizened hands. 'Find a knife. Or wait for Flo to get back and have her do it.'

The women scattered. He went to Felldir and examined him properly, fingers travelling lightly over his broken wing, seeking out the shattered places, the torn skin and flesh. He probed gently, aware that the Titan must be in tremendous pain, but Felldir did not make a sound. He stared glassily at the fabric hanging overhead, his handsome face gaunt. When Kaeto pressed the back of his hand to the Titan's forehead, he had to snatch it back quickly. Felldir was burning up.

'You have a fever,' he said tersely. 'Can you hear me, my friend?'

Felldir did not respond. From the look of the wounds, Icaraine – or whoever she had commanded to do her dirty work – had sawn through bone and skin and flesh with a blade that was likely both dirty and blunt. The Titan was left with a feathered stump about as long as Kaeto's forearm. Kaeto wished that Belise were with them.

When Flo and the kitchen attendants arrived with the hot water and other supplies, he spent some time carefully cleaning the remains of the wing; tentatively at first, and then more vigorously as he realised that Felldir was not fully conscious. One of the older servants commented at one point, in a muttered breath, that he didn't see why they should waste such effort on one of their captors – that they should let the bastard die in agony. Kaeto told him to get out.

When he'd cleaned the wound as best he could, he ordered more hot water from the kitchens, and the largest bath they could find to be brought into the room. They stripped him of the soiled rag serving as his underwear and, with a great deal of difficulty, got him into the bath. Kaeto and the servants were left sweating, dirty and exhausted by the end of it.

'What do we do now?' asked Flo. She was watching Kaeto carefully, as though she couldn't predict what he might ask of them next.

'Leave,' he said. Out of the corner of his eye, he saw the girl flinch. As the others filed out of the room, he took her arm for a moment. 'Thank you,' he said. 'You've done your best here today, and I appreciate it.'

'Will he live?'

Kaeto nodded. 'For a little longer at least, I think. Titans are notoriously difficult to kill.'

'What sort of queen is she, to treat her people like that?' Flo asked. She spat the words as if afraid of them. 'And why do they follow her at all?'

Kaeto thought of the flattened ground outside the Indigo Sky Palace, the land that had once held a thriving town. He thought of the empress sitting in her little chair in the Blue Room, telling him that it was too late. He thought of all the dark little jobs he had done for her over the years.

'I wish I knew, Flo,' he said. 'I will wash him now, and finish binding his wounds. Later, I'd like you to bring up some broth from the kitchens for him, something with a little meat if they've got it. Can you do that?'

Flo promised that she would and left the room, closing the door behind her. Kaeto took the package of herbs from Epona out of his inside pocket – he had already hidden the more dangerous ones in his own room, but he had enough on him to put together a paste that would help clean and close the cuts all over Felldir's body. He made it up quickly, taking in the astringent scent of the herbs without really paying them any attention. When he went back to Felldir, the Titan had his head back and his eyes closed.

'Heat,' he said, through cracked lips. 'I have missed it.'

'Ah, you are back with us.' Kaeto drew up a chair so that he could sit. 'I'm going to wash the rest of your wounds as best I can, Felldir. It will sting a little.' He stopped, caught by the ludicrousness of the phrase – the man had just had a limb inexpertly lopped off. 'Try not to move. I believe your wing has finally stopped bleeding and I do not want it to start again.'

He poured a little of the hot water into the bath, and soaked the cleanest rag he had. 'Just lean forward for me a little.'

There were cuts and grazes all over Felldir's skin, as well as large bruises as dark and purple as storm clouds. It hurt his heart to look at them, and it occurred to him that contrary to his earlier thought, he was glad that Belise was not here. As tough as she liked to appear, he feared that the sight of Felldir in such a sorry state would break something in her. He began to wash, methodically, cleaning each cut as much as he could. Once he was done with each cut, he would apply a little of the medicinal paste.

'Why did she do this to you?' he murmured.

For a moment he thought that Felldir had slipped out of consciousness again. Then he shifted slightly, causing the water that was gathering in the bottom of the bath to lap against the sides.

'She grew bored of the usual hurts,' he whispered. 'I should have made more of a performance for her, perhaps. Cried out more, or wept. Such entertainment might have saved my wing. But even now, I am loath to give her what she wants, and that drives her to greater and greater rages.'

'At least we have you out of her sight for the moment,' said Kaeto. He had cleaned the cuts on Felldir's left arm and torso, so he shifted to concentrate on one long leg. The muscles beneath the skin were as hard as stone. 'It gives us a chance to patch you up, as best we can. Try and bring this fever down.'

Felldir grunted, as though he did not care much either way.

'How is Belise?' he asked eventually.

'I do not see her often,' said Kaeto. 'But she is keeping out of harm's way. She continues to tend to Malakim.' He glanced at the door and lowered his voice. 'It's a clever play. To insinuate herself close to the thing that is the most important to Icaraine. But I worry about her.'

'You should,' said Felldir. 'Icaraine's spawn is more dangerous than you can imagine. He is the reason...' He trailed off, his head nodding forward.

'Try and stay with me,' said Kaeto, gripping his knee and shaking it.

'Stay with you,' murmured Felldir. 'Yes, I'll stay with you.'

'Tell me about Malakim.' Kaeto eyed the makeshift bandages uneasily. Spots of red were blossoming on the fabric, like sinister flowers. He would have to change them before he left. 'Why is he so dangerous? What did he do?'

'When he was born, we all knew... we all knew something was wrong.' Felldir's eyelids fluttered. 'The offspring of queens are often born with something that marks them out as different. There have, in the past, been many such children. They grew to be heroes, some of them. Celebrated champions of... the Othanim.' His voice was soft, and seemed to be coming in and out like the tide, but Kaeto was heartened. At least he was making sense. 'There was Achion, who could whisper to the wind and change its course – he was the fastest of our people to ever fly. Or Zeracheel, who was born with two sets of wings and four arms. She lived to be the general of our armies for generations... until Icaraine had her killed, and took over. But Malakim... when she bore him, we thought that she had been cursed. No one had ever seen a child born so unlike the heroes who came before.'

'Who was the father?' asked Kaeto, only half listening as he soaked the dirt from an especially deep cut in Felldir's thigh.

'We all were.'

Kaeto sat back. 'I'm sorry?'

'It was the *honour* of her closest advisors...' Felldir turned his head, looking at Kaeto directly for the first time. 'Our... mating practices differ from yours, light-bones.'

For reasons Kaeto didn't quite understand a creeping heat was moving up the back of his neck. 'Well. I had no idea.'

'It is not always the way with queens, but Icaraine insisted. My partner, Areel, was a special favourite of hers. It meant that we were both closer to her than we would have liked.' His voice was a little firmer, as though talking had brought him out of his stupor. 'Areel had chosen to stand with Icaraine against the old queen at the very beginning. He never felt that he could leave her after that, despite all she did. And that was not so unusual. When a new queen is born, it is natural for us to rally to this fresh blood. It is the way we have always been. And if Areel stayed with her, then I would also. There was no question.'

'Tell me about Areel.'

'He was stubborn. Passionate. Impatient.' Felldir smiled faintly, his white hair lying in limp strands across his face. Kaeto felt the urge to push them out of his eyes, but resisted. 'He wanted so much for the Othanim. Saw a great future for us, if we were bold enough to take it. I was young, and easily led. I didn't know yet what taking it might actually mean for us, for all of Enonah. I still do not know how much of it he intended, or even agreed with. The poor fool.'

'You told me once that he died fighting alongside her.'

Felldir sighed. 'A small lie, to soothe my own pain. But what does it matter now?' Felldir shifted in the bath again, moving his curtailed wing awkwardly. For the first time, Kaeto heard him grunt with pain. 'In the last days of the war on the Black City she killed him. I did not see it. I was fighting at the gates, trying to keep out the griffins and the bears and the god-boar – and failing. When I returned to her palace, I found him on the floor of her chamber, his face purple. The child, Malakim, had crushed his throat without touching him. Icaraine was furious – not that she had lost her closest advisor, but that we were losing the war. She'd goaded the child into it. We had been pushed back from the gates, and the griffins and the fire birds hung in the sky over the city. There was no getting out. We knew, too, what they meant to do. The bears had sent us missives in an attempt to stop the bloodshed – if we surrendered, they said, if we submitted to being imprisoned beneath the city, then perhaps, one day...' He trailed off. 'She told me I had to hide. That I would wait, and watch, and see how their magic could be beaten. Because the bears were always the strongest with magic.'

'I am sorry. About Areel.'

Felldir turned his head away. 'Icaraine was always half mad, I believe. But when Malakim was born, and it slowly became apparent what he could do and what his... appetites were, her megalomania quickly became impossible to navigate. She was convinced that Malakim's birth was a sign that we should destroy the other Titan races, that it was our place to be above them, and above humans too. Even Areel could not make her see that we were heading towards a war we could not win. But now...'

'Now?'

'There are only the griffins left.' He shifted in the bath again, his yellow wolf's eyes settling on Kaeto's face. 'And few enough of them. This time she could succeed.'

The water in the bath had turned grey with dirt and old blood. Kaeto contemplated getting the kitchen staff to bring up more hot water so that he could rinse Felldir down, but the Titan looked exhausted, his eyelids drooping as he spoke. He pressed the back of his hand to Felldir's forehead and found it cooler than it had been, although not by much.

'Felldir? How are you feeling now?'

'Like I've just had my wing cut off,' he said, the barest hint of a smile tugging at one corner of his mouth.

'If you can make jokes, it can't be that bad.'

One large hand came over the side of the bath and curled around the bare skin of Kaeto's forearm.

'Light-bones. Kaeto,' Felldir said heavily. 'You should run. Leave this place the first chance you get. Take Belise and go.'

'Not without you.' Kaeto stood to bend over the bath, his heart in his throat, and kissed Felldir on the forehead. The heat and the salt of it seemed to sear onto his lips.

When he'd called the servants back in and they had moved Felldir to the bed, the Titan fell unconscious again, although this time it did appear to be actual sleep. Kaeto stripped the soiled bandages and rebound the broken wing, his deft hands moving with precision and confidence – you couldn't be an assassin without learning a little about healing, perversely – while he tried to ignore the sharp feeling of sorrow that pricked at him every time he saw the ragged bones. His wings had been so beautiful, once.

Eventually he got up to leave, having assigned Flo to the room as a more permanent nurse. He paused by the door, looking back. Felldir's face was grey in the half-light under the canopied bed, and Kaeto remembered how when he had first seen him, he had thought the Titan looked like a statue come to life. *I have to get us out of here, and soon*, he thought as he closed the door behind him. *If it's not already too late.*

# 36

For her second meeting with the Imperial Envoy, Epona dressed as regally as she was able. She washed and combed her hair, and put on the circlet of gold that was the only piece of jewellery she'd managed to keep with her over the last few years. There was a coat of dark blue velvet that Jack had found in an abandoned merchant's premises in the city, which she wore over a dark tunic and trousers; a single line of gold thread circled the cuffs. She could not quite bring herself to paint her face as she used to, but even so, she felt better for the dressing up. This was a man who was used to dealing with empresses, and she was too aware that she was increasingly desperate. Her mother had very little time left, if the Othanim they caught was to be believed. She needed to present herself as a useful ally.

They met again by the wall at the bottom of the rose garden. The moon was a glowing presence behind a thin layer of cloud, and the lights of the castle seemed almost to hang suspended in the darkness. In the distance, every now and then, she could hear the laughter of the Othanim.

'They have someone,' said Jack grimly. She had insisted on coming into the garden with Epona this time. 'They've caught someone in the city, perhaps.'

'Poor sod,' said Epona, her eyes scanning the dark path. 'Look, there he is. He's coming.'

Curiously, Envoy Kaeto looked as though he had aged over the last week. There were dark shadows under his eyes and his mouth was set in a grim line. He nodded at them brusquely, taking in the presence of Jack with one twitch of an eyebrow.

'The bodyguard,' he said. 'I wondered if I would get to meet you this time.'

'Epona is our best chance to survive this,' said Jack. 'I will defend her with my life.'

'Do me a favour,' said Epona, an odd mixture of delighted and mortified. 'That's enough posturing from the pair of you, we don't have time for it. What's the plan, Envoy? We got you the things you need. I hear that you've used them to patch up your Othanim friend, which is – if you'll forgive me – almost precisely the opposite of what we need to be doing. We need to be chopping their wings off, not sewing them back on.'

The Envoy barely acknowledged that. 'If I help you secure the release of your mother, you will help me?'

'Anything you need, we will do it,' Epona said quickly.

'I need to get far away from here, with two others. The Othanim who has had his wing clipped, and another. As far away from Icaraine as possible. We will not be able to fly. Can you assist me with this?'

Epona frowned, then shrugged. 'When we retake the castle, you'll be able to do what you want. Our victory is your victory, right? We have Druin in our camp who can take you along the Paths of the Wild Wood. From there, you can get pretty much anywhere in Brittletain. Travelling with two of those flying bastards, I can't say you'd be welcomed wherever you go, but if you want to get away, that's a start. Perhaps go west to Kornwullis and get a ship from there.'

Kaeto nodded, his eyes flicking from one side to the other as he considered his options. 'It's not enough,' he said eventually. 'Too much risk for me, and too much of it hinges on an unlikely victory.'

'It's better than nothing, and it's all we can do,' replied Epona.

Kaeto sighed, and tugged at the end of his beard. 'Even if I believed you could retake the castle, I do not think I can wait that long. My friend is being torn apart, piece by piece.'

There was a soft chime from Caliburn. Epona watched with some satisfaction as the Envoy narrowed his eyes, clearly trying to guess the source of the noise.

'Caliburn says that the ancestors are on our side. The bones of Brittletain will rise up in defence of the land,' said Jack. Epona glanced at the woman, remembering what she had told her: that the Arch-Druin Merriden had been at her birth; that he had told her parents that Jack would one day kill the Green Man. She supposed she should expect stuff like this from her.

'And who, exactly, is Caliburn?' Kaeto's voice had the weary tone of someone who had just about had their fill of unexplained things.

Epona grinned. 'That is Jack's sword. It's magical.'

'Of course you have singing swords in Brittletain.'

'Listen.' She took a step towards the Envoy, resisting the urge to grab his arm. *I must not appear desperate.* 'When we have my mother back, we will be so much stronger. When people know that Queen Broudicca is alive, they will flock here, ready to take up arms themselves – even those from other kingdoms will come. They don't trust me, not fully, because my sister is a scheming idiot, but my mother? She's a symbol. The queen who will not fall. Do you not see? She is the rallying point for all of us. She is the legendary queen who marched down from the north to take the greatest city in Brittletain when she was hardly more than a child herself. When we have her back, when we have our army, we can retake the castle. You will be free to do what you want then, with your two flying companions. Sorry, I mean one flying companion and a one-winged wonder.' She took a breath, aware she was letting her nerves get the better of her. 'So. Do we have a deal, Envoy? You'll be our man on the inside, and we'll see that you and your companions make it out alive.'

There was a silence. Epona stood very still, her chin up and her gaze steady. He was weighing up his options. She found she could not guess which way he would go. If he said no, and tried to walk away, she wasn't sure what she might do. Could they take the Envoy prisoner? Would Icaraine care enough to swap him for her mother?

She already knew the answer to that: human lives were worthless to Icaraine.

'I told you that the key to Icaraine is her child, Malakim,' Envoy Kaeto said eventually. He had lowered his voice to a murmur, and Epona had to lean in to hear him. 'And I have access to him, or at least, my associate does. I propose that you take him out of the castle, and hide him.'

Caliburn chimed again, louder this time.

'You have to keep that thing quiet,' she hissed at Jack. 'If we're found here...'

'The sword says that to kill a child, any child, is an act unworthy of any warrior.'

'Magog's balls, Jack, no one is saying we kill the kid!' Epona pushed her hair out of her face. In reality, it had been the first thing she'd thought of when Kaeto had mentioned him. 'We swap him, right?' She looked at Kaeto. 'If they give us my mother, we give him back.'

He nodded. 'Do not bring Malakim to the exchange. Be sure to secure your mother first – have her brought somewhere she can escape swiftly. If Broudicca is not away before Icaraine spies her son, she will certainly kill your mother, and all of you. I feel I should tell you: there is a good chance she will kill you anyway for the brazenness of the plan alone. It is incredibly risky.'

'But it's all we've got, right?'

For the first time, Envoy Kaeto flashed a smile. It was rare and desperate, but it made her feel better. They were choosing to trust each other, and as fragile as that felt, it felt like *something*.

'How will you get a message to Icaraine?' asked Kaeto. 'It cannot be me, or my associate. I am willing to work with you, Princess Epona, but I will not put her or myself in direct danger. If Icaraine even suspects that we are involved...'

'Oh, don't worry,' said Epona, thinking of Karayné-bog's spear-throwing contraption. 'We'll come up with a way of letting her know.'

# 37

'What are you not telling me?'

Inkwort had fallen silent. When Cillian tried to question her, the little bird flew out of reach, into the upper branches of a towering oak. In front of him, his mother was still staring at the man on the far side of the pond, her eyes wide, lips slightly parted. She put him in mind of a prey animal caught under the moonlit gaze of an owl. The man had not spotted her yet. He was naked, crouched by the pond, taking handfuls of water and rubbing them over himself, across his shining tan skin and through his dark wavy hair. Even from the far side of the pond Cillian could see that his eyes were green; the deep, lustrous green of emeralds.

He opened his mouth to ask who it was, but he realised he already knew. The man shone with a vitality that wasn't human. As Cillian watched, he saw leaves unfurling in his hair, leaves of every shade of green. Where his feet had been, fresh grass was sprouting.

*The Green Man can make himself look human, then,* he thought.

Braela stepped out of cover, moving nearly silently, but the Green Man heard. His head snapped up, his movements more like those of a startled deer than a man. Antlers sprouted from his head, spreading wide and curling over at their tips. It was a warning, Cillian realised, but his mother took no notice. She stumbled down out of the wood to the edge of the pond, moving like a woman in a dream.

'Who are you?' she said. 'I must know.'

The Green Man straightened up. He was taller than a human man by perhaps two feet, and even taller with the antlers. As Cillian watched, his body moved and changed again, growing a covering of short, dun-coloured hair. Then he was a stag, already turning and leaping away into the darker part of the wood.

Braela did not hesitate. She flung herself after him, splashing through the shallowest part of the pond so that her long coat was dipped in duckweed. Already the Green Man had vanished from sight, but she fled after him as though pixen were nipping at her ankles. Inkwort flew in pursuit and after a second's hesitation Cillian ran too, moving through the wood as a Druin does – swiftly and quietly. He managed to keep Braela in sight even as she ran like a woman possessed. When eventually she stopped and he caught up with her, he saw that her face was marked with fine scratches from the brambles she had crashed through, and her coat was torn. She was breathing heavily, her eyes wild.

'Where did he go?'

Cillian blinked, and they were back at the pond. It was a different day – the light had changed, filtering through the trees in a dappled haze, and his mother had ditched the long coat, her hair unbound across her shoulders. She was standing by the edge of the water, a dreamy look on her face that Cillian recognised from the kitchen. When the Green Man appeared again, she shook all over like a horse. On this day, he was a much wilder thing. The taught muscles of his flesh were formed from reed and stick and stem, the sinews rippling as he moved, and his hair and beard were grass and leaves. His eyes, though, were human eyes, and they still shone with an inner light, like the sun through a cobweb.

'Who are you?' she asked. 'What are you?'

To Cillian's surprise, the Green Man didn't immediately flee. 'You live in these woods, girl, and you do not know me?'

Instead of answering, Braela took a step forward, and that time the Green Man did break away, startling like a flock of birds – and that was what he became, a sudden chaos of crows, sooty wings pelting through the trees. But they did not escape into the sky as birds would, and again Cillian's mother ran after the being that was the Green Man. This time, Cillian noted as she ran past, she was laughing – the high giddy laugh of a child playing a delightful game.

Another blink, another day. Cillian took a deep breath; he was starting to feel dizzy. Inkwort had reappeared by his boot, pecking meaningfully at the dirt. The forest itself had changed. The spring foliage had taken on a deeper, more summery green. Those trees that had already blossomed had shaken away the blooms, leaving a fine snow of pink and white on the ground.

'She came every day for a month,' said Inkwort. 'Always she would chase him, and always he would get away.' The little bird puffed out her chest. 'You'll notice he always came back, too.'

'Why?'

The jackdaw gave a little *tcha* of exasperation. 'I would say you'll understand when you're older, but I know full well that you know something about these complexities. Why didn't you leave Leven to her fate when she was shot with an arrow? Why did you follow her into the northern wood when you escaped from Queen Ceni? Why did you show her the Caul of the Stars that night?'

'Ah.' Cillian smiled a little, remembering those things. 'I take your point.'

His mother was at the edge of the pond again. Her hair was wild and she was grinning in anticipation of the chase. The Green Man, when he appeared, looked human again; he was even wearing clothes this time, simple brown leathers and a cotton tunic. He had a golden torc around his neck, and a pair of twin goat horns – very like Cillian's – curled up from his temples.

'Braela,' he said. 'I might let you catch me today.'

She laughed, and they were off. Cillian ran after them again, although they didn't get far this time. When they reached a swift-running stream, the Green Man leapt over it, and as he did so he changed, becoming a fleet black wolf with burning green eyes. He turned in the mud to face the girl, and Braela skidded to a halt. Cillian could feel her uncertainty and her fear. She had grown up on the edges of the Wild Wood; she would know stories of people who had been caught by wolves, would have seen livestock that had been savaged by them. And the Green Man was a vast wolf, a healthy creature with a thick black coat and sharp, sharp teeth, standing almost as tall as a horse. His claws dug into the mud as he grinned, showing all those lethal teeth.

'Well, Braela.' His voice was a deep rumble. 'Are you brave enough to claim your prize?'

For a long moment, she stood on the far side of the stream, trembling slightly like a leaf in the wind. Cillian wondered if she might break and run; if even after a month of pursuing him, the Green Man's newest form was simply too alarming. But then she took a step forward, one bare foot disappearing into the water, which must have been icy, and then another. The background noise of the forest grew louder, birds calling frantically to each other, foxes screeching – even the tiny frogs that lived in the mud raised their voices, whether in celebration or warning, Cillian couldn't tell. When she got to the far side of the bank, Braela was shivering – with cold, he guessed, but also fright – and the hand that reached out for the wolf was unsteady. Still, it found the ruff of fur around the animal's neck and sunk into it. The wolf lowered its head, its muzzle pressed against the young woman's shoulder. Here was the most dangerous time: Braela was close enough that the wolf need only turn his head to tear out her throat. She was within the circle of those lethal jaws, but he did not bite her. As Cillian watched, her arms reached around the wolf's neck, and she pressed her face into his fur.

'Come now, child,' Inkwort landed on Cillian's shoulder, a barely perceptible weight. 'There are some things you should not see.'

'What do you mean?'

Braela leaned back to look into the wolf's eyes, and the Green Man changed again, taking on his human form. He took her hand, placing it around his wrist.

'You have me,' he said, 'now what will you do with me?'

A number of things that Cillian had been vaguely aware of but trying to ignore fell into place: the colour of his eyes, his connection to the Wild Wood, the animals that came to watch him as a child. The reason why, of all the Druin under the Druidahnon's command, he had to be the one to take on the mantle of the Green Man.

He thought about what Leven was going to say.

'Magog's balls.'

# 38

*Those yenlin that survive to be yostra are to be given their own nest-pits, so they may begin their adult lives with a safe place to roost. It is right and good that the griffins that hatched them help to build this new nest-pit, whether that is with the skill of beak, or by simply providing the griffin-spit.*

The Griffin Creed, as written on the<br>Silver Death Peak by Fionovar the Red

Flayn took them to an alcove off of the main chamber, and they followed him down a short tunnel. The smell of griffin-spit was strong here; Ynis wondered how new the war-nest was. The tunnel ended in a chamber with rounded walls that met the polished surface of the mountain. There was a wide opening facing out across the valley, through which gusts of cold air blew, bringing the hard, bitter scent of mountain snow. On the floor were more clay tablets that had been etched by talon and beak and claw. It was not a cosy room. Ynis had almost forgotten what it was like to be in a place that did not cater to humans.

'When will T'vor be back?' asked T'rook. Here, alone with their father, she sounded young again, close to the petulant hatchling Ynis remembered from the nest-pit. 'When can we see him?'

'I don't know, little one,' said Flayn. He settled on the floor, and the two of them curled up next to the great bulk of his flank, as they had done when they were yenlin. 'He has been gone for two days, but patrols sometimes last five, even six. They hunt the Othanim. I could try and get a message to him, but they might be chasing their prey into Brittletain.' He sounded worried. He looked thinner than Ynis remembered. Beneath the warm brown fur of his side, she could feel the faintest push of his ribcage. 'It is dangerous.'

'T'oro said that the Othanim that come so far north are just scouts,' said Ynis.

'That little crevice-licker is right. The Othanim come in small groups, and they are just scouts, but they remain dangerous.' He sighed, the rise and fall of his chest like a wave lifting them both. 'The queen tells us that the war effort is going well, that we are decimating our ancient enemy just as our ancestor griffins did, but I fear she is covering a goat turd in honey. Though the Othanim that fly here are scouts, they are still very good at killing us. A great many griffins that go out on patrol do not return.'

Ynis exchanged a look with T'rook. *Is T'vor safe?*

'But enough of that for now. I'm sure Queen Fellvyn will want any information you might have, but I want it first. Tell me, my forvyn, where have you been? And what brings you back to us?'

It took some telling. Ynis began, falteringly, to tell of their flight north after their banishment, how the Edge Walker Brocken had found them and taken them to the Bone Fall. T'rook added her own commentary, mainly concerning the 'weirdness' of the Edge Walkers and how she had wisely spent her time hunting. They both spoke of the Imperium creatures that had arrived on the northernmost part of that landscape, how they had attacked the Edge Walkers with arrows, and how Ynis had earned a new name and title – Witch-seer Arrow. Here, Flayn insisted on more detail, his voice hoarse with wonder, and Ynis felt a strange, tight sensation in her chest: pride. T'rook spoke of her capture by the Heralds, for the first time stumbling over her words, and Ynis felt her pride shrivel up in the face of her sister's pain. *So much we have suffered*, she thought, *and now we are finally home again, we are at war.*

When she spoke of her human sister and her past in the Wild Wood of Brittletain – as brief as it was – Flayn pressed his beak to her temple, the cold smoothness of it a comfort.

'Finally, an answer to those questions,' he said. 'I told T'vor you would tell us the truth of it all one day, and I was right.'

The final part of their story they told together, although Ynis quickly moved over Leven's anger, and the way they had parted. *He doesn't need to know about her, not really*, she told herself. *Leven is only my blood sister. She has no yost.*

'Wings,' said Flayn wonderingly. 'Who would have thought? Later, we must all fly together, Ynis. I am so glad you have returned. There may be some awkward questions from our queen concerning your exile, and that ground-stuck little rat T'oro will peck away at it like a maggot at a festering wound, but I suspect it will all come to nothing. We are not so strong here that we can turn away griffins who can fight, and I think it's fair to say that Queen Fellvyn listens to me. I have made myself very useful to her over the last two years, and despite all her bluster, she trusts me.'

'You were always clever,' said T'rook fiercely. 'She *should* listen to you.'

'Thank you, little one,' said Flayn. T'rook buried her head in her father's feathers.

'What do the Othanim want?' asked Ynis. 'I'd never even heard of Titans like these, and Leven...' She faltered a little, speaking of her human sister. 'Leven hadn't either, and she lived in the Imperium, where they have whole buildings full of scrolls and books.'

'You never spoke of them, Father,' said T'rook, getting straight to the point.

Flayn stretched out his front legs, flexing the claws in his huge paws. 'Hmm. They were a dark part of our history, one I suspect we all thought never needed to be mentioned again.'

'Do you know? What it is they want, I mean? Who are they?'

'When all the Titan races still lived, oh, over two thousand years ago now, there were so many more of us. Griffins existed in pockets all over Enonah – always in high places, mountains and valleys at the top of the world. The unicorns stayed near their precious volcanoes, and the bears and the god-boars and the giants, they lived in the forests, and the kraken in the deepest part of the sea.' Ynis blinked slowly. Tiredness had come upon her like a wave, summoned by the warmth of her father's flank and the soft rumble of his voice – so dear to her, so familiar. She was safe, here, in this moment. 'The firebirds haunted the distant deserts – they didn't like to talk to other Titans, so we did not hear from them often. So the histories told us. And the Othanim...' He sighed. 'They lived in a place of deep jungles, populated with flying, buzzing things, where it was always hot, and water hung in the air like a veil. There were no mountains. We did not like it. But even so, our paths would sometimes cross. Often it ended badly. They reminded us too closely of humans.' He paused to turn his head so that he could run his beak through Ynis's hair. 'I am sorry, Ynis. And we, I think, were better suited to our wings, and more skilled in the air, which offended them.'

*Because a human body is not meant to fly*, Ynis thought. Absently her hand touched the place on her arm where the Titan-ore lozenge was buried.

'It was well known that there was no love lost between the Othanim and us, but it did not truly matter – the bears were none too fond of the god-boar either, and the unicorns hated everyone for being less beautiful than them. Then, a new queen was born among the Othanim – earlier than expected, before the reigning queen had come to the final portion of her life. It caused a civil war among them, which I'm sad to say we ignored at the time. Othanim business, we thought. It pains me to think that if we had intervened, if we had stood with the old queen against Icaraine...' He trailed off. 'I suppose that is another thing that doesn't matter. This new queen won the civil war. Too late, news reached us that she didn't just dislike griffins. She hated us. She wanted us torn from the skies – and more than that, she wanted all the other Titans gone too. We heard she had a great weapon, something that could end us all, and then we heard that it was her child, a mutant prince. The bears – always the most diplomatic of us– sent an envoy to speak with the Othanim in their hot, green country. He did not stay long in the Black City, but before he left, he did get an idea of what this child could do.'

'What was it?' asked Ynis, yawning. 'What could the child do?'

'It had control over Titan bones,' said Flayn. 'And when this creature ate, that is what it ate. Our bones.'

Ynis sat up, all sleepiness falling away from her like a blanket from her shoulders. She was thinking of how the Imperium had taken and butchered Brocken's body.

Flayn continued, caught up in his own story. 'Icaraine was not subtle. She said that she intended to feed her child, feed him every last bone of every last Titan, if that was what he needed. And she intended to start with the bears' diplomat. He fled, only just escaping with his life. From there, we went to war. It was a long and terrible conflict. It left us decimated – the bears especially. But in the end, we wore them down, and threw them into the dark space underneath their city. That should have been an end to it. Generations of griffins believed it to be so. And yet, here we are again. This time, the Othanim have come to Brittletain.'

'What will happen?' asked T'rook. 'Now that there are no other Titans but us, how will we fight?'

'Your father T'vor would say, "as griffins have always fought: in the sky, with talon and claw", or something rousing like that. I think, and have been advising Queen Fellvyn as such, that we need to find some other way. Our numbers are too low. The Othanim seem half crazed...' He trailed off again, then shook his shoulders a little, as if throwing off a chill. 'But never mind all that now. My yenlin are home. That is all that matters.'

Ynis smiled. It was good to be home. But her mind was filled with new worries: what would happen when the full force of the Othanim army arrived in the north, and would their fathers be caught up in it? And what could her role be, in a place where winged humans were an ancient enemy? She looked up and caught T'rook's eye.

'We will stay and fight,' said T'rook. 'This is where we belong, after all, sister.'

# 39

*Birds are known to move through worlds, living and dead, as easily as flying through the clouds, but jackdaws especially are said to have a close relationship with the ghost-ways. It has even been suggested that they contain the lost spirits of men and women who died young, with stories left to tell.*

*So if you're going to move those nests from the eastern atrium, I suggest you do it very carefully. Jackdaws know more than they should.*

A note from Elder Druin Jathinos,<br>Dosraiche's Master of Histories

'It makes no real difference.'

They had walked out of the dream of the past. Cillian found himself at the ruin again, his back against the old stones. He stood up and stretched, lifting his hands up to the sky. Inkwort strutted around on the dirt in front of him.

'What do you mean, it makes no difference? The Green Man is your father, child. It makes all the difference in the world.'

Cillian shook his head. 'I'm not him, and I never will be. Why should I give up who I am because of who my mother... slept with?'

'It is your birthright!'

'It is extortion, of a kind. You and the Druidahnon should

be ashamed.' But even as he said it, he knew it wasn't true. The Druidahnon had asked him out of desperation. The old bear had died to summon the Green Man.

In front of him, Inkwort was hopping around in agitation. 'Fine,' she said. 'I have one more thing to show you, and then I have done all I can to convince you. Will you follow me?'

'I will,' said Cillian. He sighed. 'But then I want you to take me back to Leven. I should never have left her in the first place.'

Instead of replying, Inkwort hopped into the air and opened a Path opposite the ruin. Cillian followed her through it, walking through a part of the Wild Wood where there were still crowds of bluebells on the ground, their soft mauve haze like a low-lying fog. The bird led him down a short slope, and to his surprise he spied Leven, lying on the ground next to a small campfire. She was curled in on herself, her eyes squeezed shut. She was shivering faintly.

'Leven?' He glanced back at Inkwort. 'I thought you had something else to show me.'

'I do,' said Inkwort. 'And this is she. Have you forgotten what her fate is, Cillianos? Right now, she is asleep, dreaming violent dreams of the Titans whose bones grace her skin. Her own memories are being obliterated as theirs return. Soon, she will not know who she is, or who you are. She will know only the deep salt of the krakens, or the fury of the unicorns. The only thing that will save her from madness is death, and that follows close on her heels too. You know this. Will you not save her from it?'

In her sleep, Leven cried out, the sound of a child lost in the dark. It hurt his heart to look at her.

In the end, there was no choice. If there was even a chance of helping her, he had to take it.

'Time is running out,' Inkwort continued. 'The Druidahnon's magic will only last so long. Eventually the Green Man will return to the Wildest Wood. He will not be so easily woken again. If we are to—'

'Enough,' he said. 'I will do it. Take me where I need to go.'

---

Cillian stood in front of a vast lake, its surface like a polished mirror. Beyond it, he could see craggy green hills, covered in grass and gorse. On one of the hills there was a white horse. He could smell blood on the wind, sharp and metallic. Overhead, the sky was in constant movement, a boiling maelstrom of clouds that could not settle. Inkwort had guided him here, then vanished.

'Hello? Is anyone there?'

He walked to the edge of the lake and peered into the water. Up close, it was a deep dark green, the sandy bottom quickly vanishing into shadow. At first, he just saw his own reflection – curling horns, green eyes, dark eyebrows – and then another face shimmered over the top of it. Startled, Cillian drew back as the Green Man climbed out of the water. He was as large as the Druidahnon, if not larger. His dark brown hair fell down his back like a mane, and from his forehead the wide antlers of a stag spread like the hands of a giant. His eyes were the green of moss, and the colour went from lid to lid. He was bearded, and handsome, and smiling.

'There you are,' he said.

The world shivered around him. Cillian sensed the grass and trees, and every living thing, reaching out towards the Green Man. When he glanced up, he saw that even the clouds had converged above their meeting place. Fear gripped him.

'*There* you are,' the Green Man said again. Without obviously changing, he was suddenly human-sized, and he swept Cillian into a hug, half lifting him off the ground. There was strength in the man's arms like a dangerous rip tide, one that could crush him at any moment. 'I could hardly wait to lay eyes on you, boy. My boy.' The Green Man let him go, grinning. He had sharp canines, like a wolf. 'The things we will do, you and I. We'll run these interlopers out of the Wild Wood. We'll split their skulls and eat their brains, we'll let their blood run into the good earth and feed the trees. We'll grind up their bones, boy, and make pottage.'

Cillian swallowed. There was a great heat coming off the man, as though he burned with an unquenchable fever.

'Can you not do that yourself? Why do you need me at all? Why do you need my body?'

'Do it myself? And where is the fun in that?' He clapped Cillian on the back heartily. 'No, I jest. The mortal world, Cillianos, is not somewhere I can exist easily – I am too wild even for the Wild Wood. You will help temper me, turn my steel to a cutting edge, lest my power turn everything to green.' He stopped, and grinned. 'Which would be, in my opinion, no bad end for this isle. But the time for that is a long distance from here. We have enemies to kill and eat and make into new things. Let us begin, boy.'

He reached for Cillian, but he took a step backwards, his heart hammering in his chest.

'Wait. My wife, Leven, is dying, and I want to save her. Can you do that? Can *we* do that? It's the only thing I ask.'

'You have a mate!' The Green Man sounded ecstatic. 'You have given her children, yes? How many?' He stopped to bellow with laughter. 'A dozen girls and boys, all with the wild green in their blood. There could be nothing better!'

'No,' Cillian said quickly. 'We've had no children. She can't. And that's not the point anyway. All I want is her life, in exchange for mine. Do you understand?'

The Green Man tipped his head to one side. In the turbulent sky above them, a flock of starlings came together and moved in an organic wave, as though riding the clouds. Cillian found he could not interpret the expression on his father's face, and it occurred to him that there was nothing human about him, not really. He reached out with his thrawn senses, trying to feel for the aura of warmth that was a part of every living thing, and felt only that tremendous heat, much too hot to get close to. He drew back, singed.

'Very well, Cillianos,' the Green Man said eventually. 'We will do all we can to save your Leven.'

Cillian nodded. This time when the Green Man came forward, he did not pull away. His father took his face in his large, calloused hands, brushing the pads of his thumbs under Cillian's eyes. He appeared to be looking for something in them.

'Ah now,' he said eventually. 'There it is. That thread of green. You can't hide it from me.'

He pushed, his thumbs sinking into Cillian's cheeks, hard enough to hurt. Cillian grunted and grabbed the man's forearms, but it was like trying to move a tree.

'Wait,' Cillian pushed the word through his lips like it was covered in barbs. 'I'm not... What are you doing?'

'There you are,' said the Green Man, taking no notice. 'Join me now, son.'

He let go. Cillian pitched forward onto his knees, his head throbbing, and then something surged up the back of his throat, something hard and fibrous and *strong*. He opened his mouth and vines poured out, spewing forward onto the ground in a torrent, a waterfall of leaves and stems and branches. He clutched at his throat and tried to speak, but couldn't.

'My son,' said the Green Man faintly. Through Cillian's watering eyes he looked even less human, a great horned figure of seething darkness, his eyes like marsh lights in a forgotten part of the forest. 'I cannot wait to walk in the mortal realm again, boy. I will use your body well, believe me.'

Cillian made a choking noise and fell sideways into the grass. He was aware of vines streaming from his nostrils and his ears, and behind his eyes he felt a terrible, agonising pressure. Alongside the green he could taste his own blood, and his lungs were burning with the need to breathe. Dark spots blossomed in his vision, growing and blotting out the daylight, his father's shape.

*I am dying*, he thought. *Leven, forgive me.*

# PART THREE

IN WHICH A HUNGER GROWS

# 40

Belise crouched on the edge of the castle wall, watching the steady progress of a fat beetle along a branch. Next to her she had a glass jar, already prepared with leaves and twigs. It would be the work of moments to catch the tiny beast. Over the last few days, she'd caught countless insects for Malakim, but she still struggled with the beetles. When she looked at them she remembered the Undertomb: a rushing sound like the sea, and thousands of tiny legs, skittering, skittering. She frowned.

'Belise? Are you up there?'

Kaeto emerged from the overgrown bushes and stood at the roots of the elm tree, looking up at her. He looked tense, the skin under his eyes drawn tight.

'I'm here, chief.'

She jumped down from the wall, letting her wings slow her descent until she landed neatly in front of him.

'How is he?'

Kaeto turned away from her slightly, only the tiny crease at the corner of his mouth any indication of the pain he was in. Belise knew that the old assassin loved Felldir, had known it for a year or more, but she could not get him to admit it. And here, in this arse-end of an island, he was being made to suffer for that love.

'He is healing well,' he said eventually. 'Titans are remarkably hard to injure, and heal quickly.' He glanced back at her. 'A fact that should cheer you, I suppose. All of his surface injuries are dealt with. It's only his wing that...' He cleared his throat. 'He won't fly again. But the wound is no longer infected, and it shouldn't give him trouble in the future. If he has one. Icaraine has been asking for him back with increased frequency, and I cannot hold her off much longer. Sooner or later, she will send her creatures to come and drag him from the room.'

Belise nodded. The queen of the Othanim was relentless. There was no way she would give up her favourite toy – she had simply paused to let it be repaired.

'We don't have much time,' he continued. 'Not if we want to leave this place with Felldir.' He paused, and she sensed his reluctance.

'So it's happening tonight?'

He nodded. Belise felt her heart sink, just a little. As if he could tell what she was thinking, he looked at her askance.

'You have reservations.'

'I'm playing a long game here, chief, and I've made progress.' She glanced along the overgrown path, and then at the sky. It was early morning, and the castle gardens were quiet. The human servants were busy getting ready for another day of misery, and the Othanim did not rise early. Belise had seen them, crowded into the rooms of the castle; they slept in big groups, their bodies pressed close, like weasels in a burrow. It made her uneasy. Luckily for her, she had been allowed to sleep in the tiny servant's quarters that adjoined Malakim's chamber. 'The boy trusts me, and that's half the war won, right? This plan of Epona's, it's bloody risky. It's like dropping an anchor in a pond—'

'What an interesting metaphor.'

'Everything going on under the surface is going to get pulverised. What if the kid doesn't trust me after this?'

'If all goes according to plan, Belise, we may not need him to. With Broudicca free, the armies of Brittletain will rally to Londus's aid. They can retake the city. Then, you and I and Felldir will escape, either when Epona has expelled the Othanim or during the chaos, I do not care which.'

Belise tipped her head to one side slightly, a gesture from the old days. 'Do you really believe that's going to happen, master? That all of Brittletain will rise up because they got some old woman out of the dungeons?'

'I don't believe Queen Broudicca is that old,' he said. Then, 'I think there's a chance. Admittedly, it's not a good chance. But Felldir's injury has changed things. What I do believe is that Epona is an honourable person, and she says the rebels will help us.'

'There's the Heralds to think about too,' said Belise. 'They're not going to just let us wander off.'

'When the rebels come, I will instruct the Heralds to fight alongside the Othanim for the sake of our *alliance*.' The word dripped with scorn. 'While they are busy, we will do what we can to get out of this place.'

Belise raised her eyebrows. 'The Heralds will massacre the rebels.'

'They will,' said Kaeto. For a long moment neither of them said anything. A host of small birds chirped from the tree by the wall. Absently, Belise wondered if they had snapped up the beetle she was after. 'Will you do it?' Kaeto asked eventually. 'Quite aside from losing the boy's trust, it could put you in direct danger. We've taken care to distance you from what's going to happen, but you are still the person Icaraine has deemed responsible for Malakim's wellbeing.'

This was interesting. In the past, there would only have been orders and instructions. These days, since their mission to the Black City, he had been treating her differently; like she was a fragile pitcher of glass that needed to be handled carefully. Once upon a time, this would have annoyed her to a significant degree, and she still felt a flicker of amusement when he behaved this way, but more and more she was aware of a change inside herself, too. When he had visited them on the ship, she'd witnessed the fear it had caused him, seeing her and Felldir in chains. It had made her want to hurt someone. Many someones, probably. She also knew that if she told him now that she did not want to go through with the plan, then he would accept it. He wouldn't even be angry with her.

'They've got hold of what they need, then?' she asked, a way to delay her answer a little longer. 'They're ready?'

'Apparently so. They are desperate enough that I believe if we asked them to source the empress's pity, they'd be able to find it.'

Normally Belise would have savoured a mild jab at the empress from Kaeto, but the weight of what they were doing meant the smile died on her lips.

'I'm impressed,' she said. 'It's a shame I won't be there to see this Druin magic in action.'

'It's extremely important that you are *not* there,' Kaeto reminded her needlessly. '*If* we go ahead with it.'

'And you've got the stuff for the diversion?'

'I have,' said Kaeto, raising an eyebrow. 'It's basic enough, and it'll be little more than a bit of light and noise, but luckily that's exactly what we need.'

'Fuck it then, let's do it,' she said. 'I hope the rebels really are ready for what's gonna happen. That big bitch is going to be furious.'

---

The first step was to take the child for a walk.

This part was easy enough. Malakim and Belise had settled into a routine that often included a walk around the castle or its grounds, usually with a couple of glass jars in hand in case they found anything interesting, and thanks to the child's peculiar rhythms, these walks could happen at any time, day or night. A late-night walk was nothing to be remarked upon. She let him lead the way mostly, until it drew closer to the time when

Kaeto would be putting the next part of the plan into action. She began shepherding Malakim towards the danker, less populated end of the castle, and the warren of corridors that led down into the dungeons.

'We've not looked around here before, have we, my prince?'

Malakim shook his head. His hands were clasped tightly around his jar, and his eyes – all six of them – were intent on the stony floor ahead of them.

'It seems to me that dark and damp places must have some interesting things for us to see. Look at those cobwebs! It looks like no one's been down here for years.'

Except that clearly wasn't true. As they passed through the heavy wooden doors that separated the dungeons from the rest of the castle, they walked under a freshly lit oil lamp. Ahead of them, Belise spied an Othanim guard, leaning against the wall. He looked up as they approached, bright eyes narrowing with suspicion, and she realised she recognised him. This was Mikeal, who had initially been tasked with caring for Malakim before vanishing from duty. On the one hand, she was surprised he was still alive after so obviously snubbing the prince. On the other, it was quite a piece of luck. After all, Mikeal had already demonstrated his negligence. Belise smiled at him.

'What are you doing down here?' snapped Mikeal. His eyes flickered to Malakim, distaste evident in every line of his face.

'Our prince is exploring,' said Belise smoothly enough.

'Is that what it is? A prince?'

This new voice came from a door off to their left. It was the single occupied cell in the castle, and as Belise watched an arm slipped through the narrow barred window. It beckoned to them.

'Come closer,' said Queen Broudicca. 'Let me get a look at the little maggot. Does he not even have wings?'

Malakim took a step back, pressing himself against Belise's legs as he had once done with Icaraine.

'You will speak with more respect, or Prince Malakim won't be the only one missing some limbs.' Belise put as much ice as she could into her voice, but Broudicca just chuckled. She had her face against the bars now too, and Belise could see the lined skin of an older woman, a pair of bright blue eyes that observed all too keenly. *She could probably have been an Envoy*, thought Belise. *She's sharp enough.*

'What's going on up there?' asked Broudicca. 'This long streak of piss won't give me any news.'

Belise turned away from the queen of Londus, one hand gently on Malakim's shoulder. From somewhere down the corridor, a faint hum had started, like lots of people talking loudly in a distant room. Mikeal frowned.

'What is that?'

'You could at least tell me what has become of my daughters?' continued Broudicca. 'I know that Epona got out, along with Lanoshea, Ennua and Eefa. The explosion from a few doors down was enough to rattle my teeth. Has there been any news of them? I know that Ceni, Green Man curse her, is spending her hours crawling up Icaraine's arsehole, for all the good it'll do her – she always was willing to do whatever it took to claw some power to herself. Bronvica is doing her best, no doubt. But what of Togi?'

It occurred to Belise that Broudicca was just talking for the sake of talking, that she'd been down here for two years in a tiny cell while her kingdom was torn to pieces. It was remarkable that she was up and talking at all. Belise had seen what happened to prisoners kept in the bowels of Stratum. It wasn't pretty.

Meanwhile, the hum had grown louder. It was really more of a buzz.

Suddenly, from somewhere above them, there was a bang and a crump, the sound of objects falling over. A flurry of shouts.

'Ho ho, are the rebels at it again?' said Broudicca. 'It would really brighten my day to see you all strung up by your wings. Tied up and thrown in the Old Father perhaps...'

'What was that?' Belise pushed Malakim behind her, looking back the way they'd come. If anything, the explosion Kaeto had managed to engineer was bigger than she'd been expecting. Dust was floating down from the ceiling. Mikeal had stepped forward, his hand on the sword at his belt, but she gave him a sharp glance.

'No, you stay here. Look after the prince and keep an eye on the prisoner. If this is another rebel incursion, they are our priority. I will go and see what the trouble is and bring others back with me.'

'Who are you to order me around—'

But Belise was already going. As she left, passing back through the wooden doors, she heard Malakim speaking, although it was only when Mikeal asked him what he was talking about and he repeated himself that she made out the words.

'Wasps,' Malakim said. 'I think it's wasps. Making that buzz.'

# 41

*Arch-Druin Merriden made many prophecies throughout his long life, most of which, we suspect, were never recorded. The following are a few of those we have multiple sources for:*

*In Wehha, at the Mount of the Sacred Hare: 'The forsaken king will search all of the deadlands, but only when he accepts the help of a young griffin will he find the Tree of All Souls.' (note: could the 'tree of all souls' be the Dosraiche?)*

*During his hermitage on the sacred isle of Indisfarne: 'In a distant forest where the rain hangs in the air and the sun does not forgive, a seal will be broken that will bring slaughter to the Wild Wood.'*

*At a settlement in Mersia, where the great city of Wodencaester was eventually built: 'On this spot, there will be a soaring tower of white bone, and it will hold within itself great treachery and glory.'*

*On the banks of the Old Father, after ingesting an unwise amount of strong mead: 'The soul of a woman will find a home in a humble jackdaw, the better to guide her son, who is as wilful as his father! May the tiny gods of the Wild Wood protect them.'*

Note from a Druin archivist,
working on the Dosraiche records

Yelm was carrying the wasps' nest as though it might explode, which Epona supposed was fairly close to the truth.

It had been an uncomfortable journey through the underbelly of Londus. Her and Jack in the lead, carrying lamps they could cover if they should need to; Larth and another rebel Epona didn't recall the name of, carrying rope and other supplies, bringing up the rear – and Yelm in the middle, singing the wasps inside the nest into a state of hazy slumber. It wasn't a Druin skill that Epona was familiar with. Yelm had explained that 'singing the hive', as it was known, was fairly uncommon amongst the order, largely because it seemed a step too close to going thrawn. She wasn't commanding the insects, however – she was simply speaking to them in their language, the language of song. Wasps, bees and all creatures who lived for the hive longed to sing, and when another came along who knew their songs, they could be very amenable. So for now, at Yelm's suggestion, the wasps slumbered.

They were picking their way through the wreckage of their previous incursion this far under the castle. Last time, Karaynébog's black powder device had littered the tunnels with rocks and dust, threatening to bring the whole thing down on their heads. Epona still wasn't certain it would stay standing. Once her mother was back on the throne and the Othanim were expelled from Londus, they would need to shore up the dungeons anew. For now, they skirted around the larger pieces of rubble until they came to the place where they had originally broken through.

'It looks as though they patched it up, but not well enough,' whispered Jack. There was a hole, around a foot and a half across. Too small for them to get through, but cavernous for a wasp. And only a mild squeeze for a child.

'No surprises there. The Othanim have no interest in the castle itself. They are like wolves squatting in a summer house. Yelm, how are you doing?'

The Druin spared her a quick glance. She was humming and chanting quietly, words that Epona could not make out. She managed a nod before closing her eyes — Epona assumed it was easier to concentrate that way.

'Alright, so, hopefully everyone is in place.' Epona glanced up at the hole. There was a faint light coming from it, and she imagined a guttering candle, or an oil lamp, somewhere up above. Thanks to her sister Ceni, she had spent more time in the dungeons than she would have liked, and the damp scent that drifted down to them was all too familiar. 'We just have to wait—'

There was an explosion, loud enough to shake everything around them — *please don't fall*, Epona thought fiercely at the ceiling, *I've got enough on my plate* — and over the hum of the wasps they heard the faint sound of shouting and panic.

'That's it.' She nodded to Yelm, realised the woman still had her eyes shut, and put a hand gently on her arm instead. 'Send them up,' she said. 'It's time.'

Yelm lifted her chin, and the peaceful hum grew in pitch and volume. Wasps, shining black and gold in the dim light, began to stream out of the hole in the bottom of the nest and head up towards the fissure in the ceiling. They went through it in an orderly line, a sight so uncanny that Epona felt a wave of unreality move through her — for a handful of heartbeats she could almost believe she was dreaming, and that the Othanim invasion was just some nightmarish joke. Jack put her hand on her arm and the sensation stopped.

'Listen,' she whispered. 'There are voices above.'

She was right. Epona heard the high, piping tones of a child, followed by the deeper voice of an Othanim adult. Their voices were louder than humans, had a deeper resonance. It wasn't hard to tell them apart.

'There's a guard up there,' she said. 'Yelm, do what you can to get rid of him.'

Kaeto's Othanim friend Belise might also still be up there, but that wasn't Epona's problem.

Yelm nodded, her eyes still shut, and the song grew a little faster, a little more urgent. A crease appeared in the centre of the woman's forehead and the corners of her mouth turned down. From somewhere over their heads, the sound of the wasps grew louder, and angrier. There was a confused shout, followed by a few rapid footsteps. The child's voice spoke, clearer than it had been.

'They want to dance with you.'

The adult Othanim shrieked. The hum of the wasps was now a furious whine; it made the hair on the back of Epona's neck stand up.

'Attack,' murmured Yelm. 'Attack this invader. It threatens the hive.'

The buzz increased in volume again, and the Othanim began to scream. They heard his footsteps quite clearly as he ran away up the unseen corridor, followed by the crash of a heavy door being thrown open.

'This is it,' said Epona. Her throat felt almost too tight to speak. 'The kid is alone. We've got one chance to do this. Yelm, can you get the wasps back under control?'

The Druin's lips twitched. 'I can do it,' she said. 'Whether it will work or not is something else.'

Her song changed again, becoming softer and full of an eerie music. The whine from the wasps softened in response, turning back into a lazy hum, and as Epona watched she saw the first of them began to drift back in through the hole in the ceiling. They moved to and fro, as though they were dancing their way back to the nest. From above them, she heard a child's cry of delight, and small footsteps coming closer.

'Move back,' she hissed to the others. 'He won't come down here if he sees us. Get those ropes ready.'

Carefully Yelm placed the wasps' nest on the ground, angled so that the hole in the bottom was still accessible, and they all moved into the deeper shadows. Epona kept her eyes on the fissure in the ceiling. Every part of this plan was dubious, a jug with so many cracks it was practically a sieve, yet this was the biggest crack of all.

*If you're there, Green Man, I'd appreciate a chunk of luck right now. We certainly need it.*

A pale shape appeared in the hole, like a small moon moving across the night sky; the child's head, bulbous and strange. Six blood-red eyes glistened wetly at the dance of the wasps, and Epona's stomach turned over. She'd never seen Malakim up close before, and he was both smaller and weirder than she had been expecting; a reminder that, yes, they were kidnapping a child, but he was a child unlike any other. One hand holding a glass jar swung into view as he tried to capture a wasp, but the insects danced away easily enough. She heard him huff with frustration.

*Come on kid*, she thought furiously. *Time is running out.*

There was a dry scuffling as the child began to manoeuvre his way through the crack in the stone. She thought it likely that he had seen the wasps' nest lying in the dark and had decided to investigate further. A pair of skinny legs dangled from the hole, pinwheeling at nothing as he tried to lower himself down. Epona looked up to catch Jack's eye, but the other woman was already moving. Jack grasped the child by the legs and firmly yanked him down into the room below. He gave a squawk of outrage, but he did not wriggle and squirm in Jack's arms, and when Yelm and the other rebel approached with the rope, he just looked at them. Or at least, appeared to look at them. It was difficult to tell what he was doing with those crimson eyes.

'Get him secured,' said Epona. Now that they had him, she felt, if anything, more nervous. 'And put the gag on him too. We need to be as quiet as mice.'

The boy raised one hand, fingers splayed, as though about to strike the women binding him in place, but instead his hand shook a little, as though he were expending great effort on something.

His eyes narrowed, and despite his strangeness it was easy enough to read the disappointment there.

'We've just got normal ol' boring human bones, I'm afraid, your majesty.' Epona smiled slightly. 'Your tricks won't work on us.' She picked up the lamp and began to head back to the tunnels. 'Follow me. Quickly now. I strongly suspect the castle is about to get a lot livelier.'

## 42

'Listen, kid, we're taking the gag off now. No one can hear you down here, so don't get any ideas.'

It unnerved Epona to speak this way to a child – but then, the child himself was unnerving. Under the warm lights of the oil lamps, he looked even paler and stranger than he had in the broken dungeon. Six red eyes, like fat blobs of ink, marked a pale forehead, and he appeared oddly frail, with stick-like arms and legs, and a head that looked too heavy for his neck. He sat with that bulbous head hanging over his chest and his hands palm up on the tops of his legs. Every now and then, his fingers would wriggle. He was boy-shaped, alright, but something about him put her in mind of a worm or a grub. She fought against the grimace that was trying to settle on her face.

'We've got water, bread, some apples,' Jack was saying. 'If you're hungry, Malakim.'

The boy didn't appear to have heard her.

'Our friend told us the child eats Titan bones, and we definitely don't have any of those immediately to hand.' Epona sighed and looked around the cavernous space. They were in the cellars that ran underneath Londus's sprawling Wardstone Market. Once, this space had been used to store a whole variety of wares, from freshly butchered meat to fine silks. It had good thick stone walls and only two entrances, making it easy enough to guard with only a handful of people. Epona had no idea how much Icaraine knew about Londus – she guessed very little – but she thought it couldn't hurt to choose a location that even most citizens of Londus were unaware existed. It was chilly down here, and a little damp. She could smell the river, which made her wonder if the cellars were in need of shoring up.

Larth came down the steps with her arms full of blankets, which she dumped onto a makeshift cot they had set up in the nearest corner. Epona saw her look at the child, then away.

'Epona? Can I have a word.'

The two of them wandered away from the boy on the chair, and after a moment Jack joined them.

'What is it, Larth?' Epona realised she was on edge. She was half expecting Icaraine herself to kick down the door any moment.

'We should not give him back.'

Epona pulled her hand through her hair. It needed a wash.

'What? The whole point is the exchange, Larth. We need him to get my mother back.'

'Yes. He's the bait. I understand that.' In the stark lighting of the cellar, the black paint across the small woman's eyes looked like an absence, an eerie slash of nothing. 'What I am saying is, we get your mother back, and then we kill him. It. That creature is too dangerous to keep alive. The Envoy said it is the key to Icaraine's plans. What better way to disrupt them?'

Epona arranged her face into a shocked expression, as if the very same thought hadn't occurred to her, too.

'Larth, we can't do that. He's just a kid. No matter how weird he looks, or who his mother is. Right?'

'It would be a dishonourable act,' said Jack. 'We'd be disgracing ourselves. You can't seriously be suggesting it?'

'We are at war,' said Larth. 'Plenty of dishonourable things happen during wars.' She glanced back at the boy, frowning slightly. 'It's not human. It eats its own kind. What if by killing it now, we save hundreds of lives? Thousands of lives? You don't want to look back on this opportunity and curse yourself for not taking it, Epona.'

'No, we won't be doing that.' Epona felt a moment of relief at how easy it was to say. 'It's not part of the plan.'

'Your mother would do it,' said Larth in a low voice. 'All of Brittletain knows she is ruthless when it comes to taking power. Londus still bears the scars of her campaign against its last queen.'

Epona heard Jack take in a sharp breath.

'No, please, do tell me more of your opinions regarding my mother.' Epona turned to Larth, a sickly heat creeping across the back of her neck. 'I'd love to know what you think.'

'It's not an opinion, it's fact,' said Larth, shaking her head. She wasn't angry – in two years, Epona had never seen the woman get angry – but she did sound exasperated. 'Even in Dwffd we knew that Queen Broudicca was wily as an old cat and twice as cunning. For the sake of Londus, and Brittletain, would she get rid of that creature? Yes, in a heartbeat, and you know I am right.' She took half a step closer. 'Think how it would look to the rest of Brittletain, Epona. The other leaders still don't trust you. But they might, if you were willing to do what needs to be done.'

There was a ringing chime from Jack's scabbard.

'Caliburn says that no true queen would kill a child.'

'It's not a child!' Larth's voice rose a notch. 'And if you won't do it, lend me the blade. I've seen more than enough friends and family torn apart in the sky by those flying bastards.'

'That's enough,' said Epona. The brief boiling fury she'd felt a moment before had sizzled away into nothing again, leaving her drained and full of dismay. 'Listen, I don't want us snapping at each other like this. We're all on edge because of…' She nodded towards Malakim, who was still sitting on the chair, fingers twitching. 'That. The next part of the plan is incredibly dangerous. We need to focus and have each other's backs. Am I being clear enough for everyone? We're so close. We just need to keep it together for a bit longer.'

Larth was still frowning, but she nodded anyway. Jack crossed her arms over her chest and looked at the floor.

'Jack, you stay here with the boy for now. Get a message to the Barrow. I want a few more bodies here before we go and collect my mother.' She had intended to take Jack with her for the next part of the plan, but the idea of leaving Larth unsupervised with their prisoner seemed foolish. She saw the hurt look Jack shot her and shook it off. She had no time for it. 'Karayné-bog should be in position by now. I'll go and join him.'

'How will we know when the message has been sent?' asked Jack.

'Oh, I think we'll all know soon enough.'

---

Outside in the streets, Londus was quiet and dark, the first blush of dawn just beginning to brush the underside of the clouds. Epona crept out of the market cellar and straight into the darkest part of the shadows, keeping close to the walls and ducking under cover wherever possible. After two years of sneaking in and out of the city she was adept at moving around it without being seen. At one point there was a flicker of movement in the skies overhead, causing her to crouch and hold still, but it was only an early flock of starlings, moving sinuously over the rooftops. So close to the ground, Epona could see plants growing up through the flagstones; some of them were getting pretty big. A few more years with no humans to tend to the place, and Londus would be another part of the Wild Wood.

The castle was visible from most places in the city. As she made her way along alleyways and streets and roofs, she glanced at it periodically, her heart in her mouth. There was a smudge of dark smoke over the kitchens, the place where the Envoy had set his small explosion, and there was the suggestion of some movement there. That mystery was still holding the attention of the Othanim, but at some point, pretty soon, they were going to discover that

Icaraine's child was gone. It was possible things would spiral out of control quickly. She had to reach Karayné-bog by then.

When she did find him – perched with his spear contraption on a roof that ran parallel to the castle's highest point – he was asleep, or at least snoozing, his back resting against the wall and his beard spread out over his chest. She kicked his boot with some force and he startled, reaching for the knife at his belt.

'You idiot,' she hissed. 'What if I was some Othanim scout, huh? You'd be looking for your guts in your beard right now.'

'I was just resting my eyes,' he said. 'It's important to have rested eyes in this line of work.'

'I'll rest your eyes for you in a minute,' said Epona. She peeked over the lip of the wall. During her journey across the city, the sun had crested over the horizon, filling the city with a hazy golden light; it illuminated a low ground mist and turned the castle windows into rectangular gold coins. 'Any movement?'

'Nothing that I've seen so far,' he said, joining her at the wall. 'But it must be soon, mustn't it?' He glanced uneasily at the open sky above them. 'If we're waiting here all day...'

'Don't fuss, it'll be fine,' she said. 'Once the message is on its way we duck down the stairs immediately and get into the sewer.' There was a large piece of sacking on the roof with them, ready to be thrown over the spear-throwing contraption until they could retrieve it later.

'Have you got the message?'

Epona pulled the piece of parchment from within her tunic. She unrolled it for a moment to check again what she had written. They had all decided on it together, and it had taken longer than she had expected. It read:

*Greetings, Icaraine the Usurper. For the crimes you have committed against the isle of Brittletain we have taken your son. He will be released, unharmed, back into your care if you follow these instructions:*

*Release Queen Broudicca from the royal dungeon. Bring her to South Stone Harbour tonight, at sunset. Remove any bindings she might have, and then leave her unguarded at the statue of the horned queen. If any Othawim are in sight when we collect her, the boy will be killed and left in the street. Once we have recovered our queen, Malakim will be released to you the following morning. We will send further instructions when the first part of the exchange has been concluded.*

Karayné-bog took the parchment and tied it to the shaft of the waiting spear, making several strong knots and then testing each one. When it was done, he grunted.

'What do you call this thing, anyway? Do you have a good name for it?' Karayné-Bog seemed twitchy. She thought it was probably a good idea to try and take his mind off it. 'Are you going to name it after yourself? The Karayné-Spear Device, something like that.'

He patted the wooden flank of the machine fondly. 'I was thinking I might call it Agnes.'

'Agnes?' Epona snorted. 'You can't call it Agnes.'

'I've known a few good Agneses,' Karayné-Bog said wistfully. 'One very good one in particular.'

'Definitely do not tell me about that.' Epona peeked over the wall again. A small plume of white smoke was rising from the chimneys over the kitchens as the human slaves began their chores for the day.

'Aye, she was a goer, was Agnes,' said Karayné-bog. 'She ran a tavern on Frith Street for years, had a stuffed owl on the bar that she used to call Treacle, and if you got enough drinks in her she'd—'

There was an abrupt and terrifying scream, so loud that Epona instinctively ducked back behind the wall, her hands over her ears. It was a sound of absolute rage and horror, completely inhuman yet utterly recognisable. It went on and on. Epona felt herself shrinking against the wall, trying to make herself as small as possible, like a mouse hiding from a cat. She glanced at Karayné-bog and saw that he was doing the same, the whites of his eyes standing out starkly against his ruddy skin. The noise finally died, only to be replaced with a rising chorus of shouts and the clattering sound of lots of armoured people moving quickly. Still half rigid with fear, Epona peeked over the edge of the wall again, just in time to catch sight of the first wave of Othanim setting off. There had to be around fifty of them, rising up from the castle walls like a plague of locusts.

'It's time,' she hissed at Karayné-bog. For a second she thought she'd have to kick him again, but to his credit he scrambled to his feet and began pulling levers and winding cranks on Agnes. He lined the spear up, aiming it at the teeming crowd over the castle.

'There's no guarantee I'll hit any of them,' he said gruffly.

'It doesn't matter,' said Epona. 'A dead Othanim is just a bonus.'

He nodded once, realigned the spear, and yanked a final lever. With a sound like a big wooden door being kicked, the spear flew up into the air. Epona watched it go, watched it arch over the space between the castle and the roof. The biggest problem was the possibility it wouldn't make it over the wall, but it sailed up and over and smack into the leg of a rising Othanim. There was a high-pitched scream, blood in the air, and then Karayné-bog was yanking at her arm. He'd already covered Agnes with the sacking.

'Come on, Princess, we have to go. Now!'

Epona scrambled up and ran to the door, a step or so behind Karayné-bog. She hadn't seen where the Othanim had fallen but she guessed in the courtyard.

'Did it work? Did we get one?' Karayné-bog had been so intent on covering the contraption and getting away he hadn't watched where his spear had landed.

They were in the gloomy stairwell heading down into the basement. From there, they could head into the defunct sewer system and head back towards the market cellar.

'Yes. You got one of them, alright. Now we wait for this evening. We haven't even got to the hard part yet.'

*This evening*, she thought to herself, *I could see my mother again.*

# 43

*'You wouldn't believe half of what we found in that place. Envoy Kaeto's reports don't do it justice, although you get the sense he tried, you know? The Black City is safe now, for want of a better word, but the locals still won't go near it, and I have to say I don't blame them. If any place is haunted, it's that one. Too many beetles, too. Some of them the size of your head. I was glad to get home.'*

Transcription of a monitored conversation
between two Imperial alchemists sent to Houraki

Kaeto watched from the window, so tense that his back was beginning to ache. All morning and into the afternoon the castle had been in uproar. Icaraine had personally demolished part of the building when she'd realised that Malakim was missing from the castle. Then, a note had been discovered, tied to a spear that had pierced the body of an Othanim soldier. Luckily for the rebels, the Othanim hadn't acted fast enough to figure out where it had come from, and now the atmosphere in the castle was even worse than it had been. Kaeto had not heard from Belise, and he didn't dare go to her. Icaraine might draw a line between the two: human with possible human sympathies, and Othanim with access to Malakim. From there, it was only a small leap to conspiracy, and even though she hadn't been the one watching Malakim when he was taken, Belise could still be the one to take the blame. Mikael, the Othanim who'd been with the prince, had been found in the stables covered in wasp stings. He had been dousing himself in cold water, by all reports. Kaeto didn't know where the guard was now, but he suspected that wasp stings were the least of his problems.

Behind him, Felldir got up from the bed slowly, the frame creaking from his weight. 'What is happening?'

'They've got the note,' said Kaeto. He had personally inspected the room several times and he was comfortably certain they could talk privately here, but he still lowered his voice. 'She has them out scouring the city anyway.'

'Hmm.' Felldir was recovering well, healing with the eerie rapidity that Kaeto was coming to associate with the Titans. He cut a strange figure, with one severely curtailed wing, but his face was no longer so gaunt and his wolfish yellow eyes were clear again. It did Kaeto good to see him that way – but always in the back of his mind he was wondering what Icaraine would do to him next. 'It's a bold play. I can hardly think of anything that would make Icaraine angrier. Do not expect her to react like a human might. She is proud to the point of insanity.'

Kaeto turned away from the window. 'Sooner or later, she will kill you, Felldir. We couldn't continue with the situation as it was, and the rebels wanted to act. I decided to help them.'

'So for my sake, you have put Belise in danger. Something I would never ask you to do.'

It was the worst thing he could have said. Kaeto crossed the room to him in a few strides, his stomach churning and his fists balled at his sides.

'How dare you say that to me. You of all people... You know what I would do to keep her safe.'

The corner of Felldir's mouth twitched. 'Is this keeping her safe, light-bones?'

He was taller and broader than Kaeto, and even severely injured as he was, Felldir was still significantly stronger, yet in that moment Kaeto wanted to strike him. He imagined it would be like hitting a marble statue. From somewhere within the castle, he could hear Icaraine bellowing. She wanted the queen brought to her. It occurred to Kaeto that she might simply have Broudicca killed out of spite.

'I've done what I had to do,' he said, looking down at the floor. 'And Belise agreed with me. She would singlehandedly fight every Othanim in Londus to keep you from harm, Felldir.'

'Not *every* Othanim, surely.'

Kaeto looked up, and was surprised to see a dry smile on the Titan's face.

'You don't know what it was like,' he said softly. 'To witness what she was doing to you, every day. Watching her kill you, piece by piece.' His eyes flickered to the stump of wing protruding from Felldir's left shoulder. 'I can't do it. Not anymore.'

'Light-bones. Kaeto... I hesitated to let her out of the Undertomb, and for that Icaraine will never forgive me. I fear this is a destiny I cannot fly away from forever. Well, I certainly can't fly away from it now.'

'Don't,' said Kaeto sharply. 'Don't make jokes about it.'

'I am sorry.' Felldir reached out and placed his hand on the side of Kaeto's neck, one large thumb brushing the underside of his beard. Kaeto swallowed. 'It is a source of comfort to me that you care so much, and I should not make light of it.' His hand moved so that it cupped the back of Kaeto's head, fingers entwined in his long, dark hair. 'I care for you, also. I am very afraid, Kaeto, that Icaraine will discover what you have done. She will think nothing of killing you. And then what will I do?'

Kaeto closed his eyes lightly and rested a hand on the Titan's arm. 'Do you remember,' he said, 'when we spoke about leaving, going west? The sun was setting on that old, broken castle, and

I thought there was a chance we could be free. But the empress already knew about the pair of you. She was just waiting for the right moment to stick the knife in. It was all just a dream.'

'I remember,' said Felldir. 'I still dream it.'

When Kaeto opened his eyes, the Titan was closer than he had been before, and despite all of it – Felldir's injury, the danger to Belise, the chaos around the castle and their own diminishing odds of escape – he felt something inside him shift and lighten. *Hope*, he realised. He felt hope. If this could still exist, in the midst of everything else...

Felldir's mouth met his tentatively, almost shyly, as though he were uncertain of the reception he would receive, so Kaeto kissed him back firmly, stepping into the circle of the Titan's arms and drawing him closer. Felldir made a small noise of pleasure and surprise, and very quickly the kiss moved from something soft and uncertain to a stronger, more urgent need. The Titan's hands moved down Kaeto's back, pulling him close in a way that reminded Kaeto of the other man's strength. Kaeto's hand found a gap in Felldir's clothing, letting him touch his bare skin; it was warm and smooth, a statue brought to life.

*We can't*, thought Kaeto. *At least, not here, not now.*

But the thoughts seemed very unimportant. They backed towards the bed a little, Felldir transferring his kisses to Kaeto's throat, when there was a flurry of knocks at the door. They moved apart, and the door flew open to reveal an Othanim warrior on the other side. Her greyish skin was flushed. She glared at them both with open disgust.

'You,' she said, jerking her chin in Kaeto's direction. 'Icaraine wants to see you. Now.'

---

Icaraine's chambers were partially demolished. One wall stood entirely open to the spring morning and a stiff breeze was barrelling around the room, tugging at the surviving tapestries and the torn bedclothes. The body of Mikael had been pinned to one of the surviving walls; long iron nails had been hammered through his wrists, ankles and wings, and the space between his sternum and his groin was a churned, bloody mess. Scraps of ropey gut were stuck to his bloody thighs, and his head hung so low his chin was pressed to his chest. Kaeto was glad he couldn't see the dead warrior's face.

*The price of incompetence*, he thought, his skin breaking out in goosebumps.

Belise, thankfully, was unharmed, standing half hidden in the shadows of the adjoining chamber. There were a handful of Othanim warriors standing fearfully by the door, their eyes returning repeatedly to the ragged corpse of Mikael. Ceni, the old queen of Galabroc, was kneeling on the flagstones with her head down, while Icaraine herself crouched by the open wall. Her black hair was loose over her shoulders, and she was splattered all over with blood; her hands and arms were red to the elbows, and there were ominous smears around her mouth.

'YOU!' Icaraine took a step down from the broken masonry, her eyes narrowing at Kaeto. 'What do you know of these rebels?'

Kaeto bowed his head, his hands held respectfully behind his back. 'Very little, your highness. As you know, I am a stranger in this country, and Brittletain has long been an enemy of the Blessed Imperium.'

She hissed and wiped the back of her hand over her mouth, only serving to smear the blood across her cheek. 'Do you know what they have done? Do you know what they have dared?'

It would be foolish to pretend he did not know – it was all the castle was talking about.

'It pains me to hear that the young Prince Malakim has been kidnapped.' He cleared his throat. 'If there is anything I can do to help you learn his whereabouts and bring about his retrieval,

I will gladly offer it. As I have said in the past, the Imperium is your friend, Icaraine Lightbringer. Especially in the face of Brittlish rebellion.'

'I have my warriors out searching,' said Icaraine. 'Some of them were not searching quickly enough for my liking.' She glanced down at her bloody hands. 'But we have this now, too. A note.' She held out one vast hand. Resting on her palm – looking no bigger than a leaf – was a piece of parchment. 'Read it.'

Kaeto came forward and carefully peeled the parchment from her hand. It was damp with blood and sweat. He read it quickly, keeping his expression neutral. The rebels had done all he had suggested, but seeing it here, inscribed in ink, made him uneasy. It was indeed a fragile, dangerous plan. He wondered if he had doomed them in his attempt to save Felldir's life. The memory of the heat of Felldir's body pressed against his felt so vivid he half imagined Icaraine would be able to see it in his eyes. He pushed the thought away.

'They wish for an exchange of prisoners, your highness. What will you do?'

'Envoy, I told you before that Malakim is the very centre of the Othanim's future. With him, we will destroy, finally, the last remaining inferior Titans. My boy will lead us into the future, will lead the Othanim when I am gone—' Kaeto sensed rather than heard a flicker of reaction amongst the gathered Othanim. Not all of them, he suspected, thought this was a great idea. '—and above all things, he is my son. It has been thousands of years since I have dealt with humans, and it's possible I've forgotten the depths of their stupidity, but to take my son from me...' She grinned, revealing bloody teeth. 'In our glorious future I imagined that humans would be a useful kind of slave, kept as pets, the performers of menial tasks. But if they are this troublesome, Envoy, it may be that they go the way of inferior Titans. It may be that we sow Enonah with their bodies and feast on their bones, as thin and soft as they are.'

She moved towards the drop on the far side of the wall, leaning out with one hand braced against the brickwork. Her eyes scoured the city beyond, as if she might spot Malakim herself.

'There was another thing,' she said, a sly softness creeping into her voice that put Kaeto on high alert. 'An explosion in the kitchens. One of the ovens, they tell me, although none of the humans could tell me why it blew up. It was late. It was dark. They tell me that it would have been many hours before they even started to bake their bread. Yet the oven blew itself to pieces, making a noise that brought many of my warriors running. Isn't that a curious thing?'

Kaeto nodded seriously. 'If you would like, your highness, I could investigate this for you? I have some knowledge of the physical sciences.'

Icaraine grunted.

'Humans. Like stinging ants. An irritation, but one I can easily deal with.' She leaned further out over the drop, and her wings flexed – an animal about to take flight.

'Where are you going?' The question was out before he'd fully considered the wisdom of what he was asking.

'I go to hunt for my child,' she said.

The vast Titan dropped from the chamber into the morning beyond, and a second later she rose again, wings spread wide as she headed into the sky. Kaeto's first impulse was to look for Belise, to ask her what she knew, but that would be incredibly careless. Instead, he let himself observe the chamber. The other Othanim were leaving, either following Icaraine out into the sky over Londus, or creeping back out the door. Ceni was climbing off the floor, her lips pressed into a thin line.

'Queen Ceni,' he said, filling his voice with the formal respect he used for the empress. 'May I have a word?'

The woman turned slowly towards him. Her eyes were a startling blue against her brown skin, and the look she gave him wasn't welcoming. *Curious*, thought Kaeto.

'What is it?'

Kaeto came closer, ushering her slightly towards the door. From the corner of his eye he saw that Belise's doorway was empty. The girl had made herself scarce, but he had no doubt she was listening from somewhere.

'What happened here? I am most curious. If there's a way I can help Icaraine retrieve her child, I believe I must know all the details.'

Ceni gave him a sharp look, as though she knew this to be nonsense.

'The prince went on one of his little nightly walks with his nursemaid. They were near the dungeons when the oven exploded, and the Othanim girl left him in the care of Mikael to investigate. There was some confusion. She had all the kitchen staff dragged from their beds to explain what had happened.' Kaeto felt a warm flush of pride. He could picture Belise doing this, stoking the confusion and the panic, obfuscating what had actually happened, winding on the hours to give the rebels more time. 'When she returned, she found no Mikael and no Malakim. The alarm was raised.'

By alarm, he assumed she meant the bellowing scream that had nearly flattened Londus itself.

'The child vanished from the dungeons?'

'Apparently so. Icaraine asked Mikael a few questions when he was found. He said that he had been attacked by flying insects that seemed intent on piercing every inch of his skin. The fool actually complained about the pain to Icaraine.' She gestured briefly at the wall where the remains of Mikael were hanging. 'Well, you can see how she received that.'

'Indeed.'

'They brought my... They brought Queen Broudicca up from her cell to answer questions too. She confirmed that there had been wasps in the corridor. There were no wasps when the Othanim went down there to look.'

'Curious. And what do you think happened?'

The former queen glared at him, before glancing around the chamber. There were no Othanim nearby, but she still lowered her voice.

'Wasps that attack on command, then vanish? Smells like Druin magic to me. My sister has done something very foolish indeed, but then you could always rely on Epona for foolishness. Headstrong little idiot.'

'You think your plan is better?' he spoke very quietly indeed, barely moving his lips. 'The Othanim will not treat with you, Ceni. They won't place you back on the throne as some convenient puppet queen.'

'If there is no chance of deals being made, then what are you doing here?' she snapped. 'The empress is no fool.'

'I do as she asks, I can do no more,' said Kaeto carefully.

'You play your game, and I'll play mine, Envoy.' She curled her lip, looking very much like a cornered animal ready to bite. 'Something happened here, and I intend to extract the details from someone. I suggest you stay out of my way. I don't want to be seen talking to you.'

She turned on her heel and stalked away from him. Kaeto watched her go with a stone of dread weighing heavy in his stomach. Ceni wanted to make herself useful to Icaraine, and he was certain that could mean terrible things for the rebels. They would have to be warned.

# 44

The air was full of an unexpected spring snow. Ynis did not feel cold, however. Her furs were thick and well lined, and she was too full of the joy of the flight to think of anything else. They were skirting the border of Brittletain, T'rook flying to one side of her, and T'vor on the other. Unlike Flayn, T'vor had been relatively reserved in his reaction to their return, but he had taken a moment to groom them both – running the sharp edge of his black beak through Ynis's untamed hair – and insisted that they join him to fly south immediately. He had heard, he said, of Ynis's wings and he wanted to see them for himself. When she had summoned them and leapt into the air to join her sister, T'vor had made a low caw of amazement before flying around her in a slow loop.

'Finally, the wings you deserve, yenlin. They are not feathered, which makes them strange to my eyes, but they work well enough.'

Now they were on the search for Othanim patrols. T'vor told them as they flew that he had personally stopped over two dozen crossing the border into Yelvynia, tearing them from the skies and shredding their guts over the stony ground.

'When did they start coming?' asked Ynis. She was thinking of the road they had seen, cutting through the Wild Wood like a scar.

'Around twenty moons ago,' he replied. 'When we first heard rumours of the Othanim's return, we dismissed it. Foolishly, perhaps. How could we know that they had escaped their prison? But these are dark days. It is time for griffins to taste Titan blood once more.'

'We told Queen Fellvyn that we saw them building something in the Wild Wood,' said T'rook importantly.

'Yes. I heard this. I can see no reason for it, aside from simple destruction.' T'vor snapped his beak in a dismissive gesture. 'But you did well. The queen was pleased to have this knowledge.'

Ynis sensed her sister preening at this praise. The wind died down abruptly, as it sometimes did in the foothills of the mountains, and they were held for a moment in a maelstrom of white flakes. Below them, Ynis caught sight of a small herd of mountain deer moving slowly across a low rise. They were clipping at the grass that poked above the thin layer of snow. She hadn't eaten mountain deer since she'd left Brittletain, and the thought of chewing on a fresh, rubbery deer kidney made her mouth fill with saliva.

'Are you hungry, Father?' she asked. When they were hatchlings, T'vor had always seemed to be hungry, eating his share of any hunt faster than the rest of them; they used to tease him for it.

T'vor rumbled with amusement.

'Does the Druidahnon leave his droppings in the Wild Wood?'

'Then we should hunt!' cried T'rook, already dropping closer to the ground.

'Yes,' said T'vor, 'but let your sister have the first grasp, T'rook. Always she has hunted from your back, but no longer. Do you have your claw-knife, Ynis?'

Ynis patted her belt where her beloved knife was stored. 'I do, Father, but...'

Was now the time? Finally? She had seen Leven's magical blade more times than she could count over the last two years, but still had yet to summon her own, and as she reached out her hand, she felt a moment of doubt: what if, in the end, it wouldn't work? But there was that familiar tingling in her arm, that sense that something waited for her just out of sight. She reached for it. 'I thought I might use this instead.'

A bright sword of light appeared in her outstretched hand. It looked to be made of clear crystal, filled with a pale blue-and-white glow that turned the snowflakes around them into tumbling diamonds and sapphires. The shape of it was different to Leven's: where her human sister's sword was wide and straight, similar to the hefty broadswords carried by the warriors they had seen guarding Tyleigh's compound, the sword Ynis had summoned was shorter and slimmer with a fine tapering point, and the crossguard flowed back over her hand like a cuff. Her father cooed with appreciation.

'A fine set of talons! You will hunt well with those, Ynis.'

Ynis caught her sister muttering under her breath something like 'just one big talon really' and 'it's too bright for any stealth', but it hardly mattered. They had started circling the herd of deer, who in the midst of the snow were yet to become aware of their presence, and she prepared herself to dive. She would, she realised, be able to take down much bigger prey with this.

'I will take one by myself,' she called to her father and sister. 'Maybe even two.'

But it didn't quite work out how she was hoping. When she swept down out of the snowflakes, sword held above her head ready for a killing blow, the deer realised she was there much faster than she was expecting. She caught sight of her shadow, blasted against the snow and grass by the light from her wings, and then the deer were scattering, running in a loose formation for the top of the hill. T'rook shot down after them, flying through the air like an arrow, and faster than a blink she had a deer in her talons. A thin line of blood splattered across the snow, raising tendrils of steam, and then she was back up in the air with the animal, cawing with delight.

Ynis rejoined them in the air, her sword hanging loosely in one hand and a flush of pink in her cheeks.

'Do not take it so hard, yenlin,' said T'vor, his gruff voice unusually soft. 'You are learning to hunt a new way. There will be new challenges.'

'Come on!' called T'rook, who was already heading east. 'Let's eat before it gets cold.'

They landed in the shelter of a pile of mountain rubble, and there swiftly split the deer carcass between them. It had been an age since she had sat on the bare mountain, the chill creeping down her neck even as she sunk her hands into the still-hot flesh of a freshly butchered kill.

'Tell me, Ynis,' said T'vor when they had eaten their first beakfuls. 'Tell me of the human world. What did you make of it?'

Ynis considered before she answered. 'It was interesting,' she said eventually. 'We were looking for T'rook for a long time, and in many places, and all those places were different to each other. But also they were the same.' Ynis frowned, sensing that she wasn't being clear. She could feel T'rook bristling; the human world had given her two years of misery, after all. 'They live in great nest-pits built from stone or wood or clay, and sometimes the nest-pits were all crammed close together, on top of each other even, and then sometimes their homes were very remote from each other. They pay very little attention to the sky. Almost all of their food they put in fires to blacken, and they combine many things to make elaborate meals. They talk a lot. And they are loud. They have no concept that they are prey animals and make no effort to hide themselves when out in the open.'

'Yes,' said T'vor. 'Once, when griffins lived all over Enonah, humans were not our prey. We lived side by side with them, often.' T'vor sounded as though he found this distasteful.

'Why did we start eating them, Father?' asked T'rook.

'As old as I am, T'rook, I am not so old that I was present when we decided this,' T'vor said dryly. 'My understanding, yenlin, is that as our numbers dwindled, we became reluctant to share our spaces with others. Our fellow Titan species diminished or retreated, and we did the same. We came here, to this beautiful place, and we closed our borders. But humans could not accept this. They would come regardless of our need for peace, and short-lived as they are, it seems it is a lesson they need to relearn every generation.' T'vor sunk his talons into the flank of the deer, neatly slicing off a long piece of venison, the meat richly marbled with fat. 'They have never been able to leave us be.'

'Because they think you are extraordinary,' Ynis said quietly. She looked down at her hands, covered in blood. It was the first time she could recall speaking of herself and the griffins as if they were separate; it was an acknowledgement that felt a little like tearing out her own heart, even as she accepted the truth of it. She had walked in the human world and no one had batted an eyelid. That would not be the case for T'rook. She swallowed. 'You are legendary. A living myth. You live so much longer than... us, and your bones are heavy with magic. It would be like asking humans not to look at the stars, or warm themselves by a fire.'

There was a long moment of silence. Ynis half expected T'rook to be angry with her for taking the side of humans in any argument, but after a moment she felt her sister's head rest on her shoulder, the fur and feathers of her ruff warm and soft against her cheek.

'You are not like them, Ynis,' she said gruffly. 'You have yost. The soul of a griffin. I know it.'

'Your sister is correct,' said T'vor. 'You belong—'

There was a shrieking peal of laughter from overhead. T'vor was instantly on his feet, wings snapping open with an audible *crack*, but the Othanim were already on them – three of the creatures, so large and unnerving up close. The one that landed nearest Ynis was a female, wearing a half-helm and a belt made of griffin feathers.

'Look at this,' she cried, 'a human! Do you keep human pets too, griffin? And we thought you so uncivilised.'

T'vor and T'rook were already fighting, talons raking across Othanim flesh as their wicked swords caught the bleak snow-light and reflected it in flashes. There was a screech as one of the blades caught T'rook a glancing blow across her back leg, and suddenly Ynis found that her hand was holding her bright sword again, and she was lunging at the Othanim warrior.

'What's this?' The Othanim laughed – Ynis could only see the lower half of her face, and her mouth was wide with merriment. 'The little human has claws!' She batted away Ynis's first lunge, but it was perhaps not as easy as she had expected it to be, because the grin faltered.

*I am strong*, thought Ynis. Her second lunge, crashing against the Othanim sword, pushed the woman back a foot or so, and this time she looked actively furious. She brought her sword arm up, bellowing something unintelligible as she prepared to chop Ynis into several pieces, but Ynis was faster, ducking in under her guard and pushing the shining Herald blade up beneath the Othanim's chest plate. The warrior faltered, a thick gurgling noise emerging from her throat. She dropped her sword and sank to her knees, her mouth hanging open. Ynis pulled her sword free, marvelling for a second at the blood on the blade – which was glowing from within like a particularly spectacular sunset – before slashing its edge across the Othanim's neck. Her head fell and rolled across the thin covering of snow, travelling so fast it barely left a bloodstain. It bumped down the hill and out of sight while the body of the warrior slumped sideways and fell. All at once, Ynis realised how quiet it was. She looked up to see her father and her sister watching her, the other two Othanim scouts little more than ragged piles of meat smeared across the ground.

'I would say,' said T'vor slowly, 'that your talons work very well indeed, yenlin.'

# 45

*They say that Magog was born from one of the twin hills that sit either side of the Old Father. That lightning struck it one day, splitting the hill down the middle, and a bear cub scrambled out of the rubble. Well, I knew him when I was a cub myself, old Magog, and he did like to be bloody mysterious, I'll give you that. Wise as anything, that old bear, and he loved his stories. I asked him about the hill story once. I asked him if that was really where he came from. He was old in those days, older than any other living creature, maybe, and he was a grumpy old fart. He cuffed me around the head and said: 'You're too old to be asking where cubs come from.' So that was that.*

Extract from *Conversations with the Druidahnon* by Elder Druin Jathinos

The statue of Magog had stood in the harbour for as long as anyone could remember. Twenty feet tall and cast in pieces of bronze, it loomed in plain sight of any ships coming up the Old Father, reminding their passengers that this country was a place of Titans, and magic, and the wisdom of the bears.

*Not anymore*, thought Epona. *Now we're a country of desperate idiots hiding inside a bear statue, and the only Titan we had left*

*is nothing more than a pile of bones waiting to be eaten by an abomination.*

She was sitting halfway up the structure on an interior ledge, her face pressed to a tiny hole where one plate of bronze met another; there were several like it all over the statue, and Jack and Larth watched from similar peepholes. It gave an unobstructed view of the harbour all the way to the statue of the horned queen, a much smaller monument that was currently being painted with the orange and pink glow of a setting sun. No one living knew who the horned queen was, only that once she had ruled the lands around the Old Father, and that she had been a Druin – back then, the Wild Wood came right down to the banks of the river, and the Druin had kings and queens amongst themselves. The horned queen statue was old indeed, made of weathered stone, her face long since rubbed to a blank stare with only a suggestion of eyes and a snub nose, but Magog was at least recent enough that some enterprising citizens had made it into a storage area and bolthole; there was a trapdoor in the base that led down into the defunct sewer system, and it was through this that they were coming and going. It made Epona immensely proud of her countryfolk – there wasn't a single part of the city that couldn't be used for some underhanded purpose. That was Londus for you.

The trapdoor popped open, and Yelm stuck her head in. There was dirt smudged over her face. The tunnels under Londus were not always clean.

'Our friend has requested a meeting,' she whispered.

'What?' Epona leaned out on her ledge, looking down at the Druin. 'Now? There's no time. She could be here any minute.'

Yelm shrugged. 'He's left two stones in the alcove, and that means he wants a meeting, right?'

'Magog's balls,' said Epona, before placing her hand against the bronze. 'I do beg your pardon, sir. I can't leave this place now. He'll have to wait.' She pressed her eye to the hole again, but the harbourside was still empty. Out there, somewhere, her mother was being brought from the dungeons, marched through the street, or flown through the sky. She was sure of it. 'It's not like he doesn't know we're busy.'

'I don't like it,' said Jack from somewhere above her. 'What if he's trying to warn us about something?'

'It's hard to imagine us being in more danger than we are already,' said Epona. 'Fine. Yelm, you go. Take this.' She reached inside her jacket and pulled out one of her last pellets of blue wax. She dropped it into Yelm's waiting hands. 'That way he'll know you're from me.'

'I don't want to go back there,' said Yelm. Since they had snatched the child, she'd been especially jumpy.

'I will go,' said Jack, already climbing down from her perch.

Epona closed her eyes briefly. 'No, Jack, I want you here with me. If things go wrong, we'll need Caliburn. Yelm, please. He won't bite. If anything, he's remarkably charming for a dog of the Imperium.'

Yelm hesitated a moment longer, then disappeared back through the trapdoor, the pellet of wax clutched in one hand.

'The sun is almost down,' said Larth. She was on the other side of the bear, watching the far end of the river. 'Perhaps they're not coming.'

'They'll come.'

The alternative was unthinkable, after all. If Icaraine ignored their message, then Epona had no idea what they would do next. She knew that Larth had been talking to other members of the rebellion. She guessed that she wasn't the only one who thought they should just kill the Othanim child – one fewer enemy for them to deal with. So far, Epona had controlled the rebellion through virtue of her royal status and sheer force of personality, but she wasn't at all sure how much longer that would last, especially with so few genuine victories under their belt. And what could be an easier victory than killing a child? Epona grimaced.

All around them, the light was dying. Inside the bear, it was getting increasingly hot and sweaty.

'How long do we wait?' asked Jack, but Epona did not answer. They would wait as long as it took.

In the end, the last hints of the sun's ruddy light had sunken into the deep purple of twilight before they came. At first, Epona thought the wind had picked up out of nowhere, but then she realised that the rushing, whirring noise was the sound of the Othanim approaching – lots of them, from the volume of it. She pressed her eye to the hole again, the harsh metal biting into her skin.

'They're coming.'

The whirring grew louder, loud enough that for a moment Epona thought the Othanim were going to land somehow directly on top of the statue of Magog, and then she saw them: around ten warriors, with Icaraine in the middle. It was too dark to see if her mother was with them. She swallowed hard, her mouth dry and scratchy. What would it be like to see her mother's face again, after two years? Would she have changed? Would she be broken? A surge of despair lapped at the back of Epona's throat, quickly followed by anger.

*It ends tonight*, she thought fiercely.

Epona hadn't been this close to Icaraine before – not many rebels had and survived. She loomed over the other Othanim, who themselves loomed over the average human, and her wings stretched across the boardwalk with ease. She was looking around the harbour with a pointed kind of fury, and the muscles across her shoulders and along her arms looked as though they were carved from stone. Then she moved, pulling something that had been behind her out into the light. Epona saw her mother stagger forward.

Epona made a noise in the back of her throat.

'Are you alright?' whispered Jack.

'Yes.' She swallowed hard. 'I just can't believe it's really her...'

Her mother had never been tall, but she had always managed to be imposing anyway; there was a solidity and a presence to her that meant every eye naturally turned to her when she was in a room. The woman standing next to Icaraine looked like a sketch of that woman, poorly done: she was thin to the point of gauntness, and her hair – once a rich, deep brown – was grey and white, and somehow ragged, as though portions of it had fallen out. Most of all, though, she looked exhausted, the chains that circled her wrists seeming to drag her towards the ground.

'She looks dead on her feet.' She dragged her eyes away from Broudicca and scanned the rest of the Othanim. 'I don't... Wait, is that Bronny?'

Bronvica stumbled into view, her arms restrained behind her back. She was bleeding from a head wound, her face half lost in blood. Bronny, who had only ever really cared about horses and had no interest in being a princess or following in her mother's footsteps. Bronvica had been kept by Icaraine as a servant rather than thrown into the dungeons, just as Ceni had, and because of this Epona had assumed she was relatively safe. A cold worm of fear was working its way up her throat.

'Something's wrong,' said Jack from somewhere above her head.

'HUMAN SCUM!' Icaraine's voice echoed off the harbour buildings, so loud that the bronze bear trembled slightly. 'Do you think you can play games with the Othanim? Do you think you are worthy to make demands of Titans? You are little more than beetles to us. Less than beetles, you are the dirt they burrow in.'

'This is just her blustering,' said Epona, although she didn't believe it. 'She can't just give my mother back without making a big show of it, that's all.'

Above her she could hear the scuffling sound of Jack beginning to climb down the interior scaffolding of the statue.

'We should leave, Princess.'

'What are you talking about? We can't leave, my mother is right there.'

Icaraine was speaking again.

'I want to see the face of the light-bones who thought they could make demands of the Othanim. Show yourself, human. Let me see the face of the bravest human in Brittletain.' The Othanim queen gave Broudicca a light shove with the tip of her finger, nearly sending her into the dirt. 'Let me see you, and perhaps I will give you your mother back, just for impressing me with your stupidity. If you don't, I will kill her right now, here on the docks. I know you will be watching, light-bones.'

'*No*,' Epona hissed between her teeth. 'What is she doing? We were clear we would kill her brat, so why is she risking it?'

Jack was on the wooden strut above her, and as Epona glanced up she lowered herself down noiselessly, the muscles on her biceps tensing.

'Jack is right,' said Larth. 'We've misplayed this. I told you we should have just killed the kid.'

'SHOW YOURSELF, LIGHT-BONES!'

'*Fuck*. I have to go out there.'

'You can't.' Jack took her arm, then seemed to think better of it and dropped it. 'Please, Epona, think about this. She'll just kill you, and then where will we be? No queen, and no leader either.' Her cheeks were very pink, and distractedly Epona noted that made her eyes look even greener. 'We can't lose you.'

'She's going to kill my mum.' Epona shook her head. 'If I go out there, maybe I can convince her that Prince Malakim is in danger, and that the best way out of that is to give our queen back. I'm just one of seven princesses, right?' She laughed a little. 'There's only one Queen Broudicca, and we already know that the other kingdoms won't follow me – they still think I had something to do with the death of Queen Ismere. If I don't go out there...'

'She's bluffing,' said Jack quickly. 'You said so yourself.'

'If I don't go out there,' Epona continued, 'she kills my mother and my sister and this has all been for nothing. Larth, go back to the market cellar, and tell them to move the kid.'

'Where?'

'I don't know, get him out of the city, take the tunnels as far as you can.' As Epona spoke she could feel the panic rising in her chest. Everything was going wrong. She had the distinct feeling that there would be one less member of the Londus royal family before sunrise. 'Get him into the Wild Wood and have Yelm and Solasach hide him along the Paths somewhere.'

Larth nodded tersely and disappeared back down the trapdoor. Epona climbed down from her own perch. Icaraine was still bellowing, making the bronze plates quiver under her fingertips. Epona could sense Jack watching her, unsaid things boiling between them.

'I will go with you,' she said.

'No.' Epona turned to the other woman and took hold of both her arms. 'I'm sorry, Jack, I know that you hate this, but I want her attention solely on me. Stay here, and watch. It might be that we have to make a run for it, and I'll need you to guide me. If I don't come back, you have to lead them.'

'Epona...'

She squeezed Jack's forearms as hard as she could. 'That's an order. A royal command, if you like.'

There was the softest chime from Caliburn, who had up until that point been largely quiet.

'He says we cannot refuse a royal command,' said Jack faintly. 'That we are bound by it.'

'Great. Good. He speaks sense for once.'

'Epona...' Jack took her hand and kissed the back of it, quickly but firmly. 'For luck.'

Epona stepped up to the back of the statue. There was a panel there that was actually a door, where no doubt the people who made the statue had come and gone while they were constructing it. It opened facing away from the Othanim, so for a few moments she would be invisible to them. She pushed it open just wide enough to squeeze out into the fresh night air, then closed it behind her before stepping boldly out into the open.

'Here I am, you ugly great brute!' she yelled. 'I've come to get my mother back.'

# 46

*Sightings of the supposed Titan were frequent enough, back in the time when the Wild Wood teemed with bears and wolves, but in the last five hundred years or so? Not a peep. If the great kraken still lives, and I sincerely hope she does, then she is sleeping somewhere at the bottom of that silty lake. I'd go and have a look myself, but Yelvynia is no place for humans, and I'm not sure a glimpse of that wily old monster is worth losing my guts for.*

Extract from the notes of Bede the Liar,<br>famed adventurer and alchemist

'How'd you get all those shiny lines on your face, then?'

Leven took a long gulp of the ale in her tankard, thinking about how to best reply. This tavern, the Griffin's Reach, was the first evidence of civilisation she'd found after wandering the Wild Wood for days, and she was teetering on the edge of exhaustion. It was a tiny place, tucked under a thickly forested hill, the hand-painted sign hanging from one fraying rope, but it was busy enough. She stood elbow to elbow with people at the bar, and the noise levels were rising as the daylight hours dwindled. She wondered where they all lived.

'I was born with them.' The barkeep made a face at that, so she kept talking to avoid more questions. 'I'm looking for a Druin. I wondered if you had seen him, or know anyone who might have.' She'd been thinking about what she would say all the time she had been walking through the wood; now her words sounded flat and heavy to her own ears. 'He's youngish, my age, with brown hair to about here.' She touched her collarbone. 'Goat's horns that curl back from his temples.' She considered mentioning the blue tint to his horns, then decided against it. Asking about a thrawn Druin might make her especially unpopular. 'He might have been... confused.'

The barkeep, a skinny young man with a straggly beard, wrinkled his nose. 'Only Druin I know of round here are the rangers that keep the Paths around the Humming Hill, but I don't think any of them look like this one you're after. What d'you want him for?'

Leven looked down into her pint. 'He's my husband.'

He chuckled at that. 'Oh, you lost him, have you? Has he done a runner?' The barkeep sucked in air over his teeth. 'My mum always used to say it was a bad business, trying to keep a Druin – too wild by half. Their hearts belong to the bloody trees and animals. You've got to be an idiot to get involved, that's what she used to say.'

Leven's fist curled around the handle of her tankard. She was exhausted and her ore-lines prickled with pain, but she thought she might have enough in her to pull this man over the bar by his beard. *He doesn't know what he's saying*, she reminded herself. *And you can hardly say he's wrong at this point, can you?*

Something of this must have shown in her face, because the barkeep began to hem and haw. 'If you ask me though, she was always a bit sore about the Druin. Had a sweetheart from the order before she met my dad and it didn't end well. People is people, that's what I think, whether you've got horns or not.'

Leven nodded wearily. So he hadn't seen Cillian, but there were other Druin nearby. That could be a place to start, at least. A wave of pain moved up her body, tracing the ore-lines with a fiery finger. She winced and downed the rest of the ale.

'Do you have rooms here?'

'We do, aye.'

'How much for a night?'

He looked at her dubiously. 'Well now, we don't exactly have any free at the moment I'm afraid. A lot of people are on the road these days, what with those flying bastard Titans. Whole towns and villages are emptying out – a lot of people are heading for Dwffd, or Kornwullis.' He had the tone of someone about to embark on their favourite activity: gossip. 'They're tearing down part of the Wild Wood, did you know that? Less than a league from here. I saw a pair of them myself the other month, flying so low over the trees I could see every feather on their wings. I came fair close to pissing myself, I don't mind telling you. But there's a rebellion in the south. Trying to take back Londus.'

'So what you're telling me is you've no rooms?'

'Not as such, no. Got to keep them available for locals.' He eyed her ore-lines again. 'And I'm guessing you're not from round here, are you?'

Leven sighed. More than anything, she wanted to find somewhere quiet to lie down. The strangeness of the Titan memories was beginning to colour her thoughts. But one of the words he'd spoken seemed to shine brighter than the others.

'A rebellion?'

'Oh yes, led by the murder princess herself, Epona. Can you believe that? After all that dark business with Mersia and their stuck-up queen. Beggars can't be choosers, I suppose.'

Leven blinked rapidly. It was like having a cup of cold sea water dashed in her face.

'Did you just say Epona? Epona's alive?'

'But maybe what you want in these times is a bloodthirsty queen, someone who's ruthless and will do what it takes.' The barman sniffed. 'Wouldn't want to be ruled by her myself, but those thick-headed Londus types are welcome to her.'

'What happened? Where has she been?' Leven rubbed a hand over her face. She was too weary for all the questions that were crashing around her head.

'A big fan of hers, are you?' The barman looked unimpressed. 'You look the type. I only know what everyone knows. Queen Ceni threw her in a dungeon, but she was too slippery to stay there. And now she fights the Othanim.'

Leven nodded slowly, trying to take this in. Her old friend was alive. Possibly not in the best situation, by the sounds of it, but this was good news. When she found Cillian again – if she found him again – they would have to head south. Epona would need help.

'You don't have a barn or a, I don't know, set of stables I could kip in?' she asked. 'I just need to rest for a little while. I'll pay you.'

The barkeep opened his mouth – too quickly, it was clear he was about to say no – when the door of the tavern crashed open. The noise of the place died down, and Leven heard a few gasps and some muttered comments. She turned to see Cillian in the doorway, his horns all tangled up with ivy and his clothes ragged and torn. His eyes were wild.

'Cillian!'

'Is that him, is it?' said the barkeep. 'You want to tell him to put a comb through his hair. It might not look like it, but we have some standards at the Griffin's Reach.'

Leven paid him no mind; she was already crossing the busy tavern, the pain in her limbs briefly forgotten.

'How did you find me?'

Cillian grinned at the sight of her. His eyes looked brighter than they had; they were the green of duckweed rather than jade.

'You, my love, I would be able to find anywhere – in the Wildest Wood, at the ends of Enonah.'

When she reached him, he half lifted her off her feet, embracing her so fiercely that she forgot to breathe. She laughed, and kissed him. For a long moment they stood, pressed closely together, the hubbub of the tavern rising again around them. To her surprise, his arms circled her waist, pulling her hips against his, and she could feel very clearly how glad he was to have found her.

'Cillian, where have you been? You just bloody disappeared on me.'

'I have a lot to tell you, my love, but we need privacy to do it. Barkeep!'

The tavern keeper was watching them with a slightly sour expression.

'Yes?'

Cillian strode to the bar and placed his hands on top of it. Leven was sure he was no taller than he had been when she'd last seen him, but somehow he seemed to take up more space. Others at the bar leaned away from him; not as you'd lean away from a dangerous person, but as you'd lean away from a fire that was too hot.

'Your finest room for my lady. At once.'

The barkeep scowled, his eyes flickering to Leven and back. 'I just told her we don't got no rooms at the moment. There are too many people on the road already.'

Cillian leaned forward. Leven grew tense. For reasons she couldn't quite name, she felt abruptly afraid for the barkeep. She wanted to touch Cillian's shoulder, draw him back, but couldn't do it.

'Come now.' Cillian's face split into a wide grin, as though he and the barkeep were sharing a secret. 'There's a room on the first floor, near the back.' He slid his hand across the wooden top of the bar as though reading words there that no one else could see. 'There's a big window that looks out onto a fine alder and a fine hazel, who have grown together for the last twenty years – I can hear them whisper to each other, words of love and devotion.' He leaned further over the bar and lowered his voice. 'And they talk of the strong box buried between their roots. The man who owned this place before you was a cautious soul and told no one of his box, so that when the pox carried him off no one even knew to look for it.'

The barkeep's eyebrows had travelled up to the middle of his forehead.

'Now, you'd be doing me and those trees a great favour if you were to dig up that strong box,' continued Cillian. 'It weighs heavy on their roots, and so it weighs heavy on my mind. Will you do that for me? Who knows what may be inside it? Something worth burying though, I reckon.'

There was a beat of silence. Several people standing close to them must have heard what Cillian had said, as Leven saw the barkeep glance anxiously at them. She could almost see him trying to remember where he kept his shovel.

'Fine.' He reached under the bar and came up with an iron key, which he dropped into Cillian's outstretched hand. 'You can have the room. Just don't do anything... weird in it.'

Cillian laughed, but the man was already leaving. His eyes were fixed on two other patrons who had made it out of the tavern door before him.

Up in the room, Leven closed the door behind her with relief. The window did indeed look out on a pair of trees dressed in their spring finery – she didn't know trees well enough to say if they were alder and hazel, but she had little doubt. Cillian went to the window and looked out. He laughed.

'There's two of them down there,' he said, clearly delighted. 'If it comes to blows, my coin is on the one with the bigger shovel.'

'Cillian.' She went to him and pulled him away from the window. She pushed his hair back from his face and plucked an ivy leaf from the tangle. '*What happened?*'

The merry expression faded, and he nodded seriously. He took hold of her hands and kissed each one.

'Oh, Deryn.'

'You promised me that you would stay. But you did it, didn't you?' The worry and then the relief had blunted her anger towards him, but it was seeping back now. Was he calling her Deryn to distract her from it? 'You found the Green Man.'

'I found him. Inkwort showed me the truth of it. The Green Man lay with my mother, Leven, and... well, she loved him, even if he didn't love her. He's my father.'

'He's your *what*?'

A smile touched the corner of his mouth and was gone again. 'I know how it sounds, but it's true. And it explains a lot. Like why the Druidahnon was insisting it had to be me.'

'You could have still walked away from it. There was still a choice.'

'I didn't want this,' he said quietly. 'But it felt inevitable in the end. Like a path I couldn't avoid. If there was a way to save you, I had to take it.'

Leven shook her head slightly. 'I never asked you to do that. Never.'

'It doesn't matter. How could I love you and not try?' He picked up her hand and kissed it again, and this time a curious thing happened: the burning pain in the ore-lines that traced her palm faded, then ceased entirely. 'And I think there could be a way, Leven, I've just got to find it.'

She watched as he kissed her other hand, and the pain faded from that one too. 'Is he... is he with you now?'

'He is. In truth, I think he's always been with me. Just in the roots somewhere, deep in the earth.' He lifted her arm and kissed the underside of her wrist, and a curl of something that definitely wasn't pain made her shiver. He pulled her closer and bent his head to her neck. The near-constant burning pinpricks faded underneath the touch of his lips.

'What are you doing?'

'Trying to find a way to heal you,' he said. 'Will you let me try?'

Later, when they lay in the small bed together in a pleasant tangle of limbs, Leven felt some measure of peace for the first time in months. The pain wasn't completely gone, but it had retreated, and for a while the ore-lines had thrummed with something else – where Cillian had traced the patterns, with his lips and fingers and tongue, pleasure had blossomed instead, as though the Titan ore under her skin were singing to some other tune. It was the dead of night, and outside she could hear an owl calling.

'There's a full moon,' said Cillian. He trailed his fingers over her stomach, no longer tracking the lines there, but following the soft curve of her. 'A good omen for this night's work.'

'Huh?' She felt almost exquisitely sleepy. 'What do you mean?'

'Never mind. How do you feel?'

'Better,' she replied, although even as she said it, she felt the pain ebb back like some terrible tide. She realised she wanted to lie to him, to tell him that he had fixed it after all. 'Better for now. So. The Green Man is part of you. I was expecting something more alarming than ivy in your hair, especially after what the old bear said. Was he trying to frighten us, do you think? I haven't noticed any hooves or fur in the last couple of hours.'

Cillian chuckled. 'I don't know. This is all new to me, Leven. There's a lot of power, just under the surface...' He grew quiet, then continued. 'When I touched the wooden top of the bar, I saw the whole life of that piece of wood, from acorn to tree to timber, and through it I felt everything that it touched, too – everything that lives in the green – the floorboards, the hard earth and stone beneath, and the roots of the trees that stand outside the tavern, and then their voices too. It is like being a Druin, but more. Like being thrawn, but more. It's like the difference between scooping out a handful of earth from the ground to make a hole, and a fissure opened in the ground from the movement of Enonah itself.'

'What do you mean?'

He sighed. 'I'm not sure I know, Leven.'

'And what are you supposed to do with this new power?' She sat up so she could see his face better. Strong moonlight filtered in through the window, turning everything to shadow and bone. 'Does the Green Man know? Does he speak to you?' It was strange to think of the Green Man being there with them, listening to their talk as the sweat dried on their bodies.

'We have to go south,' said Cillian. 'That is... That's what I feel strongly.'

Leven noticed that he hadn't exactly answered her question, yet the urge to chase it was ebbing away from her as the need to sleep grew greater. Queen Mab's face seemed to hang in front of her in the semi-dark, a warning on her lips. *He consumed my husband*, she had said.

'Epona's in the south. According to the barkeep, anyway. She's fighting the Othanim in Londus.'

'Yes, the enemy.' He pushed his hair out of his eyes. 'The ones who are murdering the Wild Wood. I can feel it, a great sundering in the wood as they chop and hack their way to the north. It's almost like a wound,' he touched a finger to his chest and drew a line from breastbone to naval, 'in my own body.'

'Does it hurt you?'

'It does.' His voice sounded very distant, as though he were on a ship and she were on the dock as he drifted away. 'So much pain, Leven.'

'Then we'll stop it,' she said. Her eyes were closed. She would not let anyone hurt him. She would impale them with her horn. She would run them through with her tusks. She would come out of the sea and grind their bones with her teeth. 'We'll run them out of the Wild Wood, Cillian.'

# 47

'There you are, tiny light-bones.' Icaraine turned her whole body slowly, a cat that has just spied something small and squeaky in her peripheral vision. 'You are so *little*, girl. Are you really the one that chose to defy me?'

Down by her feet Broudicca lifted her head, her eyes wide in the dark. She looked horrified.

'Epona?'

'Being big doesn't make you clever.' Epona strode across the wharf as though she were enjoying the night air. 'If I ever needed proof of that, Icaraine, I would look at the fact you're wasting time here when my people have your child hidden away somewhere. Leave my mother and Bronvica here, unharmed, and go. I swear you'll have Prince Malakim back before you know it.'

Icaraine smiled slowly, exposing all her teeth. 'Big words, little one. What is to stop me snatching you up and biting off pieces until you simply tell me where he is?'

'Listen, big bird, I have spent the last day talking my people out of just killing the kid. They want to hurt you, like you've hurt us over the last two years. All of the rebels have lost someone. Slitting the prince's throat might not bring them back, but it'd certainly make them feel better, and honestly that's not the worst reason in the world. Do you think that if you kill me here, they won't just do the same to him?' She paused. If she could keep the Titan distracted for long enough, it would buy time for them to move Malakim elsewhere. If they could get him to the Wild Wood, Icaraine would never find him. 'Why are you here? The rumour is that you came from a country halfway across the world, a hot place with beetles and strange fruits growing on the trees. Why come all the way here? To a place where you aren't wanted.'

'Epona,' Broudicca spoke again, her voice louder this time. 'Stop this. Get out of here while you can.'

'Be quiet,' growled Icaraine. 'We are here, light-bones, because this disgusting backwater island is the last source of Titan bones, and Malakim must feed. We will take what we need, and when we have had our fill of that, we will use up the rest of it as we see fit.'

'I'll never tell you where he is,' she said. She thought of Jack inside the bear statue, watching her defiance with horror, no doubt. It occurred to her that she was sorry she wouldn't see Jack again; her flushed cheeks, the shimmering brown-green of her eyes like the sky reflected in a still lake. She hoped she wouldn't do anything stupid.

Icaraine crouched, her huge meaty arms resting on the tops of her knees. Her long black hair hung like oiled ropes to either side of her neck, and her yellow eyes gleamed with menace.

'You don't need to tell me,' she hissed. 'I know.'

'What?' It felt as though the wooden boards under her feet were jumping and trembling, the whole world tipping off its axis.

'It was Ceni,' said Bronvica. It was the first time she'd spoken. 'I'm... I'm sorry, Epona, but I told her. She came to me, asking what had happened. I told her about the plan. I thought she would help. I didn't think...'

Epona bit down the sharp reply in her throat. If she was about to die, she didn't want her last words to her sister to be harsh ones.

'That fucking *snake*.' She was less concerned about using harsh words towards her other sister. Spinning around, she looked over the harbour buildings to the west. Although it was dark, it was still possible to make them out: a whole host of Othanim in the sky over the market square. As she watched, some of them began dropping towards the ground.

'As we speak, my warriors are retrieving my son,' said Icaraine. Her voice was suddenly much softer and consequently more alarming than it had been when she'd been shouting at the top of her lungs. 'He'll be back in time for bed. Whereas you, Princess Epona, won't see another sunrise.'

Broudicca lunged forward. 'Epona, run! Get out of here, go!'

Icaraine yanked her back easily, lifting her up into the air with one hand. Epona took a step back. She drew her sword. Above her, her mother's legs cycled in the air uselessly.

'I've had enough of the supposed royalty of this stinking island,' said Icaraine. 'So loud and nosy and troublesome. I was going to wait and feed your queen to my son as an appetizer to the bones of your bear Titan, but sometimes pests have to be swatted.' Broudicca kicked and squirmed as Icaraine took hold of her with her other hand. Too late, Epona saw what was going to happen.

'No!'

Icaraine wrung Broudicca like she was an old dishcloth, twisting her body back and forth between two enormous fists. There was a terrible crunching sound and a scream that cut off abruptly. She dropped the body. Blood began to ooze onto the boards. Epona was dimly aware that Bronvica was screaming.

'No.'

It seemed impossible. Her mother couldn't be dead. She wasn't capable of it. Such stillness was beyond her. The sword dropped from Epona's numb fingers, unnoticed.

But Icaraine wasn't done. Without another word, she snatched up Bronvica – who beat at her with her legs and fists – and twisted her head the wrong way. There was a crack, and then she was lying next to their mother, her eyes staring sightlessly up at the night sky. Icaraine took a step forward, reaching for Epona.

*It's all over*, thought Epona, watching without reacting as a huge hand filled her sight. The main emotion she was aware of in that moment was frustration. *Two years of fighting, and for what? All lost in a stupid gamble.* Her only hope was that the rebels had fled the market cellars soon enough, but it was a very slim hope indeed. Icaraine had known where they were long before she arrived at the statue of the horned queen.

'When I am finished with you,' said Icaraine, 'I will find your little sisters and eat them myself.'

There was a flash of blinding, golden light. Icaraine stumbled back, her hands no longer reaching for Epona, but covering her face. She grunted. The whole harbour was lit up like it was the middle of the day.

'What—?'

Jack was standing on the wall that ran parallel to the harbour, Caliburn held high over her head. The sword burned with a brilliant light, like sunshine at the very height of summer, and the air was full of the clamour of bells. The Othanim fell back from it, apparently confused. Jack's eyes were filled with a golden glow too.

'Jack, what are you doing?'

There was nowhere to run that the Othanim couldn't immediately get them but it was their only chance. Epona turned to flee into the buildings, but Jack was leaping down from the wall and running straight at her, Caliburn still held over her head. She caught Epona around the waist and flung her back in the other direction, and before Epona quite knew where she was they were falling, tumbling towards the murky waters of the Old Father.

---

Belise hung in the air over the market, wingtip to wingtip with the crowd of Othanim. She was watching the dusty space below them keenly, tracking each Othanim warrior as he or she dropped to the ground or emerged from the entrances they'd found. There were humans down there too, people they had dragged screaming from their hiding space below, and who were now being killed in a variety of terrible ways: disembowelled, torn to pieces, dropped from a great height. Kaeto had tried to get a message to the rebels in time, all based on a hunch that Ceni was about to do something unwise – it seemed he had failed. They were exactly where the Othanim had been expecting them to be. But then, it had always been a risky plan. No, much better to wait, and watch, and choose your moment.

Finally, the constant traffic from one of the entrances eased off, and Belise flew down, taking care not to land in a puddle of blood. She didn't want to engage any of the rebels if she could help it – she would have to kill them to avoid rousing suspicion, and although murder in the service of her work did not normally cause her any concerns, killing people who might help her down the line felt inefficient. And yes, slightly heartless. Folding her wings away neatly, she headed down the steps, her head bowed to avoid cracking it against the low ceiling. A couple of Othanim passed her, dragging a woman between them, and then she emerged into the larger space below ground. It was an impressive cellar, reminding her a little of Gynid Tyleigh's workshops underneath Stratum. Once, she was sure, it would have made an excellent base for the rebels, but now the dusty floor was slippery with blood, the stench of it mineral in her nose.

'There you are.'

Malakim was tied to a chair in a shadowy corner, his bulbous head drooping. None of the Othanim had attempted to free him, but then, Belise knew, the prince wasn't all that popular with the rank and file. When they thought she wasn't listening – and Belise was always listening – they described him as a freak, a rogue mutant that was sure to lead them to a ground-stuck future. How could anything wingless be trusted?

Belise knelt behind Malakim and untied his bonds. The boy slumped forward, shivering, so she pulled a nearby blanket from the floor and slung it around his shoulders.

'My prince,' she said. 'Are you alright?'

Six red eyes like cursed egg yolks glared up at her.

'There were...' he said. 'I saw wasps.'

'Did you?' She brushed some of his hair back from his forehead. It didn't look as though he'd been harmed, although the ropes had left deep pink marks on his wrists and arms. 'We'll have to find one for your collection. Right now, we need to get you home to bed.'

She got him up and standing, brushed the dust from his clothes and led him to the stairwell. Most of the Othanim had left already, while all that remained of the rebels was the odd disembodied scream from somewhere above their heads. Outside, the full moon hung heavy in the night sky, its light turning the puddles of blood as pale as cream.

'I'm going to fly you back to the castle now, my prince. So I'll need you to hold onto me good and tight, alright?' Belise watched as the boy processed this information. There was another version of this night, she realised, where she took Malakim back to the rebels and she and Kaeto and Felldir threw in their lot with them. But judging from the mess in the market square, there wasn't much left of Princess Epona's rebellion. 'Can you do that for me?'

The boy nodded.

'Beleeze?'

'Yes?'

He looked up at her, one hot hand grasping hers.

'I'm hungry, Beleeze.'

---

When she got back to the castle and brought Malakim to his mother's chambers, she found Icaraine already there. The queen of the Othanim had a wilder than usual look about her, and her hands were covered in dried blood. Belise wondered where Kaeto was. She'd have to check in on him as soon as she could.

'There he is. There's my boy.' Icaraine looked him up and down before settling her yellow wolf's eyes on Belise. 'He is unharmed?'

Belise nodded. Malakim kept his head down.

'You should have been with him, girl. You should not have left his side.'

Belise knelt on the flagstones, bowing her head before the giant Othanim queen.

'I know, my queen. I have failed you, and I have failed my prince. I must be punished.'

Icaraine snorted. This was a dangerous move, but Belise sensed that pleading with Icaraine, or trying to wriggle away from responsibility, would only provoke her anger. She was a predator, a wildcat that could not resist pursuing fleeing prey.

'Mikael paid for his *inattention* with his guts. Perhaps that is what you deserve, too.'

Malakim lifted his head, and shuffled over until he was leaning awkwardly on Belise's shoulder. He put his arm around her neck. This close, he smelled strange, like vegetables that had been left too long in the dark.

Icaraine sighed. 'But the boy is fond of you,' she said. 'Your true mistake was trusting Mikael to be more than a worthless maggot. In future, Beleeze, you trust no one but yourself with my son's care.'

'It is done, my queen,' said Belise. 'I swear it.'

Icaraine nodded. 'Good. The rebels have already paid in blood for their mischief, but my appetite is vast. Soon, we will head north, but until then we will entertain ourselves by scouring this stinking city for the last of the rebellion.'

'There is one more thing, your highness,' said Belise. 'The boy said he is hungry.'

A slow grin spread across Icaraine's craggy features like blood soaking into a bandage.

'*Finally*,' she said.

# 48

*There is a giant buried beneath Humming Hill. I say buried, of course I actually mean that a giant sleeps beneath the earth there, except that sometimes he is wakeful. If you are lucky – as I was – you can sit on the grassy slopes of Humming Hill, the scent of clover and buttercups in your nose, and the ground will start to vibrate. It's so soft at first you could miss it, but it grows in strength until the whole hill is rumbling and a low discordant music thrums in the air. We no longer know the name of the giant, but we know he likes to hum to himself.*

Extract from the notes of Bede the Liar,<br>famed adventurer and alchemist

Epona sat shivering on the muddy riverbank. Dimly she was aware of the cold water squelching in her boots, and the first smudge of dawn light pinking the eastern horizon, but mainly her head was filled with the same handful of images, over and over: her mother caught between Icaraine's brutal fists; her sister's eyes, staring blankly up at nothing at all; blood on the wooden boards of the harbour. Blood that should have been hers.

'Epona?' Jack sounded very far away, like she was whispering down a long tunnel. 'I know that you need to rest, but we can't do it here. I'm sorry. We're still too close to the city.'

That was true. Epona didn't know how they had made it even this far. The dark waters of the Old Father had been freezing, taking the air from her lungs in an instant, and then Jack had actually dragged her under, pushing her head down and down so that the Othanim couldn't see them, so that the arrows that came pelting after them sank into the darkness. And then Jack had dragged her – even with Caliburn slung over her back she was fast, and strong – downriver towards the sea, allowing only the briefest snatches of the surface to catch their breath. The taste of the river water was still in her mouth, silty and strange.

'Please.' Jack leaned down and took her arms, pulling her to her feet. Epona stood, her limbs oddly loose. They didn't feel attached to her. 'We have to move. Get out of sight. There will be patrols overhead any moment.'

'Where is this place?'

The other woman looked at her oddly. 'Do you not know it? There's a village not far from here. Or there used to be. Furzeworth.'

'Oh. I do know it. Looks different in this light.' *Everything looks different now*, she thought.

'Let's get moving. I want to get somewhere we can build a fire. I don't like how pale you are.'

A laugh bubbled up in Epona's chest. She swallowed it down for Jack's sake. It hardly mattered how pale she was. Everything was done. She had failed.

They climbed up the riverbank, Jack pausing frequently to haul Epona along, and then across a stretch of marsh, following paths that took them around the wide stretches of shallow water. Wading birds fled at their approach. A low mist began to pool around their feet, summoned by the rising sun. Epona thought of her sister's eyes, as unknowing and as blank as the still surface of the fen. Once, Jack spotted an Othanim patrol in the distance, a scattering of dark shapes against the pale sky, and they crouched in the water again, only the tops of their heads showing. When the patrol had moved on and they started walking, Epona was shivering even harder, her teeth clattering together.

'Are we going to the village?' she asked. It was curious, she thought, how quickly and easily she had passed leadership to Jack. In this moment, she was no longer in charge.

'It's not safe there,' Jack replied. 'None of the villages around Londus-on-Sea are free of Othanim these days.'

'So where are we going?'

Jack's eyes kept wandering up to the sky, her lips drawn into a thin line. Her hair was plastered to her head and neck. 'You'll see.'

The marsh ended eventually, and they came instead to a vast orchard, rows and rows of apple and pear trees, many of them still covered in pink and white blossom. Orchard groves were sacred to the Druin, and normally the place would have had at least one in attendance, whispering to the trees and tending them, but it was clear that this orchard had been abandoned at least a year ago. There were still the rubbery brown remains of rotten fruit underfoot. Epona wondered if this was where they would stop — there was cover here, at least. But Jack kept on walking.

Beyond the orchard there was a stretch of woodland. Epona opened her mouth to point out that neither of them were Druin, and they were likely to get lost. Then she remembered the noise she had heard when Icaraine had snapped her sister's neck, and she said nothing. By the middle of the morning, they had reached a lake, a long, cool, dark green stretch of water shielded by pine and weeping willow. Jack led her down to the edge, where she began to build a small fire. Epona sat cross-legged on the ground, staring at the water. There were dragonflies skipping across the surface, and here and there the flicker of a fish.

'I knew the village,' she said eventually. 'But I don't know this lake.' She frowned. She was trying to picture the maps in her mother's rookery, maps she had committed to memory more than a decade ago. It was hard to get a clear picture in her mind, particularly when her mind only wanted to show her blood, but she was fairly sure there was no lake on the maps. 'What is this place?'

'It's Caliburn's Lake.' Jack got the fire going, then took the sword from her back and laid it carefully on the ground. Both of them, Epona realised, were covered in river mud, but somehow it looked fetching on Jack. Her shining skin only seemed brighter between the flecks of dirt.

'That doesn't explain why I don't know it.' Epona rubbed her eyes. She was starting to feel more awake, and the full despair of their situation was approaching. She didn't want to think about it yet.

'It is... a secret place. I found Caliburn here.' She pointed at the green water. 'I stumbled across it, but it's supposed to be hidden. I only found it because...' Jack sat down next to Epona, facing the fire. She looked at her hands. 'Because I was meant to find the sword. Normally, there is a powerful magic that keeps everyone away.'

'Hold on. You're telling me you had access to a secret magical hideaway all this time? Jack, we could have kept the rebellion here. We could have hidden Malakim here!' Epona's stomach turned over, thinking of the rebels who had been hiding in the market cellar. All dead now, no doubt. 'Why wouldn't you tell us about this? Why wouldn't you tell *me*?'

Jack was shaking her head. 'I thought about it. Obviously I did. But I couldn't bring anyone else here. The magic wouldn't allow it.'

'That's nonsense. I'm here, aren't I?' Epona rubbed her hands down her face. She was trembling all over, and not from the cold. In her mind she saw her mother's body land on the wooden boards, broken beyond repair. Her sister's eyes. Blood seeping from their bodies, and then stopping. She was thinking that if they had got them out, if they had saved them, they could have brought Broudicca and Bronvica here, they could have been here now, by this fire, safe...

Epona only realised she was sobbing when Jack's arms circled around her, pulling her in and holding her tight. She tried to pull away, horrified at being exposed in this way, but Jack only laid her head on top of hers, gently.

'It's alright,' she murmured. 'It's alright.'

---

Later, when the sun had reached the vault of the sky and the lake was filled with fragile spring sunshine, Epona spoke again. She felt wrung out and exhausted, her head so heavy it was making her neck ache.

'I've been watching the sky,' she said. Jack looked up from her work. She had vanished into the wood an hour ago and brought back a pair of rabbits, which she was now cooking over the fire. They had both taken off their outermost layer of clothing to dry, and her legs were shockingly, delightfully pale, like cream. 'I've been watching the sky and I haven't seen any birds fly over. Is that part of the magic?'

She hadn't spoken since the crying had started. Jack adjusted the skewer so that the other side of the rabbit could begin to brown.

'It is. Birds are close to the Druin. This place is hidden even from them.'

Epona nodded as though this made sense. After a while she asked, 'Why?'

'Come here.' Jack stood up and went to the edge of the lake. When Epona didn't move, she waved her over. 'Look, I'll show you. It's about the right time of day to see it, if you stand on this little ledge here.'

Epona joined her, climbing to the top of the sandy bank with bare feet. Jack pointed at the lake. 'There. Under the surface. Do you see her?'

'I can't see anything but green water,' said Epona. The midday sun was bright, sending searing ripples of golden light across the lake. They dazzled the eye.

'You have to look *under*. Here.' Jack put an arm around her shoulder, lightly, and pulled her down into a slight crouching position. She put her head close to Epona's so that their eyelines matched. She pointed again. 'Don't look at the surface. Look at the water beneath. It's easier to see if you're overhead, I imagine. Which is why the magic makes the birds fly around it.'

Epona blinked. One moment she was looking at the surface of the lake, bright and quiet and alive with insect life; the next she was looking into the depths, from an angle. Everything beneath was caught in shades of green, and there, at the very bottom, a vast face in profile. It was human, more or less, its eyes closed. Hazy beams of sunlight cut through the water to splash against a cheekbone, a brow. There was a neck too, a suggestion of shoulders.

'What is that?' Epona cupped her hands around her eyes to see better. 'Is it a statue?'

'It's the lady of the lake,' said Jack, a faint smile on her face. 'One of the sleeping giants. That's who the magic is protecting. The giants went to sleep a very long time ago. That's what Caliburn tells me.'

They stood for a long time, just watching the lady sleep, until clouds moved in overhead and the sunlight vanished, taking with it the vision of the giant. The lake was murky again, only revealing a mirrored vision of the sky overhead.

'Thank you,' Epona said faintly. 'Thank you for showing me that. But I still don't understand. If this lake is hidden from birds, and hidden from random wanderers, why is it I can come here? Why can I see it at all?'

'Because you are with me,' said Jack. The tops of her cheeks had turned pink. She stepped away from Epona. The rabbits were cooked, and she passed some of the meat to her. They sat by the fire and ate it quickly, fat and juices running over their fingers.

'I am allowed to bring one person here only. I only get to choose one, and after that, no one else. So I never chose. I figured

I would know at some point who that person was supposed to be.' Caliburn chimed in from its space on the ground, but Jack ignored it.

'You were forced to choose me, then, because we had nowhere else to go. I'm sorry, Jack.'

Jack shook her head. She looked as though she wanted to say something further, but then decided not to.

'We couldn't go back to the Barrow,' she said eventually.

Epona nodded. That was true. If they had tried to make it back to the Barrow, they could have led the Othanim straight to the rest of the rebels. If there were any left.

'Your life is like a story,' she said. 'A sleeping giant, an enchanted sword, a hidden lake. The Druin Merriden arriving at your birth, to place an impossible destiny on your head – *one day you will kill the Green Man.*' She smiled a little. 'I wish my life were a story. Daughter rescues her mother from a monster. They all live happily ever after.'

'Princess... I mean, Epona.' Jack took a breath. 'I am so sorry. About Queen Broudicca and your sister. I can't imagine what that must have been like. I'd have given anything to stop it.'

Epona looked down at the rabbit meat in her hands. Her fingers were still trembling, and the crying felt very close, like a tide waiting to wash her away.

'You did what you could,' she said. She didn't say, *You should have left me there to die with them. That was where I belonged.* 'You did more than anyone else could have, I'm sure.'

'When the last of our clothes are dry, and you are rested, we can travel north again, although I suspect we should go slowly. Icaraine was in a rage. I doubt she'll stop looking for you, especially now that she knows your face.' Jack threw a rabbit bone in the fire, where it popped and blackened. 'We can meet up with the other rebels as we go. We'll just have to be cautious.' She looked up. 'What will our next step be, Epona?'

'Jack.' Epona spoke softly, hoping it would lessen the impact of her words. 'Jack, there is no next step. We are done. They have likely killed almost all of our people. My only hope is that they have killed them quickly and haven't kept any to question, but if they have then it's likely they know about the Barrow. We have no base, no bodies, no queen to rescue.' She paused, swallowing past the lump of grief in her throat. 'No leader,' she finished.

'We have you.' Jack leaned over and took her hand and squeezed it. 'You were always the heart of it, Epona. Don't you see that?'

'Jack, you might be the sweetest...' Epona sighed. 'I gave it what I had, and I got us all killed. I'm done, Jack. If anyone's going to save Brittletain from the Othanim, it won't be me.'

# 49

Ynis landed on the bare branches of the war-nest, laughing giddily as T'rook skidded to a halt next to her. The other griffins in their patrol landed around them, also chattering with good humour. It was early in the morning, and they had been flying all night. By rights Ynis knew she should be dead on her feet, but in truth she felt exhilarated. She had summoned her sword-talons four times that night, and every time they had found Othanim blood.

'That last one did not even have time to scream,' said one of the bigger griffins. 'Before our bolt of lightning had his head off with her talons.'

*Bolt of lightning* was how some of the other griffins had begun to refer to Ynis. They said that she struck like one, unnaturally fast and full of light. She grinned.

'They did not know what hit them,' added another. 'So fast we were, and so deadly.'

Other griffins had come over to greet them, including Flayn. Ynis and T'rook went to him and he groomed them, pecking away dirt from T'rook's flight feathers. Dried blood fell from them in rust-coloured flakes.

'A good hunt, my yenlin?'

'It was the best one yet,' said T'rook. 'We found a pack of six Othanim and chased them from the mountaintop before we opened their guts! After that we found a smaller patrol and when they saw Ynis's blue light they tried to flee. We did not let them.'

'They are beginning to know who you are,' said Flayn in a musing tone. 'They flee now, Ynis, but beware. They might decide that the way to deal with this bolt of lightning is to bring greater numbers, to track it and trap it. You must be careful.'

'I am, Father, I am.'

One of the newly arrived griffins butted Ynis in the shoulder with her beak.

'You'll fly with us next, won't you?' she said. 'Our patrol would be glad to have you.'

'Hoy!' The big black griffin who had initially called her the lightning bolt shouldered his way forward. 'Will you be snapping eggs out of our nests next, Forgen? You do not get to steal warriors for your patrol – if your patrol is weak, that is your problem.'

There was a smattering of laughter at this. Forgen bristled, the feathers on her ruff puffing out to make her look larger.

'It is no surprise that you seek to keep Ynis to yourself, Fasad – her prowess covers up your own inadequacies. Perhaps she can sire yenlin for you in the spring, too.'

There was even more laughter at this. Ynis watched in wonder. Once, she had thought she would forever be an outsider; now they were fighting to have her fly side by side with them. And it was all thanks to Gynid Tyleigh's implant.

Flayn, however, looked less impressed with their blustering.

'Come, you two. I came to fetch you as the war-nest has a visitor, and they wish to see you.'

'Who?' asked Ynis. Her first thought was Leven, prompting a guilty flush that crept up the back of her neck. It didn't seem possible that her sister could have made it over the border without being caught and slaughtered by a patrol, but then perhaps they had seen that her wings were like Ynis's, and they had decided to trust her. The thought made her uneasy; she wasn't sure if she wanted to see Leven or not. 'Is it... a human?'

'Here? Of course not.' Flayn led them away from the squabbling griffins. Ynis called over her shoulder to the squad that she would see them again soon, and that she was happy to fly wherever her talons were needed. Next to her she heard T'rook mutter something that sounded a little like she was suggesting some unusual places her talons could be shoved. Their father spoke over her. 'We're to go to the queen's roost immediately.'

The roost was a space at the very top of the tallest part of the war-nest, and they flew up there together in the overcast morning light. On a clear day from this viewing spot, it was possible to see right down into Brittletain, the thick green forests of the northern Wild Wood frothing at the bottom of the mountain like sea foam. Queen Fellvyn was there with a pair of her husband-advisors, and a small, frail-looking griffin in an elaborate griffin-bone headdress who Ynis found she recognised.

'Frost?'

The older griffin turned, her ear tufts raising in glad surprise. She looked older and somehow smaller than when Ynis had seen her last, and her feathers and fur had started to turn grey. The place where Ynis had once pulled an arrowhead from Frost's flesh was marked by a dart of white fur.

'Witch-seer Arrow,' said Frost. 'I had wondered if we would ever see you again. I am glad to see that your fate-ties bring you back to us. And you too, T'rook.'

Ynis let her wings vanish. Her initial impulse had been to go to Frost, to put her arms around the old griffin's neck and press their heads together as close friends do. But she was remembering the last time she had seen Frost.

'Ah, I am glad you remember my name,' said T'rook in a dry tone. 'I had thought you might have forgotten it after deciding not to help my sister find me.'

'What is this?' snapped Queen Fellvyn. 'We haven't time for sniping amongst ourselves. I won't have it.'

Witch-seer Frost lowered her head a little. 'Forgive me. We were very fond of both Arrow and T'rook at the Bone Fall, but things ended between us in a way that I regret. May I speak to the yenlin alone for a moment?'

Queen Fellvyn sniffed. 'Do what you like, Edge Walker, but you should know that both have proven their yost on the battlesky and should no longer be referred to as yenlin. They deserve that much.'

Ynis went to the edge of the lookout with Frost. T'rook snapped her beak derisively and went to speak to Flayn instead.

Frost sighed. 'That one may never forgive me, I suspect.'

'The Edge Walkers abandoned her,' said Ynis. 'Or did you expect me to coat what happened in honey? Only Festus had the yost to help me do what needed to be done.'

'As I said to you before, Arrow, it is not our place to run after the living, or to leave the Bone Fall. We have sacred duties that—'

'Arrow is not my name,' broke in Ynis. She felt strange, even feverish. She hadn't realised until that moment how much Frost's refusal to help had hurt her. 'And you are not at the Bone Fall now, are you? The same people that shot you with an arrow and killed Brocken took my sister across the sea in a crate. And once there, they kept her in a cage and tortured her. Took her blood, her feathers, fed her dead things and kept her from the sky. All of this you could have helped me prevent, but you did not. How can you expect her to forgive it? How can you expect either of us to forgive you?'

Frost nodded as though she had expected this. 'I failed you both. I see that now. I don't know if I could have made a different choice, but when you came to us, Ynis, a human with the natural talents of a witch-seer, I should have seen you as the harbinger of change that you are. And I should have changed.' She turned to face Ynis, her shoulders trembling with the effort of it, and a trill of alarm went through Ynis. Frost was old, and weak. Flying down here from the Bone Fall must have cost her enormously. 'But my mistakes should not change your path, Arrow.'

'Ynis. My fathers named me Ynis.'

'Ynis, yes, forgive me. We heard even at the Bone Fall that you had returned to Yelvynia, and that you were flying now thanks to some strange new magic. I knew how much you wanted that, young one, and I was glad to hear it. We also heard that you have been flying with other griffins and fighting the old enemy, but, Ynis... this is not your talent. Have you given up on the ways of the witch-seer entirely?'

Ynis shook her head. In the two years they had spent looking for T'rook, she had hardly thought about her witch-seer training. She had used her talent to help them find her sister, and that was all.

'None of that matters while we're at war,' she said, which was what she thought Queen Fellvyn would say. In the distance, low over the woods, she could see movement. More Othanim patrols on their way to try their luck. There were more and more every day.

'Ynis, listen to me. You have a very rare and precious talent. Your connection to the realm of the dead is extremely unusual even amongst griffins. I urge you not to throw that away. Any griffin with claws and talons and beak can be a warrior, but only a very rare few are able to see fate-ties and the shadowy places beyond. You'll always be a child of two worlds, Ynis.'

'So I should go back to living at the Bone Fall, far away from my family? Because T'rook will never agree to go back there. And I am accepted here.' She thought of how the other griffins called her their 'bolt of lightning'. 'This is all I've ever wanted.'

'They accept you because you are a weapon for them to use,' said Frost, her normally soft voice suddenly sharp. 'You are useful to them.'

'You *named* me after a weapon,' Ynis snapped. 'And I am useful to you too, right? You just want to use a different talent of mine, that's all.'

Frost sighed. All the sharpness seemed to flow out of her, leaving her even smaller and frailer than before.

'I did not come here to argue with you.'

'Then why come?'

'Your fate-ties are connected to us all, Ynis. I fear you have a larger role to play in this, something beyond shedding blood in the skies over Yelvynia. I think it's possible—'

'Witch-seer!' Queen Fellvyn's powerful call cut through all the voices in the room. 'That's enough cawing in corners. I would hear your report from the Bone Fall now.'

'Think about what I've said,' Frost said, her voice pitched just for Ynis. 'That's all I ask.'

---

Standing in front of the queen with her head bowed and her wings tucked away, Frost looked like a creature made of sticks and griffin-spit, small and frail enough to blow away in a strong gust of wind. Ynis stood off to one side with T'rook and Flayn, watching uneasily while the old witch-seer made her report. She was wondering when they could leave, and whether Fellvyn would have further use for them. They had paused to hunt and eat while they were on patrol, but her hunger was back. A few hours' sleep wouldn't hurt either. She stifled a yawn.

'...so in this time of upheaval we have been monitoring the ancestor spirits of the Bone Fall, and keeping an eye on the Lich-Way also. There have been omens and portents – a goat found with two heads, starlings flying at night. Even the Dunohi have been wandering, sending shadows of themselves into the far north, as though they were looking for something.'

One of Fellvyn's husband-advisors cocked his head at that. 'Dunohi leaving the Wild Wood? Unheard of.'

Frost nodded. 'I wouldn't have believed it if I hadn't seen it with my own eyes, Lord Consort. The Wild Wood, the very soul of this island, is unsettled in a way we haven't seen before, and under the last new moon, we felt the Druidahnon cast a powerful summoning spell.'

'That old fool,' snapped Queen Fellvyn. She looked troubled. 'Losing the rest of his kind addled his mind. And he is altogether too fond of his human pets.' Her eyes darted to Ynis and back again. 'I do not mean to offend, daughter of Flayn.' Ynis looked down at her boots, her cheeks flushing; not from shame, but from pride. This was the closest the queen had come to treating her like a griffin. 'What has he done?'

Frost hesitated. 'He has summoned the Green Man, my queen. He has risen in the form of a mortal man.'

'Ah, Brittlish superstitious nonsense,' said Fellvyn. She flexed her wings, casually batting one of her husband-advisors across the beak. 'What use is a human fertility spirit to us?'

'He is much more than that, your highness,' said Frost. 'He is the land itself, and even as creatures of the sky, we must eventually put our paws on the earth. Our leader, Witch-seer Scree, believes that the Green Man may be the key to defeating the Othanim. When—'

'Hold on.' Ynis was speaking before she was aware of what she was going to say. 'Scree is your leader? Since when?'

Every griffin turned to look at her.

Frost sighed heavily. 'Since he forced me from power, Ynis. I am old, and growing weaker all the time. Without Brocken to protect me and speak on my behalf... Things changed in the Bone Fall after you left. Now, I am his second. Which is why I am here, carrying his messages.'

'A male in charge?' Fellvyn sniffed. 'But then the Edge Walkers have always had strange ways. Continue your report, Frost.'

'Yes. The Green Man has chosen his human form. The ancestor spirits have seen him, and they tell us that his power grows every moment, and that it could end the Othanim. But he is unpredictable by his very nature, and dangerous. It would be sensible for us to seek him out and make sure that such power is under griffin control.'

'Who is he, then?' asked one of the husband-advisors. 'Who is this human?'

'One of the Druidahnon's children. A Druin with goat horns and green eyes, who once was thrawn. He is followed by a bird, a jackdaw.'

Ynis looked up to see T'rook staring at her.

'He travels with a woman,' continued Frost. 'A woman with Titan bone in her skin, formed of lines of forbidden magic. They travel now in the south, we think, and—'

'Forgive me.' Ynis took a step forward, trying not to wince as every griffin eye turned to her for a second time. 'Forgive me, but I think I know who that is.'

## 50

'Is there anything I can get you, my prince?'

Belise watched the boy from her place by the window. Since she had brought him back from the rebels' hideout, he had been behaving oddly; he was twitchy, unable to sit for more than a minute. He was roaming his chambers restlessly, picking things up and putting them down again. Each of the jars with their insect occupants had been picked up and examined, then discarded. Two he had simply dropped onto the stone floor, smashing them into pieces. Belise had picked up every shard of glass and swept the floor both times, watching with a wary eye as the liberated grasshoppers bounced away into the corners of the room. She wondered if the rebels had done something to the child, or possibly fed him something that had upset him on some fundamental level. He appeared to be unharmed, but even assassins knew that not all wounds were visible.

When he didn't answer her, she went to the kitchens and made up some of his 'nectar', heating the milk gently and slowly adding water, sugar and honey, mixing the anaemic slop while the human staff watched her from a distance. It was funny, really. In Stratum, if a kid like her had been caught in the kitchens of a palace, she would have been turfed out on her ear. In this place, in this body, she was respected. Feared, even.

She took the nectar back to his chamber, and with some difficulty got him to sit next to her on the bed while she spooned the stuff into his waiting mouth. Eventually this seemed to calm him a little, and he leaned against her, his large bulbous head resting against her arm.

'There. That's better, isn't it? I imagine you've not had much sleep, have you? Do you want a nap? It's the middle of the day but I don't reckon anyone's going to mind.'

He nuzzled further into her arm. Belise did her best not to grimace. In many ways, she told herself, he was just like a normal child. It wasn't his fault, what he was.

'That's alright, you can sleep on me if you like,' she said, trying not to let her inner revulsion seep into her words. 'And when you've rested, we can go for a walk around the grounds if you like. We can get some new jars from the kitchens and pick up some new beasties for you.'

He pressed his little face against the skin of her arm, snuffling. There was a wet sensation, and the press of teeth. He had his mouth open, she realised. She fought against the urge to throw him off.

'Here, what are you doing?'

'I can smell. Your bones.'

Belise leaned away abruptly, leaving the boy to slump awkwardly onto the bed. She stood up, her skin prickling all over.

'What?'

Six red eyes stared at her flatly. Was there something else in that gaze that hadn't been there before? Not hostility, exactly, but a need of some kind. Once, she had been a hungry child on the streets of Stratum, and she imagined that she had looked like that when she saw other kids with families, well fed and fat.

'Your bones. Under your skin. I smell them.' He took a deep breath, as though those short sentences had worn him out. 'I'm hungry.'

'Well.' She crossed her arms over her chest. 'You can't have these bones, my prince, because I am still using them.'

He looked away from her, one small hand coming up to scratch at his neck. The sound it made was too loud, as though his skin were made of sandpaper.

'I'll change soon,' he said in a small voice.

---

'It's dinner time finally, my sweet.'

They were outside the castle, on the start of the road that headed north towards the Wild Wood. There was a great platform, so newly built that the planks of white wood were still bleeding sap, and this was where Icaraine crouched. In front of her was a great pile of Titan bones, shining silver under the afternoon sun. Kaeto recognised the shape of the bear skull, great empty sockets staring at nothing. Belise, he noticed, was standing off to one side, her eyes watchful, and the prince was seated on the platform like a fat toddler who had finally run out of energy. Felldir was there too, his head lowered, his curtailed wing clasped tightly to his back. Kaeto hadn't been able to see him since Malakim had been taken. He looked stronger, but there was a stillness in him that suggested he knew that more violence could soon be heading his way. Ceni was waiting off to one side. She was dressed in finer clothes than when Kaeto had seen her last, and her hair had been freshly washed. There were fine lines of blue paint on her cheeks, the traditional sign of her family's royalty. The wages of betrayal, he thought sourly.

The Othanim guard that had hold of his arm called out to Icaraine, and her head snapped up, a hawk sighting its prey.

'There you are.' She stood up. 'It's nearly time, Envoy, and I didn't want you to miss it.'

He cleared his throat. 'You honour me, your majesty.'

'First of all though, light-bones, I thought I would give you a gift.' She nodded to an Othanim warrior who had a large sack in his hands. He stepped forward, his face hidden behind his helm.

'Since Malakim was taken from me, I have had a great deal to think about, Envoy. One of the humans I allowed to live, who I kept close to me in the castle, plotted against us. Princess Bronvica has paid the price, but it has made me consider who I should allow in my court. Clearly I have been far too lenient.'

'Your majesty...'

She raised her voice, speaking over him easily. 'Ceni, my most loyal servant, knew the right course of action to take. It occurred to me to purge my court of every creature that was not Othanim, but I have decided to keep you alive for a little longer, Envoy. The same could not be said for your associates.'

Kaeto's eyes settled on the sack. The hessian at the bottom was dark, stained with something, and when the wind blew down from the north, he caught a familiar scent. *Belise is safe*, he told himself. *Felldir is safe, for now. They are the only ones that matter to me.*

Icaraine nodded, and the warrior upended the sack. From it, six severed heads rolled out onto the dirt, their necks and faces ragged and slathered with gore. Kaeto took a careful step backwards, his mouth turning down at the corners. For an instant he didn't know who they were, but then his eyes alighted on one particular head: bald, the skin as white as cream, and now almost blue. It was Thirteen. Icaraine had killed each of the empress's new Heralds.

'I... That is unfortunate. The empress was very proud of her newest Heralds. But she can always make more.'

'Enough.' Icaraine sounded bored already. 'My boy is hungry. It's time for him to eat, and become the child of the chains. Malakim.' She moved over to where the boy was sitting, leaning down to rub one massive finger over his downy head. 'These bones are the bones of a bear Titan, one of the very Titans who imprisoned us all those years ago. He threw us down into the Undertomb and sealed us in with his filthy forest magic, and now he lies in pieces before us. How the mighty have fallen. Are you ready to taste his bones, my sweet?'

Malakim nodded jerkily. The boy's whole body, Kaeto noticed, was trembling slightly.

'Here you go then.' Icaraine picked up a small bone to start with, although given it belonged to a Titan, it was still the length of Kaeto's head. She passed it gently to the boy, who turned it over and over in his hands, his red eyes glistening with interest. His mouth dropped open, wider than Kaeto had been expecting, and he saw that the child had rows and rows of teeth that marched back towards his throat. Malakim pushed the bone over his lips.

'That's it,' said Icaraine, sounding immensely pleased with herself. 'Eat it all up like a good boy.'

And he did.

Slowly, methodically, Malakim crunched his way through the bone, his tiny, neat teeth splintering and pulverising a material that Kaeto had always found to be as hard as iron. When the bone was gone, he swallowed, runnels of drool slick on his chin, then picked up the next piece of the Druidahnon. This bone was larger than the last, much too big, Kaeto thought, for the prince to fit into his mouth, but to his creeping horror the boy's jaw opened and then dropped, expanding like a snake's. The bone went in, was crunched up, and then Malakim was onto the next.

Kaeto looked around at the other witnesses. Ceni looked faintly disgusted, like she was watching a dog eat its own vomit in the street. Felldir looked sad, as though he were watching the end of something. On Belise's face there was no judgement at all; she was watching keenly, her eyes darting back and forth as she took it all in. Later, if he asked her, she would be able to recount every unpleasant detail along with her own observations and notes. He had taught her well.

When Kaeto turned his attention back to Malakim, he had to draw on his own training not to startle. The crunching and grinding continued, but now it wasn't just Malakim's jaw that was distended – the whole shape of his head had changed, pulling his six red eyes into a new configuration, and his neck was longer and wider too. His pale skin was glistening under the sunshine; not from sweat, Kaeto thought, but from something else that seemed to be oozing from the boy's pores.

*What is happening?* For the first time in his entire career as an Envoy, he briefly wished that Gynid Tyleigh was there with him. She at least might have some idea of what all this was heading towards.

'That's it,' cooed Icaraine. 'That's my boy. Eat it all up now. There's plenty more.'

Malakim did appear to be speeding up. Bones disappeared into his gaping maw faster and faster. Meanwhile, his lower body began to change too. As they watched, his stomach swelled and his arms and legs inched out across the platform. His fingers grew longer, almost spiderlike, and the simple clothes he was wearing split along the seams. Kaeto looked away, feeling the gorge rise in the back of his throat, but his eyes alighted on the severed heads of Thirteen and his fellow Heralds. He grimaced.

'What's the matter, Envoy?' called Icaraine. 'Have you never seen a baby feed? Ha!'

No longer concerned about looking impassive, Kaeto turned to one side, watching instead the faces of the gathered Othanim. Of those he could see, most looked eager, or fascinated; however, a not insignificant number, he noted, looked vaguely repulsed. He remembered what Felldir had said about the Othanim initially believing Icaraine's child to be a runt, a mutant not worth speaking of. He wondered what they thought now.

When he turned back again, he saw that almost all the bones were gone. The final remaining part of the skeleton, saved perhaps as a child saves the best part of his pudding for last, was the Druidahnon's skull. Malakim was turning it around in his long hands, spidery fingers seeking out every crevice.

'That's it. That's your final mouthful, my sweet.'

Malakim opened his mouth, jaws falling open like a book with a broken spine, and the Druidahnon's skull disappeared within. There was further crunching, and chewing, and drool, and then the boy stopped, breathing heavily, his shoulders rising and falling.

*What an end for the Druidahnon*, thought Kaeto. *Eaten by this monstrosity.* He suppressed a shudder.

The boy could no longer truly be called that. He was the size of a fully grown man now, perhaps larger. His head was long and distended, like a bird's, his eyes planted on either side of it, and his body was long and gangly, his skin almost golden. The little wisps of white-blonde hair were gone.

'There,' said Icaraine. 'The first stage of his transformation.' She looked around at her followers, her yellow eyes as bright as new coins. 'And to think some of you doubted me. Doubted my son. Don't think I have forgotten.' The wind picked up then, sending a cool breeze from the south that smelled faintly of river water. Malakim shivered. 'Pakrinash, go and fetch a cloak for the prince. He has outgrown his clothes.'

One of the warriors stepped forward, an older Othanim with long grey hair that fell to her waist in a braid. She looked uncertain, glancing at the Titans who stood with her out of the corner of her eyes. Kaeto couldn't be sure, but he thought it very likely that Pakrinash was one of the Othanim who had expressed doubts about Icaraine's child.

But an order was an order. Pakrinash unfolded her wings and swept up into the air, heading back towards the castle. Malakim watched her go, and then reached out one long, bony arm, his fingers outstretched. There was a scream, and Pakrinash hung in the air, unmoving.

Icaraine laughed. 'Dessert, my sweet? Why not. You must be famished.'

There was a terrible popping noise, like someone cracking all the bones in their knuckles. Pakrinash screeched with pain again as her wings crumpled under some unseen force, and then she was being dragged back down to the ground, back towards Malakim and his waiting mouth.

Kaeto closed his eyes and waited for the screaming to stop. It was one thing, he thought, to watch a monster eat the bones of the dead, but quite another to watch him feed on the living.

# 51

*'I saw a kraken once. Frolicking on the edges of the Titan's Eye. I know full well you won't believe me, no one's seen a Titan of that stripe for over five hundred years, that's what you'll say. I was just a scrap of a girl, serving on the* Lost Legend, *a ship that met a bad end a few years later, along with much of her crew, so there aren't many left who could back me up, it's true... But I saw him. A vast creature, blue and white and black, eyes like moons, playing in that deadly whirlpool like a bath. They live deep, those creatures. It's no surprise to me we don't see them.'*

Conversation overheard in The Lip between Captain Elisa-Glory of the *Faded Glory* and a fellow Nost sailor

The Wild Wood had always seemed especially alive to Leven; certainly alive in a way that other places she had journeyed through as a Herald were not. Now, standing with Cillian in the heart of it, she realised that it had only been sleeping before. Now, with him, it was alive and awake.

'What is happening?' she breathed.

'The wood knows me,' Cillian said fondly. The trees were the greenest Leven had ever seen, seeming to almost thrum with power, and all around, birds were singing. It had to be every bird in the wood, given the racket. There was a constant rustling in the undergrowth, and she kept catching glimpses of animals that appeared to be snatching peeks at Cillian from the brambles and bushes: squirrels, foxes, badgers, stoats, mice and adders. It was unnerving.

'We'll just have to hope we don't need to sneak up on anyone,' she said. The ore-lines were aching again, but the pain felt muted. 'You said we were going to head south. Do you need to open a Path?'

'Oh yes. But the wood has given me all its secrets.' Cillian shook his head and laughed. 'It's incredible, Leven. I always had a good grasp of the Paths, better than most Druin, but there were still lots of places I couldn't reach, that were forbidden to me. And this morning, every one of them is open to me. I can see it all so clearly. All I have to do is ask, and the way is ours.'

He nodded to the section of wood ahead of them, and it changed in front of Leven's eyes – a trick she had almost grown used to during her travels in Brittletain. But this time the whole Wild Wood seemed to part; rather than a dense crowd of oak, sycamore and hawthorn there was a clear view down a slight incline, and at the bottom of the hill lay a city crowded around a river. Leven had only seen it once before, and then briefly, but she recognised Londus immediately.

'Hold on,' she said as they started forward. She could hear Inkwort somewhere above them, calling out a farewell to the other birds. 'We were in northern Mersia, right? And now we're in Londus? If it were that easy to cross the Wild Wood, why did you take weeks to get us to Galabroc?'

'Because I wanted to spend as much time as possible in your delightful company?' He grinned at the look she shot him. 'Back then, I couldn't have done it, my love. It's like I said before – all of the secret ways are open to me now. The Green Man knows every part of this isle, and every part of it knows him.'

Ahead of them, the city of Londus-on-Sea stood unnaturally still under an overcast sky. Leven could see the steely grey snake of the Old Father River, a twinkle on its surface suggesting some sluggish movement, but there were no trails of smoke rising from the buildings and no sign of traffic going in and out of the city on the paths that spread out from it like veins on a leaf. She swallowed, hearing the click of moisture in her own throat, and realised that it was strangely quiet too.

'The whole city looks abandoned,' she said. More than once, when she was a Herald, she and her fellow warriors had been in places like that, great towns or cities that had been left empty. Sometimes, the people had left before they arrived, looking to avoid the slaughter. And sometimes, they had not been fast enough. She frowned.

'There. Look.' Cillian pointed to the castle that rose over the city. 'Not completely abandoned.'

There were Othanim there, a group of about ten. They were hanging over the castle walls. Abruptly they scattered, like birds at a loud noise. One of them, Leven noted, seemed to freeze in mid-air, its wings suddenly stiff; then it fell away, out of sight. They watched the others in case they came in their direction, but they drew further south until they were tiny black dots in the distance. When they were sure it was safe, they began to walk out of the forest and down the hill.

'We need to find Epona,' said Leven. 'Supposedly she is here somewhere, leading a rebellion.'

'Let me see.' He stopped, then crouched, placing his hand flat against the grass. In the bright sunlight, Leven noticed that his horns were tinted greenish-blue rather than blue.

'What are you doing?'

'I'm looking for her.'

Leven raised her eyebrows. 'You can do that?'

'Apparently.' He put his other hand in the grass too. Leven had always admired his hands, strong and long-fingered, the pale dashes of scars across his knuckles. She thought of the night they had spent together in the tavern, and to her own surprise, felt herself blush. 'Huh. That's odd.'

'What is it?'

'The land is telling me she's in a secret, hidden place,' said Cillian. 'Normally I wouldn't be able to see it at all, but nothing here can be hidden from the Green Man.'

'Perhaps it's the rebels' hideout?'

'I don't know. There's a very powerful piece of magic keeping it hidden. I assume they have a few of the order amongst their ranks, but it's not something I would expect the average Druin to be able to do.' He stood up. 'I can take us there, though.'

Although it was overcast, it was still a mild spring day, and the breeze that skirted up the hill brought with it a scent of early spring flowers: snowdrops, daffodils, crocuses. Leven thought about when she had last made the journey, in the opposite direction. She had been cold and out of sorts. She had been perplexed by the open green landscape.

'Do you remember when you last brought me this way? We rode on horses that time.' She slid an arm through his, and he squeezed it. 'I thought you were a pompous arsehole.'

Cillian laughed. 'And I thought you were a savage butcher, looking down your nose at the land I loved.'

'I didn't understand it then,' said Leven, smiling faintly. 'I think I do now.'

'You are part of this land too, Leven,' said Cillian. 'Even if you hadn't been born here, you have fought for the people of Brittletain, shed blood onto the earth, made love under the Caul of Stars.' They stopped walking and she looked into his eyes, greener even than spring foliage. 'Can you feel it?'

She grinned, blushing again. 'I can feel something.'

It wasn't the safest place, and there was no cover, but the grass and clover were soft, and for a little while they didn't think about the war or the Green Man. When they were back on their feet,

Cillian doing up the buttons on his shirt and Leven pulling her fingers through her dishevelled hair, they caught each other's eyes again and laughed.

'The joke in Stratum was that you stopped wanting to do that when you were married.'

'I don't think I get the Imperial sense of humour.'

She shook her head, smiling. 'It's funny. When the Druidahnon was talking about your transformation, I imagined all sorts. I didn't think you'd be human anymore. But you just seem yourself. Only, more so. Do you feel different?'

'I... it's hard to describe.' He shook his head. 'Shall we get moving? It'd be good to get under cover before dusk.'

Leven nodded, and they began to trot down the hill. So far she hadn't told him about her run-in with the pixen and their queen. It felt wrong, to be keeping something so significant from him, but she couldn't help thinking that the Green Man would not want to hear about Queen Mab and the husband he had apparently consumed. It might even make him angry. She slipped a hand into her pocket, her fingers finding the hag stone.

*Everything is fine*, she told herself. *Who knows what weird grudges Queen Mab might have against the Green Man? She could have been exaggerating, or even lying. I should know better than to get involved in someone else's complicated marriage.* Even so, she resolved to keep what had happened to herself for now. They had enough on their plate, after all.

# 52

Belise paused, her arms full of cloth, to look at the giant chariot that stood in the road. It was vast, larger than many buildings in Stratum, and covered in elaborate scrollwork and carvings. It had at least fifteen windows that she could see, and the rich dark wood the Othanim had carved it from had been highlighted here and there with gold paint. On the side that faced her, in the very centre, the helm that Icaraine habitually wore had been carved, twice as big as it was in real life – this had been painted gold, too. At the front, in a chaotic network of reins and bits and straps, stood thirty horses in six rows of five. They had been taken, Belise knew, from the royal stables, animals bred for their strength and stamina. She glanced at the chariot again. They would need it.

'Hurry up,' a passing Othanim shouted at her. 'The Lightbringer wants this contraption moving before the sun is at its height, and if it's you slowing us down I'm sure she'll be more than glad to feed you to his highness.'

This was the dark joke among the Othanim currently, a joke born, she imagined, out of screaming terror. Three times now Malakim had decided he was still hungry, and with the Druidahnon's bones all gone, the easiest and swiftest meals were flying all around him. She nodded tersely at the warrior, then let her wings lift her up the steps to the back of the covered chariot. Inside was a sumptuous chamber. Every scrap of silk and upholstery and fine furniture had been scavenged from the castle to fill it – maybe even from every fine house in the city – and Malakim crouched in the centre of it like a vast, pale turd. He lifted his head as she entered. His eyes were both larger and narrower than they had been.

'I've got some more clothes for you,' she said. Given that he was now taller than her by a good two feet, none of his old clothes fit him, and Icaraine had ordered that the servants construct new ones. She took them to a large chest in the corner and folded them inside. 'We'll be moving soon. Is there anything else I can get you?'

He cocked his head to look at her, an oddly shaped thing on a neck that still looked too slim to support it. He put her in mind of a baby bird. If so, what did that make her? The cuckoo's mother, struggling to care for a creature that shared no blood with her kind. *Except that's not actually true, is it*, she thought to herself. *My body is a Titan body now, just like his mum's.*

'Nothing else,' he said. His voice had a croak to it since the feeding that put Belise in mind of a teenage boy whose balls were dropping. It was an unsettling thought. She realised, with a grimace that she carefully hid, that age and ageing worked differently for Malakim. Technically he was thousands of years old, but he had spent that time as a baby; he'd only 'grown up' in the last few days.

'Good. Then I think that's us done.' Belise went to the back of the carriage and leaned out the door. She caught the attention of one of the Othanim attendants and waved to let them know they were all loaded up. Beyond them she could see Icaraine, who was standing in the grey morning drizzle shouting orders, and behind the carriage itself, another, smaller, vastly less ornate carriage. This one, she knew, contained other supplies they might need on their journey north, and Icaraine's two most favoured prisoners: Master Kaeto and Felldir. For the briefest second, she considered coming up with some excuse to go to the other carriage – she could say that the prince had demanded some fresh nectar, something like that – but she decided against it. To do so would be to take an unnecessary risk, and for sentimental reasons, too. Kaeto and Felldir would have to manage by themselves for a time.

She ducked back inside, pulling the steps up behind her as she did so. 'It won't be long now, my prince,' she said, just as there was a flurry of shouts from outside. The chariot jerked, steel wheels biting into the dirt; a few horses protested, and then they were on their way. 'It's off to the north we go.'

'Where we will see the griffins,' he said in his newly unsettled voice. It wasn't just the sound of it that was different; he was talking more since he had eaten the Druidahnon's bones, and more eloquently too. 'Do you think, Beleeze, the griffins will taste different to the old bear? Will their bones have more flavour?'

'I imagine they probably taste like chicken,' said Belise, shaking her head at her own joke, which Malakim did not get. 'I don't know. I'm sure you won't have long to wait.'

'My hunger is hiding again,' he continued. *The Othanim will be glad of that*, she thought. 'I do not know when I will need more. Mother says that it will be soon. Because I am growing.'

'You've certainly done that, my prince.' Belise went to one of the windows and looked out. They were passing into the Wild Wood, the raw earth of the road stark and somehow obscene against the trees that were still standing. For a little while, they were both quiet, listening to the rattle and rumble of the chariot as it made its way down the uneven road. Every now and then Belise heard a human voice, shouting at the horses. They had brought in human servants to control the animals – the Othanim did not like horses, and horses certainly did not like them.

When Malakim did speak again, it was in a voice so quiet that Belise almost missed it.

'What was that, my prince?'

'I asked – did you give me to them?'

Belise did not answer immediately. She was considering her

options. If she ran for the back of the chariot, she might make it up and into the sky before anyone noticed something was wrong, and once up there she could go anywhere, technically. That was if she made it to the back of the chariot. Her bones were Titan bones, and if Malakim wanted to, he could hold her here with the force of his will. Or crush her. Alternatively, she could smash one of his glass jars and try to cut his throat – this idea appealed to her, but it would be messy, and possibly loud. If she were caught before she could get into the sky, they would kill her. And who was to say cutting his throat would work? His body was strange, and she could not know whether his insides would match the anatomical drawings she had studied back in Stratum. All of these considerations took less than a second. She looked into his crimson eyes, keeping an expression of mild confusion on her face.

'What do you mean? Gave you to who?'

'The rebels.' Malakim shifted where he sat amongst his silken pillows and blankets. 'You led me to the dungeons. And left me there. I think you knew they were waiting for me. Mother doesn't see it, but I do.'

'My prince!' Belise knelt on the carpeted floor, her head down and her wings folded neatly down her back. 'It is my everlasting shame that you were taken while I was caring for you, and I understand why you might have these suspicions of me, but I swear to you...'

'I think these things, but I cannot think why you would do it. You are Othanim. The humans are nothing. Why would you help them?'

'I would never, my prince. It is the honour of my life to serve you.'

'I am not sure that I believe you, Berleeze.'

Belise lifted her head slowly. She didn't dare speak.

'But... I see how the others look. At me,' he said. 'They are afraid, which is correct, but they are also disgusted. They do not want to see me. But you. You are unafraid. You do not flinch. Perhaps you made a mistake. Or perhaps I see distrust and betrayal everywhere. And you were kind to me, when I was a child.'

Belise swallowed. Malakim's childhood was only a handful of days in the past.

'Of course, my prince.' She thought about how she had lost her childhood in a matter of moments too; a twelve-year-old soul in the body of a grown Titan.

'I cannot lose my only friend,' Malakim said quietly. 'And you came for me, at the end. The others pretended not to see me. They hoped someone else would do it. But you came *looking* for me.'

'I did,' agreed Belise.

'Stay with me, and I will protect you from Mother,' he said. 'In the north. She will be busy, and the rebels are broken. I doubt she will think of it again. Save, perhaps, to torture the human.'

By human, she knew he meant Kaeto.

'What will she do when we get to the north of Brittletain, my prince?' She was keen to move the subject away from who might or might not have been assisting the rebellion.

The chariot rumbled to a halt, and there was a flurry of shouting from somewhere at the head of the caravan. Icaraine added her voice to the chorus. Belise went to the window at the front of the chariot. It was difficult to see beyond the horses, but it looked as though something were laying across the road, directly in their path. A tree – losing its brethren had loosened the soil around its roots and it had fallen. Being a tree from the Wild Wood, it was sizeable. As she watched, men and women and Othanim scattered to bring forth saws and axes and ropes. They would likely be stuck for a little while.

'She will destroy the griffins,' said Malakim, who seemed not to have noticed the ruckus outside. 'And everything they have built. She whispered to me of it, all those years we were in the Undertomb.'

'We were there for two thousand years, you know.'

'I do know. I felt every one of those years, even though I was too small to express it. My body held itself still, all that time, and all I knew was her voice in the dark, her flesh like a wall between me and the world.' He coughed and gasped, as though this long speech had used up all the air in his lungs. 'Yes. She will kill the griffins, tear down their castles and end their line. It is all she dreams about. And I will eat their bones, and become...'

He trailed off. From outside came the steady sound of sawing and chopping. The rain was coming harder too, drumming on the roof. Belise took a moment to be grateful that her place was to ride in the chariot with Malakim, and not out in the rain chivvying the horses or moving obstacles.

'What will you become eventually, my prince?'

'I don't know.' He sounded afraid. 'Something terrible, though. I feel it will be something terrible.'

*Well*, thought Belise. *I hope the griffins know they are in big fucking trouble.*

# 53

*They could be guardians or prisoners, keepers or simply residents – no one seems to be very clear what their relationship with the Lich-Way is, but the three of them have appeared to unlucky travellers a number of times across the vast stretch of history. They threaten, gossip and give the occasional portentous warning. I have found, in the very depths of the archive, a note by one of my predecessors that suggests that the bog bodies are in fact the three daughters of the 'horned queen of Londus' (who is herself a nebulous figure). It was said that these three princesses were taken prisoner during a battle, then bound and thrown into the marshes of Wehha, where they slowly drowned. I suppose that if the Lich-Way is the territory of the restless dead, this would be entirely appropriate.*

Note from Elder Druin Jathinos,<br>Dosraiche's Master of Histories

'I still don't understand. The one with the horns? The human with the horns and a soppy expression when he looked at your sister?'

'Yes. Cillian.' Ynis was kneeling next to a shallow pool of rainwater that had gathered on the balcony outside their nest-pit. She cupped both hands in the water and rubbed it briskly over her face; it was close to freezing, so cold it almost felt like burning, but the dried blood was starting to make her itch. 'Witch-seer Frost was describing him and my human sister, I'm sure of it. I don't know what happened after we left them, but we know that Cillian felt like he'd been called back to the Wild Wood for some special reason. Maybe this is what it was.'

'Hmm.' T'rook did not sound convinced. 'I did not spend as much time with him as you, I suppose. I thought him scrawny. Barely any meat on his bones. Why would a forest spirit attach itself to him?' She sniffed. 'Why would it attach itself to any ground-stuck human?'

'I don't know.' She rubbed the water over her bare arms. It was a cold day, the sky so blue and the view down across the foothills so clear it made her eyes water. 'I doubt forest spirits explain themselves often.'

'What are you doing?' T'rook butted her shoulder, half knocking her away from the puddle. 'Two years with humans and you have picked up their filthy habits.'

'There you are.'

They both turned at the voice in the entrance. Frost was there, her feathers especially grey in the clear morning light. Ynis stood up, feeling like she'd been caught unawares.

'What do you want?' snapped T'rook.

'I am leaving shortly to go and find this Cillian,' Frost said evenly. 'Scree will want him found, and if possible, treated with.'

'You are too old for such a journey,' said T'rook. 'The skies south of Yelvynia are dangerous, *eyystin*.'

Ynis winced. Eyystin meant 'one who is ready for the Bone Fall' and was usually a grievous insult. Frost, though, simply nodded as if T'rook spoke the truth.

'I'm aware it's risky, and it may well be difficult to track down the Green Man, especially if he doesn't want to be found. Which is why I came to see you before I left, Ynis. I want you to come with me.' Her eyes darted to T'rook. 'And you as well, T'rook. You would both be very valuable companions on this journey.'

'T'ch!' T'rook dug her talons into the melded wood of the nest-pit. 'Now that I am useful to you, you remember my existence!'

Frost ignored this. 'Ynis, I ask you to consider this carefully. Your talents will help me find your Cillian faster, and in doing so we may stop the Othanim before they come too far north. If you ask her, Fellvyn will let you go, I know it.'

Ynis felt her stomach twist. Frost looked so old and frail, and the thought of her travelling south without them made her deeply uneasy. On the other hand... she was making a real difference here. The griffins she patrolled with had accepted her – more than that, they valued her. Her fathers were here, and she knew T'rook would never agree to leave them and Yelvynia for the sake of the griffin who had refused to help rescue her from Gynid Tyleigh. And underneath all of that, there was the thought of seeing Leven again. Her hand drifted over the blueish patch of skin on her forearm.

'No,' she said, and then, more firmly, 'No. My place is here, Frost. I'm sorry, but that's just the way it is. Won't the queen let you take a couple of warriors with you? I'm sure that we can spare them if you think finding the Green Man is so important.'

Frost nodded, as though she'd expected nothing else. 'The Edge Walkers believe it is important, Ynis, but the queen is not convinced. I'll make the request, given there's little else I can do.' Ynis felt a pang of guilt, almost like a physical pain in her chest, but she held firm. 'Will you promise me one thing, my friend?'

The wind picked up, blowing heartily around the nest-pit and flattening Frost's feathers to her narrow chest.

'She will promise you nothing,' said T'rook, snapping her beak.

Ynis placed her hand on her sister's shoulder to calm her. 'What is it?'

'Please do not abandon your Edge Walker gifts entirely. What you have is incredibly rare, and incredibly powerful. You will need them again, those powers, I am sure of it. Perhaps sooner than you might think.'

The old griffin left them, moving into the deeper darkness of the nest-pit and then vanishing into the tunnels of the war-nest. Ynis watched her go with a tight sensation in her chest. She had the oddest feeling that she wouldn't see the old griffin again. Brocken had appeared to her as a patch of light on the wall of a cave, she suddenly remembered. She wondered what her old friend would think of all this.

'The eyystin thinks she can still order you about,' said T'rook. 'When you are their lightning bolt. T'ch! Come on. Finish your strange human rituals and we'll go out on patrol again. My beak thirsts for Othanim blood.'

Ynis smiled, despite herself. 'I know you know that this is just the human version of grooming, T'rook.'

'I know nothing of the sort, sister. Summon your talons and let us leave.'

## 54

As the sun set and the moon rose, Cillian and Leven found an old brick building with a conical roof, standing alone in the middle of a field. Inside, there was a sharp, warm scent like a tankard of ale left to stand too long, and some old sacks full of rotten hops. Leven threw them outside while Cillian cleared a space for them to sit. There was a hole in the roof that let in a little patch of the night sky.

'How much further do we have to go?' she asked when they were sat on their bedrolls.

'Two days' walk, perhaps. Epona isn't too far from here, if I'm right.'

'Imagine her face when we turn up.' Leven smiled, and then felt it fade. 'We left her in a fairly dire state, Cillian. What if she's angry with us? We left her with her bastard sister, in the middle of a civil war. We never went back.'

'What could we have done?' Cillian passed her his water skin. 'There were just two of us, both hunted by Ceni's guard and the Atchorn. And when we found your sister, well...'

'We got pulled into a whole different kettle of shit,' finished Leven. 'Even so. She deserved better from us.'

'I imagine that Epona has more important things to worry about these days, my love.'

Later, Leven woke in the darkest part of the night, the smell of sour ale strong in her nostrils. She sat up, wondering what had brought her out of her deep sleep. Cillian lay next to her, his eyes lightly closed in the odd trance state the Druin used when they needed to keep watch. There was a small patch of moonlight on the ground by her feet, let in by the hole in the roof, and in it there was a tiny shape. Leven leaned forward, wondering if it was a small rat, but as she did, it reached up with a bony hand and took off a tiny hat. The creature bowed low, revealing a pair of velvety mouse ears. *Pixen*.

'What do you want?' whispered Leven. She glanced at Cillian, but he hadn't moved.

The pixen answered with a light buzzing, the sound of a fly trapped behind a window, and reached into the tiny jacket of leaves it wore. It produced a folded piece of parchment, no bigger than her littlest fingernail, and dropped it on the ground in front of her. Leven picked it up and unfolded it. On the parchment, in smudged green ink, was a single line.

*Do not trust him.*

Leven looked back at the pixen.

'Is this from Mab?'

More buzzing. Leven turned over the parchment to check whether there was anything further. There was nothing.

'What are all these pixen doing in here?' Cillian had sat up. At that moment, Leven spotted that the darkness was crammed with pixen, hundreds of them all watching with eyes like black droplets of ink. She put the slip of parchment into her pocket.

'I think they've come to see me,' she said.

As though they'd heard her and wanted to prove her wrong, the pixen began to file out again, draining out of the oast house like water through a broken jug.

'What did they want?'

Leven sighed. It went against the spirit of the message she'd just received from the queen of the pixen, but Cillian was just Cillian. Cillian with some stranger powers, perhaps, with a deeper connection to the Wild Wood that he loved, with green horns and greener eyes, but it was still him. She didn't want to keep things from him.

'When you found me again, we had a lot to talk about,' she said. 'About what had happened, and what Inkwort had shown you. I didn't really tell you what I'd been doing for the days you were missing.'

Cillian rubbed his chin, the rasp of stubble loud in the small space. 'I thought you were lost. Looking for me.'

'I was. But the pixen came and they took me to... well, I'm not all that sure where they took me, but it wasn't any normal part of the Wild Wood as far as I could tell. I spoke to Mab, their queen. Do you... do you know of her?'

Even in the dark, Leven could see that Cillian's eyes were wide.

'Are you serious, Leven, because that's... No one speaks to Mab. No one human, anyway. Even Verbena, Verla's consort, would be honoured to have such an audience.'

'She reminded me of Verbena, actually.' Leven smiled a little in the dark. 'Cillian, she told me that her husband made a pact with the Green Man – with your father – to be the greatest hunter that ever lived. And that the Green Man agreed. But over time he consumed her husband, turning him into something new, until he was lost. I think she meant to warn me against him. The Green Man, I mean. And to be vigilant.'

Cillian was nodding. 'There are stories about Queen Mab's husband and his fate, but to hear it from her mouth... This is extraordinary, Leven.'

'I know.' She reached over and took his hand. 'I'm sorry I didn't tell you at the tavern. I'm not sure why I didn't, now. But that's why

I think they were here, the pixen. They must be keeping an eye on me.' She didn't tell him about the hag stone, or the message. Both things seemed faintly silly away from Mab's lilac wood.

He squeezed her hand. 'It's fine. I'm glad you told me eventually. And we'd best make sure we tie our packs up properly at night – pixen are fiends for stealing food.'

---

Later, when Leven was curled up on her side and snoring, lost in strange Titan-stained dreams, Cillian sat up and unclenched his fist. Inside it was a pixen no bigger than an acorn. It blinked up at him, whiskers quivering, and made to bolt, but Cillian was faster. He held the creature pinched between two fingers, its six little legs pumping madly. Just on the edge of hearing he could make out the tiny piping squeaks of its speech.

'Just a messenger are you? That's fine,' said Cillian. If Leven had been awake and listening, she might have noted that his voice was a little deeper than usual, a little raspier. 'You can carry a message for me then, back to your mistress. Tell Queen Mab to keep out of it. This is my business, my family, and I won't have her stirring the pot. Got that?'

There was a squeak, and he let the pixen go. Rather than running, it blinked out of existence, leaving behind a puff of spores.

# 55

Epona lay on the grassy earth at the edge of the lake, her eyes fixed on the face of the Lady. Now that Jack had taught her how to see it, she couldn't imagine how she had missed it. Over the last few days she had found herself drawn to the giant, especially during those hours when the view beneath the water was clearest. The giant's face was so still, and so peaceful, even as tiny lake fish flitted past her eyelashes, or when a frog rested briefly on the proud slope of her nose. Once, she had seen an air bubble slip from one nostril and bob to the surface, and Epona had startled. It was easy to forget that she was looking at a living being, not a statue.

'I have some greens for your breakfast.'

Epona did not look up, or move. What must it be like, she wondered, to be so still and so peaceful? Did the Lady of the Lake dream? Or was she blessed with a head free of images, a head free of sounds? Sounds and images like the blood spurting from a mother's lips, the hard thump of a sister's body hitting wooden boards. She squeezed her eyes closed, hard.

*Don't think about it, don't think about it, don't think about it.*

Jack crouched in front of her and tentatively placed her fingers on Epona's shoulder.

'Princess, please. You need to eat something.'

'Please don't call me that,' Epona said, desperation making her voice hoarse. *'Please.'*

'I'm sorry, I won't. I just need you to eat something. Alright?'

She opened her eyes and sat up. One side of her body felt numb. She wondered how long she'd been lying by the lake. Long enough for Jack to go and fetch food from the surrounding forest, but maybe even longer than that. She was handed a bowl of green leaves and white and yellow flowers, along with some thicker buds.

'What is it?'

'Anything I can find that's edible,' replied Jack. 'Hawthorn leaves and buds, gorse flowers, wild garlic, goosegrass, chickweed. We'll have to... we'll have to move soon, Epona. This place isn't really meant as a long-term shelter, and there isn't as much game as you'd think.'

'Hawthorn,' said Epona. She picked out one of the unopened flower buds. 'We used to call these bread-and-cheese. Me and Bronny used to... When we went riding we used to look out for hawthorn trees so we could eat these. Why did the giants go to sleep, Jack?'

Jack sat down next to her, taking the odd leaf from the bowl and chewing as she spoke.

'I'm not sure that anyone living still knows,' said Jack. 'Caliburn has been very vague on the subject. It's possible he doesn't know either.'

'Maybe they'd just had enough,' said Epona. 'I could understand that. I feel like I could happily go and sleep under a hill or in a lake. For a few thousand years.'

For a little while, neither of them spoke. They ate the greens from the bowl and washed them down with water from the lake. It tasted almost unbearably sweet.

'I know you don't want to talk about this, but we really will have to leave soon, Epona. If we've any hope of catching up with the other rebels...'

Epona smiled. It was a sickly thing on her face, like putting a jaunty hat on a corpse.

'What rebels, Jack?'

'We don't know that they're all... There's still a chance. The Barrow might have survived. Larth is a canny woman, one of the slipperiest I know. If she made it out, then she would have gathered the others to her. They could be plotting something new.'

'Then let Larth do it.' Epona stood up, stretching her legs. 'I've no doubt she'll do a better job of leading them than me.'

'Caliburn says—'

'Jack, if you tell me one more time what your bloody sword says I am going to sling it back in the lake.'

'Fine.' Jack stood up, her face downcast. 'Either way, Epona, we will have to leave this place. And I will not leave it without you.'

---

That evening the clouds moved in, bringing a deeper darkness to the lake. With no starlight or moonlight to play on its surface, it became a vast patch of emptiness that unnerved Epona, so she suggested they make a camp under the trees instead. Jack agreed, building a small fire that smelled strongly of pine needles. Not long after, it began to rain heavily, churning the lake into a half-seen haze. The temperature dropped, as it sometimes did in spring, and Epona found that she could see her own breath, little clouds of vapour that vanished almost immediately. Jack was looking at her with concern.

'You should sit closer to the fire.'

'I'm already practically sitting in its lap.'

'I should have got you somewhere warm faster,' said Jack. 'We spent too much time in wet clothes, I think.'

That afternoon Jack had caught two sizeable fish in the lake, and now she was roasting them over the small fire. The savoury fish smell mixed with the heady green scent of pine needles, and Epona found her mouth was watering.

'It's funny,' she said. 'I feel the worst I've probably ever felt in my life. I would be quite happy to go and sit in a cave and never come out again. And yet, I'm still hungry. I can still smell that fish cooking and have my mouth water.'

'Your body still wants what it wants, I suppose,' said Jack.

That night, when Epona lay down to sleep, she found that despite being as close to the fire as she could manage without being singed, she couldn't stop shivering. It was like the cold had come to stay, finding a cavern inside her heart and setting up home there. *What if I'm never warm again?*

She shuddered, curling in on her side, hugging herself with her hands tucked into her armpits. She was so cold she wanted to cry, but she found she didn't even have the energy for that.

'Here.'

A soft voice behind her. A moment later, she felt Jack lie down next to her. One arm looped over her, and she was enveloped in warmth. Heat seemed to rise from Jack's body in a way that easily rivalled the fire, and Epona felt some of the tension leave her own for the first time in days.

'Is that alright?' asked Jack. She sounded very uncertain. 'Are you warm enough now?'

'Yes. Yes, thank you.' Epona closed her eyes, luxuriating in the warmth. Already close to sleep, she placed one hand over Jack's and squeezed it. 'Thank you, Jack.'

---

Epona woke in the early hours, fuzzy-headed and confused. There was a flashing light somewhere above and the comforting shape of Jack next to her was missing. She sat up and rubbed her face. The fire had died down to a scattering of embers.

'What's going on? Did I drink too much last night or something?'

Images of her mother and sister came flooding back with wakefulness, but she pushed them aside roughly. Overhead, through the canopy of the trees, she could see something strange in the sky – not the Othanim, but something else. Something bright.

'Jack?'

She jogged down to the edge of the lake. Arching overhead were thin lines of orange fire, crisscrossing and intersecting in ways that made her head thump, and they were thrumming on and off, like a discordant heartbeat; a mirror image was reflecting in the lake, orange flames lighting up the deep green. There was a humming noise too, she realised, like some huge insect was trapped somewhere nearby. Jack was by the edge of the water, Caliburn drawn from his scabbard and held loosely in her hand.

'What is it?'

'Something is trying to break through the wards,' said Jack. When she turned to Epona her mouth was pressed into a thin line, the face of someone who expected something to go wrong very soon, and was prepared to meet it with violence, if necessary.

'The Othanim?' She pictured Icaraine crashing against those lines of fire, using brute force to get through.

'I don't know. It has to be something incredibly powerful to even know about this place, let alone to break the wards. The wisest thing might be to hide.'

'No,' said Epona. 'I'm getting my sword. If those feathered bastards are getting in here, I want to take a few of them down with me.'

The thought was delicious and sharp, like an apple taken from the tree too early. Epona ran back to their small camp, snatched up her sword from where it lay on the ground, and then sprinted back. By the time she returned, the ward lines were shaking overhead, sending everything into a chaotic dance of light and shadow. The humming, buzzing sound was loud enough that they had to shout over it.

'Where are they coming from?'

'I don't know,' Jack yelled back. 'Be ready!'

The wards broke with a snap, lines of force rolling back to the horizon and vanishing. There was a rush of wind, as though the weather too had been kept out of the lake by the giant's magic, and ripples coursed over the surface of the water. From behind them, in the treeline, there came a shout. They both turned, blades raised. Caliburn was glowing softly, orange like the ward lines, and there was an answering light in Jack's eyes.

'Who goes there?' she called. 'This is a sacred place, and you are not welcome.'

A figure stepped out of the trees, although it looked half tree itself; taller than a man but man-shaped, with curling horns and long, shaggy hair. Epona saw eyes that glowed like green coals, and a sharp, merry grin that seemed to promise both easy laughter and unspeakable violence. He came forward, bringing a shifting eldritch light with him and a powerful scent of sap, smoke and high summer. Birds were singing, everywhere.

The sword sang out, a high and eerie sound of warning.

'It's the Green Man!' Jack surged forward, her sword arm raised, and then suddenly the figure was human-sized; he was, in fact, Cillian. There was another shape behind him, rushing past him with a blade made of blue light. Epona jumped like she'd been pinched and dropped her own sword.

'Jack, wait!'

Jack faltered, half turning back to look at Epona, and then Leven hit her like a ton of bricks.

# 56

*Wings like music*
*Sky like song*
*Our feathers are the instrument*
*Sing, Othanim, and rise with the sun*

Extract from a song written in the
centuries before the Titan War

The supply carriage was cramped, filled with boxes of food, wine, weapons and other odds and ends, but Kaeto and Felldir had moved things around so they at least had space to sit comfortably. Othanim guards rode on the roof – Kaeto could hear them sometimes, talking and laughing, or the scrape of their boots as they took off into the sky again – but within the carriage they had some measure of privacy. They sat together and spoke in low voices.

'We don't know what Bronvica told Ceni, but it seems she did not mention my name, or I'd be a colourful paste decorating the castle walls. Yet I feel I dance closer and closer to the edge. And now, Icaraine packs me up like one of her bags and drags me to the north. Why?'

'You know why,' said Felldir in his low musical voice. 'She likes to wring the pleasure from things where possible. If she killed you now, that would be it – a quick moment of bliss, and all she'd have is a body to dispose of. If she keeps you around, well, the possibilities are intriguing. Torture, maiming. She could use you as a slave until your body collapses under the strain. Keep you in a dark hole for years, feeding you just enough to stay alive. Cut off bits of you for her son to play with.'

'The Othanim are certainly creative,' said Kaeto dryly. 'I note that she didn't waste time torturing the Heralds. Their deaths must have been fast, at least.'

'Icaraine did that to annoy your empress,' said Felldir. 'She is cannier than you might realise, Kaeto. Large and terrifying and bloodthirsty, yes, but not without cunning. A sharp and brutal intelligence.' He sighed. 'Areel would never have followed her if she were an idiot. She sees something between us. I doubt that she understands what it is – humans are little more than insects to her, like especially stupid beetles – but she sees the connection anyway. In the way that you watch me, in the way that I look at you.'

Kaeto felt his face grow hot. He had thought often of the kiss they had shared the morning Malakim was taken – in truth, he often felt like he could think of little else – but there had been no time since to… revisit it.

'So the monster keeps us both alive,' Felldir continued. 'I believe that she also wants us to see what Malakim will become. She wants as many people as possible to see what she has wrought upon the world.' He shook his head, long white hair hanging in his face where it had escaped his braid. 'It is because he was born so small and so strange. When they saw him, the Othanim questioned whether she was a true born queen at all, or simply some kind of giant anomaly, an accident of birth. Surely no true queen would bring a weak, sickly, wingless child into the world. My people can be cruel, Kaeto. And this small group of survivors are cruelty distilled.'

Kaeto thought of what he'd seen. The Othanim throwing human prisoners into the river to watch them drown; the Othanim descending on random servants in the castle to pull them apart for no reason that he could see. Just for sport, he supposed.

'Why are they like this?' Then he added, in a softer tone. 'You are not like this, Felldir.'

'Can I remind you that I threatened to eat you when we first met?'

*Promises, promises*, thought Kaeto. 'You know what I mean.'

Felldir shifted where he sat, pushing a box of replacement bridles out of the way with his foot. 'Many things warped my people. That is what I believe. Remember, when Icaraine rose to power, there was a civil war in the Black City. Those who supported the old queen were slaughtered. Their ways were obliterated on the orders of Icaraine – and this was not so unusual. When a new queen is born, it often changes our whole society, like a boulder dropped in a river changing its course. But Icaraine's appetites led us down a strange road. She had decided that all other Titans were inferior, and that at best they should be brought under our control – at worst, destroyed. Which led to the war, which led to our imprisonment in the Undertomb. And there, instead of our people producing a new queen to replace her, as should happen every few hundred years, we were held in place, in stasis. Left to stew over thousands of years, becoming strange and broken and warped in the dark. I, at least, escaped that fate. I saw the sun, and I flew over the Black City.' From above them, they heard a sudden blast of Othanim laughter. 'It hurts me, light-bones, to see what we have become. Once, we made music, we sang. All were welcome in the Black City, humans and Titans alike, and we shared ourselves with the world. Now we are giggling butchers, intent on feeding a monster.'

'For what it's worth, I'm sorry.' Kaeto hesitated for a moment, then placed his hand on top of Felldir's. 'I know what it is to watch something you love be destroyed.'

The Titan raised his head, a sad smile catching at his lips. They were close enough that Kaeto could feel the heat that rose from his skin, could smell the mixture of sweat and dust that seemed to be

Felldir's unique scent. It occurred to him that despite what he'd said, it was very likely that Icaraine would kill one or both of them when they reached the north, and here, in this carriage, might be his last chance to be alone with Felldir. His heart began to beat a little faster. It was stupid, and reckless, but what did it matter? There could hardly be anything more worth taking a chance for.

But before he could move, the rumbling of the carriage came to a stop, and the rear doors opened with a clatter. He and Felldir blinked at the sudden influx of daylight; there was a strong smell of wet earth, horses and freshly chopped wood. An Othanim soldier ducked his head in the door, a smirk on his handsome face.

'There's a tree in the way, so we'll be going nowhere for a while. Make yourselves useful and pass us that crate of wine.'

---

For a time, the supply carriage was a busy place, with human servants moving in and out, carrying crates and boxes full of food, the Othanim watching them like hawks – apparently Icaraine had decided she wanted to eat while they waited for the tree to be removed. Kaeto went to the lowered steps and looked out, trying to get a sense of how far they'd travelled. Beyond the jagged dirt scar of the road, the Wild Wood rose to either side, trees that had to be ancient standing vigil over the brutal stumps of their dead neighbours.

'I never thought I would end up here,' Kaeto said. Felldir had appeared at his back, still standing within the shadow of the carriage interior. 'In Brittletain. In the Wild Wood, of all places. Although whether it really counts when you're not under the trees, I don't know.'

'This is a haunted place,' said Felldir. 'The forest watches us. It does not like us.'

Kaeto turned to him. 'What do you mean?'

'Exactly what I say. We took the wood's sworn guardian from it and fed his bones to our prince. There could hardly be a bigger insult.' Felldir leaned out and looked up at the sky, which was crowded with rain clouds. 'I would not like to fly over it – not that I could now. It's waiting for something. Can you not feel it? A kind of... simmering anticipation.'

'I can't say that I do.'

'Something is coming. Icaraine is a fool to travel this way.'

Eventually the tree was moved and the carriages set off again, rumbling along the wide dirt road, heading ever north. The grey clouds let loose, and the rain drummed on the roof, making the space feel even more crowded, almost suffocating. Night came quickly in the wood, the light from the narrow slots that served as windows turning yellow, then orange, then purple before dwindling to nothing, and the procession stopped for the second time. Again, the carriage was opened up and people came and went, taking the things they needed for that night's supper. Kaeto went again to the back steps. Darkness had fallen like a velvet curtain; with the clouds overhead, he could no longer see the trees, and the caravan seemed to exist in its own fragile cocoon of light. Pushing his luck a little, he leaned out over the steps and craned his head to look at the ornate carriage that was travelling ahead of them. As he had hoped, the rear doors were open, and he caught a glimpse of Belise, her long dark hair shining in the light from the campfires. She was carrying a bowl of something, which she was bringing back into the carriage. He also saw, a much less welcome sight, the pale hulking shape of Prince Malakim, half hidden in the shadows. Even at this distance, he could see the creature's scarlet eyes glimmering wetly.

'Belise looks well enough,' he said quietly as he climbed back into the carriage.

'It is dangerous to share such close quarters with the prince,' said Felldir. 'It worries me.'

'She's tough.' Kaeto closed the doors behind him. The stream of servants and Othanim had stopped. 'Smart and ruthless, too.

Remember, she was surviving on the streets long before I took her on as my apprentice. If anyone can handle this, it's her.'

'But you worry, too.'

'Of course I do. I'm bloody terrified.'

Felldir lit a small candle and wedged it carefully in a space where nothing flammable could reach it. Outside, the sounds of people setting up camp for the night drifted in. Kaeto heard Othanim laughter, the occasional shriek of a human who hadn't performed their task swiftly enough. Every now and then, Icaraine's voice cut through them all like a blow to the head.

'I think the guards on top of the carriage are gone,' he said. The words hung between them for a long moment. In his throat, Kaeto could feel the rapid patter of his pulse quickening. 'Felldir. I don't know how much time we have left together. For all I know, she could have us both executed tomorrow. And I want...' He trailed off.

'I have been alone since the end of the war,' said Felldir. He cleared his throat. It wasn't often that Kaeto saw him at a loss for words. 'I want *you*, Kaeto. If this is the only place we get to be together, then so be it.'

They fell together onto the carriage floor, moving urgently; now that the words had been spoken and the decision made, it was like it couldn't happen quickly enough. Clothes were yanked at, even torn, until they had both shed everything they had. Felldir lifted Kaeto easily, holding him where he needed to be with a gentleness that only hinted at the power in his limbs. They were quiet at first, still mindful of the larger caravan – Kaeto thought, once or twice, about what would happen if a servant was sent back for another bottle of wine, what they would walk in on – but eventually those sorts of concerns fell away, becoming tiny and unimportant. Kaeto was sure he cried out, that Felldir did too, the kinds of noises you only made when you'd been so far from pleasure for so long that its return was a sweet kind of shock.

Eventually they lay together on the floor, the little candle almost burned down to a puddle. Kaeto ran his fingers over the Titan's feathers, marvelling at their softness.

'Thank you,' Felldir whispered. 'Whatever time I have left, I am glad to spend it with you, light-bones.'

'We will have more time,' said Kaeto. He felt as though a new fire were burning within him. 'This won't be all we get, Felldir. I intend to make sure of it.'

# 57

*Green Man grow you and keep you, sow you and reap you.*

Old Brittlish saying

'Wait a minute. You got *married*? When was this? What was it like? What did you wear?'

Leven laughed. 'Of everything I just told you, that's the bit you're struggling with?'

'Listen, I'm starting with the smaller crazy bits and working my way up to the entirely insane.' Epona was sitting cross-legged by the fire, feeding it bits of twig and grass. The woman called Jack was stood behind her, her arms crossed over her chest – she had the beginnings of a bruise on one cheek where Leven had knocked her into the grass. She felt a little guilty about that, but the woman had been running towards Cillian with a sword, and some instincts never truly faded. Cillian himself was down by the edge of the lake, his hands held over his head. He was, he had told them, restoring the wards that kept the lake hidden from random wanderers. Every now and then a flicker of green light would move across the sky. Leven assumed this was the Green Man's magic at work.

'...because the other stuff is just too wild for words,' Epona continued. 'You have a sister who was raised by griffins, only you're not talking to her anymore because your mother – who was an evil alchemist and also, let's not forget, the legendary Echni of the Druin – gave her the same powers you have.' She was ticking the points off on her fingers, and Leven laughed again, shaking her head. 'You've just spent the last two years tracking down the griffin sister of your sister, who was kidnapped, essentially by your mother. And the best bit of all, my personal favourite bit, is that the grumpy Druin who was told to guide you around the Wild Wood is the Green Man, this mythical figure that the more mystically minded members of the rebellion were convinced might turn up to save the day.'

'Sounds to me like you've got a good handle on it all, actually.'

Epona laughed then, a small fragile sound, and they leaned together, knees touching. Impulsively Leven put her arm around the shoulders of the smaller woman and squeezed her.

'I'm sorry, my friend.' Her throat felt tight all of a sudden; she swallowed past it. 'I'm sorry that I wasn't here for you. We failed you, I think. We should have come back and got you away from Ceni.'

'I don't know.' Epona rubbed the corner of her eye with the pad of her thumb and shook her head. 'All that stuff about fate-ties your sister told you about. That feels pretty true to me. I reckon there are many invisible threads binding us, and some of those are tied to certain paths, particular destinies. You were meant to find Ynis in Brittletain, Blessed Eleven. That's what I think. She's why you came here. You just happened to get embroiled in some good old-fashioned Brittlish backstabbery.'

Leven opened her mouth, meaning to say something about how her friend sounded older than when she'd left; that leadership had made her wise, perhaps. But it felt like the wrong moment. Instead she squeezed her again.

'And I'm sorry about Queen Broudicca, and Bronvica. I only knew them briefly, but I've very rarely met such impressive women. The world is poorer without them.'

'Yes. Well.' Epona leaned back, an expression of pain passing over her face that made Leven regret her words. Even kind words cut like a blade, sometimes. 'I'm not sure what Brittletain will do without my mother. The other queens and kings have gone into hiding, or are resisting where they can, but it's a battle we're surviving rather than winning.'

'The rebellion has you,' the woman called Jack said quietly.

'And now, it has me.' Cillian strode up to them, dusting his hands on his trousers. Above them, a grid of green fire was briefly visible before fading into nothing.

'If you are who you say you are,' said Jack.

'I've never known Cillian to lie,' said Epona. 'Forgive me, my friend, but I'm not sure you've got the imagination for it.' Cillian laughed. 'And we saw him, Jack. We both saw what he looked like when he broke through the wards that were guarding this place. Even the wildest Druin magic doesn't look like that.' As Leven watched, a look passed between Jack and Epona that she didn't understand. Both of them looked worried, and when she caught Jack's eye the woman turned away.

'Believe me or don't believe me,' Cillian shrugged. 'The Green Man is your most powerful weapon, and you don't have to believe it to use me.'

Caliburn chimed, and Cillian shook his head.

'Sword, I am older even than you. I knew this one when she was knee high to an oak tree.' He nodded at the giant sleeping beneath the lake. 'By the time you were forged, I had been centuries in the Wildest Wood, away from all human contact. You don't, in short, know of what you speak.'

'You can understand the sword?' asked Leven. Something about the way Cillian was speaking made her uneasy. She remembered the tiny note the pixen had smuggled to her: *Do not trust him.* 'What did it say?'

'It said that I have always been dangerous.' Cillian rolled his eyes. 'That those who have sought to control my power in the past have failed, and been destroyed. There have been stories, I'll give you that, stories that have a grain of truth at their heart, but this is what I am for. The very land is under threat. Right now, as we speak, the Othanim are clawing their way north, tearing up the Wild Wood and wounding this land down to its core. Destroying them is my purpose.'

'What will you do?' asked Jack.

'I'll rise up against them.' Cillian grinned. His horns looked greener than ever. 'We'll rise up against them together and throw them down. The earth will eat their bones and their blood will grow new trees. What is left of the rebels?'

'Honestly? Probably very little,' said Epona. 'We don't know that there's anything left of them at all.'

'No matter. The people of Brittletain *will* come when I call them. We'll go to the Othanim and destroy them, Epona. The three of us at the head of the army of the Wild Wood! We can't lose.'

'Not me,' said Epona, shaking her head. 'No more leadership, thank you. I have nothing left to give to it.'

All of them grew quiet then. Somewhere, overhead, Leven heard a jackdaw cawing. She wondered if it was Inkwort, who had been scarce since Cillian had found her again.

'We all need some rest.' Leven stood up. 'We'll talk about it again tomorrow. I don't know what our next move should be, but I'm very glad to see you, Epona.'

---

Later, in the middle of the darkest part of the night, Epona woke up with a start, her heart hammering. In her dreams she had been back at the harbour, and her mother had been the horned queen statue. Icaraine had been breaking off pieces of it and throwing them into the river. And the statue had bled, and cried out for Epona to make it stop. She got up from her bedroll and wandered down to the lake, letting the very edge of the water – like ink under the night sky, the giant entirely hidden – lap against the toes of her boots. Her own face looked up at her, as pale as the moon.

'Epona...'

Somehow, she wasn't startled. She had known, somehow, that Jack would join her. It was like the other woman knew what Epona was going to do before she did it.

'I'm fine,' she said, although she knew from the sound of her own voice that Jack would never believe it. 'Just wanted to stretch my legs a little.'

Jack appeared next to her in the lake's reflection, her blonde hair like a darting gold fish in the water. Unusually, she wasn't carrying Caliburn.

'You will go with them, I think,' she said. Her voice was little more than a murmur. 'I saw the way your face lit up when you realised who it was. I know you think you're not ready to lead again, Epona, but I think you'll join them all the same. You have a bond with them... with Leven.'

Epona took a long slow breath, held it for a few seconds, then let it out in a sigh.

'You're probably right. My... my mother never meant for me to journey around Brittletain with Leven, although sometimes I wonder if she knew that's what I would do anyway. She knew me better than I knew myself. I just couldn't resist it – the idea of seeing Brittletain through the eyes of this Imperial barbarian.' She chuckled, although there was little humour in it. 'But she was more than that, as it turned out.'

'I think it's best if I leave your service.' Jack seemed to stand up a little straighter. 'If Cillian truly is the Green Man, and if he is the key to defeating the Othanim, it's dangerous for me to be around him. Blessed Eleven will be your guardian now, as she has been in the past, and I will find other ways to help free Brittletain from the Othanim.'

Epona put her hands on her hips. 'Is this about the prophecy? You don't really believe it, do you?'

'I have to. Merriden said I would find the sword, and I did. He also said I would kill the Green Man with it one day. Your friend seems like a good man. A little full of himself maybe, but decent. The fact that he has turned up here, in the one place I thought we could hide from all the world... it can't be a coincidence. I don't want to kill him.'

'Before, he was quiet, reserved even,' said Epona. The surface of the lake rippled, disturbed by the movements of a fish or the slow breath of a giant. 'This Green Man business has changed him.' She shook her head. 'You can't seriously be thinking of leaving me – leaving my side, I mean – because of something some crazy old wanderer said on the day you were born. Why would you kill Cillian anyway? He's on our side.'

Jack looked away down the lake. 'There are other pockets of resistance. If Larth is still alive, I might journey back to Dwffd and see if the army there can't be rallied to the cause.'

'I don't want you to go.'

'My place is by your side, Epona, but...' Jack cleared her throat. 'Leven will be your guardian. You are close to her. She'll serve you well.'

Epona realised she was angry, although she couldn't have said why. 'I forbid it.' She drew herself up to her full height, which was still a good few inches shorter than Jack. 'I know I told you not to give me titles or treat me like royalty, but if you're going to do daft things, you're going to force me to use that power.'

'Epona...'

'No. That's my final word on it, Jack. If we're going to launch ourselves at the Othanim again, we will need every sensible head we can get. And every sensible talking sword, too. This stuff about the Green Man is nonsense.'

'What would your friend think about it if she knew I was fated to kill her husband?'

Epona threw her hands up. 'Why would she even find out? Because it's not going to happen.'

For a few moments they stood in silence together. Epona thought of the giant asleep beneath the lake. Did she dream of war? Could she sense that the Green Man had invaded her sanctum?

'You've decided you will fight, then?'

Overhead, the clouds moved in front of the moon, casting them into a deeper darkness. Epona found that she couldn't make out the expression on Jack's face; she could only see a faint shine on the other woman's eyes.

'I... maybe I can't stand by and do nothing, at least.' She thought of the pieces of the statue being thrown in the river, sinking without a trace. 'And if that's the case, I'll need you there.'

For a long moment they stood together in silence, until eventually Jack nodded. It was still too dark to see her face, and Epona found she was very sorry about that.

'Then I will take the risk. I will stand by you, Epona,' she said quietly, before walking away. Epona watched her go, feeling disappointed for reasons she couldn't quite put her finger on.

# 58

Ynis waited for the other griffins to sleep, their heads tucked under wings and their bodies pressed close. When she was sure, she snuck off, creeping over a rocky incline dotted with thistles and gorse.

It wasn't that she needed to be away from them – if anything, the company of griffins who thought so highly of her was an endless source of delight. There were no more jokes about her scent, or how they might like to eat her. Instead, they called her 'lightning bolt' and recounted the stories of how she had beheaded this enemy or chased down that Othanim. It was just that sometimes they wanted to rest, and she wanted to fly. She knew that it cost her less – she wasn't using muscles to move her wings, after all – and it didn't tire her as quickly. After so many years spent ground-stuck, the call of the sky was just too great to resist.

T'rook had elected to go out with a different patrol that morning – Ynis had the sense that a young male griffin with particularly fine spots on his flight feathers had something to do with that decision – which meant that no one was watching her especially closely. When she was up in the sky again, the wings of light at her back, she let herself drift for a while, enjoying the hot and cold currents of air that lifted and surged all around. It was dusk, light fading from the sky quickly in this cold, northern place, and the first stars were out. Up here, things were cold and still and silent. She felt older than she had, and powerful.

And then, things were not quite as still as they had been. In the dying light she spotted some frantic movement low over the trees to the south. It looked to be a lone Othanim soldier, their movements oddly jagged, as though they were in some kind of distress. Normally, Ynis would have reported this to the patrol immediately so that their entire group could investigate, but this was just one single Othanim. One who might even be injured. And she was the lightning bolt. She would be in and out before the unfortunate Titan knew what had spilled his guts onto the waiting trees below. He would see her coming, no doubt, because her wings lit up the night as well as the moon, but it wouldn't matter.

Ynis summoned her sword, grinning as it fizzed into life around her right hand, and then she dashed across the sky. The Othanim turned, apparently startled, but he didn't flee.

*Fool*, thought Ynis. *I'll bring your head back to my patrol and they will eat your brains.*

'Ah, it is the pretender,' called the Othanim. 'A meek little version of us, all on its own.'

Ynis darted forward, sword slashing, but he dropped below her so that the blade of light passed a few inches over the top of his head. Up close, she was always surprised by how big the Othanim were – bigger than your average human, at least.

'You're alone too,' she snapped. 'And it will be you who wishes they had assistance.'

'Alone, am I?'

Ynis looked down to where the Othanim had moved and saw, to her shock, several Othanim faces grinning up at her from the canopy of the trees. They had been hiding in the upper branches like sinister crows, their wings neatly folded away. It was an ambush.

'Stars' arses!' Shouting one of her human sister's favourite curses, Ynis leapt up into the sky, thoughts of dismembering the Othanim warrior forgotten, but the others came after her with alarming speed, and all at once she was surrounded by laughing

Titans. She could see the glimmer of their armour, the cruelty in their eyes. One of them reached out and grabbed one of her braids, yanking her head back, so Ynis spun around, letting her sword slice neatly through the soldier's arm. There was a scream and he fell away, but he was immediately replaced by another who shoved her so hard she collided with someone else. Suddenly it was hard to stay upright – she felt her wings beating against hard bodies, and she realised they were bullying her out of the sky.

'Get off of me!'

'Oh no, little bird,' one of them cooed. 'We've heard all about you, the human that thinks it can fly. We're going to have some fun with you.'

Another hand grasped the back of her neck, and this time there was no space to turn. Her sword vanished and abruptly she was crashing down through the branches of the trees, twigs and leaves lashing against her face and arms while the weight of an Othanim warrior dragged her down. She was strong now, she knew, thanks to Gynid Tyleigh's implant, but she was no match for fully grown Titans. When they smashed her into the forest floor, all the air was driven from her lungs in one go, and she lay in a heap, wheezing. Dark shapes gathered around her, still laughing.

'Look at the little bird. Where did her wings go?'

'Not so fast without them, are you?'

'Did you lose your claws too?'

Ynis groaned and tried to lift her head. A booted foot struck her in the shoulder, turning her so that she faced upwards. Little slices of the night peeked between the branches overhead. The sky had never looked so far away.

*T'rook*, she thought. *Come and find me.*

The Othanim were talking to each other now.

'What shall we do with it?'

'We should take it back as a prisoner. It might know all sorts about the griffins.'

'A human, knowing Titan affairs? Have you hit your head or something? No, we should just kill it and leave it here for the wolves to eat.'

'I want it to suffer.' This voice was louder than the rest. 'It's killed three of my brood mates alone. I want to see its blood. Let's cut it into pieces.'

'Easier for the wolves to eat, I suppose.'

Ynis tried to move, hoping that she could crawl away, but a swift kick in her side made her curl over, pain ringing through her body like a struck bell.

'We should take it back to Icaraine,' said one of them. 'See what she makes of it.'

There were a variety of noises at that suggestion, only a few of them positive.

'I'm not going back there,' said another. She lowered her voice. 'Not while that *thing* is with her. What if it gets hungry again and there's no griffins ready to feed it? We'll be served up as breakfast, lunch and dinner, that's what.'

'This is our catch then,' said one of the original voices. 'So let's have some fun.'

The pain, when it came, was a thousand times worse than the kick had been. With some difficulty Ynis looked down at her body, only to see the ornate hilt of a dagger rising up from her gut. The Othanim that had stabbed her drew the blade out slowly, and blood rushed from her like a river that had broken through its dam.

*I'm dead*, she thought. *I'm dead.*

There was another piercing pain, this time in the meaty part of her thigh, and the world around her dimmed alarmingly. She could see fate-ties, red threads that moved and shifted to their own rhythm, floating up all around her. *I'm walking the Edge again*, she thought, *and this time I won't be coming back.*

'There, stab it in the guts again, you can stab humans in the guts lots before they die, I've seen it.'

'That's not true. They die too quickly wherever you pierce them, no stamina at all—'

There was a yelp then, followed by a shriek. The looming shapes that were clustered around her fell away, shouting to each other and the dark. Abruptly, one of them vanished, apparently carried away into the forest by something Ynis couldn't see.

'What was that?' snapped one of the Othanim. 'Did you see?'

There was another scream, and then a long bony face swept into view. It looked to be the skull of an elk, with tiny points of green fire burning in the empty eye sockets. Around it was a body made of vegetation: flexible branches provided sinew; moss and leaves, skin.

'Dunohi,' Ynis croaked. She had never seen one before. She wondered if she were seeing it now because she was dying. It had, she noticed, blood splattered across the flat yellow bone of its face.

*We do not want them.*

The voice thundered through her head like a storm, too huge to escape.

*The poisoned Titans do not belong. They bring death.*

The Othanim that were left were still screaming, although they were growing more distant. Ynis wondered if any of them had escaped into the sky – the Dunohi were not known for their mercy when it came to trespassers.

'Forest soul.' She pressed one hand to her stomach. Her clothes were soaked in blood, hot and somehow awful against her chilled skin. 'Help. Please. My sister…'

But the Dunohi was already drifting away, its antlers passing through the lower branches of the trees like they were made of smoke. At the very edge of her sight, Ynis could see the body of one of the Othanim hanging from a tree. Its guts had been torn out; they hung like colourful bunting, tangled in a holly bush. For some reason the sight filled her with terror – *that will be me soon, I will be a dead thing in the trees* – and she tried to lurch to her feet. The pain that swept over her was so great that she was swallowed by darkness. When she woke, the light in the Wild Wood had changed. It was full dark, and she could hear the calls of night birds, although they seemed distorted and strange to her ear. She was thirsty enough that her throat felt like it was full of thorns, and pain lay in wait for her with every movement.

She was alone, and bleeding, in the Wild Wood.

Oddly, she didn't think immediately of T'rook, who would be likely looking for her when she hadn't returned. Instead, she thought of Leven. She had only the vaguest idea of where her older sister was – somewhere south, somewhere with Cillian – and for some reason that pained her. They had argued, and she had left with anger in her chest as sharp as thorns. It seemed wrong that she would die in the mud without getting a chance to finish that argument.

*Look at you*, Leven would say. *Look at where Gynid Tyleigh's augments have led you. Without that sword and those wings you'd never have blundered into that ambush.*

'And I'd never have flown, either,' Ynis murmured. 'I'd never have lived.'

*So stubborn*, said a voice. *The only human I ever met that reminded me of myself.*

Ynis lifted her head as best she could. She found that she wasn't all that surprised to see the ghostly image of Brocken standing near her feet. As large as ever, the griffin was painted in the blue and green tones of the Bone Fall, a creature of shifting light and shadow. Her eyes, though, were still sharp.

'The only humans you met... besides me,' croaked Ynis, 'you ate.'

*A fair point. You are close to death now, yenlin. And moving closer all the time.*

'This is stupid. To get this far. To get my wings. And then to die here. On the border of Yelvynia.' She was no longer sure she was speaking out loud. The shape of Brocken was growing more solid by the moment, while the world around her grew less distinct. Her fate-ties were clearer than she had ever seen them, and she lay in them like a fish in a net. There were so many. How was it possible there were so many?

*It might not seem like it, yenlin, but you are exactly where you need to be.*

'If I had the energy... I might be insulted.'

Brocken snorted, shaking out her wings in a very griffin expression of amusement.

*As unpleasant as it may be for you, you're closer to your talents here.* With that, Brocken began to fade. Ynis felt the first stab of real fear. Dying here was one thing, but dying here alone was unthinkable.

'Please, don't leave me.' She tried to lift her arm to reach out for the griffin, but there was no strength left in it. 'Brocken, please.'

*I'll be back again, Ynis.* The griffin's voice was fading too, becoming the breeze in the trees. *You have company now.*

'What?'

Brocken vanished. A few moments later Ynis heard a stealthy tread behind her; a human footstep, no doubt, or something that did a good job of looking human. The Othanim warriors, perhaps, come to make sure she was dead, or retrieve their fallen kin. But instead, someone much shorter than an Othanim came into view. It was too dark to see them properly, and the living world still felt out of focus. Ynis tried to reach for her claw knife anyway, her fingers scrabbling uselessly against the leather-covered hilt.

'What do we have here, then?'

A pair of hands reached down to move her, and Ynis lost consciousness for a second time.

# 59

*Let it be recorded here that Witch-seer Frost watched over the Bone Fall for a hundred and eighty turns of the world. Let it also be recorded here that her wisdom and her keen eye shepherded many spirits, and she steps down from her post only because her bones grow fragile and her eye begins to cloud. Let it be recorded here that she endorses the accession of Scree, the new witch-seer for this age.*

Extract from *The History of the Edge Walkers*,<br>carved into the side of the Eternal Glacier,<br>which overlooks the Bone Fall

'It's good for you to stretch your legs.'

Malakim made a low rumbling noise in the back of his throat that suggested he didn't quite agree with that. *Well, I need to stretch mine anyway,* thought Belise. They had been cooped up in the carriage for days, Belise leaving occasionally to fetch food for herself or to toss out his latrine bucket, and she was sick of the sight of its four walls, as lavish as they were. She had convinced Malakim that when the carriage next paused on its journey, they would venture to the very edge of the Wild Wood. There were bound to be insects there they had never seen, she told him. The castle grounds were a poor place to find such things, in her opinion. So now they stood, in a faint drizzle, at the treeline. Behind them the Othanim camp seethed with its usual energy. Icaraine was at the head of the procession as she often was, shouting instructions and demands. Here, by the trees, it was at least quieter.

It was also true, Belise considered, that Malakim's legs hardly needed any further stretching. He towered over her now, a vast slender beast in a hotchpotch of patched-together clothing, his elongated head hanging forward like the blade of an axe. They had been told to go no further than the edge of the wood itself, which was annoying, but peering into the trees Belise reluctantly conceded that seemed like sensible advice. The only place she had seen that rivalled the Wild Wood was the vast jungle of Houraki, and that had contained all manner of dangers. She thought of the beetle that had poisoned her and shuddered.

'Are you cold?'

'I'm fine, my prince. This weather gets under your skin a bit, doesn't it?'

The water had beaded on his white skin like thousands of tiny pearls. Belise crouched and peered closer at the leaflitter on the ground. There were plenty of bugs around, when you looked closely, and most of them looked like odd versions of creatures she had seen on the streets of Stratum. Snails, centipedes, slugs and tiny creatures that rolled up into a grey ball when you lifted up the stone they were hidden beneath.

'You see that there, my prince? I wonder what it's called.' She paused, wondering if this was too risky. 'I have heard that in Stratum, the human city, they call them cheese-bugs.'

'Why?'

'You know, I have no idea. Do you want me to fetch a jar from the carriage so we can collect it?' Once they were caught, Malakim seemed to lose interest in the insects, and every few days or so Belise would release the creatures that had died from their captivity. There were always spare jars.

'I can feel something,' said Malakim.

'What do you mean?'

'Something is coming,' he said. He lifted his head and looked up at the grey ceiling of cloud that hung over them. 'Can't you feel it?'

Belise looked up, squinting at the sky. Her thoughts tumbled towards Kaeto and Felldir, who she hadn't spoken to in days. What fresh trouble was this damp country about to lay at their feet?

When it came into view, she gasped – not an appropriate reaction for someone who had been Othanim all her life, perhaps, but some things were difficult to suppress. It was a griffin, flying low over the treetops, glorious wings outspread and every feather clear as daylight. Belise had a moment to note that it had a shock of white fur amongst the grey, and then Malakim was reaching up with his long bony arm. The griffin gave a piercing shriek as Malakim's will ensnared its bones. Then it was being dragged towards them, its front and back legs kicking uselessly. From the Othanim camp, there was uproar.

'My prince!' Belise backed away as the griffin was pulled down to the ground. It was bellowing with rage and struggling with all its might against the force that held it. Malakim himself seemed fascinated, his crimson eyes wet in a way that Belise was beginning to recognise meant he was excited or alarmed. Behind them, several Othanim warriors had appeared, spears at the ready, and at their backs was Icaraine, grinning widely.

'Look at what my boy has caught!' she boomed happily.

'Is this a griffin, Mother?'

'It is, it is. Watch it scrabble in the dirt like a worm. Yes, that is where you belong.' Icaraine came to loom over the griffin, which was panting heavily, its broad ribcage rising and falling. Belise stood no more than a handful of feet away, her eyes wide. Somehow, she hadn't quite believed they were real, she realised. Not until this very moment.

The griffin rolled its eyes towards them. 'What is it that has a hold of me?' she demanded. 'I feel like I am tangled in my own fate-ties.'

'How good it is to look upon your face again, old adversary.' Icaraine peered down at the Titan, her head cocked. 'I remember the griffins of old, and they had feathers of all colours. Now you are the colour of dirt. What happened? Are you fading from this world, as you deserve?'

'You.' The griffin shifted, trying to rise. Malakim twitched, and she flattened to the earth again. 'Our histories speak of the monster born to the Othanim who murdered their true queen and set her people on the path to ruin. You're smaller than I thought you'd be.'

Icaraine chuckled, her eyes glinting dangerously. 'What is your name, little bird?'

'Frost. I am Frost of the Edge Walkers, witch-seer of my clan.'

'Such titles you give yourselves. You should feel honoured, Witch-seer Frost. My son Malakim rarely bothers to learn the names of his meals.'

Malakim's eyes had yet to leave the downed griffin. He was watching her with the same ripe fascination he'd held for the first grasshopper they'd caught. Belise looked up over the heads of the gathered Othanim soldiers and wasn't entirely surprised to see Kaeto forcing his way between them, his dark face flushed. They exchanged a look: she saw the awe on his face, and the fear there too. It was rumoured that Gynid Tyleigh had a young griffin held captive in her secret compound, but of course neither of them had ever seen it. Belise felt a prickle of something like dread move across her back: what right did they have to treat one of the last Titans this way? They were magical. You only had to look at them to see it.

'Yes, this is... this is something else.' Frost lifted her head a few inches off the ground to look at Malakim. Belise expected to see fear, or revulsion. Instead, the griffin clicked her beak in a weary way. 'Your people always had strange ways. The Othanim always stood apart from the other Titans.'

'Because we are superior,' said Icaraine.

'That is what you believed, I'll give you that.' Frost sighed. She was old, Belise realised. Her fur and feathers were greying, and her skin hung on her in places. 'And you were glorious, once. Believe it or not, our oldest stories talk about the great wisdom and beauty of the Othanim, their talent for music and their curiosity about the world.'

Some muttering rose from the gathered Othanim. Belise searched their faces. Icaraine might not be fully aware of it, but there was a tide here, and it was possible she wasn't on the right side of it. She filed away the thought for future examination. It was like Kaeto had always taught her – find out everything you can and keep hold of it in a quiet place inside your head somewhere. You never knew when it might be useful.

'All gone now, of course,' Frost continued. 'The Othanim are a joke, a shadow of what you once were. You've escaped your prison in the Black City, and what are you doing with this new life? You're destroying the Wild Wood in the name of a war that the rest of Enonah has long forgotten. Enonah has forgotten you, False Queen.'

'Oh, I'm going to make them remember,' said Icaraine. The vicious good humour had dropped from her tone; the anger left in its wake was raw and ugly. 'When the griffins are nothing more than feathers in the wind, the creatures of Enonah will still be saying my name. Do you have anything left to chirp, little bird, before I snap your neck?'

'Mother.' Malakim's voice was the softest rasp, but Belise heard it clearly enough. 'Mother, can I speak?'

'Not now, my sweet.'

'Mother...'

Malakim had shuffled closer to the griffin, hands outstretched.

'I have something to say,' said Frost. Her claws flexed, as though she wanted to drag herself upright. 'Yes. I will tell you this. The Green Man is risen, and he is coming for you, False Queen. He's here in the world again and he won't rest until all of you are dead.' She laughed rustily. 'You've earned his most diabolical anger. The wood itself will eat you. And that thing,' she gestured with her beak towards Malakim, 'that thing won't save you. That thing will be your downfall. The Green Man's bones are the furthest thing from Titan. They are wood and sap and grass, and you'll have no power over him when he comes.'

'Enough,' snapped Icaraine.

'Mother,' Malakim said again, a little louder this time. 'Can we keep it, Mother? I want to talk to it some more.'

*Stars' arses*, thought Belise. *We don't have a jar big enough.*

'The Green Man is coming,' said Frost. 'And he's going to eat you alive.'

Icaraine lunged at the griffin and snapped her neck in one decisive movement, leaving her limp in the dirt. It was fast enough to make Belise jump, her heart hammering in her chest. A few of the gathered Othanim laughed. Icaraine grinned around at her soldiers.

'That is the fate of all of the griffins, left to rot in the dirt of their precious Wild Wood. You.' She gestured to one of her warriors. 'Take this carcass and strip the meat off of it. She was a scrawny old buzzard, but there might be enough for a few steaks. If not, make a stew from the innards and scraps. We will want the bones nice and clean.' She chuckled warmly, a woman thinking fondly of a long-awaited treat. 'Malakim, my sweet, you will eat well tonight.'

'I am not hungry.'

Malakim was trembling slightly all over, his hands bunched into ungainly fists at his sides.

'Then we will save them for you for when your hunger returns.' Icaraine gestured for the Othanim to take the corpse away, but before they could, Belise knelt and plucked a few feathers from the Titan's wings. They were soft in her hands, and much finer than the ones that graced her own wings. She thought of what she'd have been able to get on the streets of Stratum for a genuine griffin's feather. When she stood up, Malakim was watching mournfully as they dragged the corpse away.

'My prince,' she said to him. 'Let's get out of this rain.'

---

Back inside the carriage, Malakim was sullen and unresponsive, sitting on his cushions with his head down, ignoring her increasingly cheery comments and questions. The scent of cooking meat wafted in through the open windows. Belise felt her stomach turn over. *They're really doing it*, she thought. *They're cooking and eating a fucking griffin.* It made her feel half crazy, those thoughts, and perhaps that was why she said what she said next.

'You're certainly hard work today, my prince.'

His head twitched, like a dog scenting something, and then he snorted. And the snort became a laugh.

'You are honest, Beleeze,' he said. 'The rest of the Othanim will not speak to me, but you speak to me, and more, you speak the truth. Why are you different?'

*I'm definitely not answering that*, she thought. 'I'm just concerned that you're under the weather, that's all. You seem worn out.'

He shook his head. 'It's my mother who tires me. She does not listen to me. She throws away my thoughts as though they were nothing, yet I know I am the great centre of her world. I fear she doesn't listen to anyone.'

'Great leaders are often like that,' said Belise. *I have to tread carefully here.* It was interesting, though. This was exactly the sort of opening she'd been hoping for. 'What would you say to her if you thought she would listen?'

'I would ask her what this future of hers looks like. What she expects me to be. When I have eaten all the bones of all the griffins, what then? How will I have changed? Maybe even she doesn't know.'

'You know, my prince, you also have a say in what the future looks like.' She let the words hang on their own for a moment so that he could feel the shape of them, perhaps follow the paths they suggested. 'Your power is unique. It means that your voice has to be listened to. By anyone with Titan bones, certainly.'

There it was, out in the open. She waited to see if he would say anything further; if he would suggest that she was treasonous, or mad. He said nothing. He looked at the griffin feathers she had given him, laid like treasures across the white expanse of his palms.

# 60

Cillian sat in the bough of the tree and listened to the green seethe.

It was extraordinary. Back before he met Leven, when he was a Druin ranger in training, he had always known he had a stronger connection to the Wild Wood than most. He had been able to sink deep into the roots of the forest, listen to the moods of birds, even sense when the elusive Dunohi were near. Yet now all of that felt like half a dream in comparison to the connection the Green Man had given him.

He leaned against the bark of the tree and tasted a little of what it was feeling. It was old, an ancient oak that kept the history of every spring, summer, autumn and winter in its sap. A flurry of impressions moved through Cillian in an instant: the season that the black biting beetles had dug a nest amongst its roots; the stag that had struck his antlers against the tree's bark, full of an itching need to grow and discard; the human couple that had sheltered beneath its branches in a storm.

It was extraordinary, but it was also overwhelming, which explained the odd periods of blankness he was experiencing along with everything else. Sometimes he would just find himself in a place he wasn't expecting – like the magical lake where Epona had been hiding. If he looked back through his memories, yes, he knew that they had travelled south through the Wild Wood, and that they had stood overlooking Londus-on-Sea. He could even recall that he and Leven had talked about the last time they had been there together, when they were barely talking. Yet those memories had a fine gauze over them, as though they were from long ago, or belonged to someone else.

What did it matter though, really? There was so much else to occupy his mind. And Leven, too, was looking better than she had in months. His touch soothed her, eased away the chaos that the ore-lines brought. And he'd happily pay whatever price was asked for that little boon.

'Hey.' She appeared at the foot of the tree as though his thoughts had summoned her. She smiled up at him. 'We're ready to move if you are.'

'I'll be right down.'

He could already sense the quickening inside her, so early that she herself would not be aware of it for some time. It made him feel feverish, and strange. They had talked about it when they were first married, of course they had, and she had expressed sadness over that particular lack – it was useful for a soldier, in some ways, but it was still another thing that the ore-lines had taken from her. He shook his head and climbed swiftly down the tree, embracing her fiercely when he was back on the ground. She laughed and pushed her face into his neck.

'You smell like the forest,' she said. 'Come on.'

They walked back through the wood towards the lake. Epona and Jack had spent the morning getting ready – he was vaguely aware of this, in the way that birds note the direction the river is flowing as they fly over – and now they would venture beyond the enchanted lake with its sleeping occupant, seeking out the remnants of the rebellion. It was an overcast day, a chill on the breeze raising goosebumps across the backs of his arms. There would be rain later.

'What will you do?' asked Leven.

'The same as before,' he said easily. 'I'll open up the Wild Wood and take us to where the rebels are hiding. There aren't many of them, but enough, perhaps. The Othanim won't be expecting much of a fight at this point, and every body with a weapon counts.'

'No, I meant what will you *do*.' Her grey eyes, the colour of storms, looked troubled. 'When we march on the Othanim. Will you... what? Fight them one on one? Is the Green Man that powerful?'

'I... Honestly, I don't know. I will let him do what he needs to do.'

'You'll let him take over?'

'I will still be there, don't worry.' He squeezed her hand. 'He will fight for the Wild Wood, I know that much. How are you feeling?'

Leven sighed. 'Better. The pain is coming back again, but then it always does. At least it is bearable. I will be able to fly, and use my sword when I'm on the ground, so I won't be completely useless.'

'And your dreams?'

For a moment she didn't answer. He knew she had dreams of the Titans whose bones had been used to create her ore-lines – even if she hadn't told him, he would know from the way she tossed and turned in the darkest hours of the night, from the things she murmured in her sleep.

'They are the same,' she admitted eventually. 'Powerful. Vivid. They don't seem to fade.'

'It could be that they are a part of you forever.' He wanted to speak to her further – perhaps it was time, after all, to talk to her about what was coming – but they had reached the treeline, and Epona and Jack were waiting there for them. Epona looked more like her usual self, her face scrubbed and her black hair pushed back behind her ears, although there was a gauntness to her cheeks he did not like. Jack was watching them come with a tension around her jaw, Caliburn the legendary sword slung over her back. It was curious. When he looked at the warrior and her sword, he felt something coiled within his chest, like some presentiment of danger.

'You definitely know where they are?' There was no preamble from Epona. 'The rest of the rebels?'

Cillian nodded. 'I can feel them clearly. I know where everyone is in the Wild Wood.'

Epona shook her head, then shrugged. 'Sure. Why not. This makes as much sense as anything else. Let's go then.'

---

Epona had thought she would have some time to prepare herself for the rebels – wherever it was that they had bolted to, it would likely take several Paths to get them there, which could take days. Instead, Cillian opened up the Wild Wood like it was a book. One moment, they were in the outer fringes of the woods in Londus; the next, in the verdant forest of Mersia – on the edge of a hidden camp. A woman with dark paint across her eyes sighted them and a flurry of calls went up that sounded like frightened birds. Epona felt a stab of panic.

'We're here already?'

What was left of the rebels had retreated to the ruin of a castle, a ruin that had long since been eaten up by the Wild Wood. It was a good place to hide, because it had trees growing up through the foundations, obscuring them from anything that might be in the sky, and it had some partially intact ceilings, so the rebels had shelter when they needed it.

Leven put her hand on her shoulder and squeezed it. A number of people were leaking out of the ruin, their eyes glued to Epona. She heard someone shout her name, although she couldn't tell if it was in surprise, gladness or anger.

*All that time I spent convincing them I wasn't the traitor Ceni claimed I was, and in the end, I did betray them. I left them to an awful fate because of my terrible plan – because I had to save my mother. I failed them all.*

A couple of figures emerged from a broken doorway. A short

woman with a stern face and the smudged ash stick of Dwffd on her face – Larth – and a Druin woman. Yelm. They were both alive, and they seemed equally shocked to see her, too.

'Princess Epona!' Yelm limped over. She had one arm in a sling. 'Roots strike me blind, we were sure you'd perished. How did you get out?'

Epona took the woman's free hand and squeezed it. 'I was really bloody lucky. By which I mean that I was lucky enough to have Jack with me. What... what happened to everyone else?'

Larth nodded a simple greeting. *Never one for big gestures*, thought Epona. *Or perhaps she cannot bring herself to look at me.*

'You should come in and sit down,' said Larth, her eyes moving over Cillian and Leven, her gaze lingering on the silver-blue ore-lines etched into Leven's skin. 'There's a lot to tell you.'

---

'It was a close-run thing,' Epona said when they were sat around the fire. The stones of the ruin seemed to keep the cold in, and she found she was glad of the warmth. 'If we hadn't made it into the Old Father at that moment we would have been done for. I'm still not entirely sure how we survived even then. The Old Father isn't normally that forgiving of swimmers.'

'It is the blade,' said Yelm, eyeing Caliburn uneasily. 'It belongs to the lakes, and so the rivers won't take it. I imagine the Old Father was glad to carry you wherever you needed to go if it meant you took that sword with you.'

'Really?' said Leven. 'The rivers can have feelings about swords?'

Epona almost smiled. It was good to have her straight-talking barbarian friend back.

'My fellow Druin is right,' said Cillian. His green horns were drawing more than a few looks from the gathered rebels.

'What happened to the... what happened after that?' asked Epona. 'We were swept out of central Londus and walked through the marshes.' She didn't mention that she hadn't intended to come back.

'The Othanim came to the square where we had the child hidden,' said Larth in her steady, musical voice. 'They knew where we were. They pulled up the doors that led into the cellars and swarmed below. They killed whoever got close to them. At some point, they took the Othanim prince and disappeared, but nearly everyone who was in that cellar when they arrived died there.'

There was a long silence. Epona thought again of the sound of her mother's body hitting the wooden boards of the harbour.

'I told you to move the boy too late,' said Epona bitterly. 'I should have known we'd be betrayed.'

'I got out by the skin of my teeth,' said Larth. 'I had to... climb over the bodies of people I knew. At one point I hid beneath them until the Othanim had passed by.'

'I'm sorry,' said Epona, but Larth just shook her head as though that wasn't the point.

'Those of us that survived the cellar went to the other undercity places, and gradually made our way out. I hid in a tavern attic for several days, then I made my way to the Barrow. I watched it to make sure there were no Othanim there, but when I finally got inside, I found no rebels, either.'

'I got to the Barrow earlier,' said Yelm. 'There were a few people left there – the Othanim had come, they said, and they had dragged some of them out screaming. I got them to come with me, the survivors, and we came to this place. It took a while. I was never as good at opening the Paths as Solasach.'

'And where is he?'

Yelm lowered her head.

'He didn't make it,' said Larth. 'He was in the Barrow when the Othanim first arrived.'

'At least he was in the wood,' Yelm said quietly. 'At least he was close to the trees when he died.'

'Ah, roots strangle me.' Epona thought of how he had opened the standing stones for them so they could talk to the griffins, and she felt a wild stab of anger towards those ancient Titans. Perhaps, if they had been prepared to help, more of her people would be alive now. *And if you hadn't decided to gamble their lives for your mother's?* 'What about Karayné-bog?'

'He died in the cellar. Took one of them with him though,' said Larth. 'I saw the body afterwards. Had one of his spears wedged in its eye socket.'

Somebody came with a leather flask, pouring out shots of mead into small clay cups. The sweet warmth was very welcome; Epona felt chilled to her bones. There were lots of things she wanted to say: how sorry she was, what a huge mess the whole thing was and her deep unending sorrow for all those they had lost – especially her mother, and her sister. Yet she knew that wasn't what they needed to hear. They needed someone in all this mess to stand up and say it could still be fixed. The rebels needed to hear that it wasn't all over. When she reached for those words, though, she couldn't find them. There was only an emptiness, and an echo of loss.

*I shouldn't have come back*, she thought. *How can this work?*

She opened her mouth, preparing to spin something encouraging out of nothing, when she found that Cillian was already speaking.

'I'll take you all to where they are,' he was saying. 'The Wild Wood will open for me.'

'And what are we supposed to do?' asked Larth. 'We are, what? A hundred or so exhausted men and women, if that, against a battalion of vicious Titan bastards. Are we going to throw spears at them and hope they feel sorry for us?'

Cillian shook his head. 'I will wield the power of the Wild Wood against them. You will see.'

'Forgive me, but no one Druin, no matter how skilled, can stand against the queen of the Othanim.'

'I am no simple Druin.'

There was a tense silence around the fire. The leaders of the rebels looked at each other, expressions of confusion and annoyance passing between them. Epona sighed.

'Just tell them, Cillian.'

He grinned – had he ever grinned like that when she'd known him before? She thought not.

'What does she mean?' asked Yelm. 'What are you not telling us?'

'Look at me, child,' said Cillian. 'You know who I am, in your heart. You know it in your heartwood.'

Yelm drew back from the fire, her eyes wide.

'No. It can't be.'

'What are you talking about?' asked Larth, a trace of impatience colouring her words. 'What Druin nonsense is this?'

'I am the Green Man, come among you at your hour of need,' said Cillian easily. 'And tomorrow, or the day after, or whenever you are ready to march, I will lead you to the Othanim and help you drive them from this land. Our fight will be spun in songs for ever after – the day you stood shoulder to shoulder with the Green Man and won back the Wild Wood.'

*There*, thought Epona wearily, *those were the words we needed.*

# PART FOUR

## IN WHICH MANY THINGS ARE LOST

# 61

When Ynis awoke, she found herself in a small human dwelling, gloomily lit by a low fire burning in the hearth. The place smelled of hot human food and woodsmoke, and she was lying on a narrow bed piled with scratchy blankets. A man was talking, although it was difficult to focus on where he was.

'There you are, child,' he said. 'Perhaps you're not done for after all. Could have sworn I saw the flicker of an eyelid there.'

Ynis made to tell him that she wasn't yenlin, but found that her mouth would not obey her; it felt gummed shut, the effort of moving her jaw vast. A sharp trickle of panic flowed into her chest and she tried to wriggle free of the blankets. Strong hands came out of nowhere and held her still.

'Try not to move,' the voice said. 'I've stitched and bandaged all the places where those flying bastards tore at you but we can't have you losing any more blood. A right mess they made of you, lass. You must be stronger than you look – anyone else would surely be dead.'

Already the effort of opening her eyes was becoming too much. Ynis slipped away again, but not into sleep. Instead, the tiny cabin reformed in hues of blue and green, the colours of the Bone Fall, and a pair of familiar shapes came forward.

'Brocken? Who is that with you?'

'It gives me no pleasure to tell you this, Ynis, but an old friend has joined me here.'

'Who?'

The smaller figure came forward. Ynis realised that the difference in size should have told her who it was straight away. Frost looked even smaller and frailer than when she had seen her in the war-nest, although she shone with a powerful greenish light – she looked more present, more vital than Brocken did.

'Frost, what happened?' Ynis swallowed, her heart sinking. 'You went south, didn't you? Alone.'

Frost nodded. 'Our queen wasn't willing to waste warriors on a hare-brained search for the Green Man.' She sounded rueful. 'And, as perhaps you predicted, I wandered into the path of the Othanim. I had thought that I could outfly them, but…' She fussed at a loose feather on her chest. 'Possibly I'm not as wise as I thought. They had a terrible creature with them, one that had power over other Titans. I felt it clutch at my bones, and throw me around like I was a prey animal.'

'Frost, I am sorry. I should have gone with you. T'rook and I should have taken you.' She sat up in her distress and flung her legs over the side of the small bed. 'We knew who the Green Man was. We could have helped you…' She hung her head, ashamed. 'But I wanted to stay and fight. And look what happened to me. I'll probably never be able to fight again, and T'rook will likely get herself killed trying to find me. And you're dead.'

'Ah, old age would have taken me sooner rather than later. And at least this way I got to vex that great Othanim bitch before I died.' Frost came forward, pushing her head against Ynis's shoulder. 'Arrow. Ynis. You will fight again, child – perhaps not in the way you expected, but you will. Look at yourself.'

Ynis looked down. Her physical body was still lying on the bed, tightly wrapped in blankets, her dirty face shining with sweat. But her true self – her spirit self – was a figure made of green and blue fire, just like Brocken and Frost, and she wasn't injured. When she moved, she felt no pain.

'Am I dead?'

'No, although I will admit that you are close,' said Frost. 'And your witch-seer powers are stronger than ever. I know you didn't want to hear it before, Ynis, but this will be your great weapon against the Othanim. There will be a task that only you can complete. I don't know what it is yet, but I feel it in my bones.' The old griffin coughed. 'Although I dread to think where they are now.'

'I don't understand,' said Ynis. 'How can I do anything from here?'

'You are much more mobile in this form, Ynis,' said Frost. 'And powerful. Your unique abilities are at their strongest here, on the very edge of things. I think you will be capable of things no one else has ever dreamed of.' She paused and lifted her head. She seemed to be listening to something Ynis couldn't hear. 'We should go. Someone else is coming.'

'Who? Don't leave me here, Frost. Brocken, please.'

Frost was already fading, her light diminishing to become the faint glow from the fire reflected in the surface of a polished pot. Brocken, though, lingered for a moment.

'This is witch-seer business,' the big griffin said gruffly. 'And Fionovar knows I was never one for the deep mysticism of our order. Walking the line between life and death is your calling, Ynis, much as it pains me. And this human man who tends to you, he drags you away from that line. You will have to decide what you want to do about that, when the time comes.'

With that, Brocken faded too.

## 62

*They say she is a ruthless queen, but the truth is she surrendered to her daughter on the field in the hope of sparing her remaining warriors. I know, because I saw it myself. Broudicca knew, I expect, that she was done for and she wanted to keep her dignity intact, and when they went to meet in the middle of that muddy stretch of grass, there was a little smile on her face. Yes, I saw it. A bitter one, maybe, but a smile all the same. I think despite everything she was impressed with what Ceni had achieved. I suppose if you raise your daughters to be wild cats, there's always the chance that one will turn around and bite you.*

Account of the Battle of Londus,
by a member of the household guard

Kaeto stood in the mud of the road and looked out over the treetops. Here, the road passed over a hill, putting a great deal of strain on the horses that were pulling their carriages, so much so that some of the Othanim had been pressed into service to lighten the load. The elevated position meant that they could see for some distance all around, and off to the west, across a sweeping tapestry of impossibly green countryside, the towers of a mighty city stood, tall and white and somehow fragile.

Kaeto consulted his knowledge of Brittletain and decided it must be Wodencaester, the only city to rival Londus-on-Sea in terms of wealth and prestige.

'Then we are not so far from their northernmost state,' he said quietly. 'Galabroc. And beyond there, the land of the griffins. Once we get there...'

'Icaraine's child will have enough to feast on to last him a lifetime,' said Felldir. He and Kaeto had been permitted to leave the supplies carriage to fetch and carry food and drink for Ceni. Icaraine seemed to find this amusing – that her lowly servant had even more lowly servants. It was, Kaeto supposed, technically humiliating, but he found it infinitely preferable to, for example, Felldir having various limbs chopped off. It also meant that they had brief moments of time together when they were not observed. As if he could guess his train of thought, Felldir pushed a strand of Kaeto's hair back behind his ear, his wolf eyes searching his face.

'The griffins will fight, when we get there,' said Kaeto. It wasn't quite a question.

Felldir nodded. 'They will fight. And they will lose. The child of the chains will stop them in their tracks, and when he has eaten this latest set of Titan bones... he will likely be even more powerful than he is now.'

Kaeto grimaced, remembering the way Malakim had simply plucked the griffin from the sky and held it on the ground, like a child pulling the legs off a spider.

'Come on,' he said. 'Let's get this food to Ceni.'

The former queen of Galabroc was by one of the many campfires that littered the Othanim road, surrounded by a circle of the surviving human servants. *They still see her as a figure of authority*, Kaeto realised. *And perhaps that is enough for her – at least, enough to survive.* When they arrived every human eye turned to Felldir, who loomed over them all with his curtailed wing. Kaeto recognised the old woman who had been in his room the day Felldir had been maimed. She saw him looking and turned her head away, ashamed.

'You,' snapped Ceni. 'Pour my wine.' She held out a simple clay cup like it was a glass of purest crystal.

'It would be my pleasure.' Kaeto poured while Felldir served from the cauldron of hot stew he was carrying. Ceni nodded for them to portion some of it out to the people closest to her, and Kaeto felt a grudging glint of admiration. Ceni might be a snake and a grasping monster who had likely gotten her remaining family killed, but she knew how this game was played. Keep people grateful to you, and they will stand by you when things get harder.

'It would be your pleasure, *my queen*.'

Kaeto cleared his throat. 'Of course, my queen.'

The pair of them waited while Ceni and her small circle of loyal followers ate, and when they were done, Ceni held out her bowl without looking at them.

'Titan,' she said. 'You will wash out my bowl. Now.'

Felldir stepped forward and took it, the bowl looking like a cup in his long-fingered hand, and something inside Kaeto, something he hadn't even been aware was on the verge of breaking, snapped.

'Do you want to know what that monster did to your mother, Ceni?'

He sensed Felldir looking at him – not alarmed, but certainly curious.

Ceni turned to look at him, her nostrils flaring.

'*What* did you say to me?'

'I just thought you'd want to know. Because surely that was your intention? To have your mother and your sister murdered? I imagine that in your original plan, before the Othanim arrived, you intended to have them quietly poisoned in the dungeons – even Brittletain would balk at you openly executing your own mother, I'm sure, and you wouldn't want to be an unpopular queen.'

Ceni rose to her feet slowly. The gathered servants were muttering and eyeing each other.

'Icaraine twisted her until her back broke, until all the bones inside her snapped. That's what her soldiers are joking about around their campfires. Is that what you wanted, Ceni, queen of no one? In your deepest, darkest dreams, is that what you pictured?'

'You swine.' Ceni's face had flushed, her lips thinned into angry lines. 'I'll have Icaraine pull your spine out of your arsehole, you jumped-up little Imperial dog...'

'That's right, have Icaraine do your dirty work for you,' Kaeto said brightly. 'Speaking of spines, where's yours?' He grinned, suddenly thinking he had reminded himself of Belise. She would have enjoyed this conversation enormously. 'Did you lose it when the Othanim ran you out of your own castle, or was it before then? Did you ever have one?'

'Kaeto...' said Felldir, uncertainty in his voice.

'It's fine, I'm sure none of this is news to the great Queen Ceni.'

'No, look.' He placed one large hand on Kaeto's shoulder and turned him slightly to face the line of trees off to their right. 'What is happening there?'

Kaeto blinked, all thought of baiting Ceni dropping from his head in an instant, because the forest itself was moving. No, it was rolling back and splitting open, revealing a place that hadn't been there a moment before, and marching out of that space came a human army with Princess Epona at its head, riding in a chariot. A woman rode next to her, a glowing sword held above her head, and coming along behind them, a shifting green shape that hurt his head to look at.

'This island never ceases to surprise me,' he said faintly.

---

Leven flew out of the wood, the gathered forces of the rebels below her, and tried to take in the scene on the road. The Othanim were largely spread out in a long line, clearly not expecting this kind of sudden attack. They had two enormous carriages with them, both pulled by teams of around thirty horses each. There were humans too, some of them scattering as shouts went up from along the line – Leven saw a number of them heading for the treeline, and that was a relief. It would be better for everyone if they were out of the way.

It was almost like being a Herald again, she thought as she darted forward, except that she could no longer summon her magical sword and fly at the same time. Instead, she had borrowed a rebel sword, which felt heavy and cumbersome in her hand. And her enemies were no longer scurrying local armies being brought under the booted heel of the Imperium. As she watched, large numbers of Othanim leapt up from the ground, wings unfurling as they rose to meet her.

Leven grinned as her ore-lines hummed and crackled. This was going to be messy.

---

Epona leaned low over the front of her chariot, dashing the reins so that the horse – a dappled grey called Owllight – surged forward. The road was boggy in places from the recent rain, and not as flat as she'd have liked, but the wheels of the chariot were sturdy, and they clipped over the ruts at a pace. Next to her, Jack was clinging on with one hand, Caliburn held above her head. Already, the Othanim were turning, grabbing their own swords. The element of surprise vanished all too quickly.

'To me, rebels!' Epona called. 'To me!'

Behind them came the rest of their force, around a hundred tired men and women, many of them injured, a handful riding on their own horses or ponies, clutching a variety of weapons that had seen better days. *This is madness.* But Jack had taken up her call, and to her amazement, the rebels were shouting back, a clear, fine battle rage that spoke of two years of invasion and murder. She laughed, and Jack glanced at her.

'This is madness, but if we all die here, at least we made a decent show of it!'

Jack smiled, shook her head. 'I'll tackle those still on the ground.' She leaned over and pressed her lips to Epona's cheek in a brief, dry kiss, and then she was gone, jumping down onto the earth and landing in a roll that suggested she did such things every day. Her face flushed, Epona turned the horses towards the carriages. All around her, the rebels were swarming while the Othanim began to rise into the air, sometimes taking an unlucky human warrior with them. She could hear Icaraine shouting somewhere ahead, and then a dark shadow fell over her – glancing up, she saw the vast shape of the Othanim queen passing over, one of the rebels held by the head in one giant fist. Her brief moment of giddy humour died in her throat.

*God's arses, Cillian had better be everything he says he is,* she thought to herself, *or we're all dead.*

# 63

*Once there was a Druin child*
*Who walked the forest on the hill*
*And in her heart she kept the Green Man*
*And there she keeps him still*

*She looked high she looked low*
*And her gaze it was always fond*
*And then she spied a changing man*
*Aside the watery pond*

          Extract from a traditional Druin song

Everything was chaos. Kaeto grabbed Felldir's arm and dragged him away from Ceni's circle. The former queen and her servants were rising to their feet, combinations of confusion and hope on many faces. He spared a thought to wonder what they would do, what Ceni would do: stick with the monster that had its foot on her neck, or align herself with the rebels? Ceni could hardly be sure of a happy reception from her sister, given what she had done. Around them, the Othanim were taking to the skies with swords and spears. Icaraine herself was already snatching up the unwary – he caught a glimpse of her biting the head off a human body and then discarding the rest to fall in a bloody pulp on the road.

'Stars' arses, it's going to be a massacre,' he said in a low voice. 'What are they thinking?'

'Perhaps they aren't,' suggested Felldir. 'When you are desperate enough, even the hopeless can give you hope.'

'I don't...' Kaeto stopped. By the place where the trees had opened to expel the rebel army, the green shape he had seen was growing brighter, larger. At first it had appeared to be human, one of the horned Druin that Brittletain was famous for, but now it was something else, something large. As he watched, it grew swiftly to the size of the closest oak tree, and although it kept its horns – huge, curling horns like those of a ram, carved with glowing runes – its face was something else, something caught between human and animal. Its eyes were as green as spring grass, the pupils a horizontal line like a goat's. Its vast body looked to be made of a terrifying mixture of muscle, skin, fur, feathers and vegetation. Birds flew from a hollow in its arm. Kaeto felt a sudden, powerful desire to be at home in Stratum, in his cosy Envoy tower. The cutthroat politics of an assassin's life felt somewhat idyllic. 'What the fuck is that? Another Titan?'

'No Titan I know of,' said Felldir. 'But the griffin spoke of a Green Man, did she not?'

'The accounts of Brittletain did not do it justice,' said Kaeto dryly. 'We should find Belise. This is likely our best chance to get out of here.'

---

Belise stood on the back steps of the carriage, a spear braced ready for the next foolish rebel to attack. Two already lay on the ground, bleeding their last into the mud. Behind her, Malakim cowered at the back of the carriage, his long spidery hands pressed against his elongated head. He was making a keening sound, high and uncertain, like a kettle close to boiling.

'Get away!' Belise shouted again as a pair of rebels approached. 'I don't want to do it, but I will kill you if you get close. The prince is under my protection!'

*And my protection only, by the looks of it.* Icaraine was in the air, dipping to snatch up unfortunate rebels from the ground, breaking their backs or biting off their heads in furious, jerky movements, while the Othanim warriors were all over the place: on the ground being swarmed by humans, or in the air, fighting what appeared to be a Herald, of all things. *Where did the bloody Herald come from? I thought Icaraine killed all the ones we brought with us.*

It didn't matter. There was a sound like thunder, and a series of high-pitched screams. The rebels who had been threatening the carriage fell back, and Belise turned to see what had changed their minds. Crashing into the road with fistfuls of Othanim warriors in its hands was a huge green creature, twice as tall as the trees. As it moved, it changed, the parts of its body that were made of branches and vines twisting and sprouting buds and fruits; one bold Othanim darted in and slashed at the giant's vast bicep. The creature did not bleed; instead the material of its body surged and knitted over the injured area. It opened its mouth, and its voice was like a calling stag; the roar of a waterfall; the crash of a thunderbolt.

'*Invaders! Defilers! The Green Wood will eat you alive!*'

'Stars' arses,' said Belise in a small voice.

'What is it?' asked Malakim. 'What is that thing? I can *feel* it.'

'I don't know, my prince.' Yet she felt like she did. The griffin had spoken of the Green Man, some incredibly powerful piece of Brittletain magic they had somehow unleashed. This had to be what she had meant. 'A giant of this land, I think.'

A turning point, then. A division in the road. Kaeto had taught her to look out for these, especially the ones that weren't immediately obvious. With this Green Man, it was possible the rebels had a real chance of defeating the Othanim, even of killing Icaraine. In that case, defending Malakim and winning his loyalty was pointless – in fact, her best chance of avoiding being killed with all the other Othanim was to abandon the prince to his fate now.

'Don't worry, my prince,' she called back to him. 'Your mother will save us all.'

Yet from what she could see, Icaraine seemed reluctant to approach the Green Man. Even her huge bulk looked small in comparison, and instead she hung back, picking off the human rebels while her Othanim soldiers battered themselves to paste against the giant's vast form. It, or he, rather – there was no missing the fact that it was male, now that she looked – was laughing as he snatched the warriors from the air around his head, crushing them against palms made of oak and flesh.

'Belise!'

Kaeto and Felldir emerged from the general chaos. Felldir had his usual calm expression, as though this kind of carnage was something he had once dealt with daily – and who knew, perhaps he had – while her master's face was flushed. Not with alarm, she realised shortly, but with hope. She came down the steps towards them, her spear lowered.

'Envoy Kaeto,' she said formally. 'Have you come to offer your assistance in keeping Prince Malakim safe?'

He shook his head and reached for her. 'There's no need for that, Belise, we're hardly being watched at the moment. Come on, we have to—'

She stepped neatly back. 'If you're not here to help, I suggest you take refuge in the carriage behind me. You'll be safer there, at least for a while.'

'Belise, what are you talking about?' It was rare for Kaeto to lose patience with her, but he certainly seemed on the verge of it. Under other circumstances, she might have found it funny. 'There's no time. Me, you and Felldir need to get out of here while Icaraine is distracted. It's probably the only chance we'll get. If the rebels survive they'll get us to the coast, maybe even onto a boat, and then—'

'No.'

Kaeto looked like she'd slapped him.

'What do you mean, *no*?'

'I believe she has her own plan,' rumbled Felldir. There was an ear-splitting scream as an Othanim warrior fell to the ground, her belly cut by the Herald's blade.

'Envoy Kaeto.' Belise came down the steps until she stood in front of him. She was taller than him now, so she had to crouch slightly. 'Master,' she said in a quieter voice. 'I should stay here with Malakim. We don't yet know how this is going to end, and I still think the best play is to have the kid on my side. And after this, he'll trust me to the ends of the earth.'

'Don't know how it's going to end?' Kaeto jabbed a finger at the giant, who was merrily stamping a number of Othanim into the mud. 'Look at that great bastard!'

'Please, chief. I'm only doing what you always taught me, right? Watching the tides, choosing which wave to ride. My guts are telling me this isn't over, and I can't abandon my advantage yet.'

'We could *go* – the three of us, together.'

'If you can get away, do it,' she said. 'I'll find you. But I have to play this out.'

It looked for a moment as though he would argue with her further. But Felldir settled one of his big hands on Kaeto's shoulder, and something in him shifted.

'You always were terrifyingly clever, Belise,' he said. 'Be careful, please. That is an order.'

Belise nodded. In some other world, if he were some other person, and she were a normal child – his natural-born daughter, perhaps – she would have hugged him then. But it was this world, and they were who they were.

'I will, chief.'

# 64

Epona had been riding in chariots from the time she could walk and confidently identify a horse, and that gave her a speed on the battlefield that no one else had. Even the Othanim, swooping out of the open sky to catch her, found themselves left in the dust as her narrow chariot, built for speed, zipped up and down the road. Her sword was wet with Titan blood, a thought that still gave her a chill even two years into this disastrous war. And now her real targets were drawing close: the two huge carriages, thought to be carrying supplies and possibly even the mutant child of Icaraine Lightbringer. In the back of her chariot, strapped securely to the board, was a flask of swift-burning oil and a flint.

She approached the first carriage, the one at the back of the Othanim procession. Out of the corner of her eye she caught sight of a small group of rebels, led by Jack. They had one of the flying Titans pinned down between them, and she saw the flash of burning light as Caliburn sliced its head off.

*Even if we don't make it, we've given them a good scare*, she thought fiercely. *We made them bleed for what they did to you and Bronny, Mum.*

Skidding to a halt, her horse lathered with sweat, Epona leapt from the back of the chariot and scrambled up the steps that led to the back of the carriage. She thought initially that it had been abandoned, but as she stumbled into the darkened interior she saw an Othanim shape loom towards her. She had a moment to think that it looked wrong somehow, and then her short sword was knocked out of her hand. Epona gritted her teeth, certain she was about to have her neck broken by a Titan, when a cool voice reached her out of the gloom.

'This Othanim is not your enemy, Princess.'

'Envoy Kaeto?'

He stepped out of the shadows. The man knew how to hide, she had to admit. He had been within touching distance and she'd never spotted him.

'Well,' she said. 'I thought for sure you must be dead.' She couldn't quite drag her eyes from the Titan, a tall pale creature with yellow eyes. His shape was wrong because he was missing one of his wings. She bent and picked up her sword.

'I could say the same for you,' said Kaeto. Outside, the sounds of battle continued: screams and shouts and the thunderous footsteps of the Green Man. 'I must congratulate you. The Othanim won't soon forget this day.'

'We're not out the other side of it yet.' She looked around the inside of the carriage. There were crates and sacks and racks, all filled with food and wine and other supplies. Kaeto and the rogue Titan had clearly been packing their own bags with as much as they could find. 'Where are you two going?'

'With you, hopefully.' Kaeto gave a faint smile. 'It seems that diplomatic efforts with the Othanim have failed, and the Imperium is retracting its offer of friendship. Or at least, I am retracting myself from their delightful company.'

Epona had to laugh. 'I told you it would end that way, Envoy. Fine. If any of us are still standing at the end of this, you can consider yourself under the protection of Londus and...' For a moment it had been on her lips to say Queen Broudicca. She stopped and shook her head. 'We'll claim everything in here when it's over. I'm off to the other carriage to burn it down.'

Abruptly Envoy Kaeto's hand was gripping her forearm. He was much stronger than he looked.

'You cannot do that.'

She raised her eyebrows. 'Why the fuck shouldn't I? That mutant bastard of hers is hiding in there and the time for playing nice is far, far behind us. In fact—'

There was a shout from outside, somehow higher and louder than everything else, cutting through the noise like an arrow through water. It was Jack.

Epona went to the top of the steps, Kaeto and the mutilated Titan just behind her. Jack was still shouting, although it took Epona a moment to make sense of it.

'He's killing us,' Jack was bellowing at the top of her lungs. 'The Green Man is killing us!'

---

Cillian floated, a speck of humanity in a vast sea of tumultuous, seething green. The Green Man — his father, there was no point beating around the bush — surrounded him on all sides, feeding off Cillian's life essence and using it to be a force in the wider world. All of the Wild Wood was with him, was with the both of them, every movement galvanised by the sheer living energy of it. To say it was overwhelming was a joke; it took all of Cillian's concentration to keep his own name in his head. He looked down on the scene below them with the detachment of a bird even as his heart pounded with a sick kind of terror. Together, they were huge, and powerful, and the Othanim were dying in their dozens. His father's joy as their bones crunched and organs popped was as heady as wine, and Cillian suspected just as poisonous if taken in large amounts.

They reached, together, for an Othanim warrior that was stabbing at their horns with a spear. Together, they pinched its skull between two enormous fingers and it shattered like an egg.

*We are winning.*

The Green Man's voice spoke inside his head, oddly quiet and self-satisfied even as he bellowed challenges with the mouth and lungs that they shared.

*There is still Icaraine*, replied Cillian. *She won't be as easy.*

*Aye, that one avoids us, because she knows we are her doom. Look how they run.* He stamped a mighty foot, crushing a small horde in a single blow. Cillian saw rebels scattering, terror on their faces.

*Be careful*, he said. *Those people are our allies.*

His father's rage boiled up, a green sea threatening to drown him.

*The Wild Wood has no allies, boy. None that walk on two legs, anyway.*

*That's not true. The Druin...*

*The old bear's children? A mere shadow of what we are, boy.*

The Green Man struck out at a group of Othanim that were flying overhead; three of them were knocked bodily from the sky, and only then did Cillian see that Leven was up there with them, her bloodied blade flashing in the sun. She had narrowly avoided being struck by the Green Man herself, and she was not as strong as the Titans. Such a blow would have turned her bones to pulp.

*Father! That's Leven up there!*

He strained against the Green Man's power, determined to wrestle back some control over the chaotic surge of nature, but very quickly he realised he didn't have the strength. He'd only experienced a tiny sliver of what the Green Man was capable of.

*No human is an ally of the Wild Wood*, the Green Man said, his voice rising. *All they do is trample the shoot underfoot, take what isn't theirs, eat our fruit and cut into our bodies, and burn us, destroy us. As long as humans have lived, they have wounded us, and they will never stop. They know no other way.*

*Stop!* Cillian tried again, straining against his father's anger even as he felt it boil out of control. He could no more have stopped the buds opening in spring.

*Humans, son, will always be a blight on us. Why not rid ourselves of the creatures now?*

*Please, don't do this.* Cillian thought of Leven, so vulnerable without her magical blade and her Titan strength, and Epona on the ground, with no idea their greatest weapon was about to turn on them. He could be about to lose them both. *We're fighting the Othanim, not our own people.*

But the Green Man was no longer listening; was possibly no longer capable of listening. Cillian held on as the tide rose, desperately clinging onto a sense of himself, his name, his history, and when that was washed away in a surge of green, he summoned an image of Leven, how she had looked when they had kissed under the Caul of Stars. Then that too was gone, and he was nothing, an echo lost in a storm of leaves and fury.

# 65

*The Lilac Wood is a myth, and the stories of Mab and Beron are likewise fables. The pixen are real enough, I'll grant you that, but can you imagine those seeds of chaos obeying any figure, let alone one that took a human shape? The stories about the pair are certainly interesting enough, and it seems to me that the inclusion of the Green Man in the story of Beron's demise is simply a metaphor for the all-encompassing power of the Wild Wood. You cannot make deals with nature. You know that better than anyone, old friend.*

Extract of a letter from Allana Dale,<br>a historian of Galabroc, to Elder Druin Jathinos

Leven ducked as the Green Man's huge hand swept through the air an arm's length away, batting several unfortunate Othanim to the ground. She wasn't caught by it, but the wind from his movement buffeted her powerfully enough that for a second she lost height, putting her dangerously close to another group of Titan warriors. She flew up out of their reach, her heart hammering.

'Ah. Shit.' Her ore-lines were burning. In the heat of battle it was possible to ignore them, at least for a while, but it was becoming difficult to think. Instead, thoughts and images she knew didn't belong to her were pushing her normal thoughts aside: *protect the eggs, avenge the lost children; we will escape to the lava pits where no one can follow; we'll follow the sun to the end of the earth, on fiery wings.* The voices, she knew, of the Titans whose bones she wore embedded in her skin. It wasn't helping. Soon, she'd have to rest, and from the looks of things the battle wasn't close to over yet.

There was a scream, a high-pitched, unmistakably human scream. Leven turned in time to see the Green Man reaching down for a handful of rebels, enormous horns bowed towards the earth, and then... he crushed them like a man wringing water from a cloth. Her stomach dropped, panic seizing her throat like a vice.

'Cillian, what are you doing?'

Except of course it wasn't Cillian. Blood ran from the Green Man's fist, spattering onto the ground far below, running down his huge, gnarled forearm. There was nothing of Cillian in him now. She couldn't have said what it was that had changed exactly, but she knew her husband was no longer there, or no longer in control, and that was terrifying. She darted away, a terrible realisation flooding through her like ice water. If the Green Man wanted them dead, there was nothing they could do. Nothing at all.

---

Belise leaned out of the carriage door, watching what was happening with a creeping sense of horror. The Green Man – if that's what it was – had apparently decided that everything moving was deserving of death, stamping and grasping and tearing everything within sight. Very quickly the ground under his feet was a churned mass of blood and bodies, the mud black with it, and he was changing again, becoming larger, less human. His face lengthened, twisting into something more goat-like, and his lower legs bent back on themselves, shaggy feet turning into hooves. Spines grew from his back, long and lethally sharp, and his eyes – once so green – were black. Those who could still run were fleeing, and the forest around him was dwindling somehow, as though he were draining the life from it to fuel himself.

'He's coming, isn't he?' asked Malakim, his voice wavering. 'He's coming for me.'

'To be honest with you, my prince, it looks like he's coming for all of us.' She glanced across the teeming battlefield, and saw Kaeto and Felldir down near the other carriage. They too were watching the Green Man advance, along with a short woman with black hair. Princess Epona, she guessed, from her similarity to Queen Ceni. Icaraine had backed off further up the road, her battle rage apparently banked while she waited to see what would happen – and that was smart, thought Belise. All she had to do now was wait for the Green Man to finish off the rebels. But what then?

*Come and get your bloody child*, Belise thought fiercely. Then she ducked back in the carriage.

'We'll have to go, Malakim,' she said. 'The giant is on the warpath and we're right in the middle of it, I'm afraid.'

'Go? Where?'

'Anywhere.' Belise went over to him, trying to keep her movements soft and patient even as she heard the thunderous steps of the Green Man growing closer; every step, closer to pulverising the carriage where they hid. 'Probably, I don't know, into the wood.'

'The wood is *haunted*.'

'I... what are you talking about?'

'I can hear it, at night,' said Malakim, sniffling. He had his head down, partly covered by his spindly arms. 'It whispers. It hates us. It hates me.'

Belise felt her impatience sharpen to annoyance, and again she took a step back from it. *He's frightened. Despite his size and the thousands of years he's been alive, he's still little more than a child.*

'There's nothing to fear in the woods, my prince.' She took a breath. 'But that bloody great huge thing out there is something we have to fear *right now*. We have to make a run for it.'

Malakim made a keening noise, drawing his arms tighter around himself. His red eyes were glistening.

'I will not go,' he said, his voice a tiny croak.

'Fuck's sake,' said Belise.

---

'What in the name of Magog's sweaty balls is he doing?'

Epona watched in horror as the Green Man tore his way through the road, attacking Othanim and rebels alike. While he snatched the flying Titans from the sky with his hands, crushing them between fingers like oak trees, he was also stamping on the fleeing rebels, smashing their bodies into the dirt. Her heart felt like it was going to burst in her chest, the horror of it all threatening to drown her. Jack had run over to them, her creamy skin sweaty and covered in dirt, and as they stood, rooted to the spot with shock, Leven landed too, stumbling as she did, as though her legs wouldn't hold her. Epona rounded on her old friend, grabbed her by the shoulders.

'What the fuck is Cillian doing?'

'I don't know,' she said, and then, in the same breath, 'I think he's lost control. It's all the Green Man. The Druidahnon said it might... that the Green Man might consume him if he let him in. And the trees too. I've seen it from overhead – whatever he's doing is draining the life of the Wild Wood itself. We're in the middle of a circle of dead trees.'

Epona glanced around and saw that the Herald was right. Whereas their forces had arrived amongst a wood clad in all its spring finery, she now saw that they had lost their leaves, or were in the process of losing them; like some sort of unnaturally early autumn.

'What could have caused the giant to attack his own side?' asked Kaeto. Epona blinked. She'd practically forgotten the Envoy was there. To her surprise, Leven also looked like she'd been struck on the head with something.

'Envoy... Kaeto?' she said. 'What the fuck are you doing here? Uh, sir.'

The Envoy's lips quirked with amusement.

'I might ask you the same question, Herald Eleven.'

Jack's sword rang out, and they all turned to look at her.

'Caliburn says...' She took a deep breath. 'Caliburn says that the Green Man was always a wily god of destruction, and if we don't stop him now, he will destroy the whole Wild Wood.'

'That makes no sense!' protested Leven. 'Cillian loves the Wild Wood above everything, he would never harm it.'

'You can see what he's doing,' Epona said quietly. 'We can all see it. People are dying, Leven.'

The sword made a noise like the pealing of a great bell, loud enough that Epona winced.

'Forgive me,' said Jack. 'But Caliburn says that this is the whole point. There can be no creation without destruction, green shoots grow in the ashes, life coming from death...' She shook her head. 'Sorry, he's not normally this dramatic. Or poetic. But the Green Man's cycle always involves death. It doesn't matter to him that he'll destroy the Wild Wood – he'll simply make it all grow again.'

'And in the middle of it all, we get massacred.' Epona ran her hands through her hair, feeling the sweat and dirt there under her fingertips. 'If we're lucky, he'll kill Icaraine too, but what good will it do if we're all dead?'

'I have to stop him,' Jack said. She hefted the sword, which began to glow with a warm white light, like it was being forged anew. 'I'm the only one who can do it. I'll get one chance.'

'Over my dead body,' said Leven. She lifted her own sword, still sticky with Othanim blood, although Epona noted that she looked exhausted, the skin beneath her ore-lines almost grey. 'Cillian's still in there somewhere.'

'We can't afford to fight each other,' said Epona quickly. 'If we do that, we've already lost.'

'We losing right now,' said Jack, 'and I can't let that happen.' She turned back towards the Green Man, who was still making his slow way towards them, and when Leven tried to block her path, she simply pushed her away, making the Herald stagger. The plain rebel sword dropped from her fingers into the dirt. 'Truly, I am sorry. This was always my destiny.'

'Jack, wait!'

The woman darted away, her golden hair shining.

'She expects to defeat that thing with a single sword?' said Envoy Kaeto. 'I suggest we all retreat into the forest, now. It won't be able to find us all amongst the trees.'

'If she lays a finger on him, I'll kill her,' said Leven, breathing heavily. She dropped to her knees in the dirt, swaying. She looked as though she were about to pass out.

'Wait,' said Epona, although she didn't know what for. All she could do was watch as Jack ran directly at the Green Man, her glowing sword raised. She sprinted through the crowds of Othanim as though they were nothing more than shadows, the light of her sword turning their snarling faces into masks. Epona lost sight of her briefly, and found that her heart was in her throat until she spotted that golden head again – now closer than ever to the giant hooves of the Green Man. Epona couldn't see how she could possibly even get close to the giant without getting crushed – *we should have coordinated this*, she thought desperately, *should have got Leven to fly her over the creature* – but then Jack was leaping, up and up towards the leg of the giant and somehow the sword was pulling her after it...

'How is she doing that?' The voice belonged to the Titan who had arrived with Kaeto. He sounded genuinely curious.

'Fucked if I know,' coughed Leven.

Jack was on the creature's leg, clinging on amongst a mixture of foliage, bone, flesh and skin. She looked tiny, impossibly tiny, but Epona saw the moment she raised the sword very clearly – it was a flash of white light that cut across the space between them, briefly dazzling everyone. She heard Leven shouting something, desperate and furious, and then the blade sunk into the Green Man's flesh.

Moments ago she had seen Othanim stab the giant with their own blades only for the wounds to close up almost instantly. When Caliburn struck, the light from the sword seemed to pass into the Green Man; a pulse of pure energy that sank into the creature's flesh and expanded, causing it to ripple and swell. There was a bellow loud enough to shake the ground, and the Green Man raised one enormous fist, bringing it down on the space where Jack had been clinging. When his hand moved away Jack was gone, but Caliburn was still wedged in the giant's leg.

'Jack!'

## 66

'Cillian!'

It was an explosion of light, turning everything shades of green for an instant, then gone again. Where the Green Man had been – *Cillian*, insisted Leven in her head, *where Cillian had been* – there was a tall cyclone of swirling leaves, a maelstrom of green, yellow, red and orange and brown, moving faster than she could follow. She made to stand up and found that she couldn't. She tried again anyway, half falling into the mud.

'Where is he? *Where is he?*'

'The Green Man is gone, Herald Eleven.' Impossibly, Envoy Kaeto had his arm around her shoulders, attempting to get her to her feet. She tried to shake him off, not tearing her eyes away from the cascading leaves. 'And I suggest we also go while we still can. Felldir, can you help me lift her up? Icaraine is on her way over here.'

The leaves were slowing down, falling towards the ground in a gentle rain. The rebels who had survived were retreating into the woods, and the Othanim too were drawing back, looking confused, but there was no sign of Cillian anywhere. Not even his broken body, lying in the dirt.

'Where *is* he?' she said again.

Strong arms were lifting her to her feet as though she weighed less than a leaf herself. A group of rebels passed them bearing Jack in their arms, bleeding from a head wound. If Leven had

had the strength she would have launched herself at the woman, demanding to know what she had done with him. Epona was shouting things, giving orders, but they made very little sense to Leven. Instead, the voices of the long-dead Titans began to rise again, demanding her full attention.

'I can't,' she muttered. 'I have to stay here. I have to find him.'

A deep voice spoke just over her head. 'Kaeto, she is delirious.'

'She's been a Herald for over a decade, I'm amazed she's still standing, Felldir. Follow Princess Epona and we'll regroup from there.'

Leven tried to lift her head, but it was too much. The sea rose up in her mind, salty and bitter, and she let it take her away.

# 67

*We live long lives on the mountain. From yenlin to eyystin, our lives are filled with the hunt, with the hatching of our future, and the singing of our songs, but we must not forget the weave of what it is to be yost: justice, strength, loyalty and sacrifice.*

The Griffin Creed, as written on the
Silver Death Peak by Fionovar the Red

Ynis grew stronger under the human man's care. He told her his name was Lom, that he had lived in the Wild Wood all his life, even though he wasn't Druin. Each day he would bring her broth with meat and small, knotty vegetables, and he would check her bandages and help her to the hole in the ground outside when she needed the toilet. She grew stronger, but her connection to the dead remained, a kind of afterimage that fluttered constantly around the real world. Sometimes, Lom would help her outside and they would sit on the porch of his shack, watching the birds and the squirrels; when they moved Ynis would sometimes see a greenish-blue shadow following them – spirits of the unseen dead. Lom's fate-lines were visible to her too, although there were only two of them, and they were weak things, little more than a hair's breadth wide and so pale they were almost pink. Ynis would look at them sometimes and feel sad. Her own fate-ties were a shifting bushel of lines, as red as blood.

'What are you doing out here alone?' she asked him when she was able to speak again. 'Where is your family?'

His bushy eyebrows drew together at that, as though the words caused him pain.

'I wish I knew. We don't speak no more. I have a daughter, a woman grown with her own child, who would be your age I reckon.' He grunted. 'All that is in another life now, mind.'

'They are still out there,' said Ynis, eyeing his fate-ties. 'They still think of you.'

He grunted again, although Ynis had the idea it was supposed to be more of a chuckle. 'Not fondly though, child. Not fondly.'

'What happened?'

'Cross words. Over something foolish. I said things I shouldn't have. She told me something I didn't need to know. And there we are. I felt like I was in the right for a season or so, but what use is that to me?'

Ynis thought of Leven, and the last time she'd seen her.

'A season of righteousness, for years of being a lonely old man. What kind of a trade is that?' Lom slapped his knees and stood up. 'No use belly-achin' about it. I'll get you something hot to drink. Put some colour in those cheeks.'

Later, as Ynis was drifting off to sleep near the dying hearth, she thought Lom had returned – sometimes, if it was cold, he would bring an extra blanket. But as the figure drew closer, she saw that even though it was bearded and man-shaped, it was not Lom. This man was younger, his shoulders broader, and he was lined with green and blue fire. *Another dead loved one*, she thought.

'Father?'

Owain came to her bedside and sat, patting her blanketed legs with one hand. She felt it as a tingle in her shins.

'There you are, little squirrel. You're not looking so well.'

'You've never come to me before.'

Owain looked away, staring at something she couldn't see. He seemed only half aware of her, or only half aware of where he was.

'It's not easy for me to be here, Alaw. I've been away for such a long, long time. But there are things you need to know.' He turned back to her and he burned a little brighter, as though gathering himself. 'Your sister needs help.'

'T'rook? What's happened?'

Owain shook his head, a pained smile on his lips. 'Your human sister, Alaw, as I'm sure you know.'

'She doesn't need me. And I can't reach her, anyway. I'm stuck here for a while. I've been hurt. Badly.' Even to her own ears she sounded petulant.

'Ah, that is where you're wrong. Your big sister needs you very much. Her husband, the Druin, is lost, Alaw.'

'Cillian?' Ynis felt her stomach turn over. Cillian was good as far as humans went. He cared about the trees, and living things, and he had helped them find T'rook. She did not like to think of him hurt, or worse. Despite everything. 'What's happened?'

'It's funny to think that Deryn has married a Druin, too,' said Owain. 'Are we drawn to the wild in people in this family? Echni was... difficult. Worse than difficult, if I am being truthful with you, although I don't like to speak badly of your mother in front of you...'

'I don't mind,' said Ynis, thinking of the last time she had seen Gynid Tyleigh, the dark glint in her eye that said she knew she was getting one over on Leven. Ynis had ignored it because she was getting what she wanted.

'Difficult, yes, and cold sometimes, but so clever. Such a hunger for knowledge. If you got her talking on something, she couldn't stop. She knew everything there was to know about the Wild Wood, and it wasn't enough for her. Which is, I suppose, why she did what she did. Some people have a fire in them, Alaw, and it fuels them, even as it burns everything down around them.'

'She had Deryn cut your head off,' said Ynis.

Owain patted her leg again and nodded. 'That she did, aye. That she did.'

'And she left me in the snow to die. And made Deryn forget herself, over and over again.'

As she spoke the words out loud, she felt a terrible pang of sympathy for her sister. Leven had had her past taken from her. At least Ynis had grown up in the nest-pit with T'rook, Flayn and T'vor. She'd had a childhood, even if she'd always been an outsider.

'I've no excuses for her, my little squirrel. What Echni did, to all of us, was unforgivable. But maybe that should help us recognise when things *are* forgivable. When it's not worth throwing away a bond over a few cross words.'

Ynis narrowed her eyes at him.

'What happened to Cillian?' she asked pointedly.

'The boy who would be the Green Man,' said Owain. Outside, a sudden spring rain clattered against the wooden boards of the shack. 'He lost control of the spirit, if he ever had it in the first place, and now, poor lad, he is lost in the deepest heart of the Lich-Way.'

'The Lich-Way?'

'You have been there before, Alaw.'

'The place with the bog bodies,' she said, frowning slightly. 'They were... very strange. Cillian is a Druin. Can he not find his own way out? Leven... I mean, Deryn told me that he had taken them there once while they were travelling up the length of Brittletain. Surely he cannot be lost for long.'

Owain was shaking his head. 'The Lich-Way isn't meant for living beings, Alaw, and he's not there by choice this time. He's tangled up in the very heart of it, in a place where only the dead can go. The longer he's there, the more chance he has of being lost forever. The Green Man will not come again, and then what chance do we have of driving those flying bastards out of Brittletain?' He glanced at her. 'No offence intended, petal.'

Ynis shrugged.

'No, Cillian cannot find his way out alone. Which is why you have to go and find him, Alaw. You have a unique magic, my little squirrel. Only you can walk into the dead heart of the Lich-Way and bring him out.'

'Me?' Ynis shook her head. 'I can barely walk. I am no use to anyone. Lom says that I very nearly died, out there in the wood.'

Owain smiled and curled one forefinger under her chin. Again, she felt it; like the faintest brush of a feather. It made her feel strange. Fragile. The touch of a father she only knew through other people's memories.

'Alaw. Arrow. Ynis. You know what I'm talking about in your heart, lass. You know the path to the Lich-Way. It doesn't need your legs to walk it.'

The rain grew heavier, turning to hail. It rattled across the roof like it wanted to come in.

'I suppose I do,' she said. 'What will happen if I don't go?'

'Cillian will be lost forever, and without him there is no Green Man to force Icaraine from the island. Your sister will die, alone. And the Othanim will swarm Yelvynia, driving every griffin from its nest while their queen's mutant child eats their bones.'

'Oh,' said Ynis in a small voice. 'Is that all?'

He chuckled. 'You've grown into a fine daughter, Alaw. Smart and brave, and tougher than my old boots. I wish I'd been there to see it.'

With that, he began to fade. Ynis felt something rise in her throat, some desperate need to keep him there a touch longer. *I need your help*, she thought. *I can't do all this alone.*

In moments, though, the room was empty again, his image slipping away like water through her fingers. She lay for a moment and then sat up awkwardly, wincing at the pain in her belly. There was a scrap of charcoal on the table next to her bed, and she spent some minutes writing on the whitewashed wall, crafting each letter with care. Cillian had taught her the letters while they were away from Brittletain, and she'd never gotten good at it.

*Lom*, she wrote. *I am sorry. Not your fault. Thank you. Go and see your daughter and your grandchild. They miss you. Forgiveness is in your fate-lines.*

When that was done, she pulled the bandages away from her stomach and her legs, revealing the half-healed wounds, and then, with a grimace, she pulled away Lom's careful stitches. Very quickly her hands were streaked with gore, and her blood began soaking into the blankets. *It's so eager to get away*, thought Ynis. *Perhaps I was never meant to live in the first place.*

Eventually, the little cabin grew darker than was natural, the embers of the hearth becoming pale shadows, and a slinking kind of blackness slipped under the door, pooling around the bed like a lake on a moonless night. Ynis sat up and swung her legs over the side, leaving the pain of her body behind, and sank down into the dark.

# 68

'Come forward, Belise.'

Belise did as she was told, resisting the urge to hold her wings over her own head against the steady rain. The caravan had picked up its pieces and moved further north, to be sure of no imminent rebel interference, and eventually they had come to rest at the foot of a series of small hills. The one furthest to the west had a bear carved into its side, the lines made from slashes of chalk. Even in the rain and lowering clouds, it stood out like a bolt of lightning, and she found her eyes were constantly drawn to it. *There are many gods in this land*, she thought, *and they're watching us all the time.*

*And it's Icaraine I should be watching*, she reminded herself. The queen of the Othanim had fashioned herself a makeshift throne from a half-collapsed cottage, and she sat with the rain running down her golden helm. Malakim was crouched next to her, his awkward body all elbows and knees, and the wider guard of Othanim stood to either side. They looked uneasy, but then they always looked uneasy these days – since Malakim had started eating Titan bones, they all knew they were possible additions to the menu. Ceni had survived the attack too, more's the pity, and she stood looking dishevelled and grim at Icaraine's right foot.

'Of all my warriors, Belise, you were the one who knew her duty best. You stood your ground and protected my child, the

Prince Malakim, and did not flee into the sky when the Brittlish giant attacked. For this, you will be raised above all others.'

Icaraine gestured to Belise to come closer still. Belise went, wondering if she would live through the next few minutes. To Icaraine, being honoured could well mean providing sustenance for her son. In many ways, surviving in the Othanim camp was like sleeping in the same room as a strange dog – you didn't know if it would bite you or lick your hand.

'Here.' Icaraine held out one giant fist, then tipped it to one side so the contents fell into Belise's outstretched hands. It was a large piece of Titan bone from the griffin Malakim had captured; she guessed from the shape it had once been a piece of vertebrae. Belise held the bone up to what light there was, watching the water run from it. If she'd come across such a piece of Titan bone in Stratum, she would have been made for life. *I'll have to keep it close in case I ever get back there*, she thought. 'To gift you the food out of my child's own mouth is the highest honour I can give. I name you Belise Heartkeeper, First Knight of the Othanim.'

Belise bowed deeply, figuring it was the thing to do.

'An honour beyond all honours, your majesty.'

At that moment, the rain picked up, driving into the gathered forces and making everyone wince, as though the weather knew Belise's heart wasn't in it.

But Icaraine wasn't done with them yet.

'Not everyone covered themselves in glory.' She spoke softly, but even over the driving rain they could hear her. Her voice was the growl of a dangerous beast. 'Ceni, please read the list of names.'

There was a flurry of agitation amongst the Othanim. Belise saw some of them exchange looks or the odd muttered word. Ceni cleared her throat and began reading from a piece of parchment.

'Agrestanor, Rhodistia, Evanshod, Micanaeus...'

In the end she named ten Othanim, most of whom Belise could recognise on sight. When they started to move through the crowd to take their places in front of Icaraine, Belise moved back out of the way. She sensed that this was about to become a very bad place to be standing.

An Othanim male with hair the colour of smoke, grey skin and eerily blue eyes pushed his way to the front of the small group. Malakim raised his elongated head and regarded the winged man with each of his six crimson eyes.

'Evanshod,' purred Icaraine. 'Do you have something you want to say to me?'

'I do, Icaraine Lightbringer. We have followed you faithfully. Have slept beside you in the prison that was the Undertomb for centuries. Have risen to this new fight, on this misbegotten island.' There were some murmurs of agreement from the Titans he stood with. 'We've lowered ourselves to slaughtering humans, while our scouts engage our true enemy in the north.'

Icaraine looked down at her fingers, each tipped with a nail so long and sharp it was almost a claw.

'Do get on with it, Evanshod. Or do you think delaying this will keep me from ripping your guts out?'

'All this we have done for you, and gladly,' Evanshod continued as though she hadn't spoken, 'and what is our reward? To be fed to *that*.' He pointed at Malakim, his voice dripping with disgust. Belise winced. She thought there was a chance he could have survived arguing with Icaraine – a small chance – but his horror for her child was unforgivable. Interestingly though, the Othanim who stood with him did not back away from the speaker, as she half expected them to. Instead, they stood taller, their postures defiant. Belise glanced at the others in the crowd and saw more sedition there. Interesting. 'Icaraine, it's a queen's duty to care for all of her people, not just her mutant spawn.'

Icaraine stood up, towering over them all.

'Enough, you mewling little fool. Do you think—'

Evanshod was in the air, flying towards Icaraine like a pellet from a slingshot, and behind him, more of them came. There were cries from the crowd, some of horror and some of support. There was a thump as the smaller Titan landed on Icaraine, a blade suddenly in his hand, seeking her throat. The Titan queen roared, her hand reaching for him even as others flew forward, swords flashing.

'Stars' arses, a coup.' Belise slipped the piece of Titan bone into a pocket within her armour and prepared to rapidly be elsewhere – if power changed hands, the last Othanim to be honoured by Icaraine wouldn't be very popular. But then Evanshod was thrown back from the Titan queen, his limbs frozen in place, a stricken expression on his handsome face. Malakim had risen from his place by his mother, one long spindly arm reaching out towards them. The other rebel Othanim were also peeled off Icaraine one by one, until they all hung in the air. It was an eerie sight, Belise thought, to see them suspended that way, their wings so still. Rain ran down their bodies as though they were already ruins, lost in the wood.

'This can't continue,' said Evanshod through gritted teeth. 'Don't you see? Please, Icaraine. Your child will be the end of us all. If you can't—'

Malakim flexed his fingers, and the entire group of suspended Othanim screamed with pain as their bodies bent in ways they were not supposed to. Belise heard the snap of bones even over the rain. Another flex, and the Titans were contorted into stranger, nightmarish shapes. Blood began to pool beneath them, and there were gurgling, wheezing sounds. Behind her, Belise heard someone in the crowd sobbing. She felt her own skin grow cold.

*Don't look away*, she told herself. *Kaeto would remind you that these are the sharks you've chosen to swim with, and you shouldn't be surprised by the blood in the water.* Even so, it was a difficult thing to look at, especially when she knew that when the sun went down, she would be sharing a carriage with the creature who had summoned such horrors.

Icaraine, meanwhile, was purring with pleasure.

'You see what happens when you don't know your place?' she said, glowering round at the gathered warriors. Malakim pulled his fingers into a fist, and the suspended Titans, already broken and bleeding, drew together into a shivering tangle of bodies. Most of the ones that Belise could see looked dead already, and the one or two still left alive were bleeding from their mouths, noses and ears. As she watched, a neck twisted as though someone had wrenched it sideways, and the light disappeared from those eyes too. Malakim dropped the bodies into the mud.

'Mother,' he said into the silence that followed. 'I am hungry.'

Icaraine stood and gestured to Ceni. 'Fetch the bones of the griffin,' she commanded. 'These others can stay here and rot for a while. They do not yet deserve the honour of being consumed by Prince Malakim.'

'I would eat the griffin bones alone,' added Malakim. 'In privacy.'

His mother frowned at that, then shrugged. 'As you wish, my sweet. We'll have the bones taken to your carriage.' Her lips parted to reveal her teeth again. 'Just do not outgrow it!'

---

When they were back in the carriage, Belise found herself glancing frequently at the darkened windows, thinking about the bodies still lying out there in the mud. *You've seen worse than that,* she told herself. *Stars' arses, you've experienced worse than that yourself.* Yet the thought of the rain soaking into their feathers, pooling on their unseeing eyes... it kept returning to her when she least expected it.

Malakim had the bones of the griffin spread out on his blanket, and he was turning each one over in his hands. He hadn't started eating yet.

'That was a brave thing you did,' said Belise, hoping to distract herself. 'Saving your mother from Evanshod and his followers.'

Malakim grunted. 'She is being foolish. She divides them when she should be binding them together. Mother has decided that my *abilities* make us unstoppable, I'm afraid, and it's making her careless.' He lifted one finger and a piece of Titan bone rose into the air. 'I had to act. If they kill her, they'll kill me next. And then you. I could not let that happen.'

Outside, someone walked past the carriage sobbing. Belise wondered if it was a human or a Titan. She bowed her head.

'Your protection is an honour, my prince.'

'You are welcome, Belise Heartkeeper, First Knight of the Othanim.' She looked up to see that his long mouth had quirked up at the edges. He was teasing her.

'And now,' he continued, 'we will see what my next form will be.'

The piece of bone that had been floating in the air – a piece of rib, Belise thought – drifted sedately into his waiting mouth, and he began to chew, the sound of crunching very loud in the small space.

'Why did you want to do this in private?' she asked.

'It's a punishment,' he said, 'for Mother. She likely won't perceive it as one, but even so. I want her to realise I must have some power of my own, even if that is only a choice about what I share with her.'

He ate another piece of bone, and then another. He shifted on the bed, rolling his shoulders and stretching his legs.

'Are you in discomfort, my prince?'

'No, not exactly, it's just that...' He wriggled awkwardly, his vast body undulating and pulsing. 'It's just that...'

He groaned and a section of his chest unfolded, becoming a third arm with one too many joints. A nodule of flesh at the end of it spread seven long fingers which opened and closed like a spider's legs. Tendrils of sticky fluid hung between them.

'Well,' said Belise, holding down the urge to vomit. 'Would you look at that?'

# 69

In sleep, the Herald looked younger than she had on the battlefield, the lines at the corners of her eyes smoothed away. Yet there was no avoiding the sallow colour of her skin, or the purple bruises that darkened her arms and neck. A Herald in peak condition would not take such damage, but Eleven was a long, long way from her strongest days. There was grey in her hair, Kaeto noted. She wasn't old enough for that, either.

'When is she going to wake up?' asked the princess.

'I wish I could tell you, your highness.'

The rebels had regrouped, ragged and exhausted, in the shadow of a hill marked with a bear. They seemed to take some comfort from the symbol even as they tended to their injured, splinting broken limbs and bandaging cuts. Even Kaeto had to admit there was something about the area that was uncanny. Since they had made their sprawling camp, the weather had been better than he'd known it in Brittletain so far, the rain finally holding off and the sun growing warmer daily. He had been for a walk to the foot of the hill the previous day and almost found it pleasant.

'You know how Heralds are made,' said Epona. 'You must have some idea how to fix them.'

'My friend, I'm afraid that Herald Eleven may well be beyond fixing. The woman who made the Heralds never intended them to survive beyond their eight years of service to the Imperium.

The fact that this one is still walking around, still flying, even, is some kind of star-touched miracle.'

'She's strong,' said Epona, a stubborn tilt to her chin.

Kaeto pressed his fingers to Herald Eleven's throat. Her pulse was there, rapid and light, and her eyes moved constantly under her eyelids. *I hope her dreams are happier than her reality*, he thought.

'The real question,' he said to Epona, 'is what will the rebels do next?'

'After that debacle, you mean?' She sighed. Kaeto could see Felldir on the far side of the camp, carrying an injured man to a makeshift bed. The other rebels watched him with conflicted expressions. 'It could hardly have gone worse, could it? Our great weapon, turned on us, and one of our bravest warriors lost. Cillian was...' She paused, shook her head. 'It was a massacre, and yet... Seeing the Othanim die. Seeing them panic in the face of a force greater than themselves. Despite everything, it made me think we have a chance, somehow. I suppose you think that's ludicrous.'

Kaeto raised an eyebrow. 'Sometimes half the battle is knowing your enemy can be defeated.'

'What we need,' continued Epona, 'is a way to kill Icaraine herself. Without her I think they would lose a great deal of their power. Without a figurehead they might start to ask themselves what they are doing here at all. The Green Man might have lost control at the end, but he took plenty of them out of the game before he did so. They've suffered. They've seen their own kind die.'

'I will kill her.'

They both looked down in surprise at the Herald, who was trying to prop herself up on her elbows.

'Leven, keep still.' Epona took hold of her friend's arm and squeezed it. 'You need to rest.'

'I've done enough of that,' she said gruffly. She sat up, breathing heavily, then squinted up at Kaeto. 'So I didn't dream you after all, Envoy. What the fuck are you doing in Brittletain?'

'I am on a diplomatic mission to secure the friendship of the Othanim for her Luminance the Empress Celestinia.' He paused. 'As you can see, it's been very successful so far.'

She laughed weakly, more of a wheeze than a chuckle.

'I always wanted to ask,' she said. 'What happened to Foro? You knew, didn't you? When I came to talk to you about it that day. You and bloody... Imperator Justinia.'

'Herald Forty was beginning to experience the degradation of his ore-lines, Eleven. It was causing him pain, and likely giving him visions of his lost memories. All of which I'm sure you've experienced since then.'

'Hah. Yes. You could say that.'

'So I was ordered to kill him.' The words lingered in the air for a moment, and Kaeto wondered why he was telling the Herald these things. He could have lied. His whole life had been about lying, after all. 'Imperator Justinia was of the opinion that unstable Heralds were a danger to the Imperium. Especially if they became... dissatisfied with our leadership.'

Eleven nodded, as though she'd expected nothing less. 'Did you know, Envoy, that Gynid Tyleigh is my mother?'

'She was... I'm sorry, she was your what?'

'My dear old mum. I was her first test subject for the ore-line alchemy. She'd been perfecting it on me for years.'

'Oh.' He sniffed. 'Well. Forgive me, I had thought that I couldn't possibly dislike her more, but here we are.'

'She's a piece of work, alright. And call me Leven, please. Herald Eleven makes me want to salute things. I don't have the energy for that anymore.' The Herald ran a hand through her hair, which was still flecked with mud and scraps of leaf. 'I'll need a decent sword,' she said. 'Maybe a really good spear. Titans are tough but they're not bloody invulnerable. If I drop down on her from out of the sky when she's not looking, I'll have a good run at it. Preferably when she's not wearing that gaudy helm, so I can stick it in her eye.'

'Leven...' said Epona.

'He's gone, Epona,' she said. 'Cillian is gone. I feel like I was only holding on for him anyway. Let me try this. If I can kill her, it's like you said – maybe the rest of them will lose heart.'

The princess gnawed at a scrap of skin on her thumb, then shook her head. 'Magog's balls but you are stubborn, Leven. Let me ask you this. Will you accept that Brittletain is your home now?'

Leven looked perplexed. 'Yes. It's always been my home, really.'

'Then as your acting queen, I am telling you to bloody rest up. Even if I allow this ludicrous mission of yours – and I'm not saying I will – you'll need to be properly healed before you make an attempt. Otherwise, what's the point?'

'I don't think there is any healing me,' said Leven, but Kaeto noted she was smiling faintly at her friend. 'Acting queen, is it?'

'You took orders from the queen of Londus once before, and I'm asking you to do it again.'

The Herald didn't look convinced, but she nodded. With this new knowledge, he found he could see the shadow of Gynid Tyleigh's face in the younger woman, although her sharp features had been softened considerably by Eleven's open, honest expressions.

'Gynid Tyleigh is a monster,' he said, taking care to look the Herald in the eye. 'And I'm sorry she did that to you.'

Leven nodded. 'Me too.'

He left them to it and went to join Felldir, who was breaking up wood for a fire.

'You have spoken to the princess?'

'They are concentrating on recovering for the moment,' said Kaeto, 'and I believe that is the right call. She has sent messengers to Mersia, and Dwffd, and any other population centres that may have people left who are willing to fight.'

'But you have other ideas.'

Kaeto smiled thinly. There really was no keeping anything from Felldir. 'I want to keep an eye on the Othanim.'

Felldir raised an eyebrow. 'When we have only just escaped?'

'If I had the choice, we'd put our backs to them and keep moving until they vanish from the world again,' he said wearily. 'But...'

'Belise.'

'I believe Icaraine has more than enough to worry about without coming to look for me, and the rebels will benefit from knowing what she is up to. The Druin they have here can move me in and out of the wood as easily as breathing. I can see how Belise is doing while I'm there.'

'Don't be so sure they will not be looking for you, Kaeto,' said Felldir. 'Icaraine will not let either of us go so easily.'

'Which is why you will stay here.' When Felldir opened his mouth to protest, Kaeto held up one hand. 'I know what you will say, but I will not risk you.' Without wanting to, he glanced at Felldir's curtailed wing. 'You have already lost too much.'

---

Later, Epona found Jack also awake and sitting up, the heavy bandage on her head stained with old blood. There was a little pack of rebels around the woman, men and women who were clearly starstruck by her – they asked if they could fetch her things, if they could make her more comfortable somehow. *She is their hero*, Epona thought ruefully. *She saved them from the Green Man. Whereas I left them to his mercy*. The sword, Caliburn, had been retrieved, and lay in its scabbard to one side of Jack. People kept looking at it, too, perhaps waiting for it to glow with magic again.

'I need a word with Jack,' she said, raising her voice slightly. 'Alone.'

The rebels scattered, although not too far. Jack gave her a weak smile, and Epona sat on the edge of the makeshift bed they had crafted for the woman.

'I'm sorry,' said Jack.

'What for?'

'Your friend. Cillian. And Leven. If there had been any other way...'

Epona sighed and looked down at her hands. There was a bruise on her right knuckle, some injury that had happened during the fight that she hadn't noticed at the time.

'I think even Leven understands that the Green Man had to be stopped. He would have killed all of us, and maybe he wouldn't have stopped there either. Maybe he would have gone marching across all of Brittletain, killing every human that he could find. Power like that isn't meant to be controlled.'

'So your friend forgives me?'

'I wouldn't go that far. Just don't ask her for any favours any time soon. Or be alone in a room with her.'

Jack nodded as though she had expected this.

'How are you feeling?' asked Epona.

'Good. I'm feeling good, actually.' Jack smiled. It was, Epona thought, a little like the sun coming out from behind a cloud on a winter's day.

'You are? Because your head has taken a serious knock.'

'But my destiny is done.' Her smile broke into a proper grin. 'That prophecy has hung over me my whole life, Epona. A fixed point I knew I'd always have to face. Everything I am, always leading to the moment I would have to stand against the Green Man, a figure even the Druin don't understand. And now I am beyond it. The rest of my life is a genuine mystery, with no predictions. I feel like I could almost do anything.'

She took Epona's hand, one calloused thumb moving across her palm in a way that made Epona shiver.

'Anything?' asked Epona.

'I'd give my life to you, if I can,' said Jack. Her eyes no longer shone with the power of the magical blade, but they had their own inner light. 'I'd serve you for the rest of my days, Princess, if you'd let me. My sword arm is yours. Every... every part of me is yours.'

'Jack.' Epona swallowed. Her mouth felt very dry all of a sudden, and she wished fervently that they were miles from the camp, far away from everyone. But wasn't that ridiculous? What was the point of being the leader, of being a princess, if she couldn't occasionally do what she wanted? She brought Jack's hand up to her mouth and kissed it softly, and then she leaned forward to kiss her on the lips, as slowly as she could manage. From all around them, she sensed a slight intake of breath as the rebels caught sight of them, but Jack's lips were soft and the muscles of her arms were firm under her touch. That was all she could think about in that moment.

---

A few evenings later, Leven gathered enough energy to take herself a little way from the camp. It was harder to bear her own suffering in the face of others who had also lost loved ones, or who were in terrible physical pain, and these days the quiet of the Wild Wood was a kind of balm to her. She considered this as she walked; how much things had changed. This place had become her home, finally, just as her reason for wanting to make one had been taken away from her.

The sun was slowly easing its way from the sky, and when she lowered herself to a fallen tree trunk to rest her legs, the light had the soft uncertain quality of evenings in the spring. During their search for T'rook they had seen two springs, but across the sea the light had never been this soft, or this green, she was sure of it. Her fingers closed around the hag stone in her pocket, and she brought it out to look at it. As soon as she'd been up and about again, she had gone back to the section of the Othanim road where the battle had taken place. Epona had insisted she take a small group of warriors with her, just in case, but Icaraine and her forces were long gone. For hours, Leven had walked back and forth over that strip of mud, churned up by horses, humans, Othanim and the Green Man himself, her eye pressed to the hole in the hag stone.

She had not found him.

'Fat lot of use you were,' she told the stone. She wondered what Queen Mab would have thought of what happened. No doubt she could have guessed the outcome easily enough, but in that case, why give her the stone at all? Perhaps it had all been a bit of pixen mischief, or perhaps she had genuinely hoped it would make a difference. 'Cillian, darling, come back to me.' She paused, holding a sob in her throat until it hurt. 'This whole island can sink for all I care, but come back to me, please.'

The wood kept its silence, and Cillian did not walk out of it, so she let herself cry for a while. When she came back to herself, the evening was colder than it had been, the shadows deeper. There was a whirr of wings and a familiar dark shape landed on the tree trunk next to her.

'Inkwort?' Leven rubbed a hand over her wet face. Her head was aching. 'I thought you'd left us, old friend.'

The little jackdaw looked at her sideways and took a couple of hops along the trunk towards her. Leven looked down at the stone still in her hand.

'If Ynis was here, I'd give this to her,' she said. 'I think she'd get a kick out of it – a real pixen artefact. But I don't even know where my sister is. My husband is dead, and my sister is lost to me. The land I thought to call home is being torn apart by creatures whose bones I wear in my skin. And I'm dying too, of course. Stars' arses, what a mess.'

Inkwort flew up and landed on her outstretched hand. For a second, Leven was both startled and touched. Although the jackdaw had always been comfortable riding on Cillian's shoulder, she had never shown the same level of trust with Leven. The bird's feet were cold against her fingers, and sharp. Then Inkwort darted forward, plucked the hag stone from Leven's hand and flew off into the trees. In a blink she was gone, and Leven was left with an empty hand.

'Sure, why not?' she said to no one in particular. 'I've lost everything else.'

# 70

*I'm writing this down and sending it to every office in Dosraiche – the rangers, the questers, the historians, the hive singers and the tree listeners. This concerns all of you. The Lich-Way is a last resort. Is that clear? I don't want to hear any more stories about apprentices walking the edge of the dead realm in order to 'look at the ghosts'. Even the most skilled among us can get lost there, and some have never returned.*

General note sent around Dosraiche by Elder Tarflin

Ynis waded through black water that came up to her chest. Over the surface of the bog, tiny green lights dashed back and forth, occasionally intercepted by larger glowing orbs. The sky overhead was full of dark grey clouds that promised rain but never gave it up; they boiled and teemed like eggs in a pan. The bog was freezing, and sometimes she would have to stop to break a thin layer of ice with fingers that were already numb. Despite her spirit form, she could see her own breath in front of her in little white puffs of vapour.

'As Leven would say,' she muttered, 'fuck this place.'

The Lich-Way, she suspected, did not care one way or another what she thought of it. She took in a deep breath, and yelled Cillian's name again, something she had been doing for the last hour or so; or at least, she thought so. The concept of time in this place felt incongruous. Almost laughable, in fact. So far, she hadn't seen a single other living soul.

*Living is not quite the right word*, she reminded herself.

Out of the gloom ahead, she spotted a mound of dry land. There was a broken-down fence on it, and slung over that, a bleached human skeleton, its jaws hanging wide and a tendril of ivy growing from its eye socket. Ynis picked her way towards it, eager to be out of the water for a little while. When she dragged herself onto the gritty grass, black bog water running from her boots, the skeleton twitched.

'That's it, get your muck all over my mound,' it said. 'Why not? Excuse me for breathing.'

'I doubt that you do,' said Ynis.

'That's rude, that is,' said the skeleton. 'I wouldn't just point out that you weren't breathing. In my day we knew better. I suppose I can't expect much of...' The skeleton paused. Even though it had no face, she got the distinct impression it was squinting at her. '... whatever you are. What are you? You're human shaped but your soul has feathers on it.'

Ynis didn't bother to answer. She sat, breathing hard and trying to get her energy back. There was very little to be seen around her: black water, small, stumpy waterlogged trees, the odd little mound like the one she was on. She could see no wandering Druin idiots. Yet Owain had been very clear. She was the only one who could find Cillian. And despite everything, she trusted her human father. She just wasn't sure how she was supposed to achieve it. The heart of the Lich-Way was vast, and more treacherous than any bog. She could almost feel it changing under her feet as she sat there.

'Look at all that muck,' the skeleton was saying. 'I'll never get that out of my grass now. And it'll stink, no doubt. What can I do about random griffin-girls dragging muck all over my mound, I ask you? Nothing, that's what.'

This was more than Ynis could deal with. She turned and looked at the skeleton.

'You are in the middle of a bog,' she said. 'This whole place stinks. You are surrounded by stink.'

'That's good old-fashioned bog stink,' said the skeleton. 'That there,' it managed to indicate the puddle of water Ynis had brought with her with a roll of its skull, 'is new-fangled fresh stink, and I can't be doing with it.'

'Please shut up.'

There was a whirring of wings, and a jackdaw appeared from out of the mist. It landed on the fence next to the skeleton, then hopped hurriedly away from the thing. A second or so later, Ynis realised she recognised it.

'Inkwort?' She stood up slowly, eager but not wanting to startle the jackdaw. 'Do you know where Cillian is, bird?'

The creature had something in her beak. When Ynis approached, she hopped onto the girl's arm, tiny bird claws sinking into her sleeve. She was carrying a stone with a hole in it. Ynis held out her free hand and Inkwort dropped it onto her palm.

'What is this?'

*I cannot show you where Cillian is.*

The voice dropped directly into Ynis's head without having to go through her ears. It sounded warm, and female, and faintly impatient.

'You... you can't?'

*Like all birds I can enter and leave the Lich-Way freely, but I have no knowledge of its secrets. You are the only one who can find him, Ynis, you know that. The stone is a gift from your sister,* she continued. *It will help.*

'What has happened to Leven?' asked Ynis. 'Why is Cillian in this place?' Part of her didn't want the answers, because she suspected they were bad.

The bird didn't give her any. She flew off again, quickly disappearing into the murk of the bog, her black wings a sooty smudge in the gloom.

'Fuck me,' said the skeleton, 'a talking bird.'

---

When she had left the mound with the skeleton far behind her, patches of mostly dry ground became more frequent, until eventually it was possible to walk along meandering paths that picked their way around deeper sections of bog. There were tall grasses here, razor sharp if you happened to run your fingers through them, with heavy, fat-bottomed insects moving lazily between the blades. She had been calling for Cillian periodically, although her voice grew quieter and quieter as her enthusiasm dwindled. It was around about this time, when she stood looking at her own reflection in the water, that she remembered the fate-lines.

'Cillian would have his own fate-tie connected to me, I'm sure of it,' she said aloud. 'But how am I to know which one he is?'

Even so, as she spoke, she reached for them in her mind, and in the surface of the water she saw the familiar red strands appear over her head. There were more now than there had been the first time she'd seen them, so many more. And when she'd tried to use them to find T'rook, they had instead led her to Leven.

But it was the thing that she was uniquely talented at, she knew that. Perhaps that was what Frost and Brocken had meant. Hesitantly, she reached one hand up towards the red strands of fate, and let her fingers drift through them. In this place, in the Lich-Way, they had a solidity to them, but unlike the tall grasses, they were soft and delicate, causing the barest tickle against her skin.

Cillian. A Druin man with green eyes and the curling horns of a ram. He was patient and sometimes moody, and he loved her human sister a great deal, a fact she had become very aware of over the two years they had spent together. She called his face to mind, the expression of concentration he wore when he had been teaching her how to write, and to her surprise she felt a wave of affection for him. Although initially when they met on the border of Yelvynia he had been wary, Cillian had quickly accepted Ynis without judgement; perhaps of all humans, she realised, he was uniquely able to understand someone with a deep connection to something that very definitely wasn't human.

One of the fate-lines hummed under her fingers, and she singled it out from the others. Strong and red and as thick as a blackberry branch, this line led off to what she supposed was the east, although like time, directions were malleable in this place. It was her best lead.

Setting off across the marsh, Ynis thought about T'rook. Would she still be looking for her? Would she have found the place where Lom had taken her? The scent of her blood could have led T'rook there, and if she found... Ynis frowned. She did not particularly want to think about that. She hoped that T'rook would have the sense not to blame Lom for what had happened. She hated to think of that old man with his guts torn open.

Time passed. The sky grew darker, and then light again, as though something enormous had passed behind the clouds overhead. Once or twice, she thought she saw large shapes in the distance, shrouded in fog. They were moving, but they looked much too large to be normal beasts. She decided to keep out of their way.

Eventually she spotted another figure on a patch of dry ground. Even from a distance she could see that it had some kind of curling horn. Excited, she hurried along, picking her way through the reeds and marsh trees, but as she drew closer, she saw that the figure was much too tall to be Cillian, and he had only a single horn. He wore ragged chain mail, and he was old, his gaunt face scoured with lines, although his blue eyes were bright. He wore a huge sword slung over his back, and he sat on a tree stump with what appeared to be a wolf lying across his feet. As she approached, the wolf lifted his head, yellow eyes narrowing with interest.

'A traveller,' said the old Druin. There were shapes carved into his horn, and he wore a thin bronze circlet across his forehead. 'What are you doing out here, child?'

'I am not yenlin,' Ynis replied automatically.

The man raised his eyebrows. 'Griffin speech,' he said. 'I've not heard that in many a year.'

'You know what it means? You're the first human I've met who does.'

The man smiled. 'In my day, we spoke often to the griffins. We went to them for their wisdom, and they came to us for our crafts. In my kingdom, we wore their image on our shields and paid them the highest honours.'

Ynis stopped a few feet away, wary of the wolf, who was still watching her. From the way the man spoke, she suspected that when he said 'my kingdom', he meant that it had been a place he ruled over rather than one he belonged to.

'I didn't know Brittletain had Druin kings.'

He chuckled. 'Who better to rule the land than those who were wedded to it, my young friend, who we have established is no longer yenlin.' His smile faded. 'I had a magical sword, one that sang and advised me, and shone like the sun. I had knights that followed me, and I served the green lord. I lost the sword though, and I lost my lord, too.'

'The green lord? Do you mean the Green Man?'

'Some called him that, aye. I look for him still, in this cold, dead land.' He shifted on the stump, bony fingers resting on bony knees. 'What is it, girl? You have a look about you that I would call vexed.'

'I am looking for him too,' she said. 'The Green Man, I mean. I am following a fate-tie...' She pointed above her head, too late remembering that only witch-seers could see them, but the old man simply nodded, his blue eyes brightening.

'How extraordinary.' He stood up, then bowed stiffly. The wolf slunk around the other side of the stump, looking put out. 'My lady. I humbly ask that you do me the honour of letting me accompany you on your quest. I am Arthwr, and I offer you my sword.'

# 71

*The Envoy Order has existed as long as the Imperium has. It began with a single woman, Aralia Shay, who stood at the right hand of our first emperor. Very quickly she realised that as the Imperium took more and more territory outside of Stratum, they would need some way to deal with and process all of the resources and information streaming into the city. She spent her time sorting through reports and stacks of acquired scrolls and books to better understand the newly Blessed countries. Soon she began travelling to these places herself, often in disguise so that people would speak freely in front of her, not realising they gave their secrets to the second most powerful person in the Imperium. Eventually she began to train others in this art.*

Extract from *Imperium: The History and the Alchemy*, by Edzio Hawk

Epona crouched on the bough of the tree, holding herself very still. Next to her, the Imperial Envoy sat unmoving, his eye pressed to one of the spyglasses they had salvaged from Londus. He looked entirely comfortable in the lofty spot, and had made short work of climbing the tree itself. For the first time she wondered about the work he'd done as a spy for the empress. She had the distinct feeling that diplomacy was the very least of it.

'It looks as though they have indeed stopped for the day,' he said, before passing her the spyglass. 'They've lit campfires.'

Through the glass she saw the road again, the now familiar strip of mud and dirt and stones, although the wood around it had changed over the last few weeks; the land was becoming steeper, more prone to hills, and the Wild Wood was darker and wilder. The Othanim road had grown curves, slinking around the high places but still heading ever north. Epona thought that they had to be in western Galabroc. Climbing another tree, close to the rebel camp, she had looked to the west and seen a faint glitter on the horizon – the Broken Sea, the cold and changeable stretch of water said to be haunted by all manner of spirits. Icaraine loomed into view through the spyglass, and Epona automatically sat up straighter, her heart beating a little faster.

*Soon, you vast bitch*, she thought. *Soon you'll pay for what you did to my family.*

'Is it me or does she look less pleased with herself than she did?'

Next to her, Kaeto smiled wryly. 'In her last missive, Belise reports that there was a small uprising against her in the rank and file. Malakim's habit of occasionally eating them hasn't fostered the kind of loyalty that Icaraine was hoping for, somehow.'

'How is she giving you reports, your friend? You've not been in the camp since the battle.'

'She leaves coded notes as they travel. It's risky, but the Othanim are all about moving forward. No one is checking what they leave behind.'

'Ha.' Epona raised the glass again and watched as the creature the Othanim called 'prince' crept down the steps of his carriage. He was larger than when they had attacked the caravan, and he had more limbs. Thin white arms burst from the centre of his chest; they seemed to move independently, like lengths of seaweed caught in an unseen current. 'I never get used to the sight of that thing. Will it ever stop growing, do you think?'

'Hard to say.' Kaeto looked troubled, as he often did when they spoke of the Othanim. There was something there that made Epona think it was more than simple worry about their fate. He had a secret, which wasn't that surprising – Envoys were all about secrets – but this was something personal. 'It's possible, I suppose, that he could keep growing forever, given an endless supply of Titan bones. We'll have to hope we're ready before he rivals the mountains the griffins live on.'

'Leven claims she is ready to attack at any time, although I'm not so sure I believe her. But then, her condition, according to you, is only going to get worse...'

Kaeto kept quiet, perhaps knowing it would be painful to confirm it.

'And we still don't have as many warriors as I would like,' she continued. 'I had hoped that Queen Verla would send more, but to be honest with you it's an unexpected boon that she even replied to our message. In the past, Kornwullis would have cheerfully sent back the messenger's head as a reply. And Dwffd have sent who they can spare, I suppose.' She sighed. She couldn't entirely blame these western queens for deciding to protect their own borders – the threat was heading north, after all, and as long as that was happening, they were safe. Their trust in her was a fragile thing. 'Mersia has sent no one, of course, for... reasons previously discussed.'

Kaeto grunted. 'I have to say, Princess Epona, that your politics are much more interesting than I was led to believe.' She had explained to him what had happened in Mersia at length over a bottle of mead.

'Wehha have been the big surprise,' she continued, 'sending the biggest group of warriors of the lot. From what they've said, they've taken it as a grave dishonour that the Druidahnon was murdered on their soil. They intend to make that right.'

'You need every blade you can get, your highness.'

'Ah. Your girl is down there now.'

The Othanim called Belise had also emerged from the carriage and appeared to be leading Malakim by the arm to the edge of the wood. Epona could see her talking animatedly, pointing to things in the trees or nodding to other Othanim warriors, who seemed to keep their distance.

'She looks to be as thick as thieves with the prince.' She let the statement hang in the air for the moment. 'I'd love to know why, Kaeto, your two closest allies are Titans. Can you truly trust them?'

'I can,' he said shortly. 'Ironically, your highness, you will just have to trust me as to why.'

Epona lowered the spyglass, deciding that once and for all she would get the truth from the Envoy, when a low whistle floated up from the base of the tree. She peered down through the branches to see Jack looking back up at her, her hazel eyes the brightest thing in the wood. Leaving Kaeto where he was, Epona climbed back down until she stood opposite the woman. Since the defeat of the Green Man, she was all the more lauded by the rest of the rebels, a position she seemed to find mildly uncomfortable. There was a small cut still healing on her forehead – Epona remained amazed that she had survived the conflict at all. Amazed, and pleased.

'Epona,' she said. 'There's a... guest back at the camp.'

'Really? Who?' She searched the other woman's face. 'You look worried. What is it? Another queen?'

'Uh.' There was a humming sound from the sword slung across Jack's back. 'I think you should come and see for yourself.'

---

When they got back, the camp was in disarray. Epona's first impression was that everyone was standing around shouting. She shoved her way through the crowd, noting as she did the solid presence of the Dwffd guard and the wild, strange men and women of Wehha. In the centre, standing with her arms partly raised, was her sister Togi. She had three of the Atchorn Druin with her, and they all looked as though they'd seen hard times. Togi's hair, which she'd always worn short, had grown long enough to touch the back of her neck, and her brawny arms were slashed with new scars. Yelm, Epona noticed, was at the front of the group shouting at the newcomers, her eyes wide and her lips thin with fury.

'Sister!' shouted Togi when she spotted Epona. 'Tell your people to stand down. We're here as friends. Allies!'

Epona drew her sword, and there was an answering rasp of metal against leather as a number of the other rebels drew their own. Togi scowled.

'The last time I saw you, sister,' said Epona, 'you were dragging the bones of the Druidahnon through the streets of Londus.' As she spoke the words, she felt the fury of the crowd infect her. 'The last of the bear Titans, Togi. Reduced to a pile of remains in your cart!'

There was a howl of anger from the rebel Druin, and the ones next to Togi drew closer to her as if for protection.

'And since then I have witnessed our mother and sister murdered by the Othanim queen, a queen you have served. You come here now, calling yourself a friend?'

'I was wrong,' said Togi, who lowered her hands, then shrugged. 'That is all I can say. I made a mistake. The Atchorn too. Ceni convinced me that it was us against you, that Mother would never give us anything but the scraps from her table, while you were always the favourite. You would get it all handed to you on a plate – Londus, the richest city in Brittletain – and if we wanted anything of our own, we would have to fight for it.'

'Yes, that makes me feel so much better about what you did,' said Epona. 'You felt that it was *unfair*. I suppose that makes it all okay then, right? I should have all of you skewered and leave your corpses for the wolves to pick at.'

'Say the word,' said Leven, stepping up next to her. The Herald had her sword at the ready.

'I have something,' Togi said quickly. 'We have something. And I think you can use it against the Othanim. Isn't that enough to spare my life?'

The crowd was still calling for her sister's blood. Epona glanced at the faces of the other rebels, lingering the longest on the few remaining Druin in the group. They were furious, and rightly so. Epona thought of her journey down from Galabroc in the back of Ceni's cart, the people of Brittletain throwing rotten fruit and vegetables at her; but she also thought of Kaeto telling her they needed every blade they could get, and information, he had told her once before, was the sharpest blade of all. Togi had always been easily led. And perhaps she had seen enough of her family's blood for one lifetime.

'Tie her up,' she said to Leven. 'Let's hear what she has to say for herself.'

## 72

At first, Ynis wasn't at all sure she wanted the king with her in the Lich-Way. Even after two years of searching for T'rook with Leven and Cillian, she was still uncertain about the company of humans – they were loud, they had little sense of the space they took up in the world, and they smelled wrong. Yet as the way became darker and stranger, she found that she was sometimes glad to hear his steady footsteps alongside her own, or to see his wolves scouting off in front of them. Of the wolves there was an indeterminate number, and they seemed to come and go as they pleased, keeping up a constant escort.

Time passed – or didn't, it was hard to tell – and the red fate-line hung in the sky over them like a thin, bloody cut in the clouds.

Eventually the marshy area ended. They were in a dry, arid place, climbing hills gone dusty for a lack of grass, passing through stone circles. They paused in one of these to rest. Arthwr sat with his sword on the grass next to him and began to sing; a low, mournful tune that seemed very at home under that grey sky. At first Ynis wanted to tell him to stop. It seemed dangerous to advertise their presence in this way. Yet when the wolves began to howl along with him, creating an eerie harmony that caused all the hairs on the back of her neck to rise up, the words died unsaid on her tongue.

*'Oh where are you going?*
*I hear the bones on the coast singing,*
*All the live long day,*
*I hear the bones on the coast singing, mother,*
*And I can no longer stay.*

*'Oh, where are you going, child, your eyes as rare as jewels?*
*I hear the Green Man laughing,*
*As the dawn gives way to the morn,*
*I hear the Green Man laughing, mother,*
*And so my soul must be torn.*

*'Oh where are you going, child, your face so bare and bloody?*
*I hear the griffins in the north calling,*
*All day and into the night,*
*I hear the griffins in the north calling, mother,*
*And none can deny their might.'*

When he finished, Ynis found herself blinking, the sense of having been somewhere else for a very long time washing through her. When she stood up, her arms and legs were numb and stiff, a wave of pins and needles prickling at her hands and feet.

'How long have we been here?'

The king looked at her with hooded eyes, as though he had only just woken up himself.

'Hmm?'

'It feels... like we've been here forever.' Panic seized her throat. There truly was no way to know how long she'd been travelling in this dismal place, or how much time had passed in the world beyond the Lich-Way. She imagined Leven and T'rook growing old and dying, or even worse, the Othanim sweeping through Brittletain unopposed, both of them falling in a pointless battle that Ynis was not there to help them win. 'Come on. Come on, get up! We have to keep moving.'

Arthwr rose slowly, his patchy chainmail even more rusted than it had been before he had started his song. He turned his head to follow the fate-line, then pointed with one long finger off to the east.

'Could that be what we seek, young warrior?'

Ynis looked where he was pointing. The landscape was still its strange, dreamy self, moving in and out of a deep fog that behaved like a living thing, but there was something else out there. From this distance, it looked to be little more than a green shape, something that moved and flickered on the horizon. It was the most colour she'd seen since she'd entered the Lich-Way, and it was in the path of the fate-line.

'I think it could be,' she said. When she ran down the hill, the wolves followed her, yipping, and the king came along after.

---

The closer they got, the harder the green shape was to define. It vanished behind hills, was lost in fog, or occasionally just wasn't there at all, leading Ynis to walk a little faster, as though she could catch it out somehow.

'It taunts us,' said the king in a musing tone. 'Or the Lich-Way does. I cannot tell.' In the end, they were almost upon it before the thing revealed itself. They crested another dusty hill, larger than the rest, and as they looked out across the shifting lands it spread before them: an enormous tree, an oak, larger than any Ynis had ever seen, and every part of it green – from the roots that delved into the earth to the branches that reached for the sky, every inch was as green as its leaves. Cillian's fate-line led to the centre of its trunk.

Ynis stopped. She wasn't sure what she had expected to find, but it wasn't this.

'How am I supposed to bring him out of the Lich-Way if he's a tree?'

The king's wolves were already pouring down the hill, their bodies as grey and as fleet as knives.

'Let us go and look at it,' said the king. 'Perhaps the answer will present itself.'

Up close, it was no clearer. They stood in the shadow of the great tree, their feet amongst its roots. This close, it was the whole world. Ynis could see endless patterns in the whorls of bark, and there were things living in it too: pale luminous mushrooms, scurrying beetles of black and yellow, tiny birds nested in hollows. There was even an adder moving sinuously along the highways of bark.

'Truly, a mighty tree,' said the king.

'It's more than that,' said Ynis. 'Can't you feel it? This thing has its roots in other worlds.' She shivered. The words felt as though they had come from somewhere outside of her.

'All trees do,' said the king. When she glanced up at him, he smiled, blue eyes twinkling. She had forgotten for a moment that he was a Druin. 'All trees are gateways, that is what we used to say. But perhaps this tree more than any other.'

Ynis knelt in the dirt by the huge, twisted roots and rested her hand on one. In an instant, she received a flood of images: a grizzled old man, full of ambition and spite, hanging himself on the branches as rain lashed his naked body; a desperate young woman with shining golden hair sitting on the roots with a human child, a lethal dagger concealed in her sleeves; a man and a woman hiding within one of the tree's enormous hollows while the world outside fell to war and ruin; a serpent in the branches, coils rasping against the bark. Gasping, Ynis pulled her hand away.

'You have the sight,' the king said gravely.

'For all the good it does me.' Ynis shook her head. 'This tree has thousands of stories to tell, but will any of them tell me where Cillian is? And I don't have the time to listen.'

'My sword would have known,' said the king. 'Very knowledgeable, that sword.'

'You have your sword,' snapped Ynis.

'Ah, this?' He reached behind to tap one finger against the pommel of the huge blade he carried on his back. 'A lesser thing, useful only to defend oneself against the creatures that skulk through this dark land. My sword would sing, and give its opinion – too frequently, if truth be told – but it belonged to the lake, and to the knights who were to come after me.'

'Right.' Ynis brushed herself down. 'Let's walk around the thing. There could be something we're not seeing.'

It took them some time to circumvent the tree, climbing over the thickest parts of the roots and sliding over fallen leaves. Ynis looked back to the hill they had clambered down at one point and saw a shape watching them from between the standing stones. It was slender and not quite human, two red points of light burning where its eyes should have been. As she watched, it faded away like a shadow at midday. *We have to figure this out quickly*, she thought. *We've already been here longer than is safe.*

But there was nothing, only tree. If Ynis brushed her bare skin against its twisted roots she would get flashes of other places and times, but she saw Cillian in none of them, and all the while she was aware that beyond the Lich-Way life was moving on without her. She stopped and sat on one of the roots, and a wolf came and rested its huge head on her knee. Absently she stroked its nose.

'I do not know what to do,' she said. The wolf began to sniff at her sleeve. 'All this way I have travelled. All the things I've done...' She thought of Lom's cramped cabin, the sharp pain as she tore his stitches from her belly. 'Frost and Brocken had so much faith in me. But I have only ever failed. Not quite a griffin, not quite a witch-seer. Not good enough to be either.'

'Young warrior, I do not believe that for a moment,' said the king. 'I believe myself a fine judge of character – how else would

I select the knights that sit at my table? And I see great strength and wit in you. Beyond your years.'

Ynis felt a prickle of annoyance. Humans were so obsessed with words, and they meant nothing in the face of *action*. She could talk of flying better than anyone, but what use was that without wings? Beyond the king, she could see another of the shadow shapes, closer this time, and drawing nearer as they spoke. *Time is running out.*

'Do you have a bit of something in your pocket? Dried meat? A salt cube? She's a terror for treats, I'm afraid.'

Ynis glanced down to see that the wolf had its nose in the pocket of her jacket, snuffling noisily. Gently, she pushed the animal's head away.

'Just this,' she said, bringing out the stone with the hole that Inkwort had given her. 'It is from my sister. My human sister.'

'Ah!' The king came forward and touched his finger to the stone. The moment that he did, the carved shapes on his horn glowed with a greenish-blue light. 'A powerful gift indeed! Why didn't you mention you had a hag stone? And one from Queen Mab, no less.'

'A what?'

'Look through the hole, my young warrior. Much may be revealed!'

Ynis turned the stone over in her hand. Now that she looked at it more closely, she saw that an aura clung to it, like an after-image on the eye after looking at the sun too long. She held it up to her eye.

Through the stone, the green tree was transformed. Rather than whorls and swirls of bark, the trunk and the roots were made up of human bodies; green figures all pressed together, their eyes closed and their faces at peace, each of them different to the next. This great tide of human bodies reached up into the branches, spreading out beneath the sky. There had to be thousands of them, Ynis thought.

'The tree is made of people,' she said, ignoring the dizzy feeling this phrase gave her. 'Maybe they are all the people that have ever been the Green Man. So Cillian has to be one of them. Cillian! Cillian, are you there?'

None of the bodies so much as twitched.

How to find him? It could take forever, looking through the tiny hole at each sleeping face.

'Seek him out,' said the king. 'I will hold them off for as long as I am able.'

Ynis turned to see what he was talking about. A horde of shadowy creatures were approaching, long limbs stretched out towards them, and as they grew closer they seemed to reveal more details: a thorned back, a pair of long, pointed ears, eyes like embers in the fire.

'What are they?'

'Souls who lingered here too long,' said Arthwr. 'Their own lives bled away into the bog and now they're jealous of anyone who still smells of the world beyond the Lich-Way. They'll eat you if they can, but I will not let them.' He drew the huge sword from his back, and the wolves gathered around him, a fearsome honour guard. 'Look through the hole, my young knight, and find our lord!'

With difficulty, Ynis turned away from the shadows and pressed her eye to the stone. Once again, the tree became a thing of green flesh, and she scanned from face to face as quickly as she dared, her heart thundering in her chest. From behind her, she heard the old king grunting as he raised his sword, the yips and growls of the wolves, and a strange, agitated hiss that she assumed was the sound the shadows made as the king cut them down.

'Where are you?'

When she had looked at what she hoped was a good section of the tree, she clambered over the roots to see more, eyes skipping from face to face to face. Some of them were so strange or so beautiful she longed to linger on them, but there was no time, no time.

'Be gone, barghest!'

She glanced behind her again to see the king's blade slicing through a shadow, tattering it into pieces before it bled away into the ground. Instantly, it was replaced by two more.

'Fionovar's bloody beak, where are you, Cillian?'

She spotted him finally near the top of the trunk, where the bulk of the tree began to split off into branches. The sight of his face, framed by his horns, stopped her in her tracks, and she gave a little jump.

'Found him!' When she turned to tell the king, she came face to face with a shadow, its face full of teeth, but then Arthwr's blade split it in two.

'Get him then,' he said. There was something new about the king in battle, a vitality and a wildness in his eyes that had not been there before. He gave her a grin, and in that moment, she thought she could see why other humans would have followed him. Pledged their lives to him, even.

'How?' She pointed up into the branches. 'I could climb it, but it would take forever, and the shadows will get you long before I reach the top.'

The king laughed. 'Why, you will fly up there, ser knight! With your wings.'

Ynis blinked. She remembered how the skeleton had told her she had feathers on her soul. She remembered that she was in her spirit form, and here, she was powerful. She turned to look at her shoulder and was not all that surprised to see the curve of a wing beyond it – and not the bright glass shape of her Herald wing either, but the feathered beauty of a griffin's wing. Her feathers were black, and brown, and white, like those of her family. Some strong emotion rose in her throat. Suddenly, it was difficult to see.

'Go!' cried the king. 'Quickly now, ser knight. Even my arms must tire eventually.'

Ynis wiped a hand across her eyes, and then in a single breath she was in the air, her wings lifting her effortlessly – away from the ground that had clung to her all her life. In the joy of it she almost forgot what she was flying for until she caught a glimpse of Cillian's sleeping face again, on a level with her own. Hanging in front of him, she reached out and grasped his shoulder, shaking it.

'Cillian? Cillian, you have to wake up!'

His eyes snapped open, as though he'd been waiting for her to appear.

'Ynis?'

# 73

*Their heavy bones have always been what linked the disparate Titan races to one another, but there are other things too: their small, extraordinary magics. They live for hundreds, perhaps thousands of years, for example. The griffins can produce a saliva that melts down wood to mulch and reforms it, making a substance harder than steel. The bears are creatures of regrowth, flowers sprouting where their blood falls. The horns of the unicorns, it is said, can heal any injury, although getting close to those hotblooded creatures risks death. The giants, it's said, could sing the hills into new shapes, and the god-boar were the great travellers, able to blink from one place to another. The kraken, surely, had their own strange magics, but living beneath the waves as they did, we never witnessed it.*

Extract from the notes of Bede the Liar,<br>famed adventurer and alchemist

'Where is my sister, human?'

The cry was loud and piercing enough that the entire camp seemed to flinch. Leven stood up slowly, the spear she had been sharpening held loosely in one fist. T'rook was in the sky above them, her wings dark against the bright morning sky, and she looked furious. Although, Leven thought to herself, she had hardly seen T'rook anything but. Leven waved to the griffin even as she saw other rebels drawing back.

'She's not here,' she called up, cupping one hand around her mouth. 'Will you come down? I haven't the energy to summon my own wings.'

T'rook hung above them for a little longer, clearly uncertain about getting so close to such a large group of humans. Leven caught Epona's eye and the princess nodded. She began waving people away, clearing a space for the griffin to land. Kaeto, she noticed, was watching too, although he was too sensible to come close. When there was a good patch of clear ground available, T'rook landed lightly, tossing her head.

'I thought she was with you,' Leven said. 'What happened?'

'Ynis has gone missing from a patrol,' said T'rook. 'I was not with her. I should have been with her.' She tossed her head again, and Leven was put in mind of a horse in distress. The griffin's talons tore at the grass, leaving deep runnels in the dirt. 'The patrol say that she left while they were resting.'

Leven put the spear down. 'When was this?'

'Days ago. I tracked her scent into the wood, and I found... blood there.'

'Blood.' Leven closed her eyes, a rushing feeling moving through her. She'd failed her little sister again. *Again.* She should never have let her run off, she should have watched her like a hawk, kept her safe... An odd sound made her open her eyes. T'rook had lowered her head and was making a very soft keening noise.

*Ynis isn't the only sister I should be caring for.*

Uncertain whether the movement would earn her a disembowelment, Leven stepped forward cautiously and put her hand on the downy spot between T'rook's ear tufts. After a moment, she put her arms around the griffin's neck. T'rook leaned her head against her.

'We'll find her,' she said.

'How? I tracked her as far as I could. We cannot see the fate-lines. The Othanim... they could have taken her, as I was taken.'

'We'll think of something.' Leven thought of Cillian. He might have had some idea – while the Green Man inhabited him, he had known where everyone was in the Wild Wood. T'rook drew back from her embrace and shook herself all over, puffing up her feathers and her fur.

'Have you eaten? When did you last eat?'

'I will not eat meat that has been burned with your fires,' T'rook said, some of the familiar spark returning to her voice. 'It must be fresh.'

'That's fine. I'm sure we'll find something.' Around them, the rebels had drawn closer again, apparently having decided that the griffin wasn't about to eat them. She saw wonder on every face, even reverence. Epona wore a more speculative expression. Leven knew that they had tried to enlist the help of the griffins, and failed. 'We are going to attack the Othanim soon, T'rook. The ones who brought this war to your home.'

'I know them.' T'rook snapped her beak. 'I have killed many dozens already. They are weak, not fit to share our skies.'

'Will you stay with us for the battle?' asked Leven. 'We could really use the skill of a warrior such as yourself.' T'rook's golden eyes flashed. Leven didn't know if the flattery had pleased the griffin or irritated her. 'The Othanim leader is there. I intend to kill her myself, if I can.'

'And then we look for Ynis?'

'You have my word.'

The griffin dipped her head, once.

'Yes. I will feast on Othanim guts with you. Together.'

'I would be honoured, T'rook.' Leven looked around at the rebels. 'We have a guest! A hungry one! Let's get her something good and bloody to eat.'

Kaeto found Felldir, as he often did, sitting in the trees a little distance from the human camp. The Titan was all too aware that his presence unsettled the humans, and so he did his best to keep out of sight. It was an example of his thoughtfulness that stabbed at Kaeto's heart: Felldir was a good man, and it was entirely possible – and understandable – that the rebels would never trust him. And that, he supposed, was at the very heart of what they needed to discuss. Kaeto went to the fallen tree where Felldir was resting. Just beyond it a natural spring bubbled, clear water twinkling through the undergrowth like a hidden hoard of diamonds.

'If you stayed in the camp more, they might learn to like you.'

Felldir looked up and smiled as Kaeto seated himself on the trunk next to him.

'Like me? Light-bones, they have seen too many of their own killed to ever feel comfortable looking at this face.'

'Tolerate, then. They could learn to tolerate you.' Kaeto sighed.

'What troubles you?'

'Too many things to count. But right at this moment? I wonder about the future of your people, my love.'

'Do they have one, you mean?'

From behind them somewhere came the chatter of voices. The recent arrival of the griffin to their camp had caused a great deal of excitement.

'In her latest report, Belise notes that a growing number of the Othanim seem to be questioning Icaraine's rule. Malakim's appetites are giving them pause for thought, it seems. She says that when it's dark, and they think no one is listening, they talk about what they fear most. Who is to be eaten by their queen's mutant child. Where will it stop, they ask. How big will Malakim grow, and how many bones will keep him satiated?'

'You hope, perhaps, that the Othanim will throw her down by themselves? Take the matter out of our hands?'

Kaeto shrugged. 'These are the sorts of solutions I am used to, in the Imperium. Seek out those who have the most to gain from your treachery, and supply them with the tools to do your dirty work.'

'It would not work,' said Felldir sadly. 'There is no queen to replace Icaraine. Without another queen to follow, they will never commit fully to walking away from her.'

'That is what I feared.' Kaeto slipped a coin from his pocket and made it dance across his fingers, a trick he used to perform for Belise's amusement. He found it helped him to think. 'And these new queens of yours. They only come every few hundred years or so?'

'Our cycle has been disrupted. Who is to say when we might see another?'

'Alright. I have another question for you. Let us suppose that Herald Eleven's plan to kill Icaraine is successful. She drives the point of her spear through the old monster's eye and we defeat the Othanim. Let us suppose this happens early on in the fight, and there are a significant number of your people alive. What then?'

'How do you mean?'

'My love, *do we let them live*?'

Felldir did not answer. He went on looking at the tumble of clear water.

'That supposes that we can kill them, of course, with the limited resources we have to hand. If they are taken prisoner, it's likely the Britons will want them dead. But can they be saved, Felldir? Is it possible that without Icaraine, they will lose their lust for griffin blood?' He remembered the singing towers in the Black City; a glimpse of a civilisation that had once cared more for music than war. 'Despite everything, it feels like losing another Titan race would be a terrible thing to bear.'

'You should be more concerned with our survival,' said Felldir. He placed his hand over Kaeto's restlessly moving fingers, stilling the coin, and then kissed him firmly on the lips. 'But I thank you for thinking of it, all the same.'

'Hmm.' Kaeto sat for a moment, gathering his thoughts. It was easy to lose them when Felldir kissed him that way. 'If there were survivors, could you lead them? Would you even want to?'

Felldir looked at him for a long moment. 'I honestly don't know, light-bones. Ask me on another day, when this battle is behind us. If we're still alive.'

## 74

Leaving the tree was like pulling himself out of a hot spring on a cold day, and for a moment Cillian's body seemed to resist by itself, clinging to the trunk like a limpet. But then he looked into Ynis's face, her forehead creased with an uncharacteristic expression of concern, and with her help he climbed down, past various sleeping bodies – all of them green. *These are all the others*, he thought. *All those who took on the mantle of the Green Man and were lost to it. Just like me. At least I am not alone in my failure.* The thought was little comfort.

At the bottom of the great tree, a strange figure was waiting for them. Tall and ancient, with a single horn, the armoured Druin sketched a deep bow. Wolves pressed themselves to his legs.

'I've seen you before, haven't I?' said Cillian. 'We've met, somewhere...'

'Of course we have, my lord,' said the one-horned man. He smiled sadly. 'Finally, after all these centuries, I look upon your face again. And now I can rest.'

And with that, he faded from view. Ynis pulled her hands back through her hair and shook her head.

'I am sick of this place,' she said. 'I would like to leave. You know the way, yes? Out of the Lich-Way?'

Cillian walked a little way from the tree. Around them, the landscape shifted and churned.

'Only there were shadow creatures here just now,' continued Ynis. 'And I would like to go before they return.'

'I can't go back, Ynis.' He sat down on the ground, crossing his legs under him. 'I failed them all. When it came down to it, I couldn't control the Green Man, and he consumed me. And because of that...' He closed his eyes against the memory of crushing living, breathing people beneath his feet, of tearing them apart with his hands. 'So many people died. If I go back, I risk unleashing that on them again.'

'But I came here to find you.' Something dark passed over Ynis's face, a look of desperation he didn't quite understand. 'I did things I can't take back.'

'The Green Man isn't what I thought he was. I think the Druidahnon tried to explain it to me, but I didn't take it in. There's no thought in there really, only a mask that sounds like a human being. He's not a spirit in the way that the Dunohi are spirits. He's a force. An instinct. Like salmon going upriver to spawn and die, or seedlings growing after a forest fire, or a mother rabbit eating her young when there's not enough food for them all. We cannot hope to bend that to our will. As he rampaged, he was burning through the very life of the wood. I never imagined he would do that, but that just shows how much I misunderstood.'

'There's more to life than death,' said Ynis. She came and sat opposite him, also crossing her legs. 'There are all the parts in between. Those are the precious things.' She met his gaze furiously, as though daring him to mock her. 'There are all the connections we make.'

Ynis pointed to a space above her head, and Cillian realised he could see hundreds of red threads hanging there – some came from Ynis, and some from him, and there was a red thread that ran between them, too.

'Fate-ties?'

The girl nodded. He noticed how different she looked here. Her features were sharper, somehow clearer than he'd ever seen them, and the wings on her back – like the Othanim, he thought, but not – looked as though they belonged with her as much as her arms or legs or head.

'You're not the Green Man, Cillian. You're better than him. Do you not see it?' She sighed. 'Humans are so obstinate.'

Despite himself, Cillian grinned. '*You* are calling *me* obstinate?'

Ynis ignored this. 'You've forged new connections – to my sister, to me, even to T'rook. These will anchor you in place. And with the Green Man's power, you've grown a deeper connection to the Wild Wood. It's all open to you now. Can't you feel it?'

'How do you know all this?'

'I am a witch-seer,' she said, and then she grinned, too. He thought it might be the first true smile he had ever seen on the girl. 'And I am a griffin. We know these things. The Green Man used and dominated the Wild Wood. Used it up and burned through its life force. You, though. *You* will speak to it. You will ask for its help. And it will help you. Don't you see?'

Cillian looked down at his hands. He was no longer green, unlike the people in the tree, but he could feel the greenness there just under his skin. What if Ynis was right? Could it be that hosting the Green Man had changed him? And there was what Inkwort had shown him to consider. He wasn't simply any mortal who had been chosen to carry the spirit of the deepest forest.

'I don't know, Ynis,' he said. 'The risk is too great. You should leave me here and go. It's not safe to stay in the Lich-Way for long, certainly not this deep in its heart. Not for mortals at least, and I couldn't forgive myself if anything happened to you. Not to mention that Leven would kill me. Somehow.'

She brushed this aside. 'They're out there without us, Cillian. Leven is out there without either of us to look after her. In the middle of a war with Titans. My people... that is, the griffins, they also need the power of the Green Man, as much as they don't want to admit it. You have to go back.' Ynis lifted her hand into the air, brushing her fingers over the fate-lines that swayed above them. 'There's something else, too. A new fate-line? So new it's barely there, and it connects the three of us together...'

Knowledge washed through him like a cold spring tide. How could he have forgotten? But of course, since joining with the Green Man his mind had only been partially his own. Much of the time he had felt like an observer of his own life. Leven did not need him, she never had, but she deserved to know what had happened between them – what had been created. If she had not guessed already.

Cillian stood up and took a final look at the tree. He was already different to them, he told himself. He'd escaped the tree when none of the others had; not because of his own innate strength, but because of the strength of someone who cared about him. Perhaps there was a chance he could truly use the Green Man's power in a way that didn't destroy everything he knew.

'It's time for us to leave the Lich-Way,' he said.

# 75

*I regret to inform her Luminance that the Imperial Bone Crafter Gynid Tyleigh passed away at her compound two nights ago. It seems she finally succumbed to the poison she ingested in Houraki, although it should be noted that in recent weeks she had taken to drinking heavily and it appeared that she rarely retired to her bed chamber. During this time I asked her if something beyond the poison was bothering her, and I received the usual invective response, but when I made to leave she asked me if I'd ever done anything unforgivable. When I told Tyleigh that nothing immediately came to mind, she snorted and told me I was, I quote: 'a lucky turd floating down the sewer that is the Imperium.' Unpleasant language, to be sure, but I thought her Luminance would be interested to hear of this apparently treasonous attitude.*

Extract of correspondence from the senior healer<br>assigned to Gynid Tyleigh during the new Herald project

'We can't wait here forever,' whispered Epona. 'They will discover us sooner or later.'

She was crouched on the edge of the eastern side of the Othanim road. Behind her were all their gathered forces: the remaining rebels from Londus, the warriors from Kornwullis,

Dwffd and Wehha, the Atchorn, her sister Togi, the Envoy and his pet Othanim, and of all things, a young griffin with eyes like gold coins. Leven was a few feet away, wearing the best armour they had and holding the finest spear they could find. She had painted her eyes black as the Dwffd did, and there was an expression on her face that Epona couldn't recall seeing before: it was as though everything else had fallen away for Leven, and there was only the approaching battle. Epona wondered if that was how she had looked when she slaughtered the Unblessed for the Imperium.

'The Atchorn said they have summoned... it,' said Jack. She was crouched next to Epona, a thin scar the only sign of the head wound from their last battle. 'But its nature is unpredictable.'

'Why doesn't that surprise me?'

There was a faint hum from Caliburn. Jack cleared her throat. 'Do I even want to know?'

'The sword says that the use of this abomination is an insult to—'

'So I'm right, I don't want to know. Tell Caliburn that we take every blade we can get, even annoying self-righteous talking ones, and even... whatever this is.'

Ahead of them, through the trees, they could see snatches of the Othanim camp, the remaining human servants moving listlessly across the mud of the road; it had rained steadily for the last three days. Beyond that was a tract of dense Wild Wood that led down to the Broken Sea – the closest they had come to it since they started following the road. To the north, the mountains of Yelvynia glowered on the horizon like a jagged bruise. The rain had finally cleared away and it was a bright, sunny morning, the light dancing and winking on the distant water.

'I'm still not clear on what it is,' said Jack quietly. 'I've never seen anything like it.'

Epona sighed. 'I met... *her* briefly in Kornwullis when she tried to kill us. What happened to her on the borders of Galabroc is vague, but from Leven's face when she tried to explain it, I don't think it was pleasant. Leven and Cillian assumed she was dead, and so did the Atchorn, but then according to Togi she appeared to them in… this form. Wait, look. Something is happening. Can you see it?'

The space between the carriages shimmered as though caught in a heat haze, and then a creature appeared there. Epona had not seen the Dunohi often herself. They always gave her a cold feeling – the skull face, the body of moving vegetation, the points of green light in the empty eye sockets – but there was no avoiding the fact that this one was even more alarming. Out of the creature's moss-covered back a human body was growing, twisted and intertwined with living plant and bone. Once, Epona knew, the figure had been a beautiful Druin woman called Loveday, but little of that person was left; there was only madness in her eyes, and her mouth, when it opened, was filled with worms. Epona would never have recognised her if it weren't for the ropes of matted red hair that trailed down her back.

There was a second of stunned silence from the Othanim camp; then, as the Loveday Dunohi reared up, lethal hooves beating the sky, people began to run.

Epona stood, her own short sword held above her head. She glanced to her left and made eye contact with Leven. *Good luck, my friend*, she thought. *Come back to us.*

'To me!' she bellowed to the army behind her. 'To me! For Brittletain!'

---

Leven summoned her wings and let them take her up above the Othanim road. She'd seen many battlefields in her time, many of them unusual thanks to the Imperium's desire to take whatever village, town or city happened to be in their way, but this had to be one of the strangest – a relatively narrow strip of packed dirt and stone running through the middle of an incredibly dense forest. As she watched, the human warriors stormed across the stretch of road, following Epona and Jack, while the creature that had once been Loveday screamed and squirmed, lashing out at the Othanim with whips made of vines and teeth. The winged Titans were scattering into the air, but Leven ignored them. She had one job to do today, and that was what she was going to focus on. Already she could feel her strength draining from her. *Hold on*, she told herself. *Just hold on a little longer, and then you can rest.*

Icaraine rose up, bellowing orders. Many of the Othanim had focused their attentions on the Loveday Dunohi, perhaps fearing that this was Brittlish magic on the same level as the Green Man, while others were swooping down on the human forces, blades bared. Leven couldn't be sure, but she thought that they didn't sound as confident as they once had. There was no laughter from the Othanim now, and no taunts either.

*You made them afraid, Cillian. They don't know what could come out of this forest, and it scares them.*

And then on the heels of that, she thought: *I'll be with you soon, my love.*

She flew up higher, feeling the warm sun on her back even as the colder, higher winds chilled the skin on her bare face. Her ore-lines thrummed with pain, but she barely felt it. Below her, Icaraine was a huge shape, her black hair flying out around her as she spun back and forth. She wasn't wearing her golden helm, which was a precious piece of luck. From the corner of her eye she caught T'rook engaging with the Othanim in the air – on the wing, she was even more remarkable; a beautiful, lethal creature carrying death in her talons. Leven hefted the spear in her arm, feeling its weight and considering its use. The problem, she mused, with being able to summon a magical weapon was that you grew reliant on it. Now that she couldn't summon her wings and the sword at the same time, she had had to make a choice. In the weeks since the last battle, she had spent her time running drills with the spear. She would have to hope it had been enough. There was no more time.

Leven folded her wings and fell like a stone, the tip of her spear held out in front of her like an arrowhead. She was aiming for the top of Icaraine's head, a large enough target, but the Titan was flying too, the movement of her huge wings beating back and forth causing her to move slightly. As it was, Leven very nearly hit it dead on; at the very last moment, Icaraine reared back and the point of the spear tore down across her cheek, flaying it open in an instant. As Leven passed by, already unfolding her wings to slow her progress, she was caught in a hot blast of breath as Icaraine hollered with fury and pain. Titan blood spattered against her glowing wings.

'Stars' arses...'

A huge hand reached out to swat her like a fly, but Leven was already moving, sweeping up into the sky to get another pass.

'Who *are* you?' bellowed Icaraine.

Leven laughed. She twirled the spear in her hands. Given how much closer they were this time, she wouldn't have quite the force she'd had on her first attempt, but it hardly mattered. The sight of the Othanim queen's torn-open face was a source of great joy.

'Me? I'm a spirit of Brittletain,' she called. 'It's time you left this place, monster.'

It was Icaraine's turn to laugh. 'I will take great satisfaction in crushing all your fellow countrymen into paste.'

While she was still talking, Leven dashed forward, spear raised again, and managed to slash across Icaraine's shoulder, drawing more blood before darting away. She risked a glimpse at the ground. Epona's rebel army was keeping the Othanim solidly occupied, and none of them had thought to come to the aid of their queen. A dark figure moved across the battlefield, and she recognised Envoy Kaeto. *Who would have thought we'd ever fight together?*

The glance lasted a fraction too long. Suddenly, Icaraine was sharing the air with her, the queen's bulk alone nearly knocking her from the sky. Leven spun and turned sharply, swirling the spear around her in a protective arc, but Icaraine simply reached around it and struck her with the flat of her hand. For a dizzying handful of seconds, Leven fell, the sky and the ground spinning giddily around her. Desperate, she launched herself back into the area where she guessed the Titan still was and had the brief satisfaction of feeling her spear point bite into something hard. Icaraine bellowed again, and Leven yanked the weapon free. She saw blood spurt from the Titan's midriff, an expression of mingled surprise and rage on her face. Leven realised this was probably her last chance. She couldn't take another blow like the one she'd just taken, and soon even the distracted Othanim guard would realise their queen required aid. Steadying the spear in her arms, she focused on Icaraine's right eye.

*Stars guide my arm*, she thought.

Summoning every last bit of Titan strength, Leven surged forward, spear aimed true... and Icaraine's enormous fist careened through the air like a boulder. It struck Leven with what felt like the force of a mountain; distantly she felt her body being flung, far far away, over the treetops. She had the impression of light beneath her, of sunshine gilding the tops of waves, and of water rushing up towards her.

*I'm sorry*, she thought, thinking of Epona. And then, thinking of Cillian: *I'm nearly with you, my love.*

# 76

'Where will this bring us out?'

Cillian paused. It was a good question. They were in a marshy section of the Lich-Way, but it had grown greener with every step, and now the space ahead of them looked very much like a Path he recognised. Although the Green Man was no longer with him, he still knew all the Paths – they opened up to him like milk dropped on a cobbled street: suddenly every secret line and hidden nook was clear to him.

'It will bring us out next to the Othanim road,' he said. 'I know where they are. The Wild Wood can feel them fighting. It's like an itch.' That wasn't quite the right word. 'It's like an infection in the sap. The land wants it gone.' He glanced at Ynis. 'Will you fight too?'

The girl nodded, although he noted she didn't look convinced. 'Yes. No. I don't know. I feel like my time for fighting is over. I have other duties.'

He looked at her, expecting more, but she just shook her head. Ahead of them the listless light of the Lich-Way fell away. There was sunshine, fresh air full of the scents of spring, and the raised voices of people fighting and dying.

'There it is,' he said. He quickened his pace. Already the Wild Wood was reaching out to him, eager for him to be back in its embrace. Ynis, however, had fallen behind, a curious expression on her face.

'What is it?'

'You go. There's something else I need to do.'

'Now?' He saw her lips thin, and his stomach turned over. 'It's Leven, isn't it?'

She nodded once, sharply. 'Go. I will help her.'

'But—'

Ynis spread her wings – beautiful, feathered things – and she was skirting away from him, up into an uncertain sky. For the barest moment he watched her, wondering if he would see her again. And then he ran down the Path.

---

He emerged into chaos.

The first fight on the road he had experienced second-hand, seen through a caul of shifting emerald as the Green Man rampaged. This time, he saw the battle at human level. There were warriors of all types everywhere – Dwffd men and women with their faces smudged with black paste, Wehha warriors with their animal furs, green-clad Druin and the fighters of Kornwullis, leather armour toughened from years of sea salt. Epona was there too – he spotted her for an instant, back on board her chariot – and the woman Jack, whose sword was flaming like the sun. And there, soaring above them, blood spilling from her talons like rubies, was T'rook.

One of the carriages was on fire. There were so many of them, and yet they were still losing – he could see that at a glance. Icaraine had a mighty gash down one side of her face, her armour streaked with her own blood, but it hadn't slowed her down. There was a heap of human body parts underneath her.

He closed his eyes.

*Wild Wood*, he said. *Wild Wood, hear me*.

The Wild Wood listened. He could feel it, like a breeze on the back of his neck.

*We need you. Fight for the land. Fight for the sky. Fight for stone and leaf and wood and river.* He swallowed. He could feel his awareness sinking into the green, easier than it ever had before. *Fight for us, even as we trample you underfoot, even as we are blind to you, for we are foolish creatures, but we are made of the same things, and in our deepest hearts, we remember the taste of the green.*

There was a rumble from the deep, the vibrations travelling up his legs and into his chest. Distantly he was aware of the pitched battle going on just feet from where he stood. Other things, other presences, were turning their attention towards him, so he reached back.

Minds as old as the land itself; he felt them like the pitted surface of ancient stone. The giants.

*You were sleeping, but it's time to be awake*, he told them. *Fight for the land that you have called home for longer than any of us. Give it back the peace it deserves. Please.*

𝔚𝔢 𝔯𝔦𝔰𝔢.

The warm vegetable scent of rot rose in his nostrils, a skittering awareness that regarded him with an alien familiarity. Yes, he had spoken to these souls a few times over the years. He'd always wondered if they truly understood him. Now, he had his answer.

DRUIN, the voice of the Dunohi thundered in his head. WE KNOW YOU.

*Know me, and trust me, I beg you*, he replied. *The Wild Wood is under threat. I ask you to stand with us now, Dunohi, soul of the forest, and see no further harm come to it.*

The Dunohi did not answer in words, but Cillian heard a rising buzz, like the flight of thousands of angry bees. The Dunohi were coming.

He paused, taking a breath and opening his eyes. The rumbling of the ground he had thought was in his own head was happening on the battlefield, too. He saw the rebels looking at each other in panic, and those Othanim that were still on the ground unfolding their wings, uncertain looks on their faces. To Cillian, everything was tinged faintly green. His feet felt rooted to the spot. He had the oddest idea that he was turning back into the tree in the Lich-Way.

He closed his eyes. Immediately he sensed another presence; sharper, hot-blooded, closer in mind to human than tree, but still vastly, vastly different. To his surprise he was reminded of Ynis, and with that thought came an image: a stern griffin with grey feathers and a headdress made of griffin bone. Blue eyes the colour of glaciers narrowed with suspicion.

*What is this? What human dares to invade the mind of the Witch-seer of the Bone Fall?*

*Griffins! Our last Titans! I ask you to come and fight for the Wild Wood, for every living thing that looks to you in awe – come, I beg you, and show us why the griffins were the most celebrated of all the Titan races.*

*The impudence,* the griffin snapped. *First they use the ancient dead ways to summon us, and now they demand we defend them in their southern forests...*

Cillian winced. Of course the griffins would be difficult. He thought of Ynis, and tried to imagine what she would say.

*Your ancient enemy defies you,* he replied. He conjured an image of the Othanim, their laughing faces streaked with blood. *They have killed and eaten the bones of one of your number. Will you let this insult stand unchallenged?*

There was a moment of chilly silence. Cillian sensed other griffins coming closer, drawn by his words.

*Frost,* said a new voice.

*We have lost her,* said another.

*They have gone too far. This must end.*

The griffins did not speak again, but in his head Cillian heard a great thunder of wingbeats, a roar like a summer wind moving through ancient oaks. *It's done,* he thought, *I've called them all as best I can, and I think some of them even listened.* The best thing he could do, he suspected, was edge around the road and try to find some space where he could use his own Druin powers to aid the fight – he was no warrior, but he wasn't useless either.

Yet, when he made to move, he found that he was unable. Something was stirring beneath his feet. A mind touched his that felt completely unlike anything else. It was green and cold-blooded, full of teeth and scales and thorns and bramble. Green fire licked at its mouth, its nostrils, and eyes the colour of marsh gas rolled up to meet his.

*What are you?*

**We are the dragons of the wildest wood**, came the voice. **We rise only in the direst need. We taste the blood of Brittletain's children seeping down through the dirt. You need us, little fleshlings, so we come.**

The force holding him in place let him go, and Cillian staggered. The shaking of the Wild Wood had grown more powerful, strong enough that the branches of the trees above him were trembling violently. There was a rhythmic thudding to it, like a heartbeat... or footsteps.

'What's that?'

The shrill scream came from a few feet away, one of the Wehha warriors staggering back as though he'd been struck in the chest. Next to him, the face of a rebel had gone as pale as cream.

'It's come back,' she said. 'The Green Man has come back to finish us off.'

Cillian looked, his heart in his mouth. It wasn't the Green Man, but he could forgive them for thinking so: the figure that loomed over the trees was just as enormous, and it carried a huge studded club in one hand. Tusks sprouted from his jaws and dark hair covered the long, rangy body.

The first of the giants had come.

# 77

Leven struck the sea like an arrow, piercing the surface and soaring into the deep. The cold was the biggest shock, a blow to her entire body, and her ore-lines rung out in protest even as her arms and legs went numb. She opened her eyes onto a deep blue darkness, accompanied by a roar in her ears and the taste of salt. With difficulty, she tried to swim, but the exhaustion that came from using her Titan augments coupled with the impact of hitting the freezing water had sapped everything from her; it was all she could do to lift her head. It was also hard to tell which way was up – she had the sense that there was an area behind her where the darkness was not quite so deep, so she attempted to twist her body around towards it. The sea pushed in on her on all sides, urging her down. Already her lungs were burning.

The thought of drowning made her angry. She had expected to be killed in battle, torn apart by the Othanim or swatted by Icaraine herself. She had even considered the idea that she might just drop dead from exhaustion at the end of the battle, the failing magic of the augments finally destroying her. When they'd prepared in the light of dawn for this, drowning had been the furthest thing from her mind.

*Stars' arses*, she thought. *They'll never find my body.*

She had wanted to be buried in the Wild Wood, where she could hope to be near to Cillian and her sister in some way. Leven kicked her legs, trying to move her body towards the surface where there was a small chance it might get spotted by someone, and as she did so she caught sight of a change in the colour of the water below her. She thought at first it must be the seabed, because it filled her field of vision, but then it moved, too quickly, and she saw mottled colours on its skin: blue and yellow and black. This, she had to admit, was adding insult to injury – not just drowned, but eaten by a sea monster.

The shape below her turned and coiled, and she realised she was looking at a long flexible neck. A moment later a huge, lizard-like head came into view. Its eyes were lidless and a pale, glowing blue. When its mouth slowly opened, Leven saw rows and rows of peg-like teeth.

*Why does your blood taste of my mother, tiny human?*

Leven hung where she was, the burning in her chest almost blotting out the freezing cold of the sea. She had, she realised, nothing left to give. She could not even raise her hand.

The enormous head slipped through the water towards her, and she felt barnacled skin brush against her. It was surprisingly gentle. In that moment she felt the closeness of the sea monster in a way that was almost familiar, and the Titan dreams came back in a rush. She had been here, she had been under the water and swam through it like it was her entire world. This creature, she realised with wonder, was a Titan, and she could feel their minds bleeding together once more. As she drifted closer to death, the chance to share something with someone, anyone, was like a final gift, so Leven gave the sea Titan everything she had: every moment of her life, every memory and thought and feeling she had ever harboured or reclaimed. The Titan rose up, and the water around them warmed with its proximity.

*You fight the flying ones*, said the monster. *Our mother remembered them well, and spoke of them with venom. They killed a batch of her eggs. She never forgot.*

*I tried,* Leven told it. *We all tried to stop them.*

*My mother would have been glad to hear that, little one,* said the Titan. *And she would not have wanted you and your child to die here. Humans cannot live beneath.*

Me and my what?

But the Titan had stopped talking to her. Its huge head moved so that it was beneath her, and gently, it began to lift her through the water, pushing her up towards the shifting light that Leven was only just beginning to realise was the water-logged sun. Pressure held her in place, pinning her against the creature's leathery skin, and she put her final shreds of energy into not breathing in: a lungful of sea water would be the end of her.

And then she was out, gasping with lungs that felt like they'd been squeezed between boulders, the shock of the air electric against her skin. Before she properly knew where she was, she felt her body hit the sand. She turned her head and vomited up a stream of salty sea water. When that was done, she raised her head an inch, trying to see the Titan that had saved her, but all she saw was its long, finned tail disappearing back into the surf.

'Sister?'

A warm hand touched her shoulder.

Leven squeezed her eyes shut, then opened them again. Her view was obscured by a face she knew very well – except that Ynis appeared to have wings: real ones, with beautiful feathers of brown and yellow and black.

'I think I've lost my mind,' she said, before she passed out.

---

Her human sister looked awful, her skin so white it was almost green, the ore-lines so stark against it that they looked like the acts of violence they truly were. Ynis touched her fingers briefly to the place on her arm where their mother had placed the lozenge of Titan ore.

'Leven? Leven, can you hear me?'

Leven turned her head slowly, her eyes only half open.

'Hey.' Her voice was the barest croak. 'I missed you, kid.'

'I missed you too.' She reached out and brushed a strand of wet hair from Leven's forehead. It was remarkable, this spirit form – almost like being alive. But not quite. 'And I am sorry. I should not have left you with angry words.'

'No, I'm sorry.' Leven blinked owlishly. 'I should have tried harder to understand. I was afraid for you. Afraid the ore would kill you, too.'

Ynis nodded sadly. 'I know.'

'Ynis.' Leven paused to cough wetly. 'Why do you… uh, why do you have wings now? Feathered ones, I mean.'

'This is who I really am,' she said. 'You can see me so clearly because you are walking the line too. But you have to come back from it, Leven. Things aren't over for you yet.'

'What are you talking about?' Before Ynis could reply, she continued, 'I've got nothing left, Ynis. I'm sorry. Cillian is gone. The Green Man took him.'

'No.' Ynis hesitated, then placed the flat of her palm against her sister's forehead. Leven closed her eyes, soothed by the touch. 'He is alive, Leven. I brought him back out of the Lich-Way. He's on the road now, fighting with every part of the Wild Wood – the giants, the Dunohi, the…' She paused, sensing the arrival of her own people. She smiled. 'Even the griffins are there, Leven. T'rook is there. And Cillian is with them. He's alive.'

For a long moment, Leven lay very still, water still trickling from her clothes. And then her eyes snapped open as she processed what Ynis had said.

'What?'

'You've a distance to travel, but you can make it. You're the toughest human I know, Leven.' Her sister was trying to get up, pushing her elbows into the sand, and with it the blood was pumping again, moving her further from the Edge. Ynis felt a pang of sadness. Soon, Leven wouldn't be able to see her anymore. 'Don't give up. I love you, Deryn.'

Leven had dragged herself into a sitting position and was pushing the wet hair out of her face.

'I love you too, Alaw. I always...' She stopped, looking around the deserted beach. 'Ynis? Where did you go?'

# 78

The dragons slithered out of the wood like serpents from an old story, their long snouts lined with teeth as long as Belise's hands, green flames playing around their nostrils and mouths. From where she watched, crouched in the mouth of the overturned carriage with a spear held ready in both hands, Belise saw one of the creatures rise on its thick tail to snap a fleeing Othanim out of the air. Like the weird skull-faced creatures that had surged into the fray a few minutes earlier, the dragons appeared to be made from vegetation, their hides covered in thick, velvety moss, their spines lined with prickles and thorns. The Othanim left on the ground – the ones who had not been pulverised into paste by the clubs of the giants, at least – fought back, thrusting spears at the squirming forms, but several were already on fire, their piercing screams adding to the racket the griffins had brought. Belise risked a glance upwards at the teeming sky: griffins fought Othanim with claws and beaks and talons, blood raining down onto the battlefield. Another scene, she thought, from an old story, from a history book that no one quite believed. Amazingly, she felt a bubble of laughter rise from somewhere beneath her breastbone.

'Dragons, giants and griffins,' she muttered. 'What am I doing here?'

Yet despite all this, Icaraine was still on her feet, was still fighting. It wasn't just her size, thought Belise, it was her sheer fucking force of will. The Titan's face was split open across her cheek, exposing raw muscle and even a sliver of blue-silver bone, but it hadn't slowed her down.

'What is happening out there?'

Malakim was crouched at the back of the carriage, large spindly hands covering the top of his head.

'You should really come and have a look,' she said, still fighting the lunatic urge to laugh. 'We won't see anything like this again.' When he didn't reply, she turned back to him. 'My prince, if I'm right, your mother will call on you to help her soon. She'll want you to use your powers against the griffins and the giants.' She took a breath. This was it. There was no more time. She'd just have to hope she'd done enough. 'But I want you to think about your own freedom.'

'My what?'

Belise lay her spear down on the ground and went to the debris on the floor. Miraculously, one of the jars hadn't broken in the moment the carriage had been turned over – by a giant, she reminded herself, a fucking giant just kicked the carriage over – and she picked it up and brandished it at Malakim. Outside, Icaraine had started shouting for her son. *Bring me my son, bring me Prince Malakim.*

'This is how Icaraine thinks of you, Malakim.' She held the jar up. Inside it was a spider, crouched at the bottom, trying to make itself as small as possible. 'A thing that she keeps, held inside a tiny space, until she needs it. She's never going to let you out, Malakim. You're too useful. Your future is this.' She shook the jar lightly. 'A weapon to use against the other Titans, always by her side.' This was it, here was the big gamble. 'As long as Icaraine is alive, you will be trapped.'

Malakim's six crimson eyes widened. He did not speak. Outside, drawing closer, she could hear a section of the Othanim guard coming to collect the prince.

'Listen,' she said. 'Listen.' Beads of sweat had broken out across her back and forehead. 'I have been in the jungles of Houraki and there are beetles there the size of dogs, and all sorts of other bugs you can't imagine. Even Stratum – even Stratum, where I'm from, has stuff you've never seen, and my point, Malakim, my point is, you'll never see them while your mother is alive. She won't let you. You'll be her child of the chains forever. Don't you see? Don't you want something more than that?'

An Othanim warrior leaned in the broken carriage doorway.

'My prince? Your mother demands your presence.' He shot an irritable look at Belise. 'Can you not hear her calling, First Knight Belise? Get him out there now. The whole shit-forsaken island is turning on us.'

She turned back to Malakim, ready to say more, but he was already moving, his long ungainly body awkward in the cramped space.

'I am here,' he said to the Othanim warrior.

They left the carriage together, the warriors immediately forming a circle around the prince. For a few seconds Belise watched them leave, unable to move. She'd played the game, had danced the dance exactly as Kaeto had taught her, and in the end, she had lost. A hollow feeling opened up inside her chest.

*At any time I could have slit his throat*, she thought, *but I had to be bloody clever, didn't I? Now he's going to go out there and tear the other Titans to pieces and I could have saved them.*

The thought made her dizzy. Belatedly she ran outside into the thick of battle, a faint roaring in her head that had little to do with the fighting. Ahead of her, Malakim had reached his mother, who had returned to the ground. Icaraine grinned at him, a white slash in a crimson face.

'There you are, child of the chains,' she said in her booming voice. As she spoke, an Othanim body fell from the sky, his guts torn open by a griffin's talons. 'It's time for you to show these lesser Titans who we are, Malakim. My beloved son, pull the griffins from the sky and throw them into the dirt where they belong. Break their bones into pieces, my child, and eat them.'

Malakim raised one of his six arms, long fingers spread towards the sky. Desperate, with no ideas left, Belise threw herself forward through the guard, elbowing them out the way with a precision learned on the crowded streets of Stratum. Annoyed, a few of them shoved her back, keeping her away from the prince.

'Malakim!' she cried out. He wasn't facing her, but she saw his head tip to one side. 'Break your own chains!'

He shook his head, and his fingers trembled. Belise looked to the sky, her heart in her throat. She didn't want to see the griffins torn from the air and crushed, but she had failed them, so she had to witness what happened. She owed them that much.

For a long, agonising second, the world stood still. Belise held her breath. *Make it quick, at least*, she thought. *Let this be over soon.*

The Othanim began to scream.

Icaraine's head snapped around, a rabid dog scenting danger, but it was too late. All at once, the Othanim were falling from the sky – no, falling wasn't the right word, Belise realised in wonder. They were being yanked from the sky, snatched by an invisible hand and slammed into the mud. Slowly at first, and then faster, a rain of winged bodies hitting the ground harder than she would have thought possible, and then, their faces pressed into the mud, their limbs were twisting in on themselves, bones snapping with audible cracks.

'WHAT ARE YOU DOING?'

Icaraine lunged for the prince, but Malakim held up two of his other arms and she stopped in her tracks, her face contorting with rage until her resemblance to anything human was entirely lost.

'MALAKIM, I COMMAND YOU—'

'No,' said Malakim, so quietly Belise thought she might have been the only one to hear it. 'You'll command nothing, least of all me.'

Kaeto paused to draw breath, his shoulders aching from the effort of cutting down warrior after warrior. He saw clearly the moment the battle changed. In one second the rebels were struggling to stay alive, even with all the wild magic of Brittletain on their side; the next, the winged Titans were broken birds in the mud, screaming as their shattered bones pierced their internal organs. The green dragons – he had no idea what they were, truly – surged towards Icaraine, moving the way ivy grows, swarming up and around her. When they came into contact with the Titan, they became more plant than creature, until she was pinned in place by a tangle of bramble and thorn. The child, Malakim, had turned on her. Kaeto knew that, somehow, Belise had been behind it.

*She always was the sharpest of us all.*

He was already moving, weaving through the crowd even as the rebels realised what had happened. Princess Epona was there, standing on an overturned crate shouting at people, but shock lay heavy on them all. It didn't matter. One of the things Envoys trained for was to see the moments where action had to be taken, and taken fast. Here, their success hinged on the whim of their enemy's child – for all they knew, this could be a brief sulk, the result of a disagreement between mother and son that could be reversed at any moment. Malakim hadn't shattered his mother's bones like he had with the Othanim warriors; he was simply holding her in place. It was their job – *my job*, thought Kaeto – to make sure the situation was permanent. It was a matter of moments to climb the green wall that encircled the queen of the Othanim, a wickedly sharp short sword held in one hand. He'd snatched it off the first Othanim body he'd found, and it glinted with the familiar colours of Titan-bone ore.

When he reached the top, Icaraine's head was hanging, strands of her black hair stuck to the open wound on her face, and she was panting heavily. Her yellow eyes rolled towards him.

'You.'

'Me,' he agreed. He glanced back at the ground. The mutant prince Malakim was down there still. Belise was standing with him, her hand on one of his pale limbs. She appeared to be talking to him, saying soothing things, no doubt. He returned his attention to Icaraine. 'We spoke once, and you made me a promise. Do you remember what it was?'

'Who can recall the bleating of sheep?' she rumbled, her voice thick.

'You promised me that if I released you from your prison, I would have my child returned to me. Instead, you gave me her skeleton. You laughed as you did it, if I remember correctly.' He levelled the tip of the sword at her face. 'My daughter was returned to me, as it happens – not by you, but by Felldir, the man I love. Who, incidentally, you spent the last few weeks torturing.' He slid the tip of the sword towards her right eye, pausing when it was no more than half an inch away. Icaraine made a low, growling noise in the back of her throat. 'By rights, it should be Princess Epona who does this. It was her mother you killed, it was her kingdom you usurped, her land you have defiled. But I am going to be selfish, just this once. I want to see you die, Icaraine Lightbringer, and I want to see you die by my hand.'

'You can't kill me,' she growled. 'A worm can't kill a Titan.'

'It's my job to know how to kill anyone, your highness, and I think you'll find a sword to the eye does for most.'

He slid the blade home, pushing harder when she tried to pull her head away, pushing harder still when she screamed, continuing to push when her body thrashed. He stopped finally when he felt the tip of the sword scrape against the back of her skull and her head tipped back, staring sightlessly at a sky full of griffins.

'I did it. I did it! I'm free.'

Belise nodded, smiling faintly. Malakim was shaking all over while the rebels around them celebrated. Already, the giants were withdrawing again, disappearing back over the tops of the trees, and the dragons were gone, turning back into the seething green vegetation that was suddenly everywhere. The Dunohi, too, had faded back into the shadows as quickly as they had arrived. There were a few Othanim still alive, a dozen or so who had been out of the range of Malakim's power, but they had all thrown down their weapons. The rebels were rounding them up.

'You are free, my prince.'

'We'll go where you said,' he continued. He was looking around at the carnage, as though he'd never seen the world before. 'To that city, Stratum, you're always talking about. And Houraki. We'll go wherever we like, and no one will stop us. We'll see everything.'

'Yes.' She was thinking of that terrible moment when Malakim had walked away from her and she had seen all her plans and schemes fall into nothing. For a few agonising minutes, she thought she had failed utterly; that she should have ended his life the first moment she got, regardless of the risk to her own life, or his usefulness to them as a weapon. She weighed the dagger in her hand.

'Mother was wrong about the griffins. They share our bones. We can share the skies too. Perhaps they will let me eat their dead, so that I can grow. There doesn't need to be a war over it.'

'And what of the humans, my prince?'

His bony shoulders rose and fell. 'We will treat them kindly. Beasts of burden work better when you feed them and pet them. That is what I think.'

'So they will serve us?'

'What else are they for?' he said brightly. 'All across Enonah we will travel, and humans will bring us everything we ask for. We won't even need to search for the insects, Beleeze. They will fetch them for us.'

*Why did you have to let me think I'd failed, Malakim?* 'Yes,' she said again, placing her free hand on his skinny white arm. The griffins wouldn't suffer him to live. Why would they? 'Think of all those places, my prince. There's so much for you to see. Can you picture them?'

'I can,' he said, nodding eagerly and not quite looking at her, which was a blessing. 'We'll build a collection together, and travel in a bigger carriage, and I'll put all the names of the insects we find into a book where they can't be forgotten—'

Belise doubted that he even felt it. One moment he was chattering away, sounding happier and more talkative than she'd ever heard him; the next he was lying in the mud, his life's blood leaking away into the soil of Brittletain.

She sat with him and held his hand until it was over. And then Belise stood up, wiped her dagger on the feathers of her own wings, and walked away.

# EPILOGUE

*I understand that my partner has reached out to you over the last month. I must thank you for taking the time to consider his words. We are living now, I believe, in a new world, a raw one, where we must pick our way through a great deal of pain. My people and I must consider our guilt, our responsibility, for bringing this war to your shores. War, perhaps, is the wrong word. It was an unprovoked attack, just as it was two thousand years ago.*

*We cannot expect forgiveness from you, our griffin cousins, or from the humans that were so violently used by Icaraine and her followers. And I do not know what the future holds for the handful of my people that have survived. But I can tell you that they have, each of them, sworn an oath to me as their guide, and an oath to never raise a hand to another Titan. That means, if you wish, you could fly down out of the north and have your revenge. None of them would stand against you. I would not stand against you.*

*But I will ask you to consider a future where you are not the lone Titans on the face of Enonah. Perhaps we could rebuild something, together. It is a thought.*

Extract from a letter sent by Felldir of the Othanim<br>to Queen Fellvyn of Yelvynia

> '*Without her, we'd all be dead. It's as simple as that. Thanks to Ynis of the Edge Walkers, Icaraine and her people were defeated. I didn't know her, never met her, but Cillian told me what she sacrificed. How she found him in the very heart of the Lich-Way, and brought him out, so that he could summon all the powers of our island to aid us. So we'll honour her, and her people, in every way we can. The griffins will always have an ally in Londus.*'
>
> Princess Epona, in an address to her newly formed court

*Two moons later*

'Will it hurt?'

'More than it already hurts?'

'Alright, that is a fair point.' Leven lowered herself until she was sitting on a rock, one hand on her belly. The bump was barely showing at all but it was still big enough already that Leven felt the extra weight. Around them, the Wild Wood was still and expectant, full of the faint hush that seemed to follow Cillian wherever he went these days, like the pause before a spoken word. When the Green Man had ridden inside him, a domineering passenger, the wood had been wild and chaotic and loud. Now, the forest loved Cillian, and he loved it; they had come to a kind of peace. He came and knelt in front of Leven, taking her hand. His green eyes – their normal, beautiful jade green once again – were very serious. 'What will happen?' she asked him.

'I'm going to ask the wood to reclaim the Titan ore from you – take it into the roots and the stones and the trees – and in exchange, to give you something of itself.' He took a breath, held it, then let it out again slowly. 'It's a risk, Leven. It might not work, and even if it does, I'm not sure you'll ever be able to leave the Wild Wood again.'

Leven smiled and let the fingers of her free hand trail along his cheek. 'Would that be such a bad thing?'

He kissed her fingers. 'My lady of the green. Here we go. I love you.'

Cillian closed his eyes, and she took a moment to examine his face: the fine line of his jaw, the scar that crossed his eyebrow, the faint green tint to his horns. Having believed that he was lost to her, she still found herself startled and delighted by his presence. She was so lost in contemplating the particular arch of his eyebrows that when her ore-lines began to change, she missed it. Only when Cillian tapped her on the arm did she see it: the silvery blue lines that traced over every part of her body turning a rich, oak-leaf green. And as the ore vanished, so did the pain.

'Stars' arses, Cillian...'

He laughed. 'How does it feel?'

'Weird. But good, too, I think.'

'Can you still feel the Titans?'

Leven let her eyes drift closed and commanded her body to relax. It was strange to feel so alone inside her own body, the teeming energy of the ore-lines entirely absent. No wings waited for her to summon them, no sword hovered just out of sight by her hand. Yet the Titans had shared so much with her, especially over the last year. She felt their presence still, and when she thought of the sea, she tasted salt on her tongue.

'All the old Titan memories, they're still with me,' she said eventually, 'but it's more like the memory of a good friend you knew long ago.' Her smile faded. 'Or the memory of a sister you only knew for a handful of years.'

For a little while they just held each other, listening to the sound of the wood. Far overhead somewhere, a jackdaw was calling.

When it was time to leave, Cillian helped her to her feet unnecessarily – she elbowed him in the ribs for it, playfully – and they walked towards the Path.

'Ynis would have been glad to see you healed,' he said quietly.

'I sometimes think I can feel her, close by,' she said. Above them the sky was the fierce blue of summer, promising a long, hot afternoon. 'When I look up, I half expect to see her there, you know? Up where she belongs.'

'I only understand a little of the griffin's Edge Walker magic,' he said. 'And even less about what happened in the Lich-Way. But I don't believe she's gone. Not truly.'

Leven nodded. She wanted to cry again, so she pictured Ynis as she'd seen her last, with her griffin wings, each feather perfect.

'So. Do you think I can leave the Wild Wood now my body is part of it?'

'I don't know. Shall we find out, my lady of the green?'

---

Epona wandered down a corridor of the castle, a mop in one hand, a bucket in the other. She was hot and sweaty. Summer had arrived and started throwing its weight around, and she felt covered in every type of grime. They had been scrubbing the remnants of the Othanim from her home for what felt like forever. Every day, they found some new thing that needed cleaning or mending or throwing out. At some point soon, she hoped, it would feel like it used to feel. It just wasn't quite there yet.

'Epona.'

Jack sauntered out of an open doorway, looking as calm and as collected as ever. Caliburn had been given a place of honour in the armoury and allowed to rest there for a while. Abruptly, Epona felt especially scruffy. She put the bucket down and attempted to quickly push her hair into a slightly neater shape.

'Jack. Have you spoken to Togi about Bronvica's stable yet? I want to get some horses back in there as soon as we can. I think that's what she would have wanted. And there should be a stonemason coming about the bloody great holes in Mother's rooms. He won't be able to get stone that matches exactly because this place was built before Magog's balls had dropped, but...'

'Epona,' said Jack again. 'Have you thought any more about it? The coronation?'

'Oh, not this again.' Epona shook her head. 'Who has the time for it, Jack? Not us.'

'The people are looking for something to cheer for,' said Jack. 'Why not you, the hero of the Wild Wood Road? Queen Broudicca's heir.'

'Me? Every person on that stretch of road was a hero, Jack – you, Leven, Cillian, even the bloody Envoy from the bloody Imperium. All of us working together, pulling in the same direction. That was what got us through. And I don't know. I've been thinking...' She swallowed. These were thoughts that had no real foundation yet, nothing she could grasp onto or wield, but the idea kept occurring to her that perhaps they didn't need queens at all. Or princesses. Certainly not kings. Perhaps there was a different way for Brittletain to be. 'Look, when this place is sorted and Londus itself is functional again, I promise we'll talk about it.' *Although you might not like what I have to say,* she thought.

Jack nodded, looked at the floor. Her cheeks were flushed a delightful rose pink again, Epona noted.

'You'll always be my queen, Epona.'

'Now that is an idea I could entertain.' Epona stepped up to Jack, and tipped a finger under her chin, lifting her face to meet hers. 'I'm not sure I deserve a friend as loyal as you, Jack.'

'Just a friend?'

Standing slightly on tiptoes, Epona kissed Jack, delighting in the softness of the other woman's lips. Jack embraced her, strong arms pulling her close, and Epona forgot all about the sweat drying across her back and the bucket of dirty water at her feet. When they broke apart, both breathing hard, she grinned. 'Maybe a little more than a friend.'

---

Belise floated up to the balcony on silent wings, then perched there for a moment. Below her, a barely visible shadow that was Kaeto was moving towards one of the empress's guards; she didn't need to watch to know that man's unfortunate fate. Instead, she unlocked the doors with one of the tools hidden in her shirt and slipped inside.

As Kaeto's assistant she'd never been allowed in the observatory room, but over the last few weeks she had spent a lot of time examining the blueprints kept on file in the Envoy offices, looking for likely places to hide, places to strike from, escape routes. Below her, the gilded bubble that housed the empress's telescopes gleamed dully in the starlight. There was a faint whirr as the door that sat at its base began to open, and a small slippered foot ventured out, the diminutive form of the empress following it. She had a doll clutched under one arm.

On one level, this was madness. The three of them knew it. Felldir, who was waiting for them in a concealed cart on the deserted plains outside the observatory, had been a voice of reason at first, questioning each part of their plan and quietly picking over their motives. But in the end, both Belise and Kaeto knew that the empress would never let them go: they knew too much about the inner workings of the Imperium; they had defied her will, and they had gotten her precious Heralds killed. In many ways, Empress Celestinia was their very own Icaraine and Malakim combined – a creature with an insatiable appetite, a thing that wanted to see the whole world crushed under her boot. Or slipper.

Belise grinned to herself in the dark, sliding a throwing knife from her belt. She was about to cause a lot of trouble.

Up in the icy peaks of Yelvynia, summer is slow to take. Snow as hard as rocks remains in the shadowed crevices, a deep cold blue at its heart. T'rook sees these outposts of winter and thinks: *when that snow fell, my sister was alive.*

Sometimes, when she dreams, she hears her sister's voice, and once Ynis had felt so close she could smell her, could feel the light touch of her human fingers on the space between her eyes.

'I want to share the gift with you,' Ynis had said. 'It's easy to do, T'rook, if I show you how.'

'What gift?' she had asked. 'What do you mean?'

When she'd woken up that morning, pressed between the flanks of Flayn and T'vor, she had looked up at the sky and understood. Scarlet ribbons crossed the endless blue, joining griffin to griffin, human to human... and human to griffin.

T'rook goes flying by herself often these days, skirting the foothills and soaring over lakes, chasing a thin red line that only she can see.

Sometimes, she tells their fathers, she knows Ynis is there with her, flying wing tip to wing tip.

# ACKNOWLEDGEMENTS

It was a strange old book to write, this one. I sometimes feel like I want to turn acknowledgements into some weird therapy session where I examine what happened during the course of the draft, but that is not what these notes are for, Jennifer, get a grip. What is relevant, I suppose, is that I started writing *Titanchild* in 2023, and then due to a number of things changing in my life, I finished writing it the following year in a part of the country where it's fair to say I did not expect to be living (hello Bristol!). In the early part of the lifeimplosion, a number of people looked out for me and checked in on me, and I want you all to know I appreciate it so much. Juliet, Den, Andrew, Jenni, Roy, everyone at Clapham Books, Boo, Adam, Leslie, Jonesy, Blighty – thank you. An especially big thanks to my mum, who had to live with me for a couple of weeks when it's fair to say I wasn't at my best, and continued to make a fuss of me even when I was being a toerag. Thanks also to my aunties and my cousins, for the sympathy, support and acerbic life advice that only family can provide. Love you all.

As ever, huge thanks to the team at Titan for wrangling *Titanchild* to the finish line; Katie Dent for the wise and witty editing; Kabriya Coghlan for getting the books in people's faces; and Hayley Shepherd for eagle-eyed copyedits. My eternal gratitude to the wonder that is my agent, Juliet Mushens, who remains a spectacular force of nature and one of my very favourite people.

I dedicated *Titanchild* to the three history teachers who taught me through secondary school and post-sixteen. It might seem a little contrary to dedicate such a deeply (even defiantly) unhistorical book to a trio of history teachers, but I think I partly write fantasy because I love history, and that love was initially planted by Mrs Mongon, Mr Brannigan and Mr Mealing. So thank you!

Peter Newman was perhaps the person I spoke to the most last year while things were going sideways – and if you know me, you probably know he's the reason I moved to Bristol. Change can be chaotic and unsettling, but it also brings unexpectedly wonderful things sometimes. It was Pete who was there every day I struggled to write, who appeared with cups of tea or the right idea at the right moment, and I doubt there would be a *Titanchild* without him. Thanks, babe.

# ABOUT THE AUTHOR

JEN WILLIAMS is a writer from London currently living in Bristol with her partner and a dramatically fluffy cat. A fan of grisly fairy tales since her youth, Jen has gone on to write dark, unsettling horror thrillers with strong female leads and character-driven fantasy novels with plenty of adventure and magic. The Winnowing Flame trilogy twice won the British Fantasy Award for best novel, and she is partially responsible for the creation of Super Relaxed Fantasy Club. When she's not writing books, she enjoys messing about with video games and embroidery. She also works as a freelance copywriter and illustrator.

Find out more at www.sennydreadful.co.uk or follow her on X @sennydreadful.

**ALSO AVAILABLE FROM TITAN BOOKS**

# DARK WATER DAUGHTER

## BY H. M. LONG

A fearsome young woman stormsinger and pirate hunter join forces against a deathless pirate lord in this swashbuckling Jacobean adventure on the high seas.

Mary Firth is a Stormsinger: a woman whose voice can still hurricanes and shatter armadas. Faced with servitude to pirate lord Silvanus Lirr, Mary offers her skills to his arch-rival in exchange for protection - and, more importantly, his help sending Lirr to a watery grave. But her new ally has a vendetta of his own.

Samuel Rosser is a disgraced naval officer serving aboard *The Hart*, an infamous privateer commissioned to bring Lirr to justice. He will stop at nothing to capture Lirr, restore his good name and reclaim the only thing that stands between himself and madness: a talisman stolen by Mary. Finally, driven into the eternal ice at the limits of their world, Mary and Samuel must choose their loyalties and battle forces older and more powerful than the pirates who would make them slaves.

'A wonderful adventure! Dark Water Daughter *swept me to the high seas with its captivating story, rich original lore, fascinating characters, and slow-burn romance. Immersive from start till end, this is a hard one to put down.*'
Sue Lynn Tan, bestselling author of *Daughter of the Moon Goddess*

## TITANBOOKS.COM

**ALSO AVAILABLE FROM TITAN BOOKS**

# THE GRYPHON KING
## BY SARA OMER

**The first in a sweeping Southwest Asian-inspired epic fantasy trilogy brimming with morally ambiguous characters, terrifying ghouls and deadly monsters.**

Bataar was only a child when he killed a gryphon, making him a legend across the red steppe. Now he is the formidable Bataar Rhah, ruling over the continent that once scorned his people. After a string of improbable victories, he turns his sights on the wealthy, powerful kingdom of Dumakra.

Nohra Zultama has no fear of the infamous warlord who marches on her country. But as deceit and betrayal swirl through her father's court, she soon learns the price of complacency. With Dumakra under Bataar's rule, Nohra vows to take revenge—yet her growing closeness to the rhah's wife, Qaira, threatens to undo her resolve.

Old evils are rising. Only together will Nohra and Bataar stand a chance against the djinn, ghouls, and monsters that threaten to overrun their world.

*'A twisty feast of politics and fantastical beasts.'*
Shannon Chakraborty, bestselling author of
*The Adventures of Amina Al-Sirafi*

**TITANBOOKS.COM**

**ALSO AVAILABLE FROM TITAN BOOKS**

# ANJI KILLS A KING
## BY EVAN LEIKAM

**For fans of R.F. Kuang, H.M. Long and R.J. Barker.**

Anji works as a castle servant, cleaning laundry for a king she hates. So when a rare opportunity presents itself, she seizes the chance to cut his throat. Then she runs for her life. In her wake, the kingdom is thrown into disarray, while a bounty bigger than anyone could imagine lands on her head.

On her heels are the fabled mercenaries of the Menagerie, whose animal-shaped masks are magical relics rumored to give them superhuman powers. It's the Hawk who finds Anji first: a surly, aging swordswoman who has her own reasons for keeping Anji alive and out of the hands of her fellow bounty hunters, if only long enough to collect the reward herself.

With the rest of the Menagerie on their trail, so begins an alliance as tenuous as it is temporary - and a race against death that will decide Anji's fate, and may change the course of a kingdom.

*'A stunning debut, fast-paced and as grim as grimdark gets, relentless till the end.'*
Glen Cook, author of *The Black Company*.

**TITANBOOKS.COM**

For more fantastic fiction, author events,
exclusive excerpts, competitions, limited editions and more

VISIT OUR WEBSITE
**titanbooks.com**

LIKE US ON FACEBOOK
**facebook.com/titanbooks**

FOLLOW US ON TWITTER AND INSTAGRAM
**@TitanBooks**

EMAIL US
**readerfeedback@titanemail.com**